PRAISE FOR *THE FORCING*

'A compelling, moving story of survival in a dying world ... a novel that might have actually predicted our future' Ewan Morrison

'Fierce, thoughtful, deeply humane and always compelling. Tightly plotted, the tension builds from page one and never relents' David Whish-Wilson

'Smart, gripping, and all too plausible, *The Forcing* asks the big questions that we're running out of time to answer, and announces Paul E. Hardisty as the true heir to John Christopher' Tim Glister

'The book I've been waiting and hoping for' Paul Waters

'With the biting intensity of a thriller and the majestic world-building of a classic dystopian tale, this story is perfectly paced with peaks and valleys, never spending too much time in one place and blending the moments together like some strange dream ... This is a cataclysmic call to arms – a powerful warning about a world that could be' B. S. Casey

'An emotional, all-too prescient climate thriller, it kept me riveted to the very end. Beautifully written, in turns moving and terrifying, this is a book of our time' Eve Smith

'A riveting and suspenseful dystopian thriller/drama ... both a reality check and completely absorbing fiction, speaking of cold, harsh facts but also of love, endurance and hope. Paul E. Hardisty has a way with words that never fails to blow me away, spot-on and occasionally rather poetic, yet never even remotely close to purple prose' From Belgium with Booklove

'Not just a novel about a world that is changed by climate breakdown ... but one written by someone who knows what he's talking about' Live Many Lives

'A stark, gripping, often poignant, but undeniably thought-provoking read and another absolute winner. Loved it' Jen Med's Book Reviews

PRAISE FOR PAUL E. HARDISTY

'Beautifully written' Tim Marshall

'Vividly written, utterly tropical, totally gripping' Peter James

'This is a remarkably well-written, sophisticated novel in which the people and places … all come alive on the page' *Literary Review*

'Laces the thrills and spills with enough moral indignation to give the book heft … excellent' *Telegraph*

'Topical and fiercely intelligent. And it's not often you can say the latter of a thriller!' *The Times*

'The quality of Hardisty's writing and the underlying truth of his plots sets this above many other thrillers' *West Australian*

'Searing … at times achieves the level of genuine poetry' *Publishers Weekly*

'A trenchant and engaging thriller that unravels this mysterious land in cool, precise sentences' *Catholic Herald*

'What spoke to me more strongly than anything was the courage, integrity and passion with which this novel is written' *Cheltenham Standard*

'A gripping, page-turning thriller that is overflowing with substance to go along with Hardisty's atmospheric prose and strong narrative style' *Mystery Magazine*

'The sense of place, and the way that the climate, the landscape and the people all combine within a location very foreign to that which many of us live in is evocative' *Australian Crime*

'A solid, meaty thriller – Hardisty is a fine writer and Straker is a great lead character' Lee Child

'A page-turning adventure that grabs you from the first page and won't let go' Edward Wilson

'An exceptional and innovative novel. And an important one. Hardisty appears to know his territory intimately … I can't praise it highly enough' Susan Moody

'Beautifully written, blisteringly authentic, heart-stoppingly tense and unusually moving' Paul Johnston

'Smart, gripping, superbly crafted' Helen Giltrow *Crime Review*

'A big, bold character-driven story so emotionally literate that it doesn't ring with authenticity, it clamours. Superb and highly recommended' Eve Seymour

'Wow. Just wow. The sense of place is conjured beautifully … think John Le Carré's *A Constant Gardener* … A thriller with heart and a conscience' Michael J. Malone

The Forcing

ABOUT THE AUTHOR

Canadian Paul Hardisty has spent twenty-five years working all over the world as an environmental scientist and freelance journalist. He has roughnecked on oil rigs in Texas, explored for gold in the Arctic, mapped geology in Eastern Turkey (where he was befriended by PKK rebels), and rehabilitated water wells in the wilds of Africa. He was in Ethiopia in 1991 as the Mengistu regime fell, survived a bomb blast in a café in Sana'a in 1993, and was one of the last Westerners out of Yemen at the outbreak of the 1994 civil war. In 2022 he criss-crossed Ukraine reporting on the Russian invasion. Paul is a university professor and CEO of the Australian Institute of Marine Science (AIMS). The four novels in his Claymore Straker series, *The Abrupt Physics of Dying, The Evolution of Fear, Reconciliation for the Dead* and *Absolution*, all received great critical acclaim and *The Abrupt Physics of Dying* was shortlisted for the CWA John Creasey (New Blood) Dagger and was a *Telegraph* Book of the Year. Paul drew on his own experiences to write *Turbulent Wake*, an extraordinary departure from his high-octane, thought-provoking thrillers, and a novel that has had a profound impact on readers worldwide. Paul is a keen outdoorsman, a conservation volunteer, and lives in Western Australia. Follow him on Twitter @Hardisty_Paul.

Also by Paul E. Hardisty and available from Orenda Books

The Abrupt Physics of Dying
The Evolution of Fear
Reconciliation for the Dead
Absolution
Turbulent Wake

The Forcing

PAUL E HARDISTY

ORENDA
BOOKS

Orenda Books
16 Carson Road
West Dulwich
London SE21 8HU
www.orendabooks.co.uk

First published in the United Kingdom by Orenda Books 2023
Copyright © Paul E. Hardisty 2023

A catalogue record for this book is available from the British Library.

ISBN 978-1-914585-55-5
eISBN 978-1-914585-56-2

Typeset in Garamond by typesetter.org.uk

Printed and bound by CPI Group (UK) Ltd, Croydon CR0 4YY

For sales and distribution, please contact info@orendabooks.co.uk
or visit www.orendabooks.co.uk

To my dad
Murray Edward Hardisty 1932–2020

Forcing /fɔːˈsɪŋ/

Radiative forcing (RF) is the difference between the planet's incoming and outgoing radiation, measured in Watts per metre squared (W/m^2). If RF is positive, all other factors remaining equal, the planet will warm. Compared to 1750, RF had increased 0.57 W/m^2 by 1950, 1.25 W/m^2 by 1980, 2.29 W/m^2 by 2011, and 2.72 W/m^2 by 2019. Sometimes referred to simply as climate forcing, or just forcing, it continues to increase. Natural climate forcings include changes in the sun's energy output, regular variations in the Earth's orbital cycle, and large volcanic eruptions that throw light-reflecting particles into the atmosphere. Human induced forcings, which now dominate the Earth-atmosphere system and are responsible for the large increases over the last several decades, include emissions of heat-trapping gases such as methane and carbon dioxide, and changes to land use which make the Earth's surface reflect more or less sunlight.
[From *Intergovernmental Panel on Climate Change (IPCC) Assessment Report 6, Working Group 1*]

'I will wipe mankind, whom I have created,
from the face of the Earth.'
Genesis 6:5

PART I

Angels

A Journey into the Past

In the beginning, God created man.

And it was pretty much downhill from there.

Of course, the descent took time, and there were many points along the way at which it could have been slowed or reversed. We all watched, fascinated, unable to look away, as day by day an unwanted future became an unchangeable past.

I am not an historian. The bigger picture I will leave to others. This is the story of how I came to be here, so far from what I used to call home, and of those who shared my journey. I have tried to record it faithfully, as truly as memory allows. Some moments remain as indelible scars, despite my best attempts to forget. Others are fading even now. And parts of the story, I fear, will never be revealed.

I have attempted to see some of what happened through the eyes of my companions, out of respect for some, and in an attempt to understand others. I hope I have done them justice and apologise if I have not.

I admit to having started this tale several times over the years and having given up every attempt. Each failure has its own story, too. But now it is time. Perhaps it was watching my own children grow up in this new and changed world, that has finally brought me to the task, ending years of procrastination. Maybe it was the birth of my first grandson.

At first, and for a long time, I simply needed to heal, to forget. Years passed, a decade and another again. Slowly, with the turn of seasons, the pain began to recede. I lost myself in the task of remaking our lives, bending to the work of feeding my family, building this stone and jarrah-plank house by the sea. Now I know that I will only ever find peace in the places I least want to go.

For it is no exaggeration to say that I have crawled to the very edge of the abyss and gazed down into the depths of Hell. I do not offer this lightly. I am a scientist, a teacher. Even now, in my old age, I remain a rationalist, a determinist. But I know now that human reality lies not in the physical, the solid stuff of the world, the bones and tumours of our mortal bodies, but in the warped fabric of time where our hopes and tortured dreams live.

In truth, I am running out of time. What once obeyed without complaint now rebels. Joints ache, and old wounds throb with the coming of the rains. Fatigue, once a stranger, is now a constant and unwanted companion. Even simple tasks have become difficult, and in my two grown sons I can see glimpses of the man I was, the same man who carried and lifted and placed each of the stones in these walls, whose hands cut and shaped the sturdy beams above me, cleared the ground and planted the crops that feed us.

And so I must make this journey into the past, now, while I still can. I hope this record will help my children understand the truth of what happened and why things are the way they are, and why we decided to bring them into such a world in the first place. Because it was truth, or to be more precise a deficit of truth, that set us on this path. A truth that remained hidden for far too long, ignored by some, avoided by many, and actively concealed by a powerful few.

I will start back when we had finally begun to try to fix the problem, after it was too late, and before we really knew what was wrong.

I still remember the letter that started it all.

1

I rose early, an old habit, crept downstairs to make coffee, correct the exam papers I hadn't got to the night before. It was back when people still got up and made coffee and went to work, led what they tried to imagine were normal lives. I guess we were all doing our best to maintain the illusion of a past we couldn't quite bring ourselves to let go of.

By the time I left the house, dawn was hinting pale against the autumn trees. My wife Maybelline – May – was still in bed. I'd gone upstairs to kiss her goodbye, but when I whispered her name, she hadn't moved. The morning was cold. Dark clouds massed in the west, obscuring the mountains. Out of the gate and left towards the river, my usual route, past ragged picket-fence gardens and modest wooden houses, lights coming on in kitchen windows. It was that kind of neighbourhood. The last vestiges of the middle class, still hanging on to that dream, still pretending.

I taught my morning class, chemistry 11, and had begun physics 12 – just another Thursday among fifteen years of Thursdays. I was standing at the blackboard describing the radiative forcing effect of carbon dioxide and methane on Earth's climate when the letters arrived, placed ceremoniously on my desk by Radley, the breathless deputy principal, a short, recently-appointed administrator whose sole joy in life seemed to be the delivery of bad news. No calamity was too small to send him into paroxysms of excitement: whispered news of a recent divorce, the latest teen pregnancy, the now-ritual distribution of draft cards at the senior assembly. The kids, predictably, called him Ratley.

I knew what my letter would say, had anticipated it for months. I finished the class, left the letters unopened on my desk, acted as if nothing had changed. At lunch I sat with a few colleagues, talked about the usual stuff – the war, the shortages, the chronic lack of mobile-phone and internet service.

Later that afternoon, after the kids had settled into the physics 12 exam, I opened my letter. It was no surprise. Except the date. What I had initially thought must be a mistake, a typo of some sort, right there in ragged black ink: the last digit of the year exactly one lower than it was supposed to be, than had been repeatedly communicated by the government over the radio and the TV for the last six months.

It made no difference to me. I had always been well within the cut-off. I was clearly one of the *responsibles*, as they were being called – the old ones, those the viruses hadn't managed to kill off. I'd accepted it long ago. But for May, it made all the difference in the world.

I looked up at the kids, heads bent to their exam papers. Kazinsky with his newly razed skull of stubble, Smith with the tip of one of her long braids in her mouth, concentrating. Good kids. No, not kids anymore. Young men and women, now. Women and men, young, with a future even more uncertain than mine.

I looked at my watch, gave them all a few extra minutes. Then I stood and cleared my throat. 'Ladies and gentlemen, time is up.'

Groans from the usual suspects, eyes looking up at me, refocusing, the afternoon sunlight in each of those uniquely patterned, uniquely troubled pairs. A few smiles – Smith, inevitably, beaming at me with that beautiful mouth, those unnaturally enhanced eyes, the Cantor dust of freckles across the bridge of her nose, that haunting intermittency. I scanned the rest of the faces, raised the letter in my right hand. 'I have some good news, for some of you at least.'

Quiet, now. Thirty-two faces directed toward me.

'This will be the last class we will have together,' I said.

Even the new kids in the back row were paying attention now.

'I am being relocated.'

A guffaw from the back, Hernandez and Richards high-fiving.

'South.'

Then silence, blank stares, information being processed. All the new kids, the ones who themselves had just been relocated, knew immediately. You're going where we just came from.

I considered saying more, offering some sort of defence perhaps. Instead, I said: 'I hope you've learned something during our time together. Even you, Richards, Hernandez...'

Nervous laughter from a few.

'Remember, wherever your lives take you, that science and rational thought have always been a beacon for humanity. In reason and truth lie hope.' As I said it, I realised how old-fashioned it sounded. I hoped one day they would understand.

More sniggering from the back.

'Now, if you will please turn in your exam papers. I wish you all good luck.'

Students began shuffling to the front, placing papers on the corner of my desk. Krusch, Robertson, Ravindran, DeVilliers silent, hoisting his bag onto his shoulder; a grunt from Rouse that could have been goodbye; a clear 'good luck, Teach' from the intelligent Blewett; a tended hand and a good, firm shake from Glass, captain of the school football team. A few thankyous. Most walked out without a word.

Soon it was only Smith and Kazinsky, the two who'd been with me the longest. Smith in her trademark short skirt and black Doc Martens, fiddling with a braid, Kazinsky hovering near the back window. Smith put her paper on the pile, looked at me. She was crying.

'I don't think I did very well,' she sniffled. 'I...' She stalled, stood looking down at her feet.

'You always say that, Maddy. And you always do well. Don't worry.'

She looked up at me. The tears in her eyes refracted the low-angle light from the windows, prismed out through the yellow part of the spectrum from those cat's-eye contacts she had been wearing for a few months now, 4.7×10^{14} cycles per second, that beguiling, prescient frequency.

'Yes, but...' She stopped herself, let the end of her braid fall to her side. 'What if our new teacher is, like, a troll?'

'Don't worry, Maddy. Miss Fenyman will take over for the rest of the term. She's a lot younger than I am. I'm sure she'll be fine.'

She stood there a moment, head bowed. 'But I want you, Teach,' she said, fiddling with her braid again. 'I want to do physics at MIT. You know that. I need *you*.'

That's what everyone calls me. Teacher. Everyone who knows me. The kids just call me Teach.

I picked Maddy's paper from the pile, scanned the first answer, her invariably neat script moving across the page, building from first principles, the unit analysis helpfully displayed and balanced, the answer perfect. 'You're ready, Maddy. You'll get in. Believe me. You don't need me anymore.'

She stood there with her legs crossed above the knees the way she did . 'You're just saying that,' she said, wiping her eyes. 'Anyway, it doesn't matter. I don't want you to go.'

'I'm sorry, Maddy,' I said, struggling for words.

She straightened, glanced at Kazinsky and picked up her bag. 'Thanks, Teach. I'll never forget you.'

And then she was gone and it was only Kazinsky, half a foot taller than he'd been at the start of term, standing by the window, looking out across the mud-scarred playing fields. I stood and walked a few unsteady paces towards him, the room suddenly empty now that Smith was gone, as if all the air had been sucked from the place. The late-afternoon sky burned that bewildering shade of alder that still made me dizzy, as if the gravity of the world had been inverted, transducing earth into sky, atmosphere into ocean. Which in a way, of course, it had.

For several minutes we stood there by the window in the empty classroom, saying nothing, each looking out at whatever we could see.

After a while, Kazinsky spoke. His voice was deep, resonant. 'I've been called up for the army.'

I said nothing. The latest draft of seventeen-year-old males had just been announced to replace the catastrophic losses in Africa. There had been the earlier experiments with females, of course, but those had been an unmitigated disaster, and now, with the population plummeting, it was ridiculous to send healthy young women to be slaughtered on the battlefield.

A long silence stretched out, pierced only by the occasional shout from the hallway. 'I don't agree with what we're doing over there,' Kazinsky said. 'I don't want to kill people.'

I put my hand on the boy's shoulder, held it there a moment.

Kazinsky glanced back towards the hallway. 'I'm thinking of running away.'

'It would be dangerous, Matthew. You know what they're doing to draft evaders.' My words sounded fake, an insincere apology.

'There's no way I'm going to go over there and kill a bunch of people I don't know, have nothing against. We're only there for the food. We're stealing.'

I had been against the war from the beginning, demonstrated against it, back when that was still possible, before the Repudiation, but I continued with my fakery nonetheless. 'The new government is trying to get out, bring the troops home. But it's going to take time, Matthew, after the mess they inherited.'

'I'm scared, Teach.'

'So am I, Matthew.' It was the truth.

Kazinsky turned to face me. Tears wicked his dark lashes. 'No. That's not what I mean,' he said. 'I'm not scared for me. I'm scared for *us*. All of us.' He wiped his eyes with the back of his sleeve, glanced out towards the hallway. 'I was just a kid when the first virus hit. I thought that was bad. But it was nothing compared to this.'

I gripped the boy's shoulder, held it tight. 'The world is a fine place, Matthew, and well worth fighting for. Do you know who said that?'

He shook his head.

'I guess they don't teach you Hemingway in lit anymore.'

'My dad read *The Old Man and the Sea* to me once, when we were on holiday.'

'Did you like it?'

'It's from another time, but yeah.'

I waited for him to continue.

'You know. When everything was still pure. Not like now.'

'I know what you mean,' I said, guilt welling up inside me.

'I like the way the old man never gave up, even when the sharks came and took the fish away from him. The way the young boy loved the old man no matter what.'

'So, in the end, he won.' I hoped he couldn't hear the lack of conviction in my voice.

'Yeah, I guess he did. If you can call it winning.'

'He just went out too far.'

'I guess.'

'So,' I said, looking into the boy's eyes, 'the decision each of us has to make is: which fight? As long as you're fighting for what you know is right, and keep doing your best, there's hope. It's when you give up that you've lost. Not a minute before.'

Now this I meant. Big difference between trying and winning. I've always been quick to give advice. It is one of my many failings.

Kazinsky looked up and to the right for a moment, that thing he did when he was working something through. 'Maybe I could head to the mountains. You know, hide in the wilderness.'

'It's still pretty cold up there.'

He stared out of the window. After a while he said: 'My dad would have known what to do. He was good in the bush. Could get a fire going anywhere. He used to take me camping all the time when I was a kid.'

You still are a kid. I didn't say it. Matthew's father had died in the second pandemic. Young and fit, he defied the statistics and succumbed to what later became known as the old-people's disease. In truth no one had been safe. With so many succumbing, the tails of the distribution accounted for millions. It had been a giant crapshoot.

'You're smart, Matthew. With your marks, you could apply for engineering at university. It would keep you out of the army.'

We'd been having this conversation for a couple of years now, on and off, me trying to get him to acknowledge his obvious talent for maths and physics, him steadfastly resisting. It's not me, Teach, he'd say. I want to get out of school, not back into it. I want to *live*. Get out there and see some of the world before it's all gone.

His words saddened me in a way I still cannot describe. I couldn't blame him one bit.

'It's not right, what they're doing,' he said. 'You don't look that old.'

The truth of it was that we hadn't tried hard enough to change things, back when it mattered, when there was still time. We could have. But we didn't.

'It won't be good, Teach. You should run away, hide.' Kazinsky paused, looked into my eyes, then lowered his voice. 'Maybe we can go together?'

'It will be okay. They'll look after us.'

'Please.'

'It will be fine, Matthew. Thanks.'

And that was it.

After he left, I stood a long while and watched the sky go dark. Then I put the exam papers and the letters into my briefcase and walked out of the classroom, along the scuffed linoleum corridor and down the front steps of Churchill High School for the last time, my throat aching from holding it all back, the fear growing inside me like a tumour, the pity I felt for these unwilling inheritors I was leaving behind.

Each Windblown Mile

I stand and stretch my legs. The ache in my left hip grows worse every winter. My father had both hips replaced, back when such things were common. I remember him telling me what a difference it made. He was back walking only a few weeks after the surgery, without pain, or so he said. Less than two years later those titanium joints and a small pile of ashes were all that was left of him.

It's been a long time since I've thought about my dad, those kids too. Kazinsky and Smith. I suppose they just got erased along with everything else, all of that other, vanished world. They were about the same age then as my sons are now, a little younger. For the thousandth time I wonder if they are alive, and if so, where they are and if they are happy.

Eight hours it took me to write that first chapter.

I clump my way to the kitchen, avoid the squeaky floorboard, the one I have been meaning to replace for months. My wife is there, sitting at the table, a mug of tea between her hands. She smiles at me, each windblown mile of the past etched in her face, her eyes a timeless miracle. I pour myself a mug from the kettle simmering on the stove, sit opposite her. She reaches out across the plank-board table and takes my hand in hers. These two sets of fingers intertwine, this bone and brittle skin, these hands that together have wielded a thousand tools, and have thus conquered distance and healed the injured, cared for the helpless and buried the dead, carried and cut and killed.

Now that I have begun, I feel as if I have no choice but to continue. But starting is easy. Finishing is what's hard.

2

I walked home the long way, down to the river and then along the footpath on the south bank though Fort Calgary, past the tarpaulin-and-plywood shanty town and then across the bridge over the Elbow River, running full and ice-free now even in January, the letters heavy in my pocket. I thought of the years we'd spent here since moving from Revelstoke after getting married, both of us so young, so oblivious. We'd done our best, raised a son here, built a life. A lot of it had been good. Some of it had been bliss.

It was getting late, and I knew that May would be home from her exhibition. I hoped it had gone well, fought off the thought that it hadn't, replaced it with visions of happy art buyers leaving the studio with paintings tucked under well-fed arms. Then I realised that it wasn't going to make any difference at all.

A cold drizzle started falling. Off to my left, on the island, the zoo was quiet and dark, the animals long since gone. One day they had just shut the place up. Cost savings, they had said. By the time I reached the end of our street, the rain was coming harder. It drummed on roofs and pelted the deleveled concrete sidewalk, cracking against my jacket and through the bare capillaries of bushes and trees, washing in through the charred shell of the Walker place – the whole family killed in Africa a few years earlier, caught there when the war started, the house taken over by squatters. I remember the night of the fire, the snow falling as the fire truck arrived, standing there with May, watching the flames fork from the windows, the jets of water pouring in through the collapsed roof, the embers spinning skywards through the orange billows of steam, her face lit up and how she looked so young still, so beautiful.

Walking on, feet soaked, cold, numb. Cold, soaked feet. On. Walking.

When I reached our house, I didn't go in. I stood on the sidewalk in front of the house for a long time, watching the woodsmoke wisping from the chimney limb, smooth and laminar at first, then shuddering and separating in the wind. The mullioned windows glowed yellow, and inside I could see May moving from the kitchen to the dining room. Her hair was up, the way she wore it when she wanted to look her best. She was wearing the green dress that accentuated her figure. I knew she was happy. Standing there in the rain watching her, I had that feeling I had sometimes of being on the cusp of something, crossing over into a place you can't get back from. That feeling that things can only ever move in one direction.

I pulled back the cuff of my jacket, tilted my wristwatch to the window light, watched the second-hand journey around the dial. Water streamed from the downspout. May moved back to the kitchen. I knew I should go in. But I didn't. I just stood there, listening to the dirge in the sky and the rain in the bare trees and the sound of the river churning up its banks.

It was late by the time I summoned the courage to go inside.

'You're late,' May said. She was sitting at the kitchen table drinking a glass of wine. The table was set, the stove was lit. A tray of roasted vegetables steamed on the oven top. The smell filled the room. We ate in silence. After dinner I got up and turned on the little TV we kept in the kitchen. There wasn't much on anymore since the commercial stations had closed – government-controlled news mostly. A story came on, one they'd been playing for the last several days about the disaster in the Gulf of Mexico, the drone shots showing oil platforms on fire, pillars of black smoke bisecting a green sky. The announcer was talking about the impacts on the coastline and what remained of the economy, blaming previous governments, the historical inaction of the voting populace. It had happened before, of course, but we had learned nothing.

Faster, cheaper. Disaster. Cheaper, faster.

Always the same. Over and over. Again and again. Over and over. The present a mirror of the past, replicating, learning nothing. Was it simply a colossal lack of imagination, or something worse, some deeper failing?

'Turn that shit off,' said May. 'I bet that footage is all computer-generated.'

I didn't want to start in on it. I turned it off.

'I'm not going to be manipulated,' she continued.

I said nothing.

After I had cleaned away the plates, she said: 'Don't you want to know about my day?'

'Of course. Sorry, yes,' I blurted. 'How did the show go?'

She smiled. 'I sold four paintings.'

'That's great, May. Great.'

'Two older ones that I painted that year we camped in the Rockies, you remember?'

I smiled at the memory. So did she. We stood a moment, smiling together, and then it was over.

'And I sold three newer ones, too. Got a good price for them. People always have money for beautiful things, no matter how bad things get.' She refilled her glass, watched me watching her. 'I'm celebrating.'

'Congratulations.'

She drank. 'I hear that people have started getting letters. Quite a few on our street.'

I nodded.

'They're calling you the grey locusts.'

'Apt.'

She frowned. 'Did you get yours?'

I reached into my pocket and pulled out the envelopes, set them on the table together, one atop the other.

'When do you leave?'

I fanned out the letters so she could see.

'What's that?'

'I'm sorry, May,' I said. 'I truly am.' I was. I still am.

I remembered the day we first heard the news, about half a year earlier, maybe a bit less. We were sitting together in the living room, reading, the radio on in the background. The official announcement followed the evening news. Over the next six to twelve months, it said, those born before the cut-off date would be relocated south to make room for the millions of younger citizens streaming north. There were other details about asset confiscation to help pay for the mounting costs of the war and the efforts to adapt society to all the changes. Building resilience, they called it.

The cut-off date meant May was safe, and I wasn't. I would have to go, and she could stay. After the announcement, she turned off the radio and looked me long in the eyes. What she had been looking for I'm still not sure. Was it envy, maybe? Anger, perhaps, or fear? The fact is I can't remember feeling any of those things, and I still don't. All I felt then, and still feel now, was a profound sense of sadness. I'm going to miss you, May, was all I said. I didn't ask her to come with me. I knew that she wanted me to go, that she wanted to live her own life. So, I decided to say nothing, to leave it all unsaid. And that was the way it had stayed. Until now.

'What is it?' she said.

'Our notices. They came this morning.'

'You mean *your* notice,' she said, turning away.

'I'm sorry, May.'

'You keep saying that. Stop saying that.'

I pushed her letter across the table towards her.

'What the fuck are you talking about?' She snatched the letter up, opened it.

I watched her eyes move as she read, wide at first, then gradually narrowing into a compressed horizon of disbelief.

She looked up at me. 'No,' she said. 'This is wrong.' She stood, took a few steps and let the letter fall to the floor.

I reached out for her, but she batted me away.

'No,' she said. 'No. You've changed it. You're jealous. You want to stay and you can't.'

'May, I'm...'

I could see her trying to steady herself. She was breathing hard. 'It's a mistake,' she said, her voice quavering. 'A typo. One number, that's all it is.' She trod on the letter and ground it into the tile with a twist of her foot. 'They make mistakes all the time.'

'I checked, May. I called them today from school. It's not a mistake.'

'One number,' she whispered. I could see panic taking hold now, the blood rising to her face, the vein just below her left eye twitching the way it did when she was stressed. She reached for the wine glass, gulped it dry, tottered, reached for the edge of the table. 'No,' she said. 'It's a mistake. They told us last year, and again just a few weeks ago. Ninety, they said. Ninety.'

I reached to steady her. She pushed me away, stumbled back towards the kitchen counter.

'There were others at the school, May. Others like you. It's not a mistake. Please, May, you have to calm down. Why don't you sit for a moment?'

'Get away from me,' she screamed. 'This is your fault. What did you say to them?'

'What do you mean, my fault? How could I—'

'Asshole. You just said it. You called them. You told them I was older.' She was screaming now, at the top of her voice, the way she'd done during the worst of her episodes, back before we figured out what was wrong and got her treatment. 'You don't want to go alone. That's it, isn't it? You're such a coward.'

I pushed through it. 'Did you skip your meds, May?'

'What if I did? What fucking difference does that make? I won't be able to get them soon anyway, the way things are going.'

'Please, May. Sit down. I'll fetch your lithium.'

She leaned back against the edge of the counter, arching away from me, reaching back. Dishes clattered to the floor.

'No,' she screamed. 'Get away from me.'

'It's okay,' I whispered.

'This is what you've always wanted. To punish me. For everything.'

I reached for her hand. She screamed as she swung the knife.

That Territory of Madness

Memory is an untrustworthy thing. I am sure May would have recalled these events completely differently. It's hard to be objective. And the further away they get, the less certain I am about anything.

The scar is still there, though, a clean cut on my left deltoid. I can still remember the flash of the blade, the surprise I felt as I stared at the knife sticking out of my shoulder, May's scream as she ran from the kitchen and out into the night. It is a memory that is very clear, very clean, seemingly unblurred, and now unearthed, troublingly closer than many, more recent, events.

Dawn lights the eastern sky. Shoals of cloud hang low over the sound, wend through the dark hills that rise from the sea. A light rain is falling, has been falling all night. I stand under the covered balcony – a later addition – and watch the boys prepare the skiff. They load fishing lines and net, bait, oars, food and water. Lewis, the taller and slimmer of the two, guides the bow into the water, tresses of sun-bleached hair falling across his face. Kweku, stockier, darker, leans low and pushes the stern through the shingle. The skiff's keel rib leaves a dark channel in the shingle behind him. Soon they are in and powering their way out towards the abandoned lighthouse. I stand and watch them go, follow the swing and drop of their oars and the silver wake spooling out behind them until they reach the headland and are gone. I wish them luck, and safe return. I say this out loud, as I do each time they go, my prayer to the ocean and the sky and the ancient granite under my feet.

I turn away and go back inside. My wife has put a mug of tea on my desk. It steams in the lamplight. I whisper thanks to her, sit down. Every time they go it is this way. Every time. I lower my eyes to the page, try to calm my fear. Yesterday's words stare up at me, crying out to be banished, back to that territory of madness from whence they came.

3

I stood there for a moment not quite believing what had just happened. Then the pain came. My vision collapsed. I braced myself against the counter, let the turbulence roil through me. I remember the wind whipping in the Manitoba maple outside the back window, the blood pulsing out around the blade, the way it beaded on the stainless steel.

I staggered to the bathroom, found the first-aid kit. The knife hadn't gone in far. I knew that I should leave it in, bind around it, go to hospital. But May was out there somewhere, scared and angry and alone. It was then that I noticed it – May's prescription dispenser, the little white pills there in their slots. She had missed taking her medication for three days running.

I grabbed the handle, held it there a moment ... and pulled. It came out easily, more easily than I would have thought, with a slight sucking sound. And then the blood came, and with it another wave of pain. I pulled a towel from the rack, soaked it in hot water, pressed it to the wound. One of May's white bath towels. Shit. It would never come clean. She'd be furious. I remember thinking that.

Soon I had a bandage in place, tightened down hard, reddening already, but holding. I had to find May. The car keys were still on the hook by the back door. Her purse and raincoat were on the chair in the front hall. Twenty minutes since she'd left. I grabbed the phone, hit the speed dial – Maureen, her closest friend in Calgary, mid-forties, divorced, a couple of joint-custody kids who were 'doing fantastic', as she told me every time we met, which wasn't often. The line crackled, the weather spiking in packets of interference. A voice answered. A child.

'Is your mother there, please?'

No answer, just a yell: 'Mu-um. Phone.'

Banging, a muffled 'shit'. Then: 'Hello?'

'Maureen, it's David.'

Nothing.

'David Armstrong.' That's my name.

'Sorry?'

'David Armstrong.'

Nothing.

'Maureen, it's Teacher.'

'Oh, Teacher. Yes, of course. Sorry.'

'Is May there, Maureen?'

'May? No, why? Is something wrong?'

'No, I ... Well, yes. I ... I need to find her.'

'What happened, Teacher?'

'It's nothing. If she shows up, can you please let me know? If I'm not here, just leave a message. OK?'

'Did she get a letter?'

'Yes.'

'I'm so sorry. Really I am.'

'Sure.'

'If I hear from her, I'll let you know, okay?'

'Thanks.'

I tried everyone I could think of. Each conversation was similar: stilted, awkward, the same negatives in reply. I put the phone down, reached up and touched the bandage. The bleeding had stopped. It wasn't that bad. I ran up upstairs to the bedroom, pulled on a sweatshirt, came back downstairs, drank a glass of water, grabbed the solar-powered windup torch from its cradle on the side counter and my rain shell and cap from the hook at the front door. I whistled for Panda. He came, tail wagging. He was old, but he was willing, and he loved May. I made sure the spare key was under the mat in case she came back while I was away and stepped out into the storm.

We started towards the river, the dog pulling on his lead. Did he sense the urgency? I knew that when she wanted to be alone, she would walk along the river pathway, often with the dog. She'd go for miles sometimes, most often to the east, away from the city, following the Bow River as it curved south and broadened into gravel-strewn braids that cut through old stands of poplar and alder growing in the shelter of the valley. But the trees were mostly gone now, burned during the terrible wildfires of last summer and then hacked away by refugees who came to cut the trees for firewood.

Sometimes I would follow her. Invariably she'd stop at her favourite places: the lookout beyond the weir, the little gravel beach cut into the bank further downstream, where in summer you used to be able to wade out and let the water run cool and strong against your legs, the bench set on the point where you could look back across the river and on clear days see the Rocky Mountains rising behind the city. Early in our marriage we'd walked together, hands clasped through woollen mittens in winter, baby fingers hooked and linked in summer, stopped at these places, watched the ice crack in spring, the water flow cold and pure from the mountains in autumn. But then one day she announced that she was going alone. She returned hours later, quiet, distant, as if she'd been on a long voyage and seen things she could not describe in words. I know how that feels.

After a while, I had started to follow. I'd keep well back, lurking in the trees at the side of the path, careful not to get too close. I watched her wanderings, wondered what had gone wrong, pondered the genesis of this distance. As soon as I'd see her turn and start home, I would hurry back along the railway tracks to the house so that when she returned, I was there, busy in the garden or marking papers at the kitchen table.

And every time I did it, I felt ashamed.

But I didn't stop. I got better and better at the following, closer so I could see her clearly, watch her stop sometimes to sketch in her pocket notebook, hear fragments of a phone conversation, see the steam coming from her mouth on a winter afternoon. I got

better at the rationalisation, too. I was making sure she was safe –
the city had been getting steadily more dangerous as the economy
slumped and food prices rose and refugees flooded in. These days,
a woman walking alone was a target, no matter how much she
asserted that she should not be, that she deserved better, deserved
respect. I was watching over her, ready to spring at any would-be
assailant, and I was trying to understand what she was doing so I
could save our marriage, stop her from making a mistake that we
would both regret. But underneath, the shame lurked, bruise hot
and impossible to ignore.

But now, as far as I could tell, she was barefoot, wearing only
her green dress. She was distressed, not thinking straight, manic.
She had no money. Her phone was still in her purse. It was cold.
Not cold enough for snow, but almost. Close to enough. Soon,
maybe. If she was balanced, she'd head to Ninth Avenue. Most of
the shops would be closed now, but there was a convenience store
there, at the far end towards the city, that would still be open. But
she wasn't anything close to balanced. If she didn't find shelter
soon, she'd die of exposure. I had to find her.

It's all a blur now, looking back. I remember running through
the rain, the dog trotting beside me, the torchlight beam scattering
among the charred trunks, the supercooled droplets hanging in
the light as if ignoring the gravity pulling them groundward. Then,
like now, none of it seemed real, this place, the pain in my
shoulder, the letter crumpled on the kitchen floor, the war in
Africa, Kazinsky crying in class, all that had happened over the
last day and decade, the changes that had come so much more
quickly than I or anyone else had predicted, that non-linearity in
complex systems that shocks an apparently stable, predictable
system into a new dis-equilibrium. I ran on through the darkness,
calling her name out into the night as the rain turned to snow,
into this new strange attractor that was drawing us all in. It was
so dark.

Rain turned to sleet, cold on my face, streaking through the flashlight's dimming beam. I breathed. My heart beat. Heat diffused from my body. Minutes of my life shed into nothing. Rain fell, cooled, turned to ice. Somewhere close by a tree limb crashed to the ground. All around me, entropy doing its work.

I kept going, calling out her name, my voice disappearing into the storm. And then the bluffs across the river where the valley widened out, lights flickering along the crest, blurred and starred through the sleet, and the old Ninth Avenue bridge. The dog was pulling hard on the leash now, tail flicking back and forth, his thick black-and-white fur soaked. As we got closer, I could see the bridge abutments blistering the water. Under the main span, out of the snow, it was dry. Empty liquor bottles, plastic bags, a pile of shit with a few sheets of toilet paper scattered about, the collapsed halves of a cardboard box, a used condom. And then something exquisitely pale, a cherished limb, a green dress.

I dropped to my knees.

That Divine Welcoming

Sometime later – after the exodus but before our escape, she opened up to me in a way she hadn't since were first married. She tried to explain to me what she'd done and why she'd done it and what she'd seen there, under that bridge, as she slipped into unconsciousness.

Every colour of cold, she'd said. Those exact words. I'll never forget them. Whites and blues and the steel grey of the I-beams under the bridge. Fractured slabs and crystal flakes, the spider-web of concentric fractures there in the frozen puddle at her hand. All these patterns demanding capture. But she was too tired, too numb, too everything. It really was too bad, she told me. Too bad about all of it. She'd always thought there was going to be so much more. More love, more happiness, more of everything. It was hard to hear.

She closed her eyes, felt herself dissolving away, as if her constituent atoms were somehow disaggregating, and she told me that part of her knew that she was dying, that this was what the last moments felt like, balancing there at the edge of oblivion, so close she could feel its cold breath on her neck, its gentle voice calling to her, telling her that it was going to be alright, taking hold of her hand, picking her up to carry her across the threshold into nothingness, and that sensation of drifting, untethered to any terrestrial point, and the terror of it, the sparking fear in her bones and the raging darkness in her head because this was not what she believed it would be like, The End.

Where were the angels, she said, the bright lights of heaven? Where was God's divine welcoming, the warm, everlasting peace? She'd always believed, always prayed. But there was only this. This cold. This frozen scattering. Sweet Lord, no. Did you lie to me? Did I lie to myself?

And in that moment, that infinity contained within a fraction of a second, she knew that she'd never heard back. She'd prayed and strived and directed her soul heavenward and envied those who claimed they'd spoken directly to God, heard the word of the saviour, one to one, a private conversation. But she never had. Not once. The communication had only ever been one way. Had she been faking it the whole time, searching for someone, something that didn't exist? Terror flooded her soul, black and deep like an ocean. This was not how it was supposed to be. Now, most of all, a lifetime's devotion was supposed to be rewarded with final certainty, that divine welcoming she'd always been promised, realisation at the final breath. Darkness opened up before her, infinite and empty. She tried to speak. No. And then she was gone.

It made me shiver. It still does.

4

I sat by the bed and watched the early-morning light play over her face, ran the fingertip of my gaze over the upturned tip of her nose and down the long curve of her neck. Once, a single touch had been enough to push me off the cliff-edge of bliss. It seems like so long ago now. But then again, a lot of things seem so long ago. The time when the world had seemed to be making slow, grudging progress. A time of optimism, before the Repudiation, a time of progress despite the setbacks, the losses irretrievable and not. And then the darkness had come, the victory of denial and cowardice over truth. Surely it can't be that long ago, that far away?

I closed my eyes, listened to the sound of her breathing. If I hadn't found her, she would surely have died. It was only because I'd followed her so many times that I'd been able to guess which way she'd go. That's what I told myself. Rationalisation. The last refuge of the guilty. More likely it was the dog who'd led me to her.

It had taken me the best part of twenty minutes to get her back to the house. I'd put my jacket over her, pulled my hat over her head, lifted her and carried her back. She was heavier than I remembered, and I was certainly not as strong as I once was. I shifted her up over my shoulder, fireman style, and then back to a bridal carry every hundred metres or so, walking as quickly as I could, the dog trotting happily beside me. I could the feel the cold inside her through the layers, but she was still breathing. By the time we arrived back at the house I was sweating hard. I stripped off her dress and underwear, dried her, laid her on the bed and covered her over with as many extra blankets as I could find. Then I took off my clothes, towelled myself down, slipped in next to her, pushed myself up against her and felt the cold move from her body into mine. I stayed that way for a long time, running my hands over the familiar topography of her. Slowly, she warmed.

Sometime later, deep in the night, she woke and turned to look at me. Her eyes were wide, the pupils dilated so that there was only black. She put her arms around my neck and drew me close. I could feel her breath on my neck. She whispered something I could not make out, and for the briefest eternity it was if nothing had changed, and we were again as we had once been.

I kissed her, ran downstairs, made her a mug of hot chocolate, grabbed one of her pills, but by the time I got back she was asleep again.

In the letters, we'd been given two days to prepare. And as I sat by her bedside, I considered that despite everything, I deserved this. I could come to no other conclusion. I suppose I could say – did say back then – that I had done all I could. I'd marched, back when it was still allowed. Written everyone I could think of: ministers, representatives, mayors, business leaders – so many letters I couldn't count them all. I'd phoned into radio talk shows and posted stuff on social media, suffered the predictable ridicule. I had even done it the old-fashioned way, standing on the roadside waving signs at uninterested motorists, occasionally receiving a horn blast in what I interpreted as support, more often a shouted insult or a mute middle finger. Everything mattered, everything was part of the fight. That's what I told myself back then, told my students, even after the Repudiation and the new laws curtailing what I could teach. I'd fought on every front I could, as tirelessly as I was able, long after I'd lost hope of even partial victory. But it wasn't enough. Not nearly. It's hard to do what's required when you've convinced yourself you have too much to lose.

And now, two days was all we had. Less. I decided then, watching the predawn sky lighten, that I would prepare. I would change focus. Narrow it down. If the world was beyond saving, I'd save myself. Myself, and the woman I loved. Two standard cases. That's what we were allowed. I'd seen it coming for years. I was not unprepared. Over the last few years, despite the shortages, I'd collected every implement, tool and instrument of survival I could get my hands on. Two sturdy backpacks, military grade. Two high-quality sleeping bags good to minus fifteen that zipped together. A two-man tent with lightweight fly. Fifty metres of military-grade paracord. An all-purpose stove that could run on anything. Compass, long-blade hunting knife, Leatherman multi-tool, wire, fishing line and hooks, torch, solar PV recharger, firestarter, medical supplies, vitamins, emergency rations, water filter.

I was laying out everything in my head when there was a knock at the door. I slid out of bed, threw on trousers and a sweatshirt, and went downstairs. Through the front windows I could see snow falling in thick sheets. I pulled open the door, peered out into the weather. At first, I didn't recognise the man standing before me, an old Toyota Land Cruiser pulled up and idling at the curb, the exhaust steaming in the cold.

'Teach, it's me. Can I come in?' The man threw back the hood of his parka. It was Kazinsky.

'Matthew,' I stumbled. 'Yes of course. Come in.' I looked past him to the car. 'Who's in the car?'

'It's Maddy. Maddy Smith.'

'I didn't know you two were...'

He flashed that big-eyed, long-lashed smile of his. 'Yeah. For over a year now.'

'That's great, Matthew. Great.'

'Gotta talk to you, Teach.' The smile was gone now. 'We need your help.'

I stood back, looked towards the car. 'OK, Matthew. Tell her to come inside.'

Kazinsky turned to the car, waved a mittened hand. The engine shut down and Maddy Smith trudged up the path in Sorrels and a parka that looked two sizes too big for her.

'Hi, Teach,' she said, taking Matthew's hand. Her smile was even more beautiful than the boy's, just as fleeting.

'Hi, Maddy.' It came out as a croak.

They stepped inside and I closed the door. They stood looking at me, cheeks blushed with cold, eyelashes sprinkled with snowflakes, steam rising from wet hair.

'Have you heard?' said Kazinsky, sharing a glance with Smith.

'Heard what? I've been ... busy. Getting ready to leave.'

'Shit,' said Kazinsky. Smith reached out and took his other hand in hers.

'What is it?' I could see the fear in them both.

'Nairobi,' said Smith, tears in her eyes.

'They nuked Nairobi,' Kazinsky said. 'We heard it on the news just now.'

I felt the peripheries of my vision compress. 'Jesus.'

'Me and Maddy, we've decided we're not going to be part of it. You've taught us that. We have to stand up, any way we can.'

I stood there not saying anything, the implications of this spinning up in my mind.

'We're running away,' said Smith. 'Today.'

'We need you to cover for us at school tomorrow,' said Kazinsky. 'And we need gear. Anything you've got. Food, supplies. You told me once you collect that kind of stuff. You know, survival gear.'

I leaned back against the wall, tried to find in the hundred-year-old wood frame a stability that was not there. I looked at the two of them, so young still, and despite everything, so innocent.

'What about MIT, Maddy?' I said, choking back everything. 'You, too, Matthew. Engineering will keep you out.'

'Engineering so we can do what?' said Maddy. 'More of the same?'

'We've been through it,' said Kazinsky. 'We're out. We are going to get as far from all of it as we can. Get to the mountains, go north. Live.'

'They'll chase you,' I said, a strong feeling of admiration growing inside me now.

'Better things to do, I reckon,' said Kazinsky. 'Especially now.'

'Will you help us?' said Maddy, eyes wide. The contacts were gone.

I gave them everything I could spare. A good compass. My best knife. Waterproof matches. I rummaged through my bookshelf, found an old, weathered copy of *Bushcraft 101* by Dave Canterbury, the one I'd bought in a bookshop in Toronto, back when you could still get on a plane and travel to another city without government permission.

Kazinsky flipped through the book, a thin smile growing on his face. 'It's been a while,' he said. 'My dad could've written this, easy.'

I didn't try to talk them around to a different future. I helped them fill two duffel bags with food, gave them an axe, a good flashlight with extra batteries, and my old topographic maps of the Rocky Mountains, the border up to Jasper.

'Come with us,' Kazinsky tried again. 'You and your wife.'

'I can't do that, Matthew,' I said. 'We'll be okay.' We had been assured by the government that the relocation would be swift and dignified, that we would have comparative, though more southerly, accommodation, that we would be well looked after, continue to be employed in meaningful work. This message had been bludgeoned home over the past ten months over the radio, the TV and across what still passed for an internet, as if it had come from an Ayn Rand novel: with a numbing repetitiveness and doctrinal purity that left absolutely no room for misinterpretation. We were guilty, yes, but we would be fairly treated. After all, we were still citizens.

Smith was crying. Kazinsky looked down at the floor.

'You had better go,' I said. My throat ached. 'The sooner you get going the better. I'll cover for you as long as I can.'

They started towards the door.

'Wait,' I said, grabbing Kazinsky's arm. I went to the desk and grabbed a piece of paper and scribbled out an address, a telephone number, an email address. 'If you can, let me know how you're

doing. Nothing anyone can use to track you, just that you're okay.'
I looked at Smith, tried not to get pulled into the depths of her
eyes, failed. 'Both of you.'

I shook Matthew's hand. Smith put her arms around my neck
and reached up and kissed me on the cheek. And as she did, I
knew that I would never see them again.

A Deep Sense of Wonder

I set down my pen. A tear slides across my cheek and falls to the page, dissolving mountains and feeling. I push my chair back from the desk and run my hands through my dry, thinning hair. Not for the first time today, I question my ability to continue, to do this story justice. Despair grips me. Will this be like all the other times I have tried to make this journey, starting only to lose courage at the first obstacle?

Outside, the rain has relented. Shafts of afternoon sun strike through broken cloud, search across the surface of the sea. I stand, feel every one of my seventy-eight years in each degraded joint, every knitted fracture. That I have come to live as long as I have is a deep mystery to me. And while there is a psalm – which one I cannot remember – that gives a man seventy years, eighty if he is strong, it also warns that the span is soon gone.

It is then that I see it. Just beyond the headland where the water is cold and clear and deep. The skiff. They have a sail up. I can see the white canvas flying in the late-slanting sun, the sharp thread of their wake as they round the rocky islet we call The Hope. Something stirs deep inside my cortex, pumps thick slugs of dopamine into my bloodstream. My boys are coming home. I can see them now, closer already, running with the wind. They grew up sailing. I have taught them everything I know, and they are both already far better sailors than I ever was. I watch as they throw in a jibe, set course for home.

I call to my wife. She comes and stands next to me, smiles that beautiful smile of hers, a smile of wisdom, of hardship endured, of regrets survived. We make our way down to the beach. Juliette and Mandy have seen too. We watch them emerge from their homes further along the ridge and run down the path between the big grey boulders, through clutches of wind-bent sheoak and peppermint, down to the beach. Juliette is first, long blonde hair flying in the breeze, clutching little Leo to her chest. She is a tall girl, almost as tall as Kweku, long-limbed and athletic, with a starburst of freckles scattered across the bridge of her nose and the points of her cheekbones. Mandy, the quieter of the two, the more circumspect, follows. She moves carefully, arms cradling her growing belly.

We watch as the skiff approaches, close enough now that we can see the boys working the lines, the sun on their bare shoulders. Juliette whoops, jumps up and down waving her arms in the air. The baby squeals in delight at this game he has played before. Lewis, near the bow, smiles that big grin of his. Kweku, at the tiller, raises a hand, flashes a thumbs up. They have had luck. What I can only call a deep sense of wonder washes over me, catches in my throat.

5

May stood in the living room, looking out through the window at the snow-covered street, the phone pressed to her ear. She'd spent most of the day in bed, had emerged with a bad cold. When she appeared that afternoon dressed for outdoors and announced that she was going out, I said nothing, just nodded and tried a smile. She returned a couple of hours later, slammed the door shut, threw her coat on the floor and tramped into the kitchen. I could see she'd been crying.

She grabbed the phone and punched in a number, glancing at the bloody bandage around my arm. A moment later a voice I knew answered. It was our son, Lachie.

'It's not fair,' she said into the phone. 'Less than a month. Twenty-three days. You need to do something.'

Silence from the other end.

'I shouldn't be going,' she continued. 'None of my friends are going. Please, Lachie.'

I could hear Lachie's voice on the other end of the line. Patience there, surprise. 'The government has kept its promise, Mum. Canadians who are young enough will be allowed to stay, continue their lives, keep what's theirs.'

'I don't care about other Canadians,' she said. 'It's the date that's wrong.'

'There's nothing I can do, Mum. I'm sorry.'

'Please, Lachie.'

'No exceptions, Mum. I'm sorry.'

She was silent a moment. 'Sorry. You're sorry.' Her tone had changed. 'I almost died pushing you out, you ungrateful little shit. And you tell me you're sorry. It's not good enough, Lachie. There are always exceptions. You're a powerful man now. I know you can help me if you want to.'

'Mum, I—'

But she didn't let him finish. 'You don't want to help me, do you? That's it, isn't it?' She glared at me. 'It's your father, isn't it? You two are together on this. He doesn't want to go alone. That's it, isn't it?'

'Mum, that's—'

She slammed the receiver into its cradle and wheeled to face me. Her face was flushed, and the dark orbs of her eyes were filled with tears. 'I told my friends today,' she said. 'None of them are going. Norma's only a month younger than me. The smug bitch just sat there patting my hand like she was ... I don't know what.' She pulled a tissue from her pocket and blew her nose. 'Satisfied. That's what she was, satisfied. I could have punched her in the face.'

I stayed silent. After twenty-five years of marriage, I'd learned to stay quiet. Don't try to solve it. Don't express a view. Just listen.

'Lachie won't help me,' she said.

The last time we'd seen him, six months earlier, he'd stopped by for a day on his way to Vancouver for a conference establishing the new post-referendum transition. Unification they called it. Clearly distressed, he'd admonished us as if we were simply faceless parts of that thing he kept calling 'your generation', rather than his parents.

'You can go like a sheep if you want to,' May said to me. 'But you have no right to take me with you. This is your fault.'

I'd known for a long time that what she had always really wanted was a daughter. A confidante, a friend eventually, someone who would always be there for her. For a while she had even suggested that another baby might bring us closer, perhaps even recapture some of what we had had at the beginning. But I didn't want another child. It was irresponsible. There were too many people on the planet, then. Thirteen billion, far above the projections made early in the century. No one had quite anticipated the ferocity of China's reversal in policy, from one-child families to war-time fertility promotion. Money for babies. And then Africa's kids all grew up and started having their own at all once, HIV barely a pothole in the road. It was the root cause of all the problems we were facing: the wars, the changes, the shortages – too many people with too many desires chasing not enough of everything and doing it all the wrong way. Even in the increasingly rare moments of passion I had maintained control, even when she had assured me that it was safe.

'Let me try,' I said. 'I'll call him.'

Tears streaked her face. 'I don't want to go,' she said.

'Neither do I.'

6

The conversation with Lachie had gone pretty much as I'd expected. He couldn't say much. I knew his conversations were being monitored. Despite his position, he had to be careful. I asked him to keep track of us, if he could, forward any mail that might be directed to him for us. He agreed. I could hear the tension in his voice. I told him I loved him, that I was proud of him, told him to look after himself. What I've been saying to him since he was fifteen.

Two days isn't a lot when you are dismantling your life.

I'd notified the few colleagues, friends and relatives who didn't already know, hadn't already done the straightforward calculation. I had tried to engage May in helping to go through our stuff. There was so much that we didn't want to leave behind. Irreplaceable stuff like photographs, paintings my father had done, favourite books, May's keepsakes and clothes. But the letter had been quite clear: one case that you can carry on your own. Laptops are allowed. No phones. No weapons. No bicycles or drones. And no pets.

That was the hardest part. Not the stuff. It was the memories, the friends. And the fear. It was not as if there had been a lack of time, mind you. Twenty-five years of forewarning, as things went from difficult to numbing, should have been enough. Should have been, but never can be. And I couldn't convince her, could not make her see, that this, our penance, was just and fair, and really it was the only logical outcome. We were guilty.

And so, when they came for us, before dawn on that third day, we were as ready as we could be. I'd packed every piece of survival gear I could carry into my bag. The dog was in his favourite spot in the back garden, under the big Manitoba maple. I'd marked the spot with a river rock, said a few words as May wept.

I stood on the front porch and stared into the bailiff's hangover face, that pissed-off, dragged-out-of bed look all over him, the smell of last night's beer. Out on the street, a bus idled in the snow, half a dozen faces peering through frost-edged windows. It was one of those yellow school buses that you still see around sometimes, like the ones that took me to summer camp when I was a kid, except for the wire cages over the windows.

The bailiff frowned, shoved a clipboard and a pen at me. 'Sign this,' he said.

I took the pen, started reading the paper.

A breath escaped between the bailiff's lips: 'Asshole.'

I looked up from the clipboard, stared into the kid's eyes. 'What did you say?'

The bailiff frowned, bored again. 'Just sign it.'

'There is no need to be rude,' I said. 'Show some respect.'

The boy turned on me, glared. 'Respect?' he growled. 'You have to be fucking kidding me.'

I can still feel it now, the shame burning up inside me, thick and hot. I signed the form.

The bailiff snatched the clipboard away, handed me two yellow tags each with an elastic band looped through a hole in one end. 'Attach this to your coat,' he said. 'The other one is for your wife.' Then he turned and started down the steps towards the bus. 'Two minutes,' he said without looking back.

A police car flashed past, lights strobing, and pulled to a stop three doors down, outside Ross Steven's house, the guy with two first names. Two big cops jumped out and stood on the sidewalk, looking at the modest two-storey home, the thick plywood sheets sealing the windows, the steel gate in the ten-foot brick wall Steven had erected around the place just last year. Steven had always been a bit of a recluse, from back East people said, Ontario somewhere, an IT guy, ran his own company. Ten years we had lived on the street and not once had we socialised with Steven and his diminutive, plain-looking wife. A few hellos in the street had been about all. And then the wall started to go up. I had spoken to him a few times, standing there on the pavement as Steven mixed concrete and hammered forms, muttered monosyllabic replies to my questions, waved away my advice. And then one day the wall was finished and that was it. Other than their regular Saturday morning excursion for food, no one saw or spoke to them. The neighbours said they had gone 'survivalist', preparing for the cataclysm, rumoured that he was one of the Canadian *indépendantistes*, the rebel group that had taken to the wilderness, urban and natural, to fight American rule.

I stood on the porch, watched the cops walk to Steven's front gate and press the buzzer, stand there fiddling with nightsticks and handcuffs. Many had tried to resist. There had been the legal challenges, of course, one of which had gone all the way to the Supreme Court and had been in the news feeds for months before the war in the subcontinent stole the headlines. No one had ever expected that they would win, and in the end, the Marshank-Watson bill was passed by both houses, and the Intergenerational Equity Commission had been established. The rest was common knowledge.

The bailiff was standing under the streetlight beside the bus. He glanced at his clipboard, looked up at me and tapped the face of his watch. *Hurry up*, he mouthed. *Asshole*.

I glared back at him. I did it quickly and without conviction. Then I turned and opened the door, and walked inside for the last time, past my father's old oak roll-top desk with the square-cut front leg where Lachie had split his head open that Christmas Eve when he was three, and his blood had seeped into the gaps between the lams of the hardwood floor; down the hall past the decimated rogue's gallery of family photos – May had packed the ones she wanted into her case, peeling the photos out of the frames – and into the living room. I liked that house. I liked the floors, the big double-hung windows, the tight turns of the staircase, the snug bedroom dormer, all of it of an earlier time when there were still some things you knew would never change.

May was in the living room, sitting in her favourite chair, hands crisped around the armrest, trancing into the mute television screen where a sixty-second loop of the day's news spooled out: an armoured fighting vehicle in a ruined street blasting its long, barrelled chain gun in sustained bursts, fire and smoke spitting from the muzzle; President Lejeune's sombre face mouthing silent words unknown but by now so familiar; a drone shot of an arctic research vessel plying a green, ice-scattered sea, the ship compressing into a tiny speck as the camera panned out, revealing a foaming expanse of whitewater that engulfed the horizon, the words 'Melting clathrates venting methane from sea floor' scrolling across a bright red chyron at the bottom of the screen.

I crouched down beside her and put my hand on hers. She pulled her arm away, sat staring at the technicolour nightmare as if somewhere below that lurid surface the right world lingered, ready to open out in a warm rush of black-and-white movie happiness.

I looped May's tag through the buttonhole of her coat. 'Please, May. We have to go. They're waiting for us.'

'Leave me alone.'

'May.'

'I'm not going.'

'May, please.'

'You should have left me there.'

'Don't be ridiculous. You would have died.'

'You can't see it, can you? This is a death sentence.'

I shook my head, filled my lungs, tried to breathe it away. 'Please, May. Don't say crazy things.'

'I'm not going. Lachie will be here any minute.'

'He's not coming, Maybelline.'

'Fuck you.' On the TV, Lejeune's young-old face mouthed inevitability.

'Why do you persist with this, May?'

'Because he *owes* it to me,' she breathed, still attached to the TV screen by an invisible umbilical.

Hammering on the door now, something hard against the wood frame, and then a voice, deeper; not the bailiff. 'Get out here, now.'

'Coming,' I called over my shoulder.

I reached for her arm. This time she didn't react, just let my hand rest there as if it was of no weight, no consequence. I waited there a moment and then got to my feet and turned off the TV. She stared at it as if it were transmitting still.

Flashing lights from the street pierced the gap between the front curtains and clanged over the ceiling and the walls, painted the back of May's head in red and blue. A megaphone blared, more police cars arrived, sirens squalling.

May turned to look.

'It's Steven,' I said. 'I told him this would happen.'

'That's you, isn't it?' she said. Her look was hard, her mouth set in a flat line. 'Always lecturing, always predicting the future, never doing anything about it. Steven is fighting for his property, for his rights. That's what we should be doing.'

'The government has promised—'

'And you believe them? In my life I've never met anyone so gullible.'

How many times had she levelled that one on me over the years? 'We have no choice,' I whispered, taking it. 'Please, May.'

A detonation shook the windows, making her jump. Me too. She grabbed my arm in reflex, but recovered quickly and snatched her hand away. A few moments later two more loud bangs ripped through the neighbourhood. We watched as a cop darted from behind his car, sprinted across the road and through the front gates of Steven's place.

A flurry of shots banged out, followed by an explosion.

'Look,' she gasped.

Smoke bloomed from one of the top-floor windows, billowing white in the high-powered beams of the spotlights. And then silence. We stood transfixed, May's hand viced around my arm.

A few moments later two cops appeared at the front gate, dragging a limp body face down between them. Stephen's head hung so that his forelocks brushed the ground. There was a big hole where the back of his skull should have been. As they dragged him his legs painted a dark stain on the pavement.

'Jesus,' was all I could say.

'I. Hate. You.' She said it like that, slowly. Emphasising each word. Her eyes flicked back and forth between mine, left and right, as if comparing the imperfections and flaws of each. 'That should be you.' Then she turned and walked out of the house, past the armed soldier standing by the door and straight onto the bus, leaving her bag on the front porch for me to carry.

I stood there, fixed to the floor, unable to move. I guess I'd known for a long time, even if I had never wanted to admit it. This truth revealed in sidelong glances, the slow closing of her eyes when I'd say something particularly inconsonant. And yet May's words opened me up, pulled me apart. I closed my eyes, felt the future closing in around me, the inevitability of it. I switched off the lights and walked to the front door and closed it behind me.

My hands were shaking. Stephen's limp body was loaded into the back of a police van. I stepped back to look at the home we'd bought the year we were married, worked and saved hard to pay off, the master bedroom dormer I put in eight or nine years ago, the studio I built for May, the shiplap siding I repainted while watching Steven's wall go up. I slung my pack, picked up her bag and walked to the kerbside, loaded our bags under the bus in the designated slot, handed the house keys to the bailiff, initialled the form on the clipboard, and boarded the bus without looking back.

Across Miles and Decades

The morning sun streams through the windows, warming my face. I look out along the now familiar line of the headland and past the old lighthouse to the easternmost reaches of this protected sound that welcomed us so long ago, gave us sanctuary.

And yet, so much has been lost. More than I could ever have imagined. That it actually happened, not in some theoretical alternate universe, but here, in the only reality we will ever know, and that I of all people was witness to it, still shocks me profoundly.

I re-read what I have written so far, a few dozen longhand pages. Events captured, moved from the quantum dreamworld of memory to the physical reality of ink and paper. Names and faces and places that I have locked away for far too long, exhumed and honoured in the only way that is left to me.

I look out to sea, past the horizon, across miles and decades.

A touch on my shoulder. Are you alright, chéri?

I look up at her, the pages trembling in my hands.

She touches my face, wipes a tear from my cheek.

It is difficult, I say.

It will get worse.

Yes.

And then it will get easier.

Yes. And then much more difficult again.

7

The bus moved through the suburban streets, stopping regularly to take on more people. They carried duffel bags and suitcases and were very quiet as they got on. Some cried. Most did not.

This is the shudder, I thought, the precursor of chaos.

Soon the bus was full, and we were making our way along the parkway through town, the mostly empty skyscrapers of the central business district on our left. We crossed the Kensington Bridge and turned west. May hadn't said a word since getting on the bus. She just sat staring out of the window. By the time we arrived at the bus terminal the sky was lightening to that colour of nausea that even now I find impossible to describe. The colour of the sky gone to hell.

There was a big crowd waiting outside the station. Held back by uniformed police, they clogged both sides of the street, swarmed around the busway. As we approached, I could make out the first placards, see the odium in the faces, all so young, like children, all of that fresh battlefield beauty of youth, their white teeth and full, springtime lips screaming hate.

I flinched as the first projectiles rattled onto the side of the bus. At first, I thought it was hail pelting the windows. But these were stones, twigs, clumps of earth, bottles. An apple disintegrated against the window near my head, the juice running down the glass carrying pieces of yellow pulp, and I remember thinking how strange to be wasting food when everyone was so hungry. As we got closer to the terminal building some of the protesters broke from the crowd, jumped the barriers, ran towards us. A young man dressed in a green army jacket hurled himself at the side of the bus, a baseball bat raised in his left hand. His eyes were deep brown, the whites heavily bloodshot. It was as if he was looking right at me. His hair was long and wavy, the colour of rapeseed, like

Lachie's, and I thought of how much he looked like my own son, except for the crudely stitched scar that gaped from the hinge of one jaw to the other, as if the boy's mouth had been torn open and then sewn closed again. His right sleeve was pinned back to his jacket, empty.

The crown of the bat hit the window with a loud crunch, crazing the glass into a soup-bowl blister. Someone screamed. The man sitting next to the point of impact flinched, knocking the woman sitting next to him into the aisle. Cubes of glass pelted my face, sprayed the back of May's head. One of the protesters had plastered a sign up against the wire that covered the windows. Big red letters, crudely drawn, spelled out: *PAY FOR YOUR SINS*. Omission and commission both.

As the bus reached the station entrance and left the crowd behind, May turned to face me. She said nothing, just sat and stared at me, pushing all the disdain she felt for me out through her eyes.

The bus pulled into one of the diagonal bays and stopped with a hiss. The front door opened. A uniformed man got on. He stood at the front of the bus and raised a bullhorn to his mouth. 'Get off', he said. 'Collect your bags. Get in line.'

'Don't you see what's happening?' May said, getting to her feet. She grabbed my elbow, squeezed hard.

'Exactly what they told us would happen,' I said.

May stared at me as if I had just escaped from an asylum.

'Keep moving,' said the man with the bullhorn. 'No talking. Collect your bags. Get in line.'

'We heard you the first time,' said May, not loud enough that he could hear her.

We stepped down from the bus. I got our bags. We stood in line. We did as we were told. The line snaked its way around to the far end of the bus terminal, where big Greyhound coaches were taking on people. We shuffled along with everyone else, a few steps at a time.

'This is what the Nazis did with the Jews,' said May.

'Don't be ridiculous,' I said. 'This is Canada, or what used to be Canada.' I was going to have to monitor her medication carefully. '*You* voted for it.'

'*Everyone* voted for it. Except you.'

'Do you think this would have happened if we'd stayed independent?'

'And you've never forgiven me for it,' she said before looking away.

We shuffled along in the queue. All the people were old. Many could barely carry their own bags. Some had canes, a few shuffled along on walkers. There were hundreds of them, thousands maybe, implanted with who knew how many hearing aids and pacemakers and artificial joints, loaded down with skin creams and hair dyes, beta-blockers and renin inhibitors, thousands of daily doses of lisinopril and Zocor and Prilosec and azithromycin, all of it to be ingested and pissed out into waterways and sewage systems from Texas to Arkansas.

I don't remember how long we were there. It could have been an hour, could have been six. But I do recall the sounds: the coughs, the laboured wheezes, the hushed breeze of a thousand frightened whispers. And I remember that sense of distance that has struck me so many times before and since, a feeling that life was somehow unfurling at the wrong scale, light years instead of arm spans.

By the time we were finally herded aboard an old Greyhound bus and our luggage loaded, a least two dozen of our number had fallen from the queue and were being treated in a temporary medical station at the far end of the station. The bus left the city and headed South on Highway 2. By morning our remaining neighbours would wake and everything would look as it had the day before, but we, the eighty-niners, would be gone. All of us. No exceptions.

8

Just before noon we crossed the old border, the customs buildings empty and boarded up, the flagpoles bare. It had been portrayed as a marriage, ten more states for the Union. The papers had reported an eighty-five percent acceptance. With the world going crazy, we had sought shelter under the still-formidable American umbrella. And yes, she was right. I still hadn't forgiven her. I realised that her vote had been cast, in a way, for the same reason that she hadn't left me. As the world got more dangerous, as technology's hold on our lives diminished and things we had once considered 'everyday' got more expensive and harder to come by – things like access to the mobile telephone network, food, the internet, medicines – independence became a steadily more frightening proposition. I had a good job. And when she was balanced, she felt safe with me. That's what I told myself anyway.

We moved steadily south on the deserted highway. There were very few cars on the road these days, with gasoline rationed and so expensive. I thought she might lay her head on my shoulder, as she had done in the first years of our marriage, driving through the night across the dark prairie, but she leaned up against the glass of the window instead. The sky was darkening. I guessed we must be somewhere in Montana now, maybe Colorado, miles and miles of dry scrub, this whole area depopulated now according to the news, the forests burned away, the soil dried up and barren, and all the wild animals gone, another example of what May called God's punishment.

It had been years since we had driven down to Utah this way, the year before Lachie was born, before we were married, before everything started to go wrong. I was still at university, finishing up my teaching degree. May was at art school. It was summer, and we had camped beside lakes and in mountain forests in my little two-man dome tent, watched the stars come out through the pines, made love in the early morning when the air was prismed with dew. We were going to make a life for ourselves. I was going to change the world one young mind at a time, May was going to paint like Camille Pissarro. It was still hard to believe that we could have changed so much in twenty-five years, that the world had changed so much. But it had. All of it, and so much more still to come. I could feel the icy fog of sadness spreading inside me, and I breathed hard and fought it back in the dark although no one could see me.

The change of speed woke me from a fitful sleep. May's head was now on my shoulder. It was just gone seven pm. We had been on the road for over ten hours without a stop. The bus stank of sweat and bad breath. Thankfully, we were near the front, away from the increasingly disgusting rear toilet.

The bus pulled into a floodlit roadside compound and rolled to a stop in front of a row of fast-food outlets. We filed off the bus into the parking lot and were ushered by the guards towards the restaurants. The brightly lit plastic boxes looked like cheap children's toys, the joyful primary colours cloistering sullen uniformed staff old enough to be my parents. May slumped into one of the moulded plastic chairs, and I went to the counter and stood in line, and when it was my turn ordered the least horrible thing on the menu. The lady behind the counter had thinning grey hair and bad teeth. She frowned and handed me two red cardboard boxes and two bottles of water.

'Thanks,' I said.

'From Canada?' she said.

I nodded. 'We all are. This whole busload.'

'I figured.'

'How far are we from the border?'

She leaned towards me, lowered her voice. 'If you're thinking of running, don't. A couple tried last week. They didn't get a hundred yards.' The woman leaned back again, crossed her arms across her chest. 'Voucher,' she said.

I fumbled through my pockets, found the little books of tickets we'd been given at the station.

'Top one from each.'

I tore them off, placed them on the counter. She handed me the food. 'Thanks,' I said.

'Canadians,' she said, shaking her head. 'Always so damned polite.'

I didn't respond, turned away and started back to the seating area.

'Took your time,' someone said.

I put May's box on the table in front of her. Without looking up she opened the box and took a bite out of the sandwich. She chewed it a moment before spitting it out in disgust.

'I think I'm going to be ill.' She stood. 'I am going to look for the restrooms.'

She was gone a long time. I ate my fried vegetable sandwich in silence. When she returned her face was pale, and I could see that she had been crying.

I reached for her hand. 'Are you alright, May?'

She looked up at me through red swollen eyes but did not reply.

I left her there and followed the signs to the back of the restaurant. A dimly lit hallway led past the kitchen and its suffocating smells of frying oil and animal fat to the men's room. A strong odour of commercial-strength detergent barely masked the stench of urine and faeces. I opened the far cubicle door and stood staring down at the toilet bowl. The porcelain was adorned by a brown ring of slime that extended from water level almost to the lip. The seat was sprinkled with piss, as if someone had squatted above the seat to avoid sitting on it. The other cubicle was worse, the bowl filled with a thick brown sludge.

On the wall just above the empty toilet roll holder, someone had written in ballpoint pen: 'Welcome to a hell of your own making. Don't forget to flush.'

What Matters

We reach the top of what we still call Chicken-Head Rock and gaze out across the water. Pearl-strings of puffy white cumulus shunt in from the sea, shadow us for a moment, and then are gone. I take a swig from my water bottle, offer it to my wife. She takes a long drink, wipes her mouth with the back of her hand, flashes me a smile. I nod, smile back.

There is a spring behind our house that flows all year round. We found it on our first day here, tucked into a break in the slope near the base of these very cliffs, set among a grove of weeping tea trees and fragrant windblown peppermint. I can see it clearly from where I stand, a telltale shock of green cradled among a henge of pillared granite boulders. After months skirting the continent's seemingly endless coastline, surviving on the meagre trickle from our portable solar desalination unit, the occasional windfall of a passing raincloud harvested with desperately deployed tarpaulins and buckets, and the foul, brackish water we sometimes managed to scoop from mossy depressions within walking distance of a safe anchorage, the delicious purity of what trickled from these fissures was nothing less than a miracle. It was one of the reasons we decided to stay.

I stow my water bottle, hoist my pack. It was Kweku who named this place, that day we first sailed into the cove. He was sitting in his favourite place, astride the bowsprit, his harness tied into the deck cleat, his little legs dangling over the side so he could feel the sea spray on his toes. I had just finished bagging the jib when he looked back at me and pointed at the strange pillar of time-worn granite that towered over the bay. Look, Daddy, he said, it's a chicken head. And so it was, beak, comb and all.

We keep going. I must have walked this path a couple of hundred times, wearing a narrow but visible thread up through the bottlebrush gullies and between the big, weathered Cambrian boulders to the *summit. Every twist and turn, every tree and shrub, each rock-strewn mesa is familiar and yet changing. The living grows and dies and is born anew, the inanimate weathers and reaggregates in turn. Wood becomes soil, shingle sand. Sea creatures die and are reborn as birds, winging their way across vast oceans. Plutons erode and reaccrete and after millions of years are driven skyward to birth jagged new Anapurnas and snow-capped Kilimanjaros. Metamorphosis is everywhere, measuring the forward impulse of time, unwavering, constant, and yet, within us, completely malleable.*

I have thought about this for a long time. Ten thousand miles' worth, more. It finally crystallised for me – three or four years ago I think it was, before the girls anyway, when Lewis was swept from the skiff during a storm. We thought we'd lost him, Kweku and I. It was out there past The Hope, where the Southern Ocean swell collides with the windblown waves that bend around the point. A good ten minutes passed before we found him again, bleeding from a strike to the head but still smiling as we hauled him aboard. It was the longest six hundred seconds of my life.

That evening, safely home, I stood on the balcony and looked out at the sea, thought of the journey that had brought us here, of everything before and since. And I realised then that this is what I believe in: this cycle, this reality. The rock beneath my feet, the water that flows through it, the sea and all its creatures, the sky above me now, the mingling fragrances of pollen and seed and blossom, the turning of the heavens. The love of my wife and sons, and my responsibility to them and to all of it. It is the simplest of conclusions. Worship what matters, what is indispensable, what is beyond yourself. And know that this, in the end, is enough.

9

They put us back on the bus and we kept going, driving south through the night. Mountains appeared, dark silhouettes against the starless sky. By my best estimation, average speed and time travelled, I figured we were now somewhere in southern Colorado.

Our fellow passengers veered between exhaustion and terror. They huddled in their seats, whispering to themselves and each other. I was grateful that my father had died before he had to face this.

The first spike of a sulphur moon appeared over the mountains, bathing May's face in a wan light. She looked as pale as she did when I found her under the bridge. She hadn't said a word to me since the rest stop.

It was a straight run. Three days. We stopped twice a day, in the morning and evening, slept in our seats as the darkened country flew by. Days were hardest, looking out at drought-riven plains and smoking charcoal forests, all the shuttered and abandoned towns. When we slowed and turned onto a dirt road, my best estimate put us somewhere in Texas.

After a few miles we arrived at what I can only describe as a refugee camp. It appeared slowly out of the heat haze, as if from a nightmare. Rows of green canvas tents as far as you could see, a cluster of plywood and corrugated steel shacks centred on a massive central building that looked like a warehouse or a discount outlet, all of it surrounded by a double line of twelve-foot barbed-wire fence stretching across the dry ground like a hastily sutured scar.

Silence smothered us as we were waved through the entrance. The bus stopped in front of the large building. The doors opened. We stood in turn, gathered our things, and advanced to the front of the bus. I stepped to the tarmac. A wall of heat hit me, snatched the air from my lungs. I stood breathless, squinting in the sun. A uniformed man with a bullhorn was telling us to get in line. I spun around, searching for May. She should have been right behind me.

'Hey look,' someone shouted. 'They're taking our stuff.'

Our luggage was being unloaded from the bus and piled onto a trolley. I couldn't see May anywhere. Other buses were arriving now, buses full of people like us, old people, the displaced, the responsible. Fear etched in their faces. Arthritis like sand in their joints. Regret piled heavy on brittle bones.

Get in line. No talking.

I scanned the line, up and back as it formed. May wasn't there. Panic rose inside me, clutched at my throat, that same feeling I'd had by the river that day, searching for her in the rain. I broke from the line, turned back towards the bus.

'Hey, you,' shouted the voice. 'Get back in line.'

I was about to climb aboard when she appeared.

'I dropped something,' she said as she walked past me and joined the line.

We were marched into the warehouse building, corrugated steel walls enclosing acres of concrete. If anything, it was hotter inside than it had been under the sun. Hundreds-long queues snaked between ropework barriers. The murmur of voices rose and blended and echoed back down from the steel roof, drowning out every individual sound. After a few minutes I was drenched in sweat.

The queue inched forward, the woman in front of us alternately pushing her walker ahead and kicking a battered little bag along the concrete. Her hair was thin, fell in grey wisps from a flaking pink scalp. I asked her if she wanted help, but she just shook her head and muttered something I couldn't make out and nudged her bag ahead a few more inches with her foot. After about thirty minutes, the queue stalled altogether.

'What's the holdup?' someone shouted from further back.

'Yeah,' came another voice. 'Get a move on up there.'

I looked back in the direction of the voices.

'Get a move on.' The same voice again.

The old woman with the battered bag twisted in her walker and glared back in the direction of the voices. 'What's the rush?' she shouted back, her voice as thin and dry as the skin stretched across her face.

'So impatient, these people,' she said, fixing me with a watery stare.

After a while the queue started forward again. Two big policemen channelled us towards a desk occupied by a young nurse in a white facemask. She was partially hidden behind two big computer screens and a carousel device of the kind you see in medical laboratories. It took us another hour to reach her.

'Name and National Identification Number?' she asked.

I told her.

She tapped the keyboard, waited a moment, then withdrew a syringe from the carousel.

'Roll up your sleeve,' she said.

I did as I was asked. I didn't ask what was to be injected into my body, or why. I should have, of course, but I didn't. I just let it happen. The nurse pushed the large-diameter needle into the fleshy part of my hand between thumb and forefinger, depressed the syringe.

'Next,' she said.

I moved on to the next desk. A young woman in uniform tapped on a keyboard. A printer hummed. She handed me a ticket. 'Your accommodation,' she said. 'Bay twelve, Group A29.'

I turned and waited for May.

She had not rolled up her sleeve. She was standing before the nurse, shoulders back, jaw set hard. 'What is this?'

'Microchip,' said the nurse.

'What for?'

'It has all of your information on it. So we can make sure you are looked after.'

'Track us, you mean.' She crossed her arms. 'Nobody said anything about microchipping. This cannot be legal.'

One of the big cops took a step towards her.

'Please, May,' I called back across the desks. 'Not now.'

The cop hesitated. May looked at me and back at the cop. 'This is bullshit,' she said, offering her arm.

The nurse administered the injection. When she was finished, she glanced up at May then lowered her eyes. 'I'm sorry about this,' she said.

'Sure you are,' said May.

*

It was there, standing in the queue at bay twelve, waiting for transport to our new home, that I met Derek Argent for the first time.

I'd heard about of him, of course. A mega-wealthy industrialist, he had become a bit of a celebrity during the Repudiation as a high-level advisor to multiple governments, famous for his extravagant tastes and entrepreneurial cunning. He'd even financed his own space-tourism company, been the third civilian to make multiple orbits of Earth in his own ship. There had been some high-profile philanthropy too, I remembered, large donations to children's charities and art foundations. But reputation seldom describes reality. I had no way of preparing for what Derek Argent would eventually reveal to me, and how it would change my life.

He was sitting on a bench next to a big black cop, not far from the bay twelve gate. As we got closer, I could see him staring at May. I stared back, but he didn't look away, only smirked at me and then made a point of exaggerating his inspection of my wife, head to foot. I looked down at the chain that linked his wrist to the cop's, up at the second cop standing behind him. May was looking too. Argent shrugged and gave her a big grin.

A woman emerged from the crowd and handed Argent a paper cup patterned with a familiar brand. 'Here's your coffee, if you can call it that,' she said.

She handed one to the cop, who thanked her in a surprised tone.

'Why are you giving him one, for Christ's sake?' Argent said.

'Don't get shirty, Derek,' the woman replied. She was dressed in tight black leather trousers and an expensive-looking jacket and black stiletto boots that made her look taller than she was. Her face was pale and gaunt in an over-trained way, and I thought she must have been beautiful once. I recognised her from the TV. Her name was Samantha Tyler-Argent, a top lawyer, famous for leading one of the failed supreme-court challenges to the Marshank-Watson bill.

'Man's just trying to do his job,' I heard her say. 'We wouldn't be here in the first place if you had listened to me. I told you not to trust Stephenson.'

'Fucking traitors, all of them.'

'We could have been there by now, home free.'

Argent jerked his left hand, jolting the cop's arm. The policeman jumped up and looked down at the coffee dripping over the front of his uniform. With his free hand he started to brush the liquid to the floor.

'Asshole,' he muttered.

Argent smiled. 'You call this shit coffee?' he said, dumping the contents of his cup on the floor, splashing the cop's shoes.

The woman stood looking at the puddle of coffee spreading on the concrete. 'Fuck you, Derek,' she said, turning and walking away.

'Yeah, fuck you, Derek,' said the cop.

The public address system droned, the bored voice of a semi-literate young woman who seemed incapable of pronouncing any word in its entirety. 'Once assigned accommodation, please proceed to your transport,' I interpreted her to say. 'Check the cards provided when you started your journey. Your personal effects will follow.'

'That's right, everyone,' said Argent, loudly enough for everyone nearby to hear. 'Follow the voice. Do any of you idiots really believe you are ever going to see your stuff again?'

10

'He's right,' May said to me. 'They'll take everything. Every last thing.'

I ignored her, then made the mistake of turning towards Argent.

'Yeah, I mean you,' he said, pointing at me with his free hand. He was staring right at me. His eyes were strong, very blue, like the sky used to be. 'You have no idea what is going on here, do you? All of you idiots being shifted around like cattle,' he glanced at the cop. 'The herders as ignorant as the herd.'

'Damn right,' someone shouted back.

I turned towards the voice. An older guy was staring past me, looking at Argent. His hair was pulled back into a ponytail, his long grey beard stained with nicotine. An army-surplus jacket hung from his bony frame. The patch over his breast pocket read *Esposito*.

'They're digging mass graves right now,' shouted Esposito. 'Just outside.'

May looked at me, fear in her eyes.

'Don't listen to him,' I said.

'What about you?' shouted Argent, still staring right at me. 'Do you have an opinion?'

I looked away, said nothing. What could I say? Most people had no idea what was happening, or why. Some days I even doubted my own understanding. Truth of any kind seemed a distant memory. I relied now only on first principles – physics, mathematics – anything to keep from being sucked into the quagmire of disinformation, conspiracy theories and bullshit. After the second pandemic, there had been such hope all around the world. Hope that perhaps, finally, people would see the perils of ignoring science, the compounding dangers of inequality and global biodiversity loss, of delaying action on the really big challenges, the folly of putting the economy ahead of people, as if somehow we existed to serve the economy, rather than the other way around. If the pandemics had shown us anything, it was that we could make massive changes quickly, deploy huge resources to tackle a problem. In a crisis, everyone is a socialist. It all seemed so clear.

But every group saw it differently, saw in the rolling calamities a different message. And so, instead of a new dawn, entrenched leaders and despots alike doubled down hard on the old ways, used the newly introduced public-health restrictions to control people in ways they never had before. Most went along with it, too tired and poor and frightened to resist, even if they had wanted to. Getting the economy going again became the all-encompassing goal. Environmental laws were wound back everywhere; huge sums were pumped into industry; resources of all kinds were opened up to rapid exploitation. And anyone who tried to stand in the way was bulldozed aside. The Repudiation had lasted almost a decade: ten years of outright lies, a literal war on science, reason, and fact – plenty of time to cement the disaster.

Then the kids had taken over, inheriting a ruined economy and a war on multiple fronts. I thought of my son. I prayed that he was alive and well, and as happy as he could be. It helped me to know that he was part of it, this new government of youth – 'the kids' I called them. That last time I'd spoken to him he told me that they were trying their best, that they'd made massive investments in green energy and sustainable agriculture, things so many of us had spent decades advocating. I hoped they would get the chance to keep at it, to make it work. I really did.

And as for all of us here, well, everyone needed a scapegoat.

When May and I boarded, Argent and his wife were already in the van, seated in the front row just behind the driver. Argent was rubbing his wrist where the handcuff had been. 'Rot in hell, pig,' he shouted out at the cop.

The bailiff checked names off on a clipboard. May and me, then another couple – a broad-shouldered African man and his seemingly much younger partner – and a single guy – older, grey hair, trimmed grey beard, slim.

The bailiff closed the door and faced us. 'Welcome, ladies and gentlemen, to your new home. We'll be arriving at your accommodation in about thirty minutes. So please just sit tight and—'

'How about telling us where the fuck we are?' Argent said, loud enough so everyone could hear.

The bailiff blanched, hesitated. He was young, like all of them now. An angry pimple festered somewhere just beneath the skin at the edge of his lower lip.

'You are in Texas,' he said.

'Where in Texas?' said the big African.

'Not far from Fort Worth,' said the bailiff. 'So, like I said, just sit tight.'

The van crawled through a series of wire and concrete chicanes, emerged from the depot. After half an hour of featureless desert, we reached the outskirts of a town, rolled through a checkpoint, this time with patches of green grass and flags flying and a sign saying *Welcome to Brownwood*.

Soon, we were trundling over cracked and potholed pavement through a once-prosperous district. There were no other vehicles on the road. We stopped at an intersection. There was no other traffic. Four traffic lights swung from the quadrangle cabling, extinguished. We kept going, turned onto a long boulevard, the trees all chainsawed down to stumps, the empty sidewalks baking in the sun. We passed a boarded-up church, the cross on the roof standing white against the clear green sky, and then over the rusted steelwork of a last-century bridge. Below, a dried-out riverbed, a shopping cart half-buried in the cracked mud, its wire frame clogged with shreds of photodegraded plastic, and further on, the rusted hulk of an abandoned car, windowless now, useless.

As the van slowed in front of a row of low-slung apartment

buildings, the bailiff stood and clutched the rail. 'You are lucky,' he said. 'You will be sharing one of the bigger, nicer apartments. Each couple will get their own room.'

The van rolled to a stop, and the driver shut down the engine. I felt May flinch beside me.

The bailiff reached into his bag and produced a stack of booklets and handed one to Argent. 'Pass these back. One each. These are your ration coupons for the next month. This is only temporary until we fix you up with an electronic system. Food distribution is weekly from the Admin centre marked on the map.' He tapped the back cover of one of the booklets. 'The hospital is next to the Admin centre. Be aware that it's short-staffed right now. The Green Zone is strictly no go – officials only. You need a special pass to enter, so don't even try.' Muttering from Argent.

The bailiff ignored it, kept going. 'And be careful with water. The building has one main tank that will be filled twice a week, on Mondays and Thursdays. Other than that, all regular laws apply. Any questions?'

'When the hell do we get out of here?' Argent again.

'I'm sorry folks, I can only answer questions about the relocation.'

'When will our stuff arrive?' Murmurs of agreement from the back of the bus.

The Bailiff shook his head. 'Should be along real soon.'

'An apartment, you say. Shared. Not exactly what I call comparative accommodation,' said Argent, louder now.

'Where is my house?' said May. 'I was promised a house.'

Other voices from behind us, chanting in agreement.

The Bailiff raised his hands, palms out. 'Look everyone, I'm sorry. I'm just here to get you into the apartment. We'll let you know soon what the next step is. This is only temporary.'

Argent was standing now, staring right at the bailiff. 'You don't know shit, do you? Fucking typical. This is the biggest government fuck-up I've ever seen. If they had their heads any farther up their asses they'd turn into doughnuts.'

May sniggered.

'Alright folks,' said the bailiff, visibly rattled. 'Here we are. You're in apartment four, ground floor. Thanks, and have a good day.'

It was a five-storey corner building with a dark-brown brick exterior and 1950s-style mouldings and windows. Above the double glass doors a name was embossed in brick: *The Hamptons*.

Argent whispered something to his wife and pushed her towards the door. She jumped to the pavement and hurried to the building's front entrance. He grabbed his bag and followed her. The rest of us straggled behind, blinking in the mid-afternoon sunshine. I tried to take May's hand, reassure her, but she pushed me away, stood staring at the building.

Argent stood outside the main entrance facing the rest of us. As the van rolled away, he opened his arms wide and smiled at us. 'Hi,' he said. 'Sorry if we got off to a bad start. I'm Derek. Might as well get to know each other if we're going to be living together for a while.'

He thrust out his hand to me. 'Sorry about all that back there,' he said.

I nodded, shook. 'Call me Teacher. This is my wife, May.'

His grip was strong. He looked to be about my age, perhaps a few years older, with thick grey hair combed up in a flamboyant pompadour, a square, clean-shaven face that exuded well-kept vitality, and those strangely luminescent glacier-blue eyes.

He greeted us each in turn, as if he were our host. We all took his lead, stood there on the pavement outside the building and introduced ourselves. Everyone was polite and shook hands. Kwesi and Francoise were the other couple. She was very pretty and had a French accent. He was built like a rugby player and sounded like he was from somewhere in Africa. The single guy was called Lance – Lan – from Seattle, quiet and polite. It was as if we were at a dinner party.

This Little Time-Bound Corner We Call Home

I sit at my writing desk and look out across the dark water. Cold starlight reflects across the bay. The first measures of day appear. Mornings are becoming progressively cooler now as the season turns. Fairweather Orion has disappeared for another winter, along with Rigel, my old companion. Aldebaran, the follower, has returned to the northern horizon, faithfully tracking the Seven Sisters across the skies. It's not that far away, as stars go. Sixty-five light years. I was alive when the light I am seeing now started its journey. Not so Electra, whose present beauty is centuries old.

I can hear my wife working in the kitchen. It is Lewis's birthday today, and she is baking him a cake. She rose early, as she always does, and got the fire going. Baking a cake in a wood-fired stove is not, I am told, a simple thing. Nor are the ingredients easy to come by. Later, I will grill up a beautiful dhufish the boys caught on their last trip out, throw in some garlic and thyme, some wild capers. We will top it off with fresh cornbread and green beans from the garden.

The kids will be coming over sometime after midday. It is important to mark these occasions, to punctuate the flow of time. To give thanks. To recognise our place in the universe and our responsibility to care for this little time-bound corner of it we call home.

11

The French woman's name was Francoise Abachwa. She had long fair hair and wide-set hazel-green eyes that seemed to smile even when the rest of her face did not. She looked young, far too young to have been relocated with the rest of us. Her husband's name was Kwesi Abachwa. May and I followed them down the hall and into the apartment. They walked hand in hand.

The main living room had two threadbare sofas and a big bank of south facing windows and doors that opened onto a walled back garden with a patch of burnt grass and a few small trees. The kitchen let off from the living room and looked out onto the garden. Three bedrooms fronted the street, accessed from a hallway that ran the length of the apartment. Argent's wife was standing in the doorway of the first bedroom, and she smiled at us as we entered. May walked past her without so much as a glance and disappeared down the hallway. Francoise and Kwesi said hello, dropped their cases and went out into the back garden. I watched them walking around the garden together, inspecting the trees. It was late afternoon, and the winter sun cast long shadows across the dead grass. Francoise bent over and picked up some of the earth and rubbed it between her fingers. After a moment she stood and took her husband's hands in hers. They spoke awhile. I couldn't hear what they were saying. I watched him kiss her and take her in his arms. The man who had introduced himself as Lance put his case on the fold-out bed at the far end of the living room and surveyed his new accommodation with a bewildered look on his face.

When May returned, I knew something was wrong. She stood facing me, hands on hips. She pointed at Samantha, Argent's wife. Argent had joined her, and they stood together just outside the doorway of the first bedroom.

'They did it on purpose,' May said, loud enough so that

everyone could hear. 'He distracted us so she could get in here first and claim the best room.'

Samantha arched her cherry-red lips into a wide grin. 'Don't get your knickers steamed up, honey,' she said. 'You've got to think ahead.'

'It's not fair,' said May, staring at me. 'Why don't you stand up to them? You let everyone walk all over us. You always have.' The words raked over her vocal cords. 'They took our home, for God's sake, and you just signed it over to them without a fight. Why can't we have the master suite? Why does that bitch get her own bathroom, while we have to share with...' she looked over at Francoise and Kwesi, who had just come back in from the garden '...with them.' She slumped forward, seemingly resigned, and then suddenly straightened and landed a full handed slap across my face.

Argent laughed.

'Coward,' May hissed. Then she turned and ran.

I put my hand to my cheek, stood silent. I looked down for a moment, and then back up at Francoise and Kwesi. 'I'm sorry,' I said. 'She doesn't mean it. About sharing the bathroom, I mean.'

Francoise smiled at me. I could tell she pitied me, that she was wondering how relationships could deteriorate so. They must have loved each other once, she was thinking. I knew she could tell that we had been married a long time, the way we seemed so familiar in our conflict, so settled in our dissatisfaction. Bathrooms were going to be least of our worries.

I faced Argent. 'She's right you know. The fair thing would be to flip for the rooms. If we're all going to be living here together, we had better start working together. We are going to have to have rules, a fair way of sharing what we have.'

Argent laughed, his gaze carving out the space between us. 'You go right ahead, mister. I approve. The two of you can flip for the other rooms. I am staying where I am. It ain't the Kempinski, but it'll do for now, until I get out of this shit hole.' He turned and disappeared into the master bedroom, leaving his wife facing the rest of us.

Kwesi sat on the tattered sofa. 'Teacher is correct. We must work together, all of us.'

Samantha regarded us all for a while. 'I think you'll find that my husband has absolutely no interest in working for anyone but himself. I advise you not to waste your time. Now if you will excuse me, I have business to attend to.' She walked to the front door and left the apartment.

Despite Argent's prediction, our bags arrived a couple of hours later, dumped in a pile on the front verge. We collected them from the sidewalk, carried them to our rooms. It was clear that they had been inspected, turned through. A clasp knife and the solar charger were missing from my pack, but otherwise everything else seemed to have survived the trip. I spent the rest of the afternoon exploring the apartment and meeting some of our neighbours in the building. Everyone's story was similar. We were all dealing with it differently.

By six o'clock the sky was darkening, and the worst of the heat was dissipating. May had reappeared and sat sulking on the couch. Argent was still in his room, and Samantha had not returned. Francoise and Kwesi were in the kitchen, preparing dinner. They'd found a big pot, were cooking for everyone. I offered a few potatoes and a chicken cube from my supplies. Soon the room filled with the wonderful smell of hot food. We found bowls and spoons in the cupboards, some old tin mugs, enough for seven but no more, the minimum of everything according to the rules. I set the kitchen table and filled an earthenware jug with water from the tap and placed it in the middle. Francoise cut seven slices of heavy dark-seed bread that she said she had baked in her own oven just last week and balanced one on the edge of each bowl.

'There are no fresh greens for a salad,' she said. 'But that will change soon. We will make a garden in the back. We will eat well.' And then: 'Dinner's ready, May, Lance. Please, come and join us.'

May looked up. Her eyes were swollen, the whites laced with angry red veins. 'I shouldn't be here you know.'

Francoise glanced at me. 'I'm sorry to hear that,' she said.

'I only missed the cut-off by three days.'

Francoise frowned, walked to the master bedroom and knocked on the door. Argent answered. I could see that it was a big room, with curtained bay windows looking out onto the street and a big double bed.

Argent looked Francoise up and down, lingering on her bust, and grinned with big white teeth. 'I'm Derek,' he said, sticking out his hand. 'Derek Argent.'

'Yes, I know,' Francoise said. 'You introduced yourself outside, remember?'

'Blocking our way so your wife could snatch the best room,' said May.

Argent glanced past Francoise. 'And that's your husband?'

Francoise looked back at us over her shoulder. 'Yes,' she said. 'Kwesi. Born on Tuesday.'

'Where is he from, originally? If you don't mind me asking.'

'He's from Ghana. We met while I was working there, in the war,' she said. 'We were wondering if you would like to join us for dinner. We have made a stew.'

'Actually, I was just about to eat,' Argent said, smiling again, showing off ten years of an average salary, too perfect and much too white. 'I have some pâté, a couple of cheeses, tinned peaches for dessert.' He was staring at her now, examining her face. I saw him reach up and touch her jaw. She recoiled as he did it, but she did not back away. Kwesi stood.

'You're way too young to be here, aren't you?' said Argent. 'Either that or you have one helluva plastic surgeon. Would you like to join *me* for dinner, beautiful?'

'Please don't,' she said in a clear voice. 'I am married.'

'Leave her alone,' said Kwesi, pushing back his chair.

Argent laughed. 'I know you're married, baby.'

Francoise spun around and walked back to the table. Her face was flushed.

'Anytime,' Argent called after her. 'Open invitation.'

We ate in silence.

12

When I woke, it was cold and dark. I could hear May breathing from the far side of the room, where she had pushed the other single bed. This was part of the treatment, a familiar pattern of enforced silence, eternal sulks and that 'you ruined my life' attitude designed to inflict maximum punishment. I'd known for some time that this behaviour was driven by her condition and that it wasn't really her, and I tried my best to accept it. Knowing how amazing she could be, and had been, only it made it harder.

I pulled on track pants, a thermal running vest, my old Gel Kayanos and a black wool skull cap, and slipped out of the room. Francoise was sitting at the kitchen table, working under the glow of a small portable lamp. Her hair was tied up in a thick braid. Before her was a row of small cardboard pots filled with earth. She looked up and smiled.

'Oh, bonjour,' she said. 'It is a bit chilly, no?'

'Solar?' I asked.

'Oh, the lamp. Yes. Kwesi and I have been using it for years, very good technology from Germany. I understand such things were banned here.'

All I could do was frown. 'During the Repudiation, yes. Are you planting?'

'Some of my favourites from our farm: aubergine, Roma tomatoes, Lebanese cucumbers, rocket, oregano.'

'If we're here that long.' I went to the sink and filled my water bottle from the tap.

'Do you think we will be moved?'

'I don't know. Maybe.'

'You are going out?'

'For a run.' I would go long this morning, twenty K. Even with all the strife and the changes and the lack of food, running was one of the few things I was still not prepared to give up. It kept me sane, made every other part of my life more manageable.

'She looked up from her seed pots. There was a smudge of soil on her chin. 'There is a curfew, no?'

'This early, I'm guessing not,' I said. 'We'll see.'

She frowned, a little twitch of her lip.

Yellow pools of streetlight stretched away down the road in both directions for as far as I could see. It still seemed strange to see a city street so completely devoid of cars, so deserted. If only I could have brought my bicycle. I took a compass bearing along the road, looked at my watch, the fluorescent dial showing 0512, synced the chronometer to the footpod and started walking east towards the mountains. No GPS since they re-tasked the civilian satellites.

By the look of the place, we were in some town-become-suburb, swallowed by urban sprawl sometime in the last century, spat out again the next. Why we'd been dumped here, and how long they intended to keep us here, I could only guess. Questions queued up in my head like tech-tragics waiting to buy the latest phone in happier times. What did they expect us to do, now that they'd shipped us halfway across the continent? Start businesses? Find jobs? There were no kids here, that was certain, no schools. From what I'd seen of the place so far, there was little in the way of economic activity of any kind. The fact that we'd been issued ration books suggested that the government was planning to feed us, for now at least. And then what? I determined that I was going to get answers. Like I always did, I was going to figure it out – collect the data, do the analysis, test the hypotheses and deduce the truth. That's what a scientist did, a man of logic in a world gone crazy.

After five minutes I was warm. I started a slow run past boarded-up shops, the familiar names of enterprises now defunct, the sources of their goods closed off, their customers no longer able to afford the continuous cycle of cheap, ever-changing disposable fashion, the permanent upgrade cycle of consumer electronics, even, sadly, the books and magazines and confections of my adolescence. I passed a string of bars with neon signs, the sidewalk littered with broken bottles and plastic cups, the occasionally syringe. A faint whiff of smoke came on the breeze, the smell vaguely industrial, burning plastic.

As I ran, I thought of Kazinsky and Smith, that day they came to the house. They had been determined, and I sympathetic. In their place, I would have done the same thing. Now I wondered where they were, if they were alright, and if I would ever hear from them again.

I upped the pace, aiming for an even five-minute K. Shops and apartment buildings gave way to run down single family dwellings, apparently empty, the lawns scorched, the trees bare and forlorn. Perhaps we would soon be given one of these houses. With a little work I could make it comfortable, I thought, maybe even build May a little studio again. The thought gave me a little boost of adrenaline, upped my pace. A police cruiser flashed through a cross-street intersection ahead, the blue-and-red strobe light lingering on my retina. I looked at my watch. Seven K and a bit, feeling stronger now. The streets slipped by, one after the other, a dark gridwork of lost opportunities, the concrete spooling out in front of me, section after section, like some hard-paved destiny.

Soon I was in an old industrial area, warehouses and fenced yards, wooden power poles strung with sagging wires, gravel shoulders now, my feet crunching out a steady rhythm. Ahead, the grey pre-dawn sky glowed orange. The odour of burning refuse intensified. A kilometre later, a fine ash began to fall, covering my hat and jacket and filming my face.

A garbage truck rumbled past towards the lights, and a few minutes later another. I followed the red tail-lights as they contracted towards the glow. After a while I could make out the first fingertips of orange flame flickering behind the black hulk of a factory building. Fire-lit smoke billowed into the starless sky. I pulled my bandana up over my mouth and kept running, drawn by the glow.

An underpass loomed up ahead, a rail line above. Beneath the tracks, the reek of piss and shit and fear, a pair of ragged boots sticking out from beneath a sheet of cardboard wedged under the big concrete beams. I kept going towards the fire. Soon I was running through a blizzard of ash, spinning scraps of charred paper, partially melted plastic bags, glowing embers of wood and rubber, half-burnt shreds of Styrofoam. I stopped, gazed at the steadily accumulating layer of burn around me. Another truck passed, heading towards the glow.

I looked at my watch. I'd gone ten and a half kilometres. I decided to go another half K, and then turn back. I reached a junction, took the turn to the right, away from the glow and into the wind, towards a series of older factory buildings, their brick chimneys glowing in the orange firelight. Soon I'd left the worst of the smoke and ash behind. I dusted myself off, kept going. The road was narrower here, the chain-link factory gates pushed into gravel shoulders, the overhanging crown of razor wire freshly hung, and here a hole in the base of the fence where the wire had been pulled back, as if someone had tried to dig their way out.

Eleven kilometres, even, flashed up on my watch, and I slowed to a walk, looking for a place to stretch. Ahead was a recess in the fence, the entranceway to an old brick warehouse. An empty wooden cable spool lay on end next to the gate. I stopped and leaned against its curved edge, stretching my calves. Beyond the fence, I could see a big black SUV parked in front of the building's main cargo bay, its distinctive Chevrolet emblem glinting in the new flaring dawn. It was starting to get warm. I pulled off my cap and put it in the pocket of my vest, rolled up my sleeves.

I was about to start back when I heard it. A high-pitched wail, a scream perhaps. I quietened my breathing, listened. After a while, I reassessed. No, it must have been something else. A dog's bark, maybe. It had sounded like a bark. No, more like a yelp. I faced the warehouse. It had come from there. I stood and watched the sky lighten behind the building, heard the cawing of a solitary crow and the rumbling of machinery in the distance, back from where the fire was.

And then I heard it again, louder this time, more distinct. A man's voice, raised. Please, I heard. *Please.* It was coming from inside the warehouse. The gate to the compound was closed, but the lock chain hung loose. I pushed the gate open and walked towards the building. I had just reached the vehicle when the voice resumed, pleading again, and then another voice, lower, steady, answering. I skirted a pile of packing crates, cleared the cargo-bay entrance, and reached the front wall and a window of smashed panes. I pushed myself up against the wall, waited a moment, then peered inside.

Two soldiers – they looked like soldiers, or paramilitaries of some sort, in dark uniforms of a pattern I hadn't seen before – were directing a pair of ragged-looking men towards the back of the warehouse. One of the soldiers was tall, broad-shouldered, powerful-looking. The other was squat, thick-legged, walked with a slight waddle. The men's hands were tied behind their backs, wrist over wrist. One had long grey hair that hung in wisps over stooped shoulders. The other had a ponytail, was dressed in an old army-surplus jacket. He stumbled to the floor.

'Get up,' barked one of the soldiers, the tall one, jabbing a handgun into the man's back.

'Please,' cried the man. It was the voice I'd heard from outside. 'I didn't know,' he said. 'I swear. *Please.*'

The soldier pulled the man to his feet and pushed him forward. 'Fucking coward,' he spat.

The man stumbled, turned his head briefly. The profile was familiar. It was Esposito, from the queue at the transfer camp, the one who'd chimed in with Argent. They were almost to the far wall now, a place where the concrete floor fell away into what looked like a vehicle-servicing well. Sweat ran cold from my temples. I put my hand over my mouth to prevent the condensation from my breath forming on the shard of glass that still hung in the window frame.

The soldiers stopped and pushed the men to their knees, facing the pit. The tall one reached into his pocket and produced a packet of cigarettes and lit two at once and handed one to his partner. His partner took the cigarette, turning briefly into profile. I gasped. It hit me hard, seeing that face. At the time I wasn't sure why exactly, and I had the vague thought that it shouldn't have shocked me but that it did. Things had changed a lot. I watched her raise the cigarette to her mouth, fill her lungs, then exhale blue smoke down onto the back of her prisoner's balding head. I noticed there was a red, heart-shaped patch on her shoulder. The heart was bisected by a jagged break.

'You fuckers deserve a lot worse,' she said. 'You will never be forgiven.' Then she raised her handgun to the back of the man's head, just below the base of the skull, and fired. Esposito toppled into the pit with a splash, the empty brass casing clinking on the floor.

Then her companion took a draw on his smoke and fired and kicked the other body into the pit.

I sank to the ground with my back against the wall. I was breathing so fast and loud I was sure that the soldiers, or whatever they were, would hear me. Run, was all I could think. Run as fast as you can. I tried to stand, but I slumped back to the ground as a wave of nausea turned my stomach inside out. I could hear footfall echoing inside the building. They were on their way back to the vehicle. If I ran now, they would see me. I had to stay put, here behind the crates. I was trapped, hemmed in. There was no way they could know I was here. I would wait until they were gone. I curled up, tried to make myself small. I could hear the low murmur of voices getting closer, then the sound of the cargo-bay door rolling closed, the click of a lock. Now car doors opening and closing. My head was spinning. I thought I was going to pass out. I heard the engine start, the wheels rolling along the wrecked concrete.

Then the car stopped, and I heard the woman say: 'Hey, didn't you close the gate behind you?'

Jesus, had I left it open? My mind raced. I had. Shit. I trembled in my hiding place, listening to the sound of the idling engine.

Then the grate of rusty hinges and the clang of steel tubing. A dozen loping heartbeats later I heard the car door close, and then the sound of the vehicle moving away across the gravel and onto the road.

I sat there for a long time, huddled against the brick wall behind those crates, my arms wrapped around my shins, my eyes closed and my face buried in my knees. What had I just witnessed? To what end, this execution of two old codgers? What had been their crime? The words echoed in my head: *You will never be forgiven*.

I looked up at the ruined sky. To the east, a billowing column of smoke rose high into the troposphere. I got to my feet, peered out over the crates to the loading yard. There was no one. I ran to the gate. It was locked. There was no way over. Then I remembered the hole in the base of the fence. I crouched and ran along the fence until I found it, near a rack of rusting pipes. I knelt, but the opening was too small. I started digging with my hands, scanning the road both ways. I scrabbled like a dog, tearing at the packed sand with my fingernails, pushing the loosenings back with my forearms, scratching away as fast as I could.

I recoiled in pain and looked down at my hand. The nail of my left index finger hung from the cuticle, ripped clean off. Blood welled up in the pores of the newly-exposed flesh. Dirt filled some of the fleshy holes. I shuddered and tried to choke back a wave of nausea, my lifelong trypophobia returning with a scream. I pushed the nail back in place and squeezed the digit hard in my other hand, trying to push away the offending image. I needed something to dig with. I scanned the ground behind me. An engine rumbled in the distance. They could be back any moment. I spun around and looked down the road. A pair of headlights loomed in the direction of the garbage facility, coming towards me.

I flattened myself to the ground and snaked back from the fence until I was hidden behind the pipe rack. Through the base of the wooden pallet, I watched as an old Humvee sped past and disappeared down the road. I closed my eyes and tried to steady my breathing. When I looked out again, I saw that one of the pallet's rough-cut two-by-fours had split. I cracked it open wider with my foot and pulled off a long dagger-shaped piece about the length of my forearm, the wood splitting with the grain.

In a few minutes I had opened the hole enough to snake under the fence. I stood, chucked the dagger back into the hole, straightened my vest, pulled my cap down close to my eyes and started running as fast as I could back to the centre of town.

PART II

Fighters

The Destruction of Order

I can see it now, and it still makes me shiver. A vision that has haunted my nights ever since. That young woman — for she was young, very young; the same age as my daughters-in-law are now, I would guess — ending that man's life with such calm zeal.

I stare down at the pages, a month's toil. Work as difficult as I have ever done. And now, for the first time, I know that I will finish. It is as if the lock has been broken and the doorway forced open. And now, every morning when I wake, the events are there, ready to be captured. It is my own exercise in quantum mechanics. Through the act of writing, I have somehow fixed on the page what had increasingly become blurred and indeterminate.

And for those few hours, time seems to stand still. No, that's not right. The time I spend writing seems to pass without register. I begin before dawn, take up my pen, look out across the sound, let it all come back, and then begin. And when I look up again a moment later, the sun is at its apogee. And yet, back there in the story, whole days have passed, or sometimes only minutes.

It took me a long time to understand that time is not what we grow up believing it is. Physics has long since proved that there is no such thing as time, in the sense I understood it as a child, that slow, even, inexorable flow that converts future into present and then, almost instantaneously, into past. Time itself, as a quantity, does not exist. What we perceive as time is, rather, merely a sequencing of events, big and small, microscopic and planetary. We watch the sun rise, climb in the sky as our beloved Earth spins on its axis in the darkness of space, and then set again. A day has passed. Stars burn away their mass and then collapse into themselves. Time is nothing more than the destruction of order, the flying apart of the universe, of galaxies, suns, planets, people.

13

I'd known May a long time, since we were kids. I'd seen her grow and change, and develop as a person and as an artist, and then was with her as her illness came on and deepened and changed her. We used to talk, at the beginning. I mean really talk, about things that mattered. But as the years passed, the real talking slowly died away. I would tell myself that the disease and the effects of her medication hadn't changed her that much. I told myself that if only I could understand, I might be able to reconnect. I tried to imagine being her, seeing the world through her eyes. I spent hours and days watching her, following her, trying to imagine what she was thinking, what she was going through. I wanted to understand her so I could support her, help her get well. That's what I told myself.

When I arrived back at the apartment, May was still in bed. As I opened the door, she glanced up at me and then covered her head with her pillow. I stood there a moment in the doorway, steam already rising from my running gear, sweat running from my temples. I closed the door and walked to my bed and sat down with my forearms on my knees and stared at the floor. The smell of smoke tiptoed across the room with me. Ash covered my clothes. Bits of charred paper stuck to my bare forearms. My finger was bleeding, the nail levered open.

May continued to feign sleep. She was not going to speak to me. I did not move, just sat there watching blood drip from the end of my finger, time meted out with every droplet's pulsing accumulation, annihilated as each impact with the steadily growing pool on the floor locked away another moment, louder and louder until the sound of it was like a hammering in my brain, relentless and uncaring.

By the time she pulled back the covers, put on her slippers and threw on her housecoat my finger had stopped bleeding. She walked across the room and sat beside me. I did not react, just sat staring at the small pool of blood at my feet. She put her hand on my shoulder. It surprised me.

'You've hurt your finger,' she said.

I let her take my hand. 'I don't know what to do, May. I...'

'It's okay.' Her voice was warm, gentle. 'This needs to be cleaned and bandaged.' She got up, went to the other side of the room, rummaged in her bag a moment and returned with a water bottle and a hand towel.

'I'm a coward,' I said.

She leaned over and kissed my cheek the way she used to do, the way she had done so many times before. 'I know it's hard. It's hard for me too. I'm glad you can see that now.'

'I just stood by and let it happen.'

'I understand,' she said, reaching for my hand, dabbing at my finger with the wet towel. 'I forgive you.'

I looked into her eyes. 'I saw something.' My voice sounded brittle, shaky. 'This morning. On my run.'

'There is no need to apologise. Together we can do this.'

'Do what?'

She squeezed my hand. 'If only I'd prayed harder. If only everyone had prayed harder, God would not have done this to us. Everything was so good before. So *normal*. But it's never too late to be redeemed. I'm glad you can see that now.' She finished cleaning my finger, applied some antiseptic cream, pushed the nail back down over the wound and bandaged it. 'There,' she said, brushing a piece of charred paper from my cheek. 'We can make things better. We will fight this, together.'

'No,' I said. 'You don't understand. Something has happened.'

'What do you mean?'

'Something terrible has happened.'

She looked at me as if I had just declared apostasy after a lifetime of devotion. 'No,' she said, moving her head slowly from side to side. 'No. That's not what I meant.'

'I don't understand, May. I...'

But I didn't get a chance to finish. She pushed me away and stormed back across the room. 'You are such an asshole,' she screamed. 'I should have known better than to believe that you were thinking of me. It has always been about you. You, you, you.'

She grabbed her toiletry bag and marched to the door, flung it closed behind her. The sound echoed through the flat.

When I finally followed her out, Kwesi and Francoise were sitting at the kitchen table with packets of seeds, planting pots and what looked like a hand-drawn map spread before them. Lan was with them at the table, a grey hoodie pulled up over his head. Samantha was leaning up against the kitchen counter, made up for day, hair perfect, holding a steaming mug in her hands. Argent was sitting in one of the lounge chairs at the back of the room, fiddling with an unlit cigar. They all looked up at me. They had heard everything.

Kwesi and Francoise smiled a moment then turned back to their work. Lance was staring at my hand. My finger had started to bleed again. He nodded, pointed to the bathroom. I mouthed thanks, jammed my finger into my shirtfront.

From the bathroom, the sound of falling water. Wisps of steam escaping from under the door. And then, suddenly, a muffled scream.

I tried the door, but it was locked. 'May,' I called. 'Are you okay?'

Curses through the door.

'May, what's the matter?'

'Someone has used up all the hot water,' she shouted. 'That's what's wrong.' A crash echoed from behind the door, then a deadened thud, followed by more muffled curses.

'May, please,' I called through the door.

Sobs. 'Just leave me alone.' Another scream, more objects hitting the walls, the crash of glass.

'Jesus,' I heard Samantha say.

I leaned back against the wall, sank down to my haunches, buried my head in my arms. How long I waited there I cannot recall.

When May finally emerged from the bathroom, she seemed to have regained some composure. Her hair was brushed, and she had put on some eye makeup. Everyone looked up at her. She ignored us, marched straight to our room, then back out a few seconds later clutching a plastic bag. Without saying a word, she walked to the kitchen, placed the bag on the countertop and pulled out a carton of UHT milk, wrote her name on it with an indelible black marker pen and put it in the fridge. Then she tagged each remaining item and put them in the fridge and turned and stared at Francoise.

'Next time,' she said, her voice trembling, 'I would appreciate if you would leave some hot water for the rest of us, if it's not too much trouble.'

Francoise glanced at Kwesi. 'I didn't shower this morning. Water is precious. We intend to use our share to grow extra food. We sponge bath in the evenings.'

'Nice job on the bathroom,' Argent smirked. 'What is it they say about breaking a mirror?'

Samantha shook her head. 'You should get your fat derrière out of bed earlier, dear.' A broad lipstick grin bisected her face.

May's face crumpled. She stared at Samantha a moment and then grabbed her bag and ran from the room. The slam of the bedroom door rattled the kitchen windows.

When I found her, she was sitting on her bed, hands covering her face. I sat beside her.

'That bitch used up all the hot water,' she spat through her tears. 'She called me fat. We can't live here. I won't live here. I don't care what you do. I am going to the authorities to ask to be moved. We should at least get our own house. That's what they promised.'

I said nothing.

'I'm talking to you,' she said. 'I'm leaving.'

I grabbed her wrist. She tried to wriggle free, but I held her fast. She raised her other hand as if she was going to hit me. I braced, held her gaze. She lowered her hand.

'You can't leave, May. None of us can.'

'I don't care what you say. I'm leaving.'

'For God's sake, May. Listen to me, please. Something happened this morning.'

'I was stuck in the shower covered in soap with no hot water, that's what happened.'

'No, May. It was murder. Cold-blooded execution.'

She looked at me as if I was crazy. 'What did you say?'

'I said, execution. Two.'

'What on earth are you talking about? Don't be melodramatic.' She looked worried now, truly afraid. I knew she was down to her last few packets of medication and had already halved her daily dose to make it last longer. But she had to know.

'I saw it. Out by the edge of town, in an old factory building. I was hiding.'

I could see the implications of this starting to run through her head, chaining up into consequences. She was quiet a moment and then she whispered: 'Did they see you? Could they have followed you back here?'

'I don't think so. I don't know. I just ran.' I let go of her wrist and stood. 'We need to be very careful, May. That's all I can say. We need to keep quiet and do what we're told.'

'Just do what we're told? Look where that has landed us.' She paused for effect, made a point of looking around the room, at the bare radiator, the peeling wallpaper, the steel-framed beds that looked as if they had been salvaged from a prison. 'As far as I'm concerned, what you saw is more reason for us to stand up for ourselves. I warned you this would happen.'

I was about to answer when there was a knock at the door. I was going to tell her about what the soldiers had said before killing those men, about how terrified I'd been watching it happen, how guilty I'd felt not doing something, anything, to intervene somehow. But I didn't get the chance. May walked over and opened the door.

It was Argent. He was wearing an expensive suede jacket and gleaming snakeskin boots. He smiled and put out a hand heavy with gold rings.

'We seem to have got off to a bad start,' he said. 'I wanted to apologise for my wife.'

May shook his hand. I couldn't see if she was smiling or not.

'Do you have a moment?' said Argent. 'I'd like to show you something I think you'll enjoy.'

'What is it?' said May.

'A surprise. For you. Game?'

May looked back over her shoulder at me a moment. Her expression was flat, perfectly neutral. 'OK,' she said. 'Sounds fun.'

When they left the apartment together, May was holding his hand.

$$a = dv/dt$$

Ever since I was young, I had an image of the man I wanted to be. For a time, I came to believe that this image was crafted carefully by my father, an expression of all the things he believed in, of the life he had wished for himself. A career civil servant, he had wanted to be a pilot but was kept out of the air force by a congenital heart defect. I knew how disappointed he was when, after giving up on my doctorate in engineering, I had announced that I would become a teacher. When he died, alone and sedated to unconsciousness after fifteen days on a ventilator, all I got was a text message from the hospital. I never even got to go to the funeral.

Later, after he was gone, I came to understand how different we were, he and I, and yet, how similar. And the farther away I got from him, the faster everything seemed to change. Acceleration. It was something I used to teach my year-eleven students. One of the simplest concepts in physics, but also one of the most powerful. A change in velocity: go faster, accelerate. Go slower, decelerate. Simple. And since velocity measures distance covered in a certain time in a certain direction, what's called a first derivative (dx/dt), acceleration, which measures the change in velocity achieved over a certain time, becomes a second derivative (dx/dt^2), or a function of time squared. Keep the same speed but change direction, that's acceleration, too. It's a vector, Newton's brilliant approximation of reality.

That was where we were, back then. Everything moving faster and faster, red-shifting to a place where thresholds are crossed and barriers shattered, to a time where predictability becomes mayhem and chaos rules. And the biggest problem was, once you were in, there was no way back.

14

When the notice arrived, I was in the back with Kwesi and Francoise, working on the garden. The afternoon sun slanted across the buildings of the neighbourhood, and the garden wall made a long wedge of shade across the dead grass. Kwesi and I were lifting a rough-cut two-by-eight plank and were about to lower it into place between a series of paired steel rebar uprights we'd hammered into the hard-packed ground. The raised bed was taking shape. Francoise wiped the sweat from her eyes with a dirty hand and held up the envelope.

It had taken me a while to get my head something close to straight after May had left with Argent. I stayed in our room most of the morning reorganising my gear, thinking about before, when we were good together, wondering where we'd gone wrong. The abandoned factory loomed in my memory, and the images of those men toppling into the pit wove themselves through my unwanted imaginings of what May was doing with Argent. It was mid-morning when I finally got myself together enough to leave the room. Kwesi and Francoise were in the kitchen, still planning their garden. Francoise made me a cup of tea. She asked me if I was alright. I said I was and thanked her, but I could tell she knew I was lying. She'd seen May leave with Argent, but I didn't say anything about it, and she didn't mention it. Kwesi showed me their plans for the garden, and I shared the sketch map of the area I had started in my notebook, mostly from observations I'd made during my run. I had mapped out a few key buildings, landmarks, park areas, an old scrap yard. Kwesi quizzed me about the scrap yard. They needed materials for the garden. The yard wasn't far away, and I told him it hadn't looked as if it was guarded, so we decided to check it out together. Kwesi and I spent most of the rest of the day scouring the yard for materials. We were careful to stay out of sight as much as we could, but the town seemed deserted, and we only saw one police car rumbling past in the distance, and the cops didn't seem to care that we were there. We carried the stuff back on our shoulders, the bigger things together. It was hot work, and by the time we were finished we were both covered in sweat. I didn't share what I'd seen earlier that morning.

Over the course of the day, the garden had steadily filled with a collection of lumber, wire, sheet metal and rusted sections of pipe, and now Francoise's plans were starting to take shape: raised vegetable beds, trellises along the walls next to the kitchen windows, a series of compost bins next to the far wall. Francoise had watered and pruned the lemon tree, cleared out a nice depression around its trunk and collected leaf litter to mulch the root area. She was confident it would start to flourish.

We looked up at her now, wiping dirt from our hands.

Kwesi said: 'Only two things come in brown-paper envelopes like that.'

'It's addressed to all of us,' said Francoise. 'The occupants of apartment four. We should wait until the others get back before opening it.'

Kwesi and I agreed.

Francoise put the envelope in her apron, wiped her hands and went into the kitchen. 'Anyone for a glass of water?' she called out from the kitchen window.

'Thanks, yes,' Kwesi said. 'Both of us.'

A few moments later Francoise appeared in the doorway, a water jug hanging loose from one hand. 'There's no water,' she said.

'Maybe there's a blockage in the tank,' said Kwesi. 'Let's take a look.' He looked at me. 'Coming?'

Kwesi and I started up the stairs. Francoise followed us. When we reached the roof, a dozen or so residents were milling around a pair of big tanks, tapping on the steel, listening to the hollow reverberating echo. Two tanks, two thousand gallons each, someone said. Everyone stood around looking at each other.

'How many of us are there in the building?' asked one of the residents, a small woman with wiry grey hair and leather skin.

Each room had sent a representative. We tallied it up. Forty-four. Four thousand gallons for three and half days for forty-four people.

'Almost exactly thirty gallons a day each,' I said. 'One hundred and fourteen litres. It should be plenty.'

'How could it have disappeared in less than a day?' someone said.

'I've seen you working in the garden,' said the woman, staring at Francoise. 'You used a lot of water.'

I could see Francoise flinch, see her cheeks and lips flush.

'That explains it,' said someone else.

Francoise tried to answer but she was drowned out.

'Wait a moment,' said Kwesi. He had a big voice. Everyone quietened down. 'What matters is what we do from now. The important thing is that we come to an agreement, all of us. Everyone gets the same share. Each of us can use it as we like.'

A few murmurs of agreement. Some dissention, too: how can we be sure that some people won't cheat, use more than their share? What about those of us who don't need thirty gallons a day? The discussion continued for some time. Finally, a consensus was reached: there should be enough to go around. Everyone agreed that each apartment would limit its use. We would have to rely on the honour system.

'It's a long time since I heard that one,' someone quipped.

When we returned to the apartment, I could see Francoise was crying. 'They are right. I used a lot of water today. I must have filled my water jug more than a dozen times. I didn't think.'

'The garden is for all of us,' I said.

She tried a smile, failed. 'I feel horrible.'

'We are going to be without water for at least a day and half,' Kwesi said. 'We are going to have to make provisions.'

'There is still a ten-litre watering jug outside that I filled earlier,' she said. 'We can share.'

Kwesi smiled and kissed her. 'Teacher is right. It's for all of us.'
Francoise nodded. 'Thanks for helping today, Teacher.'
I wasn't listening. I was thinking of May. 'Sorry?'
'Thanks for today.'
'We have to work together, don't we?'
'I hope everyone understands this,' said Kwesi.

By the time dinner was ready, Samantha had returned, and we drew four kitchen chairs around the table, sitting each with a bowl of vegetable stew. We ate. No one spoke. After I finished, I wiped the bowl clean with a corner of bread.

Samantha pushed away her bowl and leaned back in her chair. 'Not bad,' she said, 'given the conditions.'

Kwesi looked at Samantha. 'I think it's delicious,' he said. 'Under any conditions.'

Francoise smiled at him.

Samantha leaned forward. 'From what I've seen today, darlings, conditions are very bad.' She had everyone's attention now, and she knew it. 'I've been down at what they call "Administration" today, trying to get some answers. It seems we have no communications. There is no phone service – no surprise there – and there isn't going to be any, as far as I can tell. The network is cut off, too.' She looked around at everyone as if to make sure we had heard and understood.

'They told us we would be able to communicate freely,' said Kwesi.

'And you can,' Samantha said with half a smile. 'You can send and receive as many letters as you like – the old-fashioned way. They are blaming the war, the need for security, the strain on resources.'

There was silence as everyone considered this.

'Has anyone seen Lan?' asked Francoise after a time.

'He left early,' said Samantha. 'Something about trying to locate a friend.'

'Seems a nice man,' said Francoise.

'Quiet,' said Kwesi.

'Lonely,' said Francoise.

We were interrupted by the sound of a woman's laughter in the hall outside. The door opened and Argent stood teetering against the doorframe, a half-empty bottle of whisky hanging from one hand, the other wrapped around my wife's, May's, waist. May was carrying a small steel case in her free hand.

'You all look as if you've just lost your homes,' said Argent. His face split into a wide implant-filled grin.

May's morning makeup was gone, and her face was flushed. She looked plainer, older.

My head was reeling. I knew what I was seeing but I didn't want to believe it. I pushed back my chair, tried to stand, but my legs felt like they were going to give way. I braced myself against the edge of the table. 'May, what are you doing?' I spluttered.

Argent raised his hands. 'Just a few drinks, that's all. Nothing to worry about. Is there, doll?' May squealed as he slapped her behind.

I took a few steps towards Argent. I am not a violent man. I've always shunned confrontation, but I could feel the anger rising inside me, viscous, alien. 'Leave her alone,' I heard myself say.

'Here, take her,' said Argent, grabbing the case and pushing May towards me so that she lost her balance and stumbled forward. I managed to catch her before she hit the ground.

'I was just being friendly, making up for my wife's rudeness,' Argent said.

By now Samantha was on her feet too. 'You asshole, Derek,' she hissed. 'Look at where we are. Look at what's going on. We need to be fighting this, and here you are wasting your time chasing dairy cattle. Besides, isn't she a bit old for you?'

Samantha glanced at Francoise, an almost imperceptible dart of the eyes, and then looked over at May. 'Sorry, dear.'

Argent pushed past us, slammed the case down on the Formica counter and glared at his wife. The case was made from polished steel and was about the size and shape of a briefcase.

Next to the handle was what looked like a small window and a keypad.

Samantha stood for a moment gazing at the case. 'Is that what I think it is?'

Argent nodded. 'Sure is.'

She skipped over to where he stood and threw her arms around his neck and kissed him on the mouth. But he pushed her away and walked to the stove and helped himself to a bowl of stew. I guided May to the living room. She was unsteady and smelled of booze. She closed her eyes and slumped down onto the sofa.

Just then the front door opened. It was Lan. He stood in the entrance, staring at us, breathing heavily. A bright red scrape bloomed across one cheek, and his hair was matted with blood. His white shirt was stained and torn in a couple of places. A poster of some sort hung from one hand.

'Lan,' said Francoise, starting towards him. She helped him to the table, sat him down, inspected the gash on his head.

'What happened?' says Kwesi.

Lan put the poster on the table. It was crudely made, quickly sketched and run off on an old photocopier. But the image was clear enough. Two men, naked. One bent over, the other thrusting himself in from behind. Above them, in bold red letters: *An Abomination in the Eyes of God*, and below: *His Wrath Is Coming. Repent, or None Will Be Spared*.

'This happened,' said Lan.

I had already seen a few of these posters around the area, stapled to telephone poles, pasted up on walls.

'My friend and I were taking them down when we were attacked.'

Francoise ran to her room and returned with a medical kit. She stood over Lan, cleaning his wound. 'It's not too bad,' she said. 'But I will need to put in a couple of stitches.'

Lan nodded, closed his eyes. His hands were shaking.

'Leviticus,' said May, slurring the word.

Everyone turned to look at her.

'Word for word,' she said.

'She's right,' said Argent. 'It's all in the Bible. Everything that's happening. Look around, you idiots. It's God's wrath.' He looked at Lan a moment, then turned his head and spat on the floor.

'That's ridiculous,' I said.

'What's ridiculous?' said Argent, squaring up, puffing out his chest.

I said nothing.

'Teacher is right,' said Kwesi. He towered over the smaller, older man. 'To think that all of this is some form of divine retribution. It makes no sense.'

Argent wheeled around to face Kwesi. 'And you're his spokesman now, are you, after a few hours of pissing around in the dirt together?'

Francoise touched Kwesi on the forearm the way I'd seen her do before. 'Please, Kwes. Don't provoke him.'

'That's good advice,' said Argent, pushing his face closer to Kwesi's. 'Do as your mistress commands.' His face was flushed, probably from the booze, his pupils heavily dilated.

Kwesi bristled, a ripple running across his back and neck. 'What is that supposed to mean?'

Before Argent could respond, Francoise pulled the notice from her apron and held it up for everyone to see. 'We received a letter today, for all of us. Does anyone want to know what's so important that they sent a marshal to deliver it?'

A Note Held

I watch the sharp front of the squall move across the water. It makes a line on the surface of the sound that extends from The Hope as far as I can see towards the hills of what was once a national park. In front of the line the water is dark and flat. Behind, the surface comes up silver and rippled. I watch as it approaches, a long way off still but moving fast, a note held, out there on the sea. I imagine I can slow its progress, make this moment last just a little bit longer. But the future arrives soon enough, and the squall hits the shore, and I feel the raindrops hard and cold on my face, hear the wind in the trees, and then turn and watch it climb the hill and pass over the ridge.

The past lives, affixed here in my memory, in those of my wife and sons. Resonating too in the synapses of countless millions of others who have also lived to record their own versions of this story. And it is those memories, able to be recalled and reconstructed and so made real again, that are allowing us, each in our own scattered, semi-isolated way, to begin the long task of rebuilding.

15

Francoise put the letter on the table. Everyone calmed down. Argent backed away with a smirk. Kwesi sat. Francoise set to stitching Lan's wound. I picked up the envelope, opened it. It was a work roster. I read out the assignments.

May and Francoise were assigned to something called energy systems. Argent and Samantha were to work in Administration, whatever that was. Kwesi and I were to report to the sanitation services depot for garbage duty. Lan was assigned to the hospital. Work was to commence tomorrow morning at seven am. We were expected to put in six nine-hour days each week. We would be paid monthly in something the letter called 'commission credits'. If we didn't work, we would forfeit our rations.

When I finished reading the letter, Argent took a long swig of whisky and slammed the bottle down on the table. 'You didn't really think this was gonna be a holiday, did you?' he said, looking at us each in turn. 'Slave labour, that's what this is. This whole fucking thing has been planned all along. The entire bullshit story is nothing but a big hoax, designed to justify robbery and slavery. I worked my ass off my whole life, and these liberal youthic motherfuckers just think they can take it all away. I say fuck them all. We gotta stand up for ourselves. I for one have no goddam intention of working for these assholes for one hour a week, let alone fifty.'

'You're wrong, Argent,' I said. 'Look around you. Surely even you can see what's happening.' Suddenly, I felt exhausted, as if I hadn't slept in days, weeks.

Argent laughed. 'I agree. Just look around you. Do you really think that all of this has been caused by us? It's plain stupidity.'

May opened her eyes, giggled. 'That's what I've been telling him for years. He never listens to me.'

'The science is—' said Lan, but Argent cut him off.

'The bullshit, you mean.' Argent took another drink. He was just getting started. 'This isn't about science, idiot, it's about economics, about money. A whole generation of indolent, lazy assholes who want someone to blame. And they blame you.' He looked around the room at each of us. 'All of you. They've convinced themselves that they can do better, but only if they can have it all now. If you can't make it yourself, then steal it.'

'That's not true,' said Lan, persisting. 'What about all the damage we've done, the debt we've accumulated? It's the young people who are going to have to—'

Again Argent didn't let him finish, talked right over him. 'Don't give me that tired old bullshit. It's just another excuse for robbery, nothing more.'

Lan hung his head, offered no further resistance.

I was thinking about how many times I'd had this conversation. First, back when we were starting to make slow, grudging progress, and then secretly during the years of the Repudiation when fear dripped from every message. Fear of economic collapse, fear of change, of ochlocracy, of any way of living that offered something different. Growth was the only way. If we wanted to protect our precious way of life, we had to grow demand, grow supply, grow output and turnover and GDP. It didn't matter how, or what the consequences were. And there was no alternative.

'We knew what was happening,' I said, my voice riven with tremors. I sounded weak, frightened. 'And we did nothing.' I fought back the grief, kept going. 'Despite all the warnings, we just couldn't find the courage to change. The Repudiation was the final nail.' I gathered the courage to look straight into Argent's eyes. 'The government, the government *you* owned, told us it was okay to keep doing what we were doing. That everything was fine. No one wanted to rock the boat. The economy had to grow, even if it cost us the planet.'

I realised that Argent was smiling at me. He broke into a laugh, rubbed his knuckles in his eyes. 'So sensitive,' he said. 'So sincere.'

There *were* tears in my eyes. I wiped them away. 'Some work for the common good doesn't seem too much to ask.' I sank into my chair. I'd said it. I wanted to run, hide.

May rolled her eyes. 'Boring, self-righteous idiot,' she slurred. 'Thirty years I've had to put up with that.'

'To think that we, humble human beings that we are, could actually affect the planet,' said Samantha. 'It's the height of arrogance.'

All I could manage was a hoarse gasp. 'We are the cause – of all of it. And it's irreversible.' I could feel my resolve disappearing like sand from an eroding shore.

'God controls the world,' said May. 'Not us.'

'Just look at the sky these days,' said Kwesi. 'God definitely did not do that.'

I gave a nod to Kwesi, liking him more and more.

'And who did that?' said Samantha. 'Lejeune and his cabal. Hopeless.'

Argent hefted the metal case in his hands as if it held the answers to all our questions. 'What this is, my hysterical greenie friend, is a money grab, plain and simple.'

Kwesi was standing now, clearly roused. 'And what you and your friends did in Africa, what was that, if not a money grab?'

Argent waved this away. 'The Lejeune government is using natural phenomena to justify the biggest swindle in history.'

'We were there,' said Francoise. 'In Africa. We saw what you did.'

Argent wheeled to face Francoise. 'Me? You saw me?' Something in his voice had changed. His left eye started to twitch.

'We saw the results of what you did,' said Francoise. 'At first, I wasn't sure. Now I am.'

Argent seemed to brace himself, stood straighter. 'That was an unfortunate accident. We were trying to help.'

'Accident.' Kwesi spat it out, glared at Argent. 'From what I've heard, you made a fortune.'

I stood. My legs were shaking. 'We all saw you on TV. At every step, you tried to hide the truth by sowing doubt, spreading disinformation and lies. You spent millions to make scientific fact look like a debate. First, none of it was happening at all. Then when it was obvious even to the dullest moron that it was happening, you started blaming anything and anyone.'

'Even God,' said Kwesi.

'Even people who are different than you are,' said Lan.

May looked at me as if I was a stranger.

'I agree with Teacher,' said Francoise. 'We have to work, do our part. It's the only way things will improve.'

'You naïve little thing,' said Samantha, glaring at Francoise. 'You just don't have a clue do you? I suggest you stick to your mud pies, darling. And keep your tits out of my husband's way.'

Argent grinned at Samantha, then at Francoise.

'And I suggest that *you* show some restraint with your morning showers,' Francoise answered, very composed, very cool. 'We're already out of water.'

'I'm not surprised,' Samantha shot back, 'with your ridiculous little hobby farm out there.'

'That was rude,' said Kwesi. 'The garden is for all of us. We all have to live together. Basic manners are a good start.'

Samantha scoffed.

'Don't be so dismissive, Mrs Argent,' said, Lance. 'We all have a right to our opinion, but we are not entitled to our own facts. I've read about your case, the so-called evidence you dredged up, the bribery and tampering, those bogus scientists you paid to testify. That you lost is the one sensible thing that's happened in the last ten years.'

Samantha glared at him. 'Deviancy was once a crime,' she said, courtroom. 'And I assure you it will be again.'

Lan stared at Samantha a moment, as if trying to decide how he would make sense of what he had just heard, then turned and walked away. The front door closed with a click behind him.

'From what I can see, nobody has any rights now,' said Argent. 'And the sooner we figure that out and start to organise ourselves against these bastards, the better.'

May lay slumped on the sofa. It looked as if she had passed out. I leaned forward, put my forearms on my knees and stared at the floor. For a while, no one spoke, and the only sound was the wind outside and May's occasional bursts of snoring.

Finally, I looked up at Argent and his wife. I had to say it. 'You know, I dedicated my whole life to science, to helping people become scientifically literate, to understand the power of logic and reason. And you are living proof that I failed. I pity you, and I pity us all.'

Argent stared at me like he wanted me dead. 'You snivelling little zero,' he shouted. 'If you're so fucking smart why is your wife getting her bone somewhere else?'

May jerked her head up, awake now, a wild look in her eyes. She seemed unsure of where she was, of what she had just missed. Samantha took two steps towards Argent and slapped him hard across the face. The sharp crack echoed through the room. Then she turned and paced to the front door and walked out, slamming the door behind her.

'May,' I stuttered, trying to process what I had just heard.

Argent raised his hand, index and forefinger extended, thumb up in the shape of a gun, and pointed it at my face. 'Now back off, asshole, unless you want an eighth hole in that oh-so-scientifically-literate brain of yours.'

I realised at that moment that I was not scared. It surprised me. What I felt, more than anything, was a sense of futility. For a moment we all stood there staring at each other, as if surprised at our sudden descent into the unlit depths of anarchy. May sat open-mouthed, eyes wide. No one spoke. Then Argent tucked the case under his arm, winked at May, and followed his wife out into the night.

Time for Such a World

I put another piece of wood on the fire and sit back down next to my wife. The flames jump and crackle as the dry-split jarrah takes, flaring copper green and ionised blue. The night is dark. There is no moon. Rain pelts the roof, channels along the wooden gutters and into our water tanks. Up the hill, the light from Lewis's window shimmers through the rain, soft and yellow. We smile at each other, knowing that he and Mandy are dry and warm and safe.

We pull the blanket up over our legs and go back to our stolen books.

My wife is re-reading Jane Eyre *– for the fourth time, I think. I am re-reading* Macbeth, *from a 1984 paperback edition of* The Complete Works of William Shakespeare. *It is an old volume now, dog-eared, the binding long since cracked and repaired with tape, the pages cured deep brown from hours and years of sun and salt, swollen from the time Kweku dropped it into the sea off New Caledonia when he was four, the margins crowded with notes in four hands, passages underlined, starred, adorned with exclamation marks, pencilled queries.*

It is an old habit of mine, this writing in books, inherited from my father, passed on to my sons. Books are meant to be used, he always said. So, use them. Record your thoughts, how a particular passage makes you feel. Note something that strikes you, that you want to remember. That's what margins and end sheets are for. Record where you were, what you were doing, who you were with. Books aren't just stories written by others, they are a part of your story.

I run my fingertip over the faint graphite scrawl at the top of the flyleaf. Daniel Menzels, November 17, 1989. For the ten-thousandth time I wonder about him and his family, who they were and how they lived, about what became of them. What little we do know about them we know from their library – our library, now. We know that they loved each other and loved their children. We know that they cared about the world, that they loved life and looked to the future with hope. We know their birthdates, and where they were on Christmas Day of 2017 – Eleuthera Island in the Bahamas. And now their stories are forever entwined with ours.

16

I hunched over the conveyor belt and watched the junked remains of our civilisation trundle past, semi-conductors and hard-drives and every kind of wasted opportunity. I was still trying to process what I'd seen on my run that morning, how to explain it. No, that's not right. I was still trying to deny the meaning of what I'd seen.

'A lot more people coming now,' Kwesi said, picking an old PC motherboard from the belt and throwing it into the bin marked *precious metals*.

Every day the stream of garbage was different. Today it was mostly old computer equipment and electrical gear, as if someone had just demolished a server centre and sent it all here for processing. In the old world, the one we'd left behind, I recalled reading that every year we landfilled over two billion dollars' worth of gold and platinum in the form of discarded computer and smart-phone components. I remember thinking then that someone should do something about it, start recovering some of that treasure. Surely there was money to be made for an enterprising individual. I allowed myself a rueful half-smile. Little had I known it would be me.

'That must be why they've cut the water allowance in half.'

'Must be.' Kwesi wiped his brow with the sleeve of his coveralls. The coveralls we wore were orange, like the ones prisoners had, and were permanently covered in ash. 'And the food.'

Six others, similarly clad, hunched over the belt that carried the waste from the unloading area towards the incinerator. Through the shifting smoke I could see the brick smokestack and the roof of the warehouse, and above, the cloudless sulphur-dioxide sky. The execution replayed itself in my head, the casual almost offhand demeanour of the soldiers, Esposito and the other man shoved like garbage into the pit. Fear and revulsion tore at my guts. The toxic smell of burning refuse made me gag.

As the weeks had passed, the weather had become noticeably hotter. More and more people streamed into the city. Every room in every apartment building was now full. People were sleeping in corridors. Squatters had taken over the derelict houses in the neighbourhoods to the west. Food deliveries became increasingly erratic. Kwesi, Francoise, Lan and I started taking turns queuing for rations each morning, the initial weekly system having long since devolved into a daily scrum. This morning, it had been me. The ration centre was disorganised and under-staffed. I stood in line for over an hour, came away with one loaf of bread, a small jar of peanut butter, three potatoes, five oranges and half a pound of what they said was hamburger, for four of us for the day. Ignoring hunger had become a full time activity. And the water situation in our building was deteriorating steadily; people were simply not following the rules.

We had settled into an uneasy rhythm. I ran most mornings, despite everything, early when the town was still quiet and relatively cool, pushing out further towards the grim boundaries of the place, occasionally skirting the Green Zone, peering through the double line of wire fencing at the tidy newish buildings and still-green trees. By the time I returned to the apartment, the others were usually up and preparing to go to work. Evenings, everyone was too tired to do anything but eat and go to bed. Argent had kept out of my way, and I'd kept out of his.

I had come to accept that May was gone. When I woke in the mornings her bed was empty. The few times I saw her, sometimes at dinner, she was with Argent. She looked good, well fed, happy, like she used to when she was with me at the beginning. Francoise told me May was painting again. I was happy for her, but it hurt all the same. As for Argent, that case never left his side. I knew he had contacts, money. And I knew that he was able to help May in ways I couldn't. I hoped that he was helping her get more of her medication.

Samantha no longer seemed to care about what was going on between May and her husband. The last time I'd seen her, three days ago over dinner at the apartment, she spoke about a rash of disappearances. She said there was a common thread to them. Anyone who had publicly opposed the new government's reforms was a target. I hadn't seen her since. Kwesi said she had moved in with a fellow from Administration who lived in a big place all his own inside the Green Zone. We didn't see much of Lan anymore, either. Just occasionally for meals. He was working as a nurse in the hospital. Most nights after dinner he went out, returning just before curfew and sometimes not at all.

That morning, I received my first letter.

Dear Dad,

I hope this reaches you, and that you and Mum are well. I know Mum was angry with me when we spoke last. Please tell her I am sorry, but that there was nothing I could do. The president is doing the best he can under terrible circumstances. He is an ethical man, Dad. That's why he's here. After decades of lies, cowardice and bullshit, we finally have someone who has the courage to face the truth, see it for what it is, and do what is right, not just what is expedient. Most importantly, no one owns him. He listens to the experts, acts for the common good. All of us in the government must maintain the same standards. It is the only way we are going to salvage something out of the mess we've made. And yes, Dad, I say we, not just you.

Dad, the news is very bad. We are doing our best to stabilise the situation at home and globally, but it is not going well. There has been a second continental crop failure of just about every variety. The new genetically engineered strains designed to grow in the rapidly evolving northern climate have not taken, either here or in Russia. Only the supplies coming in from the newly 'acquired' territories in Africa are keeping the population fed. Please Dad, if you can, stockpile food. It's going to get a lot worse before it gets better.

The Antarctic ice cap, while much reduced, is still stable at its core, for now, we think, so that's a bit of good news. It means that Southern Hemisphere conditions are more favourable overall. That's why we can't quit Africa. No one wants to be there, but right now we have no choice. The whole thing makes me so sad. Some days I don't know if I can go on.

A letter came for you last week. I have enclosed it. Please tell Mum not to worry. I will try to write soon.

Lachie.

God how I missed my little fair-haired boy, the Saturday afternoons kicking the ball around in summer, the January mornings at the ice rink, pulling his skate laces tight. The enclosed letter was addressed to Lachie, postmarked Canmore, Alberta, six weeks ago. It was scratched on a piece of packing cardboard in blue ink. *Dear Tech*, it said, misspelled. *We are both fine. We got to where we were going. Thanks for the gear and everything. I am going to be a father. M&M.*

17

As the day went on, the temperature soared. We sweated inside our coveralls, fought to keep our flimsy paper facemasks free of ash so we could breathe. Towards noon, one of the men in our team collapsed beside the belt. Kwesi and I helped him up, half carried half dragged him to the shade of the loading ramp and propped him against the wall. Kwesi was about to go and get him some water when the foreman arrived and told us to get back to work. Half an hour later two men in blue coveralls came and carried him away.

I adjusted my facemask and looked over at Kwesi. He was levering what looked like a hardware rack from the belt. Several of the components remained bolted to the frame and a tendon-work of red, blue and yellow wires spilled from the back. He set it on the ground next to the belt. It was almost as big as he was.

'Grab a couple of sledgehammers,' said the foreman. 'Break it up and sort it.'

At the lunch break, we sat on the ground near the fence at the far edge of the facility, upwind of the incinerator, and leaned our backs against a concrete road barrier. I offered Kwesi my water bottle.

'No thanks. Some shade would be nice though.'

A lettuce sandwich with a little butter, a carrot, and a wizened apple barely dented my hunger.

'I'm sorry about May,' Kwesi said after a while.

'Thanks.'

Kwesi offered me a tomato from Francoise's garden. 'Argent is right, you know. They told us we would be able to live normal lives. Does this look normal to you?'

'I can't remember what normal is.'

'Things are getting worse, not better. We should do something. Complain.'

I nibbled away every bit of flesh from the apple's core and sat looking at the hard cartilage of the thing.

'Argent is organising a demonstration,' said Kwesi, wiping his mouth with the back of his hand. 'He said it was going to be soon. I'm thinking of going.'

I had seen posters going up around town, watched the cops tearing them down. 'Argent's a crook,' I said. 'Whatever he's doing, he's doing it for himself.'

Kwesi thought about this a while. 'I don't like the way he looks at Francoise.'

'I know what you mean.'

'Sorry,' he said, going quiet a moment. 'Maybe you're right.'

We sat and rested, and didn't speak again until our break was almost over.

'Was it very bad,' I asked. 'In Africa, I mean.'

Kwesi nodded. 'Yes. Very.'

'I think what we are doing there is wrong.'

'I live here now,' said Kwesi. 'What's happening here is wrong.'

I pulled the stem from what was left of the apple and crunched down on the core, swallowing hard.

'I ran west this morning,' I said finally. I needed to share it. The others needed to know. 'Before lining up for food. Ten kilometres straight out along our road. Do you remember the entrance we came through that first day on the bus?'

Kwesi folded the piece of wax paper his sandwich had been wrapped in and tucked it into his shirt pocket. 'Yes. Like a checkpoint. Flags and grass.'

I nodded. 'I followed the same road, but in the other direction, away from the entrance. It was early, still dark.' I stopped, thought back. 'It was the strangest thing. At about nine kilometres, the road just ended. All the asphalt had been torn up. The town ended too. Like someone had drawn a straight line and just erased everything beyond it.'

Kwesi waited for me to continue.

'I kept going. There was just enough moonlight to see. It was bare ground, dirt, nothing growing. I ran another kilometre or so and came to a huge berm, soil and rubble bulldozed up three, maybe four metres high for as far as I could see, both ways. I scrambled to the top and looked over the edge.' It felt as if my throat was closing up. I took a sip of water.

'What was it, Teacher? What did you see?' Kwesi's deep brown eyes were focused, intent.

'Wire, Kwesi.'

'What do you mean?'

'Razor wire, as far as I could see in either direction, guard towers, lights, soldiers with guns.'

'What are they protecting us against? Do the people outside really hate us that much?'

'They're not protecting us, Kwesi. There's no one out there. The guns are pointing in.'

He stared at me a moment, said nothing.

'We're in a concentration camp.' I didn't tell him about the executions I'd witnessed, but I should have.

He swallowed, looked into my eyes. 'Then Argent is right,' he said after a while. 'We have to get out of here.'

We went back to work. For four and a half more hours we picked junk from the conveyors with our hands, watching the sun slant lower in the sky, but all I could think of was May, dancing in the rain in her hiking shorts and tank top all those years ago on the Mount Washington trail with the dark spruce valley stretched out below us, deep and wide and silent in the time of our favour.

She was right. About everything.

Strain Comes On

Kweku and Lewis haul on the ropes, and Providence *settles slowly into her cradle. I wade into the water and secure the hull to the cradle's ribs, then give Lewis the thumbs-up. He ties off his line and walks back up to where Starburst and Cassiopeia are waiting. They whinny as he approaches, nuzzle his face. Steam rises from the back of his neck, wicks from the horses' flanks. He caresses their flat, steaming cheeks a moment, then checks their skidding harnesses. I can hear him talking to them in that secret language of theirs, words lost in the fine steady rain. He tugs on their collars to make sure they are snug, gives each straight trace a rattle, and leads the pair down over the shingle to the water's edge.*

Soon, Kweku has Star and Cass hooked up to the cradle. Lewis is talking to them now, getting them ready. He nods at me. Kweku stands back. I reach down through the cold water, feel for the smooth rock of the skidway. The flat-planed ridges of the wooden skids are aligned. I whisk away a few small pieces of shingle. Go ahead, I say. Get her out.

Lewis whispers a word, and the horses lean into their harnesses. Hooves scrape into the shingle, find rock. The strain comes on, shudders through bone and wood, jolts leather and muscle. Horsepower against friction. I nod to Kweku and we each grab a rib and start pushing.

Soon the cradle is moving, polished ribs grinding over rock. We pick up speed as the horses get into their rhythm. Kweku and I jump back, let Star and Cass take it. Water pours from the ribs and braces, trickles from the hull as Providence *emerges from the Southern Ocean.*

It is nearly a year since we last had her out, and her hull is fouled thick. Clumps of mussels zebra the keel. Barnacles plate the mahogany plankwork from bow to stern. A layer of thick green algae rings the waterline. I signal Lewis to stop, and the cradle judders to a halt, notches into the rock bevels I set that very first year. Kweku sets the chocks and checks the lines.

Lewis unhooks the horses and palms them each half an apple. I'll take these two back, he says.

Kweku and I stand side by side and inspect Providence. *He reaches up and touches the unfouled wood just above the waterline, holds his hand there a moment. He was born on this ship, took his first steps in her cabin, learned to read up on her bow. On the certificate we made up for him, she is listed as his place of birth.*

Left it too long, he says. Again.

I smile. He says this every year.

We set to work. I take the bow, Kweku the stern. We work from the waterline down, one plank at a time, careful not to damage the wood with our steel scrapers. Lewis joins us a while later. We work in the rain until dark, scything living tissue from the hull.

18

And on the seventh day, we rested. Ten and half weeks we'd been here now. Seventy-four days gone, spinning inexorably into summer.

I slept late, woke to a dull, overcast sky and May's empty bed. I tried to read for a while – Stephen Hawking – but hunger and the smell of freshly baked bread eventually drove me to the kitchen. The mysteries of space-time remain beyond me, even now. Kwesi, Francoise and Lan were at the kitchen table admiring a steaming loaf.

'We were going to have lunch,' said Kwesi. 'Want some?'

'Jeez, yes. Please', I said, drawn to the table.

There were vegetables from the garden: spicy rocket, some red chilies, a couple of big ripe tomatoes. Kwesi had produced a small brick of cheddar cheese, and Lan a tin of salmon he'd traded for with someone at the hospital.

'Wait a sec.' I ran back to my room and returned with half a packet of Oreo cookies, set them on the table. Francoise smiled. Earlier in the week I'd traded our foreman for them, a whole packet. It cost me a pack of triple-A batteries. I probably overpaid, but I couldn't help myself. In the trading game, it was all about food, now. Tinned fruit was particularly prized, as was any kind of meat, and, not surprisingly, real coffee. As the weeks went by everything was becoming scarcer, and accordingly, more expensive. The laws of supply and demand offer no mercy.

I sat and Francoise sliced me a piece of bread, placed a sliver of butter on top. Just looking at it was like witnessing a small miracle. Just as were about to start eating, Argent arrived. He was wearing his fancy boots and leather jacket, carried the steel case as before, close and precious. Dark circles dragged at his eyes, drained them of colour. He looked as if he'd been up all night. May was not with him. He closed the door behind him, stood looking at us, at the feast spread before us.

'Join us?' said Francoise. 'There is plenty.'

Argent didn't answer, just stood there, watching us. No one spoke. He seemed to be calculating, assessing the advantages of this clearly unexpected invitation. When he turned and disappeared into his room without uttering a syllable, Lan flashed Francoise a 'what did you do that for?' look.

She shrugged, handed round the plates. Lan opened the tin, offered it to Francoise. Kwesi sliced the cheese into four equal chunks. I bit into the bread, closed my eyes and savoured the saltiness of the butter and the energy-dense bulk of the wheat, the sublime taste of living another day.

After a while, Argent reappeared. We all turned to face him.

'For you,' was all he said, handing Francoise a bottle of wine.

She held out one of the tomatoes. He looked at it a time, then took it in his hand, inspected it carefully.

'Have you seen Samantha?' said Francoise.

The question seemed to confuse him. He blinked a few times in rapid succession, raked his fingers back through his hair. 'You don't have to worry about her. She always looks after herself.'

'Is she alright?' Francoise pressed. 'We haven't seen her for a while.'

'I saw her last week. She's shacked up with some asshole on the other side of town,' said Argent. 'She looked old.' He hesitated a moment. 'Make sure you come out to the demonstration. Two weeks from today. Thursday.' Then he turned and left. A moment later we heard the front door close.

'Well, I'll be burnt,' Kwesi said, opening the bottle, a nice Chablis.

We ate and drank in silence, with dedication. Two slices of bread each, a quarter of a tomato, three Oreos each for dessert with Francoise's peppermint tea.

'That's it for the rest of the day,' Francoise said after we'd finished.

'It was worth it,' said Lan, wiping the corner of his mouth with a small white handkerchief. 'The tomato was great.'

'The garden has started well,' said Kwesi. 'But there has been no rain. If we don't do something soon, everything will wilt and die, just as it is coming good.'

'There is plenty of water at the solar plant,' said Francoise. 'They use it to make steam for the turbines.'

'They send the power north,' said Kwesi.

'We also use it to clean the mirrors,' said Francoise. 'Hundreds of litres a day. Thousands. That's what we do all day. All of us women – artists, doctors, musicians, teachers, insurance analysts – now window cleaners.'

'Apparently it's work robots can't do,' said Kwesi.

'*Azaa*.'

Kwesi smiled at her, nodded. 'Dubious, she means.'

'They ration us so they can keep churning out power,' said Francoise.

The tanks in our building were now empty less than a day after the weekly delivery. And the hotter it got, the worse the hoarding became.

'And people are disappearing,' Lan whispered. 'Everyone at the hospital is talking about it. A woman from this building, fourth floor, vanished yesterday. A gentleman from the building across the street the day before that. They come in the middle of the night, they say. The "Broken Hearts" people are calling them.'

The words knocked the breath from my lungs. What I'd seen in the old warehouse was no one-off.

'Maybe they're just holding them for a few days, questioning them,' said Kwesi. 'Maybe they did something wrong.'

'We've all done something wrong,' I said, choking on the words.

Changed

The day dawns clear and cold. I put aside my manuscript and walk down the hill to the boat ramp. Kweku and Lewis are already at work, preparing Providence for her annual trip north. In the first years, when the boys were very young, we would all go, and then for a while it was just me, north along the coast to Albany. Two or three days going, if the winds were fair, more coming back unless you had luck and the winds veered and then held. As the boys grew older and more capable, I started to take them along. And then that year I broke my leg falling from the roof – I was trying to fix a leak during a storm – the boys convinced me that they could do the trip alone. Kweku was seventeen and Lewis fifteen. They made the journey in record time, there and back in six days, including all the bartering in town. Every item on the list was safely packed into the cabin – paint, tar, black powder, an ingot of lead, seeds, a new saw blade, flour, everything. They even managed to find a couple of books, an old copy of Jude the Obscure, and a beaten-up old paperback called Batavia about the Dutch ship of the same name that was shipwrecked on the Abrolhos Islands in Western Australia in 1629, and how the survivors, fighting for survival, turned on each other.

After that, I never did the trip again. And it's okay. It's good. I trust them. They've done it more than a dozen times since, and they've always managed it fine, always rounded The Hope and trimmed up for home within a week of leaving. It was on one of those trips that they met Juliette and Mandy. Close friends, the two girls had grown up in an orphanage, like so many other children of their generation. The trips became more frequent for a while, and then two years ago the four of them all came back together, announcing to us there on the beach as they stepped from the skiff that they were married. A justice of the peace in Albany had done the honours. It still seems so old-fashioned to me, them wanting to get married like *that. Their mother and I were never married, never even gave it a thought. But everything is different now. Circumstances have changed, and so have we all.*

19

Another week passed. And then another. Moments blended into hours, days into nights. Despite the lack of food, I had never felt fitter.

Passing the Irish pub, its windows boarded up and scrawled with graffiti, I glanced at my watch and calculated an average pace. The pavement was hard under my feet, and I could feel the rhythm take control of my thoughts, pushing away the ache that lived with me now like an unwanted guest who would not leave.

May had always complained about that – my need to create a visualised geometric construct around everything, even my emotions. And now she was gone, no longer even bothering to conceal the fact that she was with Argent, that insufferable pretentious prick. Some nights she disappeared without saying a word, and I didn't see her again until morning, when she'd sit smug and satisfied at the kitchen table with a pastry and a mug of freshly brewed coffee, knowing that all of it was driving me crazy: her doing what she was doing; the smell of the coffee that she didn't offer to share; the delicacies she could get while the rest of us starved. But most days now I didn't see her at all.

It was only the running that was keeping me together now, and I let my legs carry me along, the endorphins coursing through me like a merciful salve. Every ounce of fat had gone from my body. With the lack of food, the long runs were eating away muscle now, but I kept at it. I knew the whole town, had it all drawn up in my notebook, the alleyways and backstreets, the shortcuts across what were once parks and now looked more like refugee camps – because they were refugee camps.

I ran each morning, unobstructed by officialdom, ignored, sliding through the darkness in my black track suit and skull cap, sublimating myself. Sometimes I glimpsed a police car, or a soldier at a checkpoint, but either they didn't see me, or they were simply not interested. I was sure they had other, more important things to worry about.

That day I was thirty minutes into my run when I realised that I was heading out towards the garbage plant, carried along on autopilot, lost in thought. Here was the underpass, the same feet sticking out from under the sheet of cardboard, the row of old brickwork factories. I knew that I was taking myself there again, despite having sketched an off-limits hashwork over the place, fighting against the fascination, my natural inclination to know.

It was still dark, half an hour at least until sunrise. The glow from the incinerator painted an oblique geometry of walls and chimneys, dark, gaping shadows. I found the hole under the fence, checked the road both ways and squirmed under. The main door was locked, and the building was dark. I threaded my way between the pallets and boxes piled in the yard towards the side of the building. The windows on this side were boarded up, the heavy plywood affixed from inside, the remnant shards of the panes grey with soot and dust. A black iron stairway squared its way up to the roof. It looked like one of those city-block fire escapes you used to see in some parts of New York and Chicago, or downtown Vancouver. The bottom steps were missing, but it looked solid enough. I reached up and hoisted myself to the first intact step and started climbing. After four flights I reached a grated landing and stood looking back out across the darkened road to the row of derelict factory buildings and beyond, the lines of houses and the streets riveted with the stumps of dead trees. A canalised stream, now more of a sewer, emerged from a culvert just beyond the road and snaked westward, black in its shroud of weeds. In the other direction, away from the town, about a kilometre away, I could just make out the pushed-up rubble of the perimeter berm, and beyond, the wire stretching away in either direction.

I kept climbing. At the next landing there was a windowless steel door. I tried to open it, but it was locked. To the left, just

beyond the railing, was a window. Some of the panes were
smashed. I leaned over the rail and looked down to the ground. It
was a long way. Six more flights brought me to a wide flat roof.
Vents and chimneys lanced the black tar surface of the roof,
tumours ravaging sunburnt skin. About halfway across, a shed-
like structure protruded from the slab, a steel door recessed into
one side. I crouched and pressed the tip of my finger to the tar. It
was still solid from the night's relative coolness. I moved towards
the doorway, first light birthing on the horizon.

I pushed on the door. It swung open. I stepped inside. There
was a second door. It grated as I pushed, but it too had been left
unlocked. A foul chemistry invaded my nostrils. The smell
reminded me vaguely of the sulphuric acid from my lab at school,
but there was something else there, too, something I could not
place, and I was aware of a recklessness taking hold of me, a sense
that my own fate no longer mattered. I started down the stairs.
Soon darkness enveloped me, and I was moving by feel, my feet
searching for the steps, the paint of the handrail flaking away in
my palm, my footfall echoing down into the well below, the fetor
growing as I descended. I counted the steps, fifteen per flight,
three flights now, feeling out for the walls at each landing like a
blind man, finding the handrail again, the edge of the next flight
down. By now I was past questioning what was driving me on,
past any analysis. It was momentum that carried me, pure inertia.

At the next landing I stopped, rubbed my eyes. I looked back
up the way I'd come. The darkness was complete. I felt along each
wall, looking for a door, but found nothing. Five flights down I'd
counted. I must be close. I kept going, cursing myself for not
bringing my Maglite. It was sitting at home in my pack, useless.
Another landing, and then a door. I found the handle, creaked it
down, pushed. The hinges groaned and the sound of it echoed
back at me as my eyes adjusted. I was standing on a railed
mezzanine that overlooked the factory floor. By the incinerator
light I could make out the main sliding doors, the window

through which I had been witness before. To my right, a steel stairway led down to the floor.

I stepped to the railing and peered over the side. The pit was directly below me, a dark pool about the size and shape of a freight container. The smell was almost unbearable. I tried to breathe through my mouth as I followed the stairs down towards the polished concrete of the main floor.

I stood at the edge of the pit and stared down at the dark, oily surface of the liquid. Here, the stench was palpable, no longer an odour but a vapour, an aerosol of death. Those men had been pushed into concentrated acid. Their frail bodies would have burned away in a matter of minutes. Their molecules were still there, changed, hydrolysed, but there nonetheless, swimming in a chemical purgatory from which there was no escape. A violent spasm caught me, and I doubled over, retching a thin stream of bile into the pit. When I opened my eyes a beam of white light was moving across the ceiling. I whirled around to face the main doors. The muffled sound of a car door closing echoed through the building. Gasping, I stumbled towards the stairs. Outside, another car door slammed.

I climbed the stairs on wobbly legs, reached the mezzanine, found the stairwell and ducked back into the darkness. The big doors rolled open. It was the Broken Hearts, the same two as before, one brush cut and marine-shouldered, the other broad-hipped and squat. This time there was only one prisoner, small and frail next to her handlers. They pushed her forward a few steps, but she stopped, defiant, until they pushed her again, like that, a few steps at a time, across the floor towards the pit, the vehicle's headlights shining behind them. The prisoner turned to face her captors, screamed something at them that I could not make out. As she did, her face caught the light. I put my hand to my mouth and stifled a groan. It was Samantha.

I closed my eyes. I was breathing so hard I knew that if I didn't control myself, I was going to hyperventilate. I wanted to run but stood transfixed as I watched the Broken Hearts push Samantha towards the pit.

'On your knees, bitch,' the man barked, pushing her down by the head.

'Fuck you, assholes,' she screamed. 'Fucking criminals.'

I knew what was coming. The last time I was here I had stayed hidden. I'd watched and done nothing. Shame burned through me, my cowardice incandescent. My hands were shaking, my legs trembling. The man laughed and tapped a cigarette from a pack and lit it and blew the smoke onto the back of Sam's head. 'No, you are the criminal, babe. You deserve a lot worse. You will never be forgiven.'

I moved to the railing, in full view now, stood looking down at them.

I remembered the last time I'd seen her on TV, back when she was leading the Supreme Court challenge against the Marshank-Watson bill. May and I and Lachie had all been watching together. It was summer, and hot. We'd flung open all the doors, and a breeze was flowing from the mountains. It was the crucial phase of the trial. She'd been so confident, so sure of her position, her witnesses credible, at least on the surface. I remembered how angry I had been with her, how much I had hated her, thinking: she's going to win. She's actually going to win. She didn't. And now she was kneeling before a pit of acid with a gun to her head.

'Stop,' I shouted.

Samantha and the two Broken Hearts looked up at me at the same time. I knew I would never forget those faces, the look in Samantha's eyes. I still don't know what I had hoped to accomplish with that momentary act of defiance, but after years trying to convince myself that I did it for her, I know now that my motivations were entirely selfish.

She was still looking at me when the side of her head exploded. I will never forget the sound of it, the echoing crash of the gunshot, the treble of the copper casing dancing on the concrete and the splash as Samantha's body slumped into the pit, me running into the stairwell, dizzy, the detonation ringing in my ears, running for my life. And then, a moment later, the sound of footfall, rapid, boots on concrete, and then the metallic ting of hard soles on steel.

I took the stairs three at a time, one hand on the railing, swinging up and around the corners, climbing higher and higher. I didn't think. I ran. I was almost to the roof when I heard the groan of the hinges and a crash as the steel door was flung open. They were in the stairwell now and I could hear their heavy boots scuffing on the cement. I sprinted across the roof towards the fire escape. The sky was lightening now into a pale green. I took the fire escape stairs a flight at a time, flying down, one hand on the railing, vaulting around each corner, not caring about the noise now, down and down. I hit the ground hard and rolled and looked back up to the roof. Still no one.

I ran towards the stacks of crates. There was a shout from above and behind. One of the Broken Hearts was standing on the rooftop looking down. He raised his arm, pointed at me. There was a gun in his hand. A shot ripped the air, that same sickening crack of before. Another. I ran on, waiting for the impact. I had never been shot at before. I expected the whine and hum of the movies, but there was just the splitting thud of the bullets hitting the wood of the pallets around me. I wove through the stacks of crates and pallets. The canal was there, just ahead, running brown and opaque. I jumped in. My knees buckled as my feet hit the concrete bottom. Thigh deep, I waded towards the culvert, glancing back over my shoulder. The man was racing down the fire escape now. Where was the woman? Had they split up? Had she come out through the front? Was she already on the road, ready to intercept me? The culvert yawned black, and soon I was through and to the other side of the road, and there was no sign of the woman. I kept moving, wading as fast as I could, now into a leafy green ravine, newly sprouted trees lining the banks among a tangle of vines and grass surviving on the trickle of sewage, and then I was running again, as fast as I could, back towards town along the abandoned sidestreets of a once-happy neighbourhood, looking back but seeing no one.

20

Heat poured in silver waves from the corrugated-steel jacket of the incinerator, enveloping us in a dancing mirage. Kwesi and I worked together, shovelling the combustible mash from a huge pile onto a short-tracked conveyor that led to the glowing mouth of the chamber. The roar of the steam turbine obliterated every sound, and even through the ear protectors the cycling roar filled my head, rising and falling. There was no end to it, no respite. And to this unspoken rhythm we moved, communicating with our eyes and our bodies, a nod or a glance, one loading at the pile while the other tipped a shovelful onto the belt, crossing as we switched positions, and then back again, for hours and days and weeks now.

From where we worked, I could see the rusted metal of the fire escape and the edge of the roof where the Broken Heart had stood shooting down at me, and the place where the culvert was and the shot of green weeds and scrub that choked the canal. And each time I looked up I became more convinced that they had seen my face and had gone through the database and identified me and even now were coming to get me. This part of our civilisation, the part that catalogued and controlled, I was sure had survived.

We sat in the dust with our backs against the wall and opened our lunches. A tomato for each of us, a carrot, some bread. No butter, no meat. I held the tomato in my hand. It was ripe and fresh and the colour of blood.

The big man had not spoken all day. Even walking to work in the morning he had been uncharacteristically reserved, shuffling along with his head bowed, listless. I had let him be. You had to do that, then. Everyone was fighting in their own way, and some had given up fighting and either way you needed to let them do it.

Kwesi drew his knees up to his chest and turned his head. His eyes were red and swollen, a murky tannin sea shot with blood. Dark shadows stained the soft skin under his eyes. He let out a hoarse sob and buried his head between his knees. I reached out and put my hand on his thickly muscled shoulder. He would talk if he wanted to.

'It's Francoise,' Kwesi mumbled into his legs.

My stomach turned. 'What happened, Kwes?'

He zipped open his coveralls, pointed to his chest. An L-shaped scar ran in thick welts from just below his sternum to the base of his ribcage and across. 'She did this. In the war. I would have died. She saved me.' He rubbed his eyes. 'Me and so many others. I don't know how she did it. Operating for days on end without a break. It was utter chaos. You can't imagine.' He broke down, the sobs coming thick and heavy now.

After a while he pulled himself together. 'After my convalescence, I started helping out in the hospital. One night I watched her pull over two hundred fléchettes from one man. Can you imagine? One at a time, snipping off the barbs, removing the dart. She'd been at it for over twenty hours when I went to lie down. Six hours later when I came back, she was still at it. She was covered in blood, head to foot. It was as if she was possessed. As if God was working through her. I believe that, Teacher. That God was at work that day. The man survived. It was a miracle.'

I said nothing, tried to imagine.

'She didn't come home last night,' he said.

I had been too busy with my own problems to notice.

'When was the last time you saw her?'

'Going to work yesterday morning. To the plant. She never came back.'

Knowledge of the Future

Lewis smiles at me as I approach. Kweku just raises his eyebrows. They know I am trying to put it all down on paper, and that I am struggling. In some ways the journey back is harder that the journey forward. It's like living with knowledge of the future but knowing you can do nothing to change it.

I close my eyes and turn my face to the sun, let its warmth bathe my face. The air is cool and clean. I breathe it into my lungs. The smells of the sea come to me: iodine, sodium chloride, fresh kelp. The redolence of the hills is there, too, the healing diversity of heathland and coastal dune and far-off hints of still-surviving karri forests.

We've seen them, those forests. Trees so tall that they seem to reach right up to the stars. Trees that have outlasted any human being. The oldest were alive when Shakespeare was writing, when Newton was showing us the way out from ignorance and superstition. We camped under them, all four of us, that one time, when the boys were still young. At night we lay on our backs and watched the stars turn behind the treetops, and we were looking deep back into time, to the earliest echoes of the universe.

I pick up a sanding block and join the boys. They have made good progress. Tomorrow she will be ready for the primer. I run my hand along the hull, feeling its newfound smoothness. I visualise Providence *freed, slipping through the water like a dolphin. After velocity and acceleration, force and mass, it was the first physics I taught them. For a given speed through the water, the force acting against you is proportional to the density of the fluid you are travelling through, the wetted surface area of the hull, and a scalar quantity called the drag coefficient, which describes the roughness of the surface. You can't control the density of the water, and you can't easily reshape your boat's hull, but you can reduce the drag, a lot. So, keep the wetted surface clean. Newtonian, yes, but for planet-bound mortals, sufficient.*

I pause near the stern, run my fingertips over the bullet holes. They have long since been plugged and caulked, and just now, freshly sanded over. And yet here is the evidence that it was all real. Not exactly as I am recounting it, perhaps, but close enough. These traces tell the story. This ship is full of them: holed sails, gouged and splintered woodwork, torn clothing patched and sewn. The evidence is everywhere. In books and maps and tools, in the long scar on the back of my head and the construction of my son's shoulders. Each of these echoes that fill our lives every day, and that slowly, over years, I have learned to ignore.

21

Francoise still hadn't returned by the time we got back from work. Kwesi and I waited for May to return, hoping that she might provide some clue about Francoise, but by nightfall she still wasn't back either, so we decided to go down to the Administration building. By the time we got there, the place was closed. We went to the police station, but the cops were dismissive and unhelpful. No one knew where Francoise was, and if they did, they weren't saying.

I didn't tell Kwesi about Samantha. All that night we waited for our wives to return. Sometime after two o'clock Kwesi fell into a fitful sleep on the couch. I went to bed, but it's hard to sleep when you're trying to chase away reality with nightmares.

When I got up early to run, the women still hadn't returned. Kwesi was still on the couch, and I didn't wake him. I didn't run long. Everything hurt, and I couldn't find any sort of rhythm. When I returned, May was in Argent's bedroom, rummaging through a bag. I stood in the doorway watching her for a moment, hoping she would look up and engage, but she ignored me. I couldn't see Kwesi, and his bedroom door was closed, so I went to the kitchen, fried myself an egg, the last of my ration for the week. I was filling my water bottle from a jug we kept on the counter when, to my surprise, May joined me.

'Still running,' she said. It was a statement, so I figured it didn't require an answer.

'Where have you been?' I asked. It didn't come out right.

She picked up the electric kettle, swirled it a moment and then flicked the switch. 'Out.'

'I was worried.'

'Well, you don't need to be.'

'It's good to see you,' I said.

'It's good to see you too.'

I was sure she could see the surprise on my face. 'You look good,' I said. She did.

She smiled, put a teabag into a mug. 'Want some?'

I nodded. She poured two cups.

'I'm painting again,' she said. 'Some of it is good.'

'That's great, May. I'm happy for you.' I was.

'How are you?'

'I miss you.'

She dangled the teabag in her cup, then mine. We talked for a while. She told me about the night under the bridge back in Calgary, apologised for what she had done, touched me on the shoulder, spoke a little about her painting and how she was seeing it all so clearly now, the patterns in the chaos.

And then it came: 'I've come to collect my things. Derek and I are moving out.'

The fact that it wasn't a surprise and there was nothing I could do to change it didn't lessen the blow. It felt as if someone had hit me in the ribs with a baseball bat. I stood a moment breathing through it.

'He's found a house for us, inside the Green Zone.'

'I'm happy for you,' I lied.

'I have my own studio.'

We stood there a while, sipping our tea.

After a while I said: 'Francoise is missing.'

She looked past me.

'Did you hear what I said? Francoise is missing.'

'I heard you.'

'Do you know what happened to her?'

May blew steam from the edge of her mug. 'They took her off the bus.'

'Jesus, May. Where?'

'At the solar plant. They caught her stealing water. The last time I saw her they were leading her away towards the plant.'

I stood staring at her.

'They arrested another woman also.'

'Why the hell didn't you say something earlier? Kwesi has been worried sick.'

'I haven't seen him. Or you.'

'That's it?'

'Why do you care so much?'

'They are my friends.'

'I can see why.'

'What is that supposed to mean?'

'Nothing. I've seen the way you look at her.'

'How can you even say that?' I could feel the anger rising inside me.

'It's the truth.'

'Is that why you're moving in with Argent, because of the way I look at Francoise? Come on, May.'

'Well, it's what I see.'

'You're seriously trying to make me believe that's the reason you've taken up with that asshole?'

'You're just jealous.'

I stood there and shook my head. This was how she always did it. Turned everything around. Accused me of exactly what she was doing. 'Fuck it, May. Just fuck it. You know what, I don't care. Do what you like.' I went to close my water bottle but cross-threaded the cap. Water spilled to the floor. 'Shit,' I hissed.

I rarely swear, but it didn't seem to faze her.

She sipped her tea. 'I intend to.'

'Good.'

'Good.'

'What else do you know about Francoise?'

'See. All of this, and you're still thinking about *her*.'

'She's disappeared, for Christ's sake. It's been forty-eight hours now.'

May finished her tea and shrugged. 'I told you. That's all I know. I'm not working at the plant anymore. Derek got me a job in Administration.'

22

We walked to work. Kwesi trudged along, head down, saying nothing. It was as if time had compressed, as if an entire lifetime had run by in those few days since Francoise had disappeared. And somehow, this compression was folding back on us now. We were caught in an eddy, devolving, reverting to an earlier form. We had become our ancestors, early hominids wandering an empty plain, heavy-jawed and broad-shouldered, driven by hunger, tortured by thirst, supreme in our maladapted ignorance. Knowing nothing of ourselves, of the working of our bodies, unaware of our own consciousness or of the stars above us and the forces which keep them in place, we shivered in the cold, alone in the universe.

Bent to my toil, I burrowed among the detritus, digging out the valuable circuit boards with my hands, hurling aside the plastic and the insulation. I worked in silence, May's words echoing in my head, Samantha's last screams searing deeper into me as the day went on, the hideous symphony playing over and over until there was nothing else.

When our lunch break came, we sat together in our usual spot. We unwrapped our rations, ate.

'She didn't tell me,' Kwesi said. 'About the water.'

'It couldn't have been much,' I said. 'A few litres. I can't imagine—'

'For this,' he choked, crushing a tomato in his fist. The juice sprayed red from between his fingers and onto his face and my bare forearm. I watched the seeds drip to the barren ground, slick in their glutinous envelopes.

'She shouldn't be here,' he said. His lips were trembling. 'Did you know that? She is much younger than me, well below the cut-off. I told her not to come with me. She could have stayed at our farm, kept it going. But she wouldn't listen.'

I put my hand on his shoulder.

'It's my fault she's here. God, if anything has happened...'

I sat and listened to him cry.

'Hey, Teacher.' It was the foreman.

I looked up, nodded.

'What's with him?'

I shook my head. 'His wife has disappeared.'

'A lot of that going around,' said the foreman.

I said nothing.

'They want you to report to Admin right away,' said the foreman.

'Now?' was all I could manage. And I knew. Somehow, despite the bad light and the distance, they had managed to identify me. I should never have looked back when he yelled from the roof. Why had I looked back? What ingrained sense of respect for authority had made me turn my head, automatically, without thinking. They had been trying to kill me, and still, like a frightened schoolboy, I had responded to the headmaster's call.

'Get going', said the foreman. 'There's a car waiting for you at the front gate. Must be important.'

I grabbed my friend's shoulder, held him a moment. I wanted him to know – what? I realised I wasn't sure. Was it that I cared? That his pain mattered to me, that I wished there were something that I could do? I knew that I was powerless to help and so I said nothing. And as I started towards the front gate, I had no doubt about what awaited me.

Do Not Worry

Providence *is ready. Freshly painted, re-launched, she lies head to wind on her mooring out in the cove. The weather is fair, the wind fresh from the southwest. Kweku and I have talked it over. He will leave on tomorrow morning's ebb, early, before dawn, when the wind is still light, and then catch the rising sou'westerlies once he has cleared The Hope. We will say our goodbyes tonight, all of us.*

This will be the first time he has done the trip alone. He tells me not to worry, but I do. I taught them both to single-hand years ago, when they were teenagers, and they are both good at it. Kweku's navigation skills are excellent, better than mine. He can fix a noon sight before I've even finished setting up the sextant. That's not what I worry about. It's everything else; the things he can't control. The radically shifted coastline that has submerged islands and cities, reshaped harbours. The still-volatile weather patterns. The brigands and thieves that still occasionally venture this far south. All of it.

I place the handgun on the table. Take it, I say.

He picks it up, pulls back the slide, checks the chamber like I taught him. It's a Desert Eagle 1911, made in Israel. The man I stole it from is dead. I place two empty magazines on the table, a box of fifty rounds of nine-millimetre ammunition. All of it looks as new as when I first took it. Some things don't age.

I give him the list of what we need, count out five gold sovereigns. That should be plenty, he says. Just in case, I say. You never know.

Don't worry, he says. But I always do.

23

When I got to the Administration building, a police officer escorted me down a long corridor, through a locked gate, and down two flights of stairs. With each step I could feel the fear boiling up inside me. The cop opened a door and ushered me into a small, windowless room. I don't remember how long I waited. I do remember thinking: they have me. This is it. I have seen things I should not have, and now I too will be killed. Once again, I have gone quietly. I should have run when I had the chance, fought back like Argent said. I tried to prepare myself, find some peace somewhere inside myself, but there was none.

After what might have been an hour, maybe more, the door opened. A burly cop walked in, fixed me with a stare. A woman followed him. She looked as surprised to see me as I was her. The cop stepped back out, closed the door, and we were alone.

'What are you doing here?'

'I have no idea,' said May.

'Are you alright?' I sounded breathless, frightened.

'Never been better, actually.' She smiled in that way that she knew would hurt me.

I did not react, scanned the ceiling and the corners of the room.

'I was at a hotel.'

'What?'

'A hotel. You asked me the other day where I had been. Did you know there is a hotel here? It's in the Green Zone. Derek takes me there sometimes. He pays a lot of money. We order champagne and fine food. I take hot baths.'

I absorb this but don't take the bait. 'He's using you.'

'He is going to leave his wife. They were already separated, before. They were only thrown back together during the relocation. He is going to get out of this place, and I am going to go with him. He has people on the outside, people who work for him.'

'May, please listen,' I whispered. 'They've killed Samantha. I saw it. At that same place.'

She hesitated, spun this through, came out the other end. 'When?'

'A couple of days ago.' It seemed like forever.

'What did you expect?' she said with a new ferocity. 'Did you really believe that any of this was going to end well? I told you, David. I told you again and again, and you wouldn't listen, and you wouldn't do anything.'

I slumped into a chair, covered my face with my hands. 'It wasn't supposed to be like this.' A frisson of disgust shuddered through me. The story of my life: the eternal optimist, his folly revealed.

She shook her head. 'That's why we should have fought them. That's why tomorrow we all need to get out there and stand up for our rights.'

'Argent's demonstration?'

'We're going to march, to protest like they used to. Derek's been organising it for days.'

'I can't believe you're falling for his con.'

'We're not criminals. They can't treat us like this.'

'I can see Samantha setting up something like this, but Argent?' I tried not to use that superior tone that she hated, but I knew she would hear it anyway.

She turned away and walked to the far side of the room, arms crossed tight over her chest. I could feel the jealousy corroding me from the inside out, knew she could see it.

The door opened. A man in a blue suit and tie stood in the doorway. He waved away the cop and closed the door. He was tall and well built, with broad shoulders and his mother's straw-coloured hair turned up in a cowlick. His intelligent brown eyes and handsome face were set hard. He looked older than I remembered.

'Hello Mum, Dad.'

May hung back. I reached for him, took him in my arms, overcome. I clapped him on the back, closed my eyes, choked back tears. After a while he disengaged, went to May. He towered over her. I can still remember the day not long after his fourteenth birthday when we officially declared him taller. He stood before her now, arms open. But his face was set hard, and I knew that despite being here, he had not forgiven us. That he would never forgive us.

Tears welled up in her eyes. She blinked and wiped her face, and took a step forward and looked up into his eyes, so like mine. Then she shaped her hand and slapped his face as hard as she could. Lachie didn't flinch, just stood there looking down at her.

'Look at what you've done to us,' May screamed before collapsing to the floor.

We helped her into the chair.

'Look, I don't have much time,' Lachie said. 'I have to be back in Washington tomorrow morning. I need to talk to you.' He glanced around the room. 'Come with me.'

Lachie took May by the arm and knocked on the door, calling for the cop. The door opened, and Lachie led us along the corridor, down another flight of stairs and through a steel door. I followed close behind. We emerged into an underground parking garage where a black armoured car was waiting, engine running, rear doors open. We climbed in, and the doors swung closed. Inside, there were no windows, only two benches along each side.

I sat facing Lachie. 'Where are we going?'

'Somewhere we can talk.'

Soon the vehicle rolled to a stop. The doors opened. Outside it was now dark. Lachie spoke to the driver and took May by the hand. She tried to pull away, but he held her fast.

'Please, Mum,' he said. 'It's important.'

We walked three abreast along the deserted pavement, May between Lachie and me. At the end of the street, we turned right.

The Hamptons was just a block away now on the other side of the road. A single streetlight cast a pool of yellow over the crumbling tarmac. Lachie stopped just outside the light, glanced right and then left, and turned to face us.

'Mum, Dad,' he began, 'I'll make this as plain as I can. Please listen. Things are going badly, much worse than most people know or are willing to acknowledge. Very soon, within a month, unless something dramatic happens, we are going to start running out of food. Everything we have done to try and compensate for the massive shifts in climate has failed. The atmospheric sulphur seeding intended to cool the planet has been an unmitigated disaster – wholesale acidification of lakes and rivers, huge losses of agricultural productivity. The war has entered a new and deadly phase. The rhetoric coming out of Africa, Russia and China is increasingly hostile.'

'Jesus,' I said. I had no idea things were quite that bad.

'The Greenland ice sheet has destabilised much faster than we predicted. Bangladesh is underwater. A quarter of a billion people displaced, flooded out, starving, pouring across the border into India. International aid has completely dried up. Richer countries like Australia have pulled up the drawbridge, sunk into isolationism, barely able to feed themselves. And now India has issued an ultimatum: stop the refugees, or they will take military action.'

'It's a nightmare.'

'You can see why the relocation cities are the government's last priority.'

'No, Lachie,' I said. 'Look around. Not relocation cities. Concentration camps.'

'Call them what you like. It was not what was intended, at the beginning. But a new more radical faction has taken control of the government. Lejeune is a principled man, but he is being marginalised.' He looked down at his feet for a moment, then up again and along the street. 'It was never supposed to be like this,' he murmured.

'What did you think was going to happen,' May cried. 'Did you really think that they were just going to take everything we owned and pack us off happily to our own little holiday home in the sun?'

'Please don't shout, Mum. I'm trying to help you.' Lachie reached into the breast pocket of his coat and handed me an envelope. 'What I'm trying to tell you is that if you stay here, you're dead. You have to get out.'

Our Very Best

The heartbeats of Schumann's magical Kinderszenen wander through the house. Number seven begins, slow and mournful – my favourite. I put down my pen, look out at the everchanging play of light across the sound, then close my eyes and let the notes linger inside me. Time slows, resonates, and for a brief glimmer stops altogether, suspended high above me like a long-winged gull aloft in a perfect, cloud-strewn sky.

The movement ends and I press replay. The technology obeys. I don't want this to end, this suspension of moments vaulted forward. For this music, composed in 1838, played with consummate skill and passion by Martha Argerich in 1984 and transcribed to CD in 2007, is the past. Beautiful, yes. Sublime, even. But the past sure enough, sent forward to remind us of all we have lost and of all that has yet survived. Our collection of CDs, twenty-seven in all, and the player itself, are another of these markers, these signposts of the future's inevitability. Mozart, Beethoven, Chopin, Schubert, Kinderszenen Op. 15. This is the music the Menzels chose to have accompany us on our journey. Whether inherited or earned, stolen or perhaps just salvaged, matters little now. As time goes on, I grow more grateful to fate, understand how lucky I have been.

Even the technology reminds me. These wires and solenoids, chips and transistors, are in this way no different from the music they help to create. The CD player has worked for years with little need of repair. Solar power runs the 12-volt system we arrived here with and has done so faithfully now for over three decades. The discs themselves will probably outlast humanity, and be played in some distant epoch when the ruins of the Anthropocene have been covered over and Earth is finally visited by an alien race. If it ever happens, I hope they find the seventh movement of opus fifteen and play it for themselves. They would surely see us at our best.

24

I folded the envelope and slipped it unopened into my pocket.

'I've arranged it,' said Lachie, his voice strained. 'The details are in the letter. Three days from now you'll get out on an outbound freight truck. The driver is sympathetic and has been well paid. Tell no one. Head south. The information we have suggests that the southern hemisphere has been far less affected by the changes.'

'Jesus, Lachie, that's a long way.'

'You can't go north.'

May clutched Lachie's hand and moved close to him. 'Come with us, darling,' she said. 'Please.'

Lachie looked down at her. His face hardened. 'I can't. Someone has to try and fix this mess.' He looked up as if searching for the stars of his childhood. 'No,' he said. 'Every time your generation had a chance to do something about this, you ran away. You keep doing what you're good at, Mum. Run.'

'I know you're upset, son,' I said. 'But that's unfair.' I regretted it as soon as I'd said it.

Lachie wheeled on me, brought his face very close to mine, bore into my eyes. 'Is it, Dad? Is it really?'

I didn't answer. We were past words now.

'Look, Dad. I don't want to argue. Here,' he said, reaching into his pocket. He pulled out a small leather bag and put it into my hand. 'This is all I could scrape up.'

He glanced at his watch and looked back in the direction of the armoured car. 'Take me to your building,' he said. 'I've got another twenty minutes. It'll look good, an inspection visit.'

I realised then what a big risk he was taking just coming here. We trudged along the pavement, past the old apartment blocks. All along the street, the lights in the windows were blinking out as the power was cut first to one side of the street and then the other. Soon the street was dark. It was a bit cooler now, some of the day's heat flowing back out to the heavens.

I led Lachie to the apartment, opened the door. A hurricane lamp was set on the table, casting a wavering glow across the room. Kwesi was there on the couch. He looked up, smiled. Francoise sat beside him, huddled close to his big body like a frightened little girl. Argent was there too, splayed out in the armchair, smoking a cigar.

'Look who's back,' said Argent, grinning at May.

'Francoise,' I said.

She looked up at me.

'I'm so glad...' I started. But I didn't finish. 'What's wrong?'

She looked away, buried her face in Kwesi's chest.

Argent stood, opened his arms. May skipped across the room and threw herself into him. He wrapped his arms around her and kissed her on the neck. Lachie's eyes widened for a moment, and he glanced over at me.

'Lachie, this is Derek Argent,' May said.

Lachie's face darkened. 'Argent Industries.'

'That's right, sonny. And who might you be?'

'Lachie's with the government,' said May.

'That's my mother you have your hands all over,' Lachie growled.

May pulled herself from Argent's embrace. 'Please, Lachie. Your father and I...' She looked down at her feet. 'We haven't been together for some time.'

'Lachie, this is my friend Kwesi,' I said, 'and his wife Francoise. Great to see you back, Francoise.' She glanced up at me and curled the edge of her mouth into a weak smile that was gone as quickly as it had appeared, and it was as if she was looking back at me from across a deep, mile-wide chasm.

Lachie shook hands with Kwesi, but didn't approach Argent. We all pulled up chairs and sat, watching the flame burn behind the lantern glass. For a time, no one spoke.

It was Argent who broke the silence. 'So, what is someone from our illustrious government of youth doing here in Auschwitz, Texas?'

'That reference is inappropriate,' said Lachie. 'And inaccurate. This is a relocation town.' It sounded as if he was addressing a press conference.

'That's bullshit, and you know it,' said Argent.

'If you hadn't wasted the last thirty years, it never would have come to this.'

Argent whistled between his teeth. 'Here we go,' he said, the lantern flame burning red in his eyes. 'The justification. The big hoax. Do we get to hear it again? Is that why you've come here? Or was it only to see Mummy and Daddy?'

Lachie stared into the lantern for what seemed like a long time. 'Hoax, you call it. The work of thousands of our best scientists, compiled over decades. Surely someone of your obvious intelligence can't believe that.'

'You heard me. The biggest lie ever told. But you got what you wanted, didn't you?'

'And what do you think we wanted, exactly, Mr Argent?'

'Control.'

Lachie shook his head. 'Control? Of a ruined economy and a dying planet? No, Mr Argent. What we wanted was the chance to clean up your mess, before it was too late.'

'Our mess? You think all of this,' he made a sweeping left-to-right motion with his open hand, 'is because of us?' He looked around the room at each of us in turn, his fellow prisoners. 'You blame an entire generation for something caused by natural phenomena, and then confiscate everything they have as penance. You make me sick.'

Lachie shook his head, clearly exasperated.

Argent stood a little taller. 'No way. You can't pin this on me, you fucking mandarin. This has been going on for a long time. Long before we came along.'

May nodded. 'He's right. God created the planet. Only he can change it.'

I said nothing. What was there to say?

'What about nuclear war?' said Kwesi. 'Is that changing the planet? If we choose to be misled, that is our fault.'

Argent moved his gaze from person to person, a politician working a room. 'We have been accused of a crime that never existed and convicted without regard to rights or due process.' He turned and faced Lachie, took two steps towards him so that he was close, fists bunched. 'And you, sonny, have the balls to come here and start lecturing us.'

My son held his ground.

May sprang to her feet and placed herself between them. 'Derek, please,' she said, holding the palms of her outstretched hands to his chest and pushing him gently back until she had guided him into a chair. Then she turned to face her son. 'Please, Lachie, don't provoke him. Not now.'

Lachie seemed not to even register her presence. It was as if he was looking right through her.

'What a wonderful illusion, Mr Argent,' he said. 'To believe that everything we have done has somehow had no effect whatsoever, that we are blameless. If it were only true, Mr Argent, I could have had a normal life. But it never was.'

Argent waved his hand dismissively. 'Propaganda,' was all he said.

'And you were one of those who had the most to lose if we changed, weren't you, Mr Argent? You made a fortune exploiting the system, preying on ignorance and fear, keeping the profits for yourself, making sure others paid for the losses. Your coal-fired power stations and refineries and mines pumped shit into the atmosphere as fast as they could. Your plantations cleared forest so fast regulators couldn't even keep up. And when the world finally started to wake up and do something about it, you bribed governments, financed campaigns designed to cast doubt in the minds of people everywhere, paid celebrities and bogus scientists to confuse the public, convince them it was all okay. You want people to think that black is white? No problem. That bad is good? That's just what they did. And then, when it was clear to everyone that it was happening, you convinced the wilfully ignorant majority that there was nothing we could do about it anyway, and that your way was the only way. And then, to seal off any remaining dissent, you bought the government and launched the Repudiation. How much money did you need, anyway? It was never enough, was it?'

Lachie's voice was trembling now.

'What about us? The generations who have to live with the consequences. Us, the people who are facing that reality right now. You wouldn't listen to the warnings, would you? You didn't *want* to listen.'

He spun around, hands on the back of one of the plastic chairs, glaring at us.

'You,' he shouted. 'All of you. Old and wizened and cynical. Cowards. You ruined everything ... everything. You destroyed the future, my future.' Lachie picked up the chair with one hand and flung it against the wall, his cheeks glistening in the lanternlight.

May stepped back, took Argent's hand.

'And now look at us, you miserable, ignorant, selfish little man. Hundreds of millions dead, thousands of species extinct. Mumbai, New York, Dhaka, half underwater. The whole Nile Delta inundated. Australia burned to ash. War breaking out everywhere as despots fight over the scraps.' Lachie was screaming now, his fists curled, his arms coiled, the veins in his neck bulging. 'There are no more elephants, for God's sake, no more tigers, blue whales, koalas, orangutans, narwhals, coral reefs. The everglades are gone, and the tundra is thawing so fast that there is nothing we can do to control it. Everything is spiralling out of control. All in the last twenty years, and all because you were too fucking stupid and selfish and ignorant to get off your rich, fat fucking asses and do something.'

Lachie took a deep breath, seemed to steady himself a moment. My heart was breaking from the inside out.

'And so now, you have to pay. All of you who could have done something but didn't.' He glanced at May. 'And there can be no exceptions.'

'But people here are starving,' said Kwesi. 'Surely this can't be right.'

'No exceptions,' said Lachie. 'Each of you should have considered the consequences long ago.'

The ferocity of Lachie's words shocked me. Not only because of what he was describing, but because of the effect all of this had clearly had on him. I could see the pain in his eyes, the damage. I was about to reach out to him, put my arm around him, when Argent sprang to his feet.

'Back off, you fucking lunatic,' he said, flicking open a switchblade.

May screamed. Lachie took a step back, breathing heavily.

It's strange, but right then I had the distinct feeling that I was starting to regress. I had seen it happening all around me, to everyone else, but I guess I had always thought I would be immune. As a boy I never fought, no matter how much the other boys taunted me. Even as a young man I always shunned physical violence, embraced the irenic. I considered myself a pacifist. So everything about what I did next surprised me. There was nothing premeditated about it. One moment, I was standing there, watching my son, and the next I was charging towards Argent. I was a lot bigger than him, and younger. I was going to tear him apart. I caught him in the chest with my shoulder and drove him into the wall. He grunted with the impact as the knife rattled across the floor. I raised my fist. I'd never hit anyone with one of my fists before, but I was going to now. I was about to strike when something hard jabbed into my chest, rocking me back. I looked down, went rigid. Argent was pointing a gun at my chest. It looked like the ones the spies used in the old movies, short-barrelled and black. He raised the pistol until it was pointing at my face, held it there a moment, and so quickly I barely registered the movement, whipped it down hard into my jaw. I crashed to the floor. When my vision returned Lachie was pointing a big square-ended handgun at Argent's chest.

I reached for my jaw, staggered to my feet. My hand came away red with blood.

'Put that down,' growled Lachie. 'Now.'

May gasped and stumbled back a few steps. Argent dropped his pistol to the floor.

Lachie stepped over, crouched slowly, picked it up and shoved it into his belt. 'What you have coming, Mr Argent, is too good for you. You will never be forgiven.'

It was as if I had been pistol-whipped a second time. 'What did you just say?' I stammered.

Lachie seemed not to hear me. He walked over to May and gave her a hug. She was crying. I followed Lachie out to the street. We stood outside the building.

'You okay?' he asked.

I nodded.

'Remember, Dad. You have to get out. It's all in the letter.'

'What did you say, Lachie, just then?'

'Dad, please. We don't have time.'

'You will never be forgiven.'

'It's the truth.'

The realisation hit me physically. I doubled over, closed my eyes. 'I don't want to leave,' I said. 'You're right, Lachie, about everything. I agree with you. We deserve this.' I was crying now. I couldn't help it. 'If anyone finds out, you could—'

He didn't let me finish. 'No, Dad. You have to go. You'll die here. Get Mum out. Follow the instructions. Go south.'

I looked into his eyes, searching the familiar landscape of autumn colours and the deep black wells so familiar but suddenly now as alien as the surface of another world, and I knew that he had been irrevocably changed. He was hardened, all his boyhood sweetness flensed away. I knew at that moment that I would never see my son again.

PART III
Horsemen

Lost Territories

I stand on the shore and watch Kweku slip the mooring and move away. His mother squeezes my hand, moves closer. Day is still a few hours away, and the moon has set. Stars reflect from the dark water, the farthest constellations. Providence rounds Vega, then with Arcturus rising and the Milky Way shimmering in her wake, she tacks back towards the Southern Cross, making for The Hope.

We keep our vigil until he slips behind the point, heading north. As we turn away and start walking back up the hill, I see Lewis. He is standing at the top of Chicken Head Rock, looking out to sea.

Now the waiting begins. We will have no word again until he reappears in the sound in a week or so. There is still no working telephone network here. Perhaps there will be one day, but there have been other, far more pressing concerns over the past years, basic survival chief among them. The dead have been buried. The Earth is swollen with them. And now, slowly, the signs of healing are beginning to appear. The air is clearer. Forests slowly reclaim their lost territories. And down here, at least, the sky is blue again.

25

I stood in the bathroom and looked in the mirror. A stranger's face stared back out at me. Eyes sunk deep into bony sockets. A scraggly, greying beard. Skin stretched over Neanderthal cheekbones. Dirty, torn clothes. And the violence, the hatred I could feel growing inside me. All of it a betrayal, a betrayal of everything I believed in, of everything I had always believed myself to be. And it had happened so fast.

Argent had been organising the demonstration for weeks now. May had finally admitted to me that she was helping him. I pleaded with her not to put herself in danger, especially now, when we had a way out, but she wouldn't listen. The demonstration was set for seven o'clock that morning, before everyone was supposed to report for work, as people still called it. Any fiction that we were being paid had long since been abandoned. I had decided I wasn't going to go.

It wasn't that I didn't care. Of course I did. And it wasn't that I couldn't see what was happening. I saw it every day. But I had decided that I was going to take my son's advice. I was going to get out. And I didn't trust Argent. If he was involved there was an angle. I wouldn't join his protest.

It was Kwesi and Francoise who finally convinced me to change my mind. Whatever I thought of Argent, they argued, whatever we were guilty of, we all deserved to be treated with decency. We had to stand up for ourselves. Whatever we thought of Argent, it was the right thing to do. And I couldn't tell them I was getting out.

So Kwesi, Francoise and I walked together that morning to the rally point at the old Bank of America building at the corner of Main and Third. Lan was with us. He had brought along a friend, a slightly younger man he introduced as Dave. I hadn't seen Argent or May since the confrontation with Lachie. By the time we arrived there must have been over three hundred people milling about at the intersection. More were streaming in from every direction. Some carried handmade placards: *We Are Citizens*, one proclaimed in red handwritten letters on cardboard. *Food*, another read. *Freedom. Justice. Medicine. We Are Not Animals.*

Three police cars had been drawn up across one end of the intersection behind a row of wooden trestle barriers. One of the troopers stood beside his car, speaking into a radio handset. My watch showed 06:55. The din of voices rose as a man dressed in black climbed onto a stack of pallets in front of the bank building and faced the crowd. He was holding a megaphone in one hand, and a black duffel bag was slung over his shoulder. It was Argent.

The crowd had grown quickly, and now spread back along the road for several hundred metres and spilled out down both sides of the intersecting street. Some people started chanting. Argent looked up at the sky as if searching for something. Then he raised the megaphone.

It didn't take him long. They were hungry, they had been wronged, and they were frightened. He told them what they already knew, what they wanted to hear. He told them the truth. They were prisoners here. They were being starved. The government had no intention of honouring their commitments. They were never going to be set free. The crowd cheered and yelled. From along the street directly ahead I heard the whoop of sirens and then another metallic voice in the distance ordering the crowd to disperse.

'They are hoarding food,' Argent screamed into the megaphone. 'Right here.'

The crowd roared and bustled, pushed in towards the inter-section. Bodies crushed up against us.

'And medicine,' said Argent.

Sirens shrieked. A wave rolled through the crowd. People were being forced back by the cops.

'There,' shouted Argent, pointing to the building across the street. 'The food's in there. We want it,' he yelled.

Someone in the crowd threw a brick. It arced through the air towards the building. For a moment I thought it would fall short, land back in the crowd. But it hit the lower part of one of the front windows, shattering the glass. People cheered. More bricks flew. People streamed into the building, yelling and screaming, trampling those who fell. The cops were trying to push back the crowd, but there were too many people.

I fought to keep my footing. I saw Argent drop the megaphone and jump from the pallets into the demonstrators just as they overwhelmed the police barrier. I watched as he started working his way back against the crowd, away from the police cordon. For a moment I lost sight of him, then he reappeared at the corner of the bank building. I saw him flatten himself against the wall just inside a narrow alleyway, standing there as he watched the crowd stream by, and for a brief moment I thought he was looking right at me. But there was no sign of recognition, no change of expression, just that flat, dispassionate stare. It was as if he was contemplating his work, transfixed by this setting in motion of his will.

A group of people surged past me, some carrying cardboard signs, and for a few panicked heartbeats I was swept along towards the police barrier. By the time I finally fought my way clear, Argent was gone, and Kwesi and Francoise were nowhere to be seen. A loud cheer rose from the crowd. The cops were in full retreat. A middle-aged man wearing jeans and a brown cardigan was standing on the roof of one of the abandoned police cars, kicking in the windscreen. Others followed. There was the flash of a baseball bat and another cheer. Beyond, perhaps half a block behind the crumbling police cordon, an armoured car appeared, like the one Lachie had taken us in. A soldier emerged from the top hatch, raised a weapon and fired a canister of some sort. I watched as it looped, spinning, through the air and burst in the crowd. People screamed. Tear gas filled the street. The crowd moved as one, like a school of fish trying to avoid a predator, away from the curling smoke. And then, suddenly, from somewhere above, clear above the cries and screams, the sound of gunfire. Rounds clattered off the armoured car's black hull. The soldier in the hatch slumped away, and the vehicle reversed back down the street. Behind it I could see troops massing, some with riot shields, but most without. Somewhere overhead I could hear a helicopter approaching. Buildings were blazing now on both sides of the street. Smoke poured from the windows, engulfed the street. The smell of woodsmoke and the acrid bite of burning tyres filled my nostrils; tear gas stung my eyes. I was swept along. Bodies crushed into me and then slipped past and were gone, caught in eddies, channelled by the burning buildings. Gunfire erupted again, close by this time. Someone in the crowd was shooting back at the soldiers. A woman screamed. My foot thumped into something soft, but before I could look down the crowd had swept me on. People were screaming now all around, calling out in strangled voices, driving the others along, desperate to escape.

'Run,' someone yelled close by. 'They're killing us.'

The ground underfoot was littered with bodies now, and there was no place I could step without feeling the sickening give of flesh. I kept moving, my eyes streaming, aghast at what I was doing, driven on by the crowd. An explosion shattered the air above me. The concussion knocked the air from my lungs. Milliseconds later a shower of glass poured down. The man next to me groaned, a sabre of window glass buried to the hilt in his back. He stood a moment looking down at the point dripping from his chest. I reached out to him, but he slumped to the ground and was gone, trampled under by the shifting crowd.

That was when I saw Kwesi. Francoise was clinging to his arm as he bulldozed his way through the crowd. I called out to him, scrambled towards them.

Kwesi looked back. 'You okay?'

I drew closer, gave a thumbs-up.

'Keep moving and stay on your feet,' he shouted. 'Follow me.'

Shielding Francoise, he pushed hard into the dense pack of bodies. I followed close behind. It was then that I noticed the tear in his shirt, right across his broad back, the dark West African skin showing through. The cotton was frayed and wicking blood. A bright crimson stain spread across his back.

'Kwes,' I yelled, 'you're hurt.'

But he didn't answer, just kept going, opening up space for us with sheer mass and muscle, pushing aside the old and frail. Gunfire rattled somewhere behind us, closer now, but more sporadic. A helicopter loomed just above the building tops, close, unbelievably loud. I could see the pilot peering down at us through the billowing smoke. And then a voice telling us to put down our weapons and disperse. But there was nowhere to go. We were wedged in, stalled. Kwesi roared and pushed into the crowd. More shots now, so close that I ducked my head and looked over towards the sound. When I turned back, Kwesi and Francoise were gone, swallowed up by the crowd. I kept going, moving along with the mass, hundreds of people streaming away from the noise and smoke, hemmed in by the buildings. Some were bleeding, hobbling along, propped up by friends or loved ones, others wandered in a daze, cast away from the world they had known and counted on to protect them.

I worked my way to the far side of the street and started down the alleyway I'd seen Argent disappear into. I remember the crumbling buildings rising on both sides and the smoke from the riot drifting around me and the thin strip of green sky above, and it was as if I was scrambling along a gassed battlefield trench in some forgotten war. I remember the wreckage piled up on both sides of the alleyway, punctured tin cylinders and pushed-in cubes of cardboard, the smashed planes of television screens, all the wrecked geometry of a doomed civilisation. And strangely, I remember a discarded washing machine. I still dream about it sometimes. The front door was gone, and its dark mouth gaped open in a silent scream. It reminded me of that painting by Edvard Munch. I think it is called *Angoisse*. Anguish.

I hadn't gone far when I came across a small man with thick glasses. He was slumped up against the wall. Blood seeped from a wound to his abdomen, pooled fresh on the ground about his legs. Two gold coins lay cradled in his lap, as if someone had thrown them there, rich man to beggar. And clutched in his hand, blue light still glowing on its screen, something you didn't see much anymore, a mobile phone. He stared up at me, tried to speak. Blood frothed from his mouth, bubbled down his chin onto his shirt.

There was nothing I could do for him. I started to run. And then, suddenly, I was alone. I was almost to the end of the alley when through the smoke I saw a figure hurrying up one of the fire escapes. He was dressed in dark clothing and carried a duffel bag. He was a long way above me now, sprinting up the last few stairs. As he neared the top of the building, he stopped and glanced back. It was just a moment, a fraction of a second, but long enough to be sure. I would have recognised that sneer anywhere. And then he was gone, up onto the roof.

Silent Thanks

Some things you never forget. The surroundings might fade, the faces blur, the circumstances of weather and place and time dissolving away as the decades pass. But other, seemingly random details somehow remain immune to the ravages of time and distance, and conscious, destructive will. Even now, thirty years and half a world later, those images come hot and brutal and bled through with fear. I double over at my desk, suddenly breathless, choking. I can taste the gas, smell the blood and the shattered glass, feel the smoke burning in my lungs. And I know that I am trapped, that I must continue, and that what comes next is worse yet than I could ever have imagined back then, when I was someone else and the world was becoming what I now realise it was always destined to be.

I slump to the floor and let it all shudder through me. Slowly, it ebbs away. The shaking stops. My breathing slows, deepens. I open my eyes, offer silent thanks to the sky and the hills behind the house and the miracle of the blue ocean.

I am here, now. Somehow, I have survived the transit of time and distance and the loss of the old world. Amazement is too subtle a word.

26

May returned to the apartment later that day. She was alone. Her face was covered in grime and streaked with tears. I tried to talk to her, but she pushed past me and retreated to Argent's room. Argent appeared not long afterwards, still carrying the duffel bag I'd seen him with before. He scowled at me, marched to his room and slammed the door behind him.

Within moments I could hear May's voice. I couldn't make out the words, but I could tell she was angry. The argument continued for a while, half an hour perhaps, before he came storming out, slammed the door again and disappeared into the street.

Kwesi and Francoise were still not back. I waited a time and then knocked on the door to Argent's room.

'May, we need to talk,' I said through the hollow particle board. 'Please open the door. We need to discuss Lachie's plan. There is a lot to go through. We need to talk about it and prepare, make sure we don't screw it up.'

Silence.

I tried to open the door, but it was locked. 'May, please. This could be our only chance. We have to work together.'

The sound of a closet door closing.

'Go away. I don't want to go anywhere with you.'

'May, be reasonable, please.'

'Fuck off, you coward. I have no intention of having anything to do with you.'

'Even if it means dying here?'

A pause, and then: 'Derek will look after me. He is rich, and he stands up for himself.'

'Like today?'

'Some people in the crowd got out of hand.'

'Out of hand? It was a massacre.'

The muffled reply: 'Leave me alone.'

'Then why are you here, May? I thought you two had moved in together, found yourself a cosy little place in the Green Zone?' Now I was being mean. I pulled back, tried to push down the frustration I could hear in my voice, feel in my chest. 'It doesn't matter, May. I'm sorry. I just want to get out of here. You heard what Lachie said.' All of this through the door.

'May, please.'

Nothing. Silence.

'Kwesi and Francoise aren't back yet. Did you see them?'

'No. Go away.'

After all these years I knew better than to confront her head-on. 'If you change your mind, just tell me. But come Wednesday night, I'm leaving, with or without you.' I'd made that decision there in the alley contemplating the meaning of anguish.

By late afternoon, I had made no progress with May. Kwesi and Francoise were still not back. Neither was Lan. I waited till dusk, then set off to find them. The scene that confronted me is here with me still.

The streets are littered with the fallout from the demonstration. The authorities have managed to regain some level of control of the situation, but the curfew cannot be enforced. People wander the streets like refugees, alone or in small groups, dazed and bloody, searching for their loved ones. Bodies lie scattered singly or in small clumps along the roadside, bloated in the heat. Some have been dragged there and abandoned, others lie where they fell. It reminds me of the photos in the papers of the aftermath of the Atlanta riots. Except that this is real, in a way images or words can never capture. And yet, as with so much that has happened, I cannot quite bring myself to believe that it is real, that it *was* real, that the world I had known, grown up with, had been so completely obliterated.

I found Francoise slumped over Kwesi's body on the side of the road about half a kilometre from the hospital. She had managed to drag him that far before collapsing exhausted to the ground. Kwesi's hardened corpse lay in a pool of half-congealed blood.

I picked her up in my arms, like a bride to bed, and carried her home. She seemed so thin and frail. I laid her on the couch, washed the blood from her face and hands, and made her drink. She fell asleep almost immediately. I went out into the garden and pulled up two of the sturdy wooden poles we had used for her bean trellis, grabbed a blanket from my bed and set out into the gathering dusk to bring Kwesi home.

He lay where we had left him, alone and cold. I realised, as I sat on the kerb beside my friend and started to fashion a crude stretcher from the blanket and the two poles, that I was crying. I could not stop. And then suddenly it was as if some line holding me together frayed, then parted. I was sobbing uncontrollably, groaning under the weight of everything I had seen, of all I had lost and left undone.

By the time I pulled myself together, it was almost dark. Cursing myself, I set to work. With my knife I cut holes for the pole ends in the doubled cloth and cut lengths of paracord to fasten the blanket to the poles. I knelt on the pavement and heaved Kwesi's lifeless body onto the stretcher. The flesh was cold and stiff, the ebony skin already the colour of weathered concrete.

Then I grasped the ends of each pole and pushed myself up. He was heavy. I steadied myself and started to walk, dragging the stretcher behind me across the pavement. The ends of the poles bumped and scraped over each rut and crack. After just a few minutes my shoulders and forearms were burning with the effort, the insides of my knuckles numb. I wondered how Francoise could possibly have moved him so far all alone, he twice her weight.

After three blocks I set down the stretcher. I was trembling, soaked from the exertion, despite the coolness of evening. I sat on the curb with my feet in the gutter and looked at my friend. I had known him for such a short time but had come to consider him one of the people closest to me in all the world.

I kept going. I'd gone maybe half a kilometre when a police car pulled up beside me. A young cop stared out of the half-open window, a shotgun gripped across his chest. His eyes were stretched wide. Fear etched his face, exhaustion too, and something else: disbelief. 'Get home,' the cop said. 'You're violating curfew.'

'I'm close,' I said.

The cop looked down at Kwesi and frowned. He couldn't have been more than thirty, but everything about him seemed old. 'Do it fast. We're locking down the whole town. There's a fallout cloud on the way.'

He saw the question form in my eyes.

'There's been a nuclear exchange in India. Four bombs they're telling us. Dhaka's gone, Delhi too, they're saying. Stay inside. Once it passes over, we'll give the all-clear.'

I heard the words, but they didn't register. I had been to Delhi once, as a teenager, backpacking through India. It didn't seem possible. All those people. All that magnificent squalor. Gone. The police car rolled away in the gloom, its tail-lights glowing in the darkness like the embers of a burning city.

I trudged on, dragging my dead friend across the fractured pavement, the poles scraping across the concrete.

It took me the best part of an hour to reach the Hamptons, and another two to dig the grave in the garden, next to Francoise's wizened strawberries and shrivelled tomatoes, the dried-out tangle of peas and beans. Francoise stood weeping in May's arms as I slid the big man into the dark hole in as dignified a way as I could.

I said a few words. I hadn't known Kwesi long, but he was an honest man, a good friend and a loving husband. The god he believed in was just and good. And then, although I was not qualified to do so, I commended his soul to the hereafter, whatever that was, if it still even existed.

Francoise threw a handful of sand into the grave and collapsed to her knees, sobbing uncontrollably. It didn't take me long to cover him over. When I was done, I drove a steel stake Kwesi had found on one of our foraging excursions into the soil at the head of the grave and stood looking down at the raised mound.

Lachie had been right. First Samantha, now Kwesi. It was intended that we never leave this place.

A Good Omen

I rise early, as usual, and set to work. Most days, I write from just before daybreak to sometime after noon. Once the sun begins its downward trajectory, fatigue starts setting in. The words become harder to find and then dry up altogether. By the time I set down my pen, I am drained, an empty shell. It takes me the rest of the day to recover. Exercise, manual labour, tending the animals and sleep restore me. And somehow, for now at least, when I wake again the next morning it is all there, ready to be transcribed. Today, I write well.

Later that afternoon, we receive a good omen. Juliette spots a pod of Right whales in the sound. We congregate, all of us, up on Chicken-Head Rock and watch them come closer to shore. It is a big group, well over a hundred individuals, the largest we have seen. Smaller juveniles dominate the pod, but there are a few large, older whales. When we first arrived here whales were scarce, like so many other creatures. And then slowly, about fifteen years ago, their numbers started to increase, and it became so we could reckon the seasons and the days of the month by their return. The humpbacks came too, and then the huge blue whales, and with them the seabirds arrived, and the dolphins too, and the pilotfish and yellowfin and all the other fishes.

We watch them for a long time as they transit the bay and then slowly head back out to deeper water. For now, the winds are holding, fair from the southwest. With any luck, Kweku will be nearing Albany soon.

27

I don't know what it was – perhaps the shock of the riot, of seeing Kwesi lowered into his grave – but later that night May finally opened up to me, in a way she hadn't done for a long time.

'So much death' she said into the darkness. 'It's as if I am surrounded by it.'

I waited for her to continue. My ears were still ringing from the explosions.

She set a canvas on the table. 'I finished it just a few hours ago. The best thing I have ever done.'

I stared down at the painting, tried to take it all in. I breathed in hard, steadied myself against the edge of the table. Pigment burst across the canvas in shattered swathes. Broken bodies bled onto bare concrete, eyes wide like planets, mouths drawn in fear, the sky ripped apart by burning metal and flying glass.

'May,' I stumbled. 'It's ... I don't know what to say. It's amazing.' There it was, screaming from the canvas, everything I had witnessed. And more. So much more.

'I tried to follow him,' she whispered as if in a trance. 'But he disappeared into the crowd. I looked for him everywhere.' Tears poured from her eyes, caught the lamplight. It was then that I knew that she loved him.

And then a calm came over her. She wiped her face with her hand, steadied herself. 'We're taking him with us.'

'What did you say?'

She faced me and took my hand. 'The Broken Hearts are after him,' she said. 'We have to take him with us.'

'You heard what Lachie said. There is only room for the two of us.'

She shook her head. 'No, David. I am going to ask him tonight. I thought I should tell you first.'

'Absolutely not.' I could feel the anger rising inside me, more than anger. There was fear there, too, unmistakable. And something else. The sick pang of jealousy. Skin pain, Kwesi called it. 'You said you wanted to get out of here, May. Well, this is your chance. If you tell him, you'll jeopardise the only chance we have.'

She was sobbing now, shaking. 'But you don't understand. It's because of him that I ... I ... I can't leave him.'

I let her cry.

'There has to be a way,' she gasped.

'We can't tell anyone, May. Anyone.'

'He has a place we can go,' she pleaded. 'He told me. Somewhere down south. Paradise, he calls it. Do *you* have anywhere to go?'

'And you trust him? Where was he this morning, May? Do you know? While everyone else was getting cut down by the police, where was he?'

A confused look came over her. 'I ... We got separated. I couldn't find him.'

'That's because he left, May. He ran. I saw him, climbing up to the top of one of the buildings. I'm pretty sure he shot someone on the way.'

'What?' she hissed. 'You're lying.'

'No, May. I'm not.'

'You're jealous. You always have been.'

I grabbed her by the shoulders, shook her hard. Her head bobbed around on her neck as if she was drugged. 'Are you crazy?' I shouted. 'You'll ruin everything.'

'Stop,' she cried. 'You're hurting me.'

I let her go, aghast.

'Leave me alone.'

'May, I ... I didn't mean to...'

She stepped back, composed herself. 'Then you stay,' she said, crossing her arms over her chest. 'You wanted to come here. You agreed with it.'

I pulled myself back, sought to regain control. 'Look, May,' I said, searching for a lower octave. 'Please see reason. You don't know where the rendezvous is, who we're meeting, or how we're getting out. You can't do it without me.'

'Give me the letter,' she said. 'It was for both of us.'

It was my turn for defiance. 'I can't do that. I won't.'

She hung her head.

'If you want to get out, meet me here in two days' time, early evening. Pack light. Bare essentials only. And come alone.' And then for the first time in my life, I turned and walked away from her.

A Moment of Reflection

I leave my clothes on the rocks and walk naked across the shingle. The sun warms me, shooting through between two banks of high cloud. The winds have continued to hold, and barring an unforeseen problem, Kweku is surely in Albany by now. I think of him walking up the main street from the harbour, strong and tall and sure, and I am proud of him, proud of the man he has become.

The water is cold, getting noticeably colder now with the slow glide of the year. I step carefully across the larger, flatter stones, feel the barnacles push into the soles of my feet. Soon I am up to my waist, feeling the cold track up my spine. And then I am in and under, and the familiar cold pulse comes, the pain in my temples that takes my breath away. I open my eyes, gaze through the clear water at the familiar underwater topography. A few strokes later and I am moving well, head above water, working my way out to the rocks that mark the edge of our little cove. A seal pops his head above the surface, watches me. His eyes are very big and round under dark lashes. Water beads bright on his long whiskers. I greet him, tell him that it is good to see him. And then he slips under the water and is gone.

Past the rocks I have an unobstructed view across the sound, south towards the big national park – it is marked as a national park on the map, anyway, and I assume that it is still one, if only because so few are left to worry about such things. Beyond the hulking Ordovician hills, a thin plume of smoke rises from the camp of our nearest neighbours. We see him only rarely now, and seemingly at random.

The first time we met Uncle Liberty was a few days after we first arrived here. We were transferring equipment and food from Providence *to our newly established shore camp, not far from where our house is now situated, when he wandered down the beach. He was much younger then, of course, wiry and lithe with long dark hair*

piled on his head and a fire-red beard. Other than a pair of West
Coast Eagles shorts, he was naked. But it was the way he moved that
was unforgettable. Coiled like a big cat, he seemed to bounce from
one rock to the other, a long handmade spear balanced in one hand.
Even standing still, you got the impression of potential energy being
stored, accumulating, ready to be unleashed.

We stopped what we were doing, gathered the boys to us. We'd seen
enough over those last few years to be wary of any stranger. He seemed
to sense our fear, and stopped short, set his spear down on the sand,
and opened his hands and smiled. I will never forget that moment.
That beautiful, infectious smile, that simple gesture of friendship. I
approached him, put out my hand. We shook.

I'm Liberty, he said. Welcome to my country. He pointed back the
way he had come. My family lives over those hills. We've been there
for a long time. Your little tackers can call me Uncle.

We invited him to eat with us, and we talked until nightfall,
shared stories of the upheaval, of our journey. Liberty loved the boys,
kept making faces at them, poking their tummies with his finger. They
squealed in delight every time he wrapped his beard across his eyes
and pretended to disappear. He was friendly and open with us in a
way we had learned to distrust. Looking back now, I realise how
guarded we were with him at the beginning, how suspicious, and
how we ourselves only opened up to him slowly, over years.

Before the upheaval he taught social anthropology at university,
and for a while he had played professional football – Australian
Rules – 'footy' he called it. But that was all done. Things were bad
in much of the country, he said. His people had retreated to their
traditional lands and ways of life.

The white fellas spent two hundred years destroying our culture,
he said in a moment of reflection, staring into the fire. Took 'em less
than half that to destroy their own.

28

Argent didn't return to the apartment until the night before we were supposed to leave. May was with him. When they came in, I was sitting at the kitchen table with Francoise, trying to get her to eat. She hadn't uttered a word since Kwesi's death.

May went straight to Argent's room and closed the door behind her. Argent dropped his bags on the landing and walked toward us.

'So, it's on for tomorrow night?' he said.

His words cut through me. I knew he could see it.

'What are you talking about?' I blurted, trying to stay composed – failing.

Argent smiled. 'Drop it, Teach. I know all about it. Your son has pulled us some strings. A little nepotism never hurt anyone, right? Guess he's not as principled as he would have us believe.'

Francoise was staring at me now, her jaw tightened in concentration, her eyes narrowing.

Argent dropped the smile and looked at Francoise and said: 'I was very sorry to hear about your husband. It all went horribly wrong. It was supposed to have been a peaceful demonstration, nothing more, to let them know that we still have rights. The soldiers panicked, started shooting without orders.' He tended a hand and placed it gently on her shoulder.

I glared at him, glad of the reprieve. 'From what I saw, there were people in the crowd shooting at the cops.'

Argent shrugged, sat down next to Francoise and took her hand, ran his index finger along the smooth clear skin of her wrist. He pushed a strand of hair from her face and plucked a tear from her cheek with the tip of his index finger and placed it on his tongue. 'I heard what happened to you,' he whispered. 'At the power plant.'

She stared at him a moment, a look of surprise, then hid her face in her hands. '*Mon Dieu,*' she gasped.

'I can get you out of there,' he said.

She looked up. 'Really?'

Argent glanced over at me. 'I can arrange it tomorrow, if you like.' That rat-like grin again.

'I'll die before I go back there,' she said. Her voice was cracked and dry, but there was no trace of hesitation. 'I won't go back. They can kill me if they like, but I won't go.'

'I don't know what May told you, Argent, but there is no way you're coming with us. It's set up for two people only.'

Francoise's face twisted into a question.

Argent sat back and folded his arms behind his head. 'It's very simple. Tell me where, when and how, or I'll go to the authorities.'

'Go ahead,' I said. 'Turn yourself in. They'll do to you what they did to your wife.'

That shook him. I could see it.

'What are you talking about?'

'You mean you don't know?'

He shook his head.

'She was executed by the Broken Hearts three days ago. I saw it myself.' My triumphalism disgusted me, and still does even now – that I had sunk so far. But it felt good to hit him this way, with something so final, so definite.

Argent sat a while as if contemplating all that this meant to him. And then he stood, reached behind his back, pulled out a pistol and pointed it at me. 'Fuck you,' he rasped. 'And fuck her. Now tell me, or I'll blow your fucking head off.'

I got my feet and slowly backed away. Francoise followed me, stood close, holding my hand.

'No,' I told her. 'Stay away.'

'I'm not going to hurt her, you idiot.' Argent laughed, shook his head. 'Get over there,' he waved at her.

She moved away and stood with her back planked to the wall, a look of horror distorting her face.

'Now hand over the instructions your fascist son gave you.'

I worked up what I hoped would look like a smile and tapped the side of my head with my finger. 'It's all in here now, Argent,' I heard myself say.

He processed that for a while, then motioned with the pistol towards Francoise, still pinned to the wall. 'What about her? Were you going to leave her behind too?'

I hadn't told Francoise about the plan, and the guilt had grown inside me like a cancer.

Argent laughed and looked over at Francoise, her mouth open in silent, fading hope, and then swung his gaze back toward me. 'You were, weren't you? You were just going to abandon her. All those nice words, such a good friend.'

He was right. There was nothing I could say.

'Well, I'll tell you what, Francoise,' said Argent. 'I do care about you. I will not only get you out of working at that power plant, but tomorrow night I'll get you out of this place altogether. How would you like that? I know a place we can go where we can be safe. A paradise, untouched by all this shit. Does that sound good?'

Francoise glanced over at me. 'Yes. It does sound good,' she whispered. 'But if there is only place for two, Teacher must take his wife.' She slumped to the floor and dropped her head between her knees.

'Okay, Teacher,' said Argent, putting the gun back into his belt. 'Maybe there is a way we can work this out for everyone. We'll go out together, all four of us.'

Francoise looked up, searched my eyes with her gaze. 'Truly, is this possible?'

'You heard her, Teach. She'd rather die than stay. Is that what you want? You want her to die?'

'No, of course not,' I blurted out. 'But—'

'There's always a way, Teach. Always. One of my rules of life. We just have to find it. And we will.'

I hung my head. He was right, I couldn't leave her. 'Okay, Argent. You win.'

'Good,' he said. 'Good. We'll see you back here tomorrow at dusk, as planned. You'll lead us all to the rendezvous point, and we'll take it from there. Okay?'

Francoise stood beside me, squeezed my arm.

'Okay.'

'And just to make sure you don't change your plans, I'm taking the wife with me.' Then he turned and walked to the bedroom and closed the door behind him

29

We sat on the couch, close but not touching, gazing into the dirty kerosene flame of the lantern, watching it flicker behind the glass. Kwesi lay just outside, deep in the parched ground upon which no rain had fallen since we arrived, and for longer before.

'You are leaving tomorrow,' she said.

'We.'

'Are you sure? I do not want to burden you.'

'It's not you who is the burden.'

She nodded. 'And the fallout?'

'We have no choice. It's tomorrow or never.'

'I will not go back to the power plant,' she said. 'I am not telling you this so you will take me with you. I just want you to know. I have no one else to tell.'

'What happened to you out there, Francoise?' I looked into her eyes, noticed a submerged topography there I hadn't seen before, the cobble bed of a clear, flowing stream. The damage was there, too, all that she had suffered. 'I'm sorry,' I said. 'It's not my business.'

'Kwesi didn't want to participate in the demonstration,' she said, voice quivering. 'It was because of me that he went.'

I kept quiet, let her continue.

'I told him what happened at the plant.' She lowered her eyes, hung her head. A tremor shook her, a silent quake that seemed to run through every part of her. I reached out and put my hand on hers. She looked up at me through those swirling currents.

'That was when he decided to go,' she whispered, choking back a sob. 'Because of me. Because of what I said. I should never have told him. I knew how he would react. I *knew*.'

'It's not your fault, Francoise.' My words sounded empty, hackneyed. There was so much I wanted to tell her, back then. If only I had known what it was, perhaps I could have found a way to say it.

And then she looked me right in the eyes, very close. 'I want to die,' she said. 'There is nothing to live for.'

'You don't mean that.'

'I do. You don't need to take me with you. There is no point.'

'Don't say that, Francoise, please.'

We were quiet a long time, sitting like that side by side, watching the lantern flame slowly burn down.

Then she said: 'We met in a hospital in West Africa. I was working with Médecins Sans Frontières, he was with the UN. He came in badly wounded. Months it took him to recover. And then one night we were walking along the beach in Takoradi. The surf was coming up, all glowing, and the moon was out and the breeze was blowing in the palm fronds.' She stopped, wiped away her tears. 'It was almost as if the world was healed, as if nothing had ever happened. We made love for the first time there on the beach, and I knew then that this was my *grand amour*, the great love of my life, the one I had waited for since before I could remember. And now there is nothing. Just a world ripping itself to pieces.'

She gasped, as if surprised at what she had just said. 'I should have saved him. I have saved people with worse injuries. He was too heavy. I ran to the hospital, begged them for the tools I needed.' She was quiet a moment and then continued. 'It was terrible. As bad as I've seen. Shattered bodies lining the corridors, the staff overwhelmed, wandering around shocked and helpless behind bloodied masks. I should have gone back and helped them, but I can't anymore.' She turned to me. 'I might have been able to save Kwesi, but for them ... Do you understand? I can't do it anymore.' She folded her arms on the table and buried her face. 'I can't.'

A low moan came from Argent's room. It was May. I knew that sound, hadn't heard it for a long time. It wound itself around my intestines and tightened down hard. Francoise had heard it too.

'I have been married for almost thirty years,' I said. 'I love my wife.'

She looked up at me.

'I won't let him take her from me.'

She reached out and touched my hand again, very gently, like before. 'What will you do?'

'I don't know.'

'Please,' she said. 'Don't leave me alone tonight.'

I put my arm around her shoulder, and she leaned into me and lay her head on my chest, and I sat and listened to the slow regular beating of her heart until the nightmares took her.

Knowledge of Sin

This morning I wake feeling as if I have just run a marathon. Pain lances my joints. Rather than the usual dawn clarity everything seems shrouded in fog. I don't usually take painkillers, but I take a couple of ibuprofen from our carefully managed supply. I wait for the dulling, but it does not come. The writing is difficult. I stumble over simple sentences. Words skitter away from me. Memories materialise only to vanish again, leaving nothing but lost shadows and scents on the breeze.

Rather than remembering, writing, I find myself sitting at my desk looking out to sea. I think of the forests, the trees, of all the creatures we have assigned to oblivion, species after species, each of those magnificent individuals. And the weight of it is beyond me, the crushing gravity of stars, and I feel as if my heart will implode. For I was there, watched with everyone else as hell arrived one betrayal at a time.

I stand, try to push it all away. I have let it get too close. And yet I must keep going. The truth must be told, for Kweku and Juliette, for Leo, for Lewis and Mandy and their unborn child, for everyone.

After years of holding it all at bay, the knowledge of my sin is killing me.

I am dying.

30

As soon as I heard Argent and May leave the flat, I slid out from under Francoise, let her collapse gently onto the couch and covered her with a blanket. Then I walked to my room, grabbed my hunting knife and slipped out into the darkened hallway.

By the time I reached the front doors, they were moving off down the street, hand in hand, keeping away from the few streetlights that still burned. When they were far enough away, I followed.

After a few blocks they turned south, towards one of the residential areas now occupied by squatters. By now, the authorities had given up trying to keep people in their assigned billets. I followed May and Argent through a slum of once prim suburban properties, the gardens now withered and baked dry, the carefully trimmed and fertilised lawns now patchworks of dun mange, the houses cannibalised, whole sections of wooden siding ripped away, the wall studs showing like exposed ribs, the windows empty or boarded over with hastily nailed up plywood sprayed with graffiti epitaphs. Each wreck had been someone's life. And now the parasites were tearing them down, board by board, doing what they had always done, what they had been trained to do since childhood: consume.

I followed them along one street after another. They were heading in the direction of the garbage plant now and the place where Samantha had been killed. Up ahead I could already make out the shock of vegetation that flourished around the stream. Just beyond the burned-out hulk of a car, Argent stopped in front of a series of three identical bungalows. May stood beside him, both hands latched to his arm. I crouched behind an old refrigerator that had been dumped on the verge and watched as Argent led her across the front lawn and up the stairs onto the front porch of the middle bungalow. The door opened and they disappeared inside. It was just gone three-thirty in the morning. Less than twenty-four hours to go. I moved to the opposite side of the street and into the shadows between a pair of duplexes. From here I had an unrestricted view of the front of the house.

By four-thirty they had not reappeared. No lights showed. I took out my notebook and scribbled down the address. Until that moment, my plan, if you could call it that, had been simple. I would find out where he was hiding and report him to the authorities. The police would take Argent away, let May go, and we would escape together as planned. With Francoise.

But now the whole idea seemed to unravel before me. What if the police detained May, too? What if Argent tried to bargain, and told them about Lachie and the escape plan? He didn't know much, but he knew enough to kill it, to condemn me, and, inevitably, Lachie. Even if the Broken Hearts were after him, as May had said, he was still powerful, had connections. The riot proved that. The more I thought about it, the more I realised that there was only one course of action left to me.

I started across the street, keeping to the dark edges. A newish moon had risen above the rooftops. The gravel alleyway behind the bungalow was lined with old steel garbage cans, and the dented lids reflected the moonlight onto the fences and the stumps of trees. I counted out the dwellings, all dark and boarded up and silver-roofed, until I came to the bungalow. The back garden was strewn with junk. Three cars of various makes and in different stages of dismemberment hulked in the dirt, surrounded by a litter of parts. And beyond, the house still dark and quiet like before.

I slipped through a gap in the fence and picked my way through the junk towards the bungalow's back door. I eased the screen door open with a hiss of the sprung piston and placed my hand on the inner door handle. It was locked. What did I expect? Stupid. My resolve crumbled. I would wait for Argent to come to me, later today when he returned to the apartment to rendezvous for the escape. When he did, I would be ready. I removed my hand from the doorknob and eased the screen door closed. But in the darkness, I misjudged the gap, and the piston sucked the door closed with a clap.

I jumped back and stumbled on the step. I stood there a moment, listening, trying to stare through the walls into the house. A minute passed, maybe more. I stayed perfectly still, not daring to move. The house was quiet. I was about to turn and retrace my steps back through the yard to the alley when I heard a creak from beyond the door. I froze. Another creak. And then another. Someone was moving towards the door, slowly, carefully.

I unsheathed my knife, stepped to the latch side of the door and flattened myself against the vinyl siding, an arm's length from the edge of the doorframe. The handle started to turn and there was a muffled click as the lock was released. The door eased open. I held my breath. Someone was standing just inside the threshold, looking out through the screen door. A hand reached out, pushed it open. I crouched low and stepped out, ready to strike.

It was May.

She gasped, staggered back. Even in the darkness I could see the fear in her eyes. 'What are you doing here?' she gasped.

'May...' I began. 'I can't...'

She glanced at the knife.

'I love you,' I said, lowering the weapon.

'Go away,' she whispered. 'If Derek sees you—'

'He'll what?' said Argent, appearing behind her.

'Derek, please,' said May.

He glanced at the knife in my hand. 'Did you really think that you could just walk in here and what, kill me? How stupid do you think I am?'

'I just want my wife back, Argent. I have nothing against you.'

A smile curled across Argent's lips. 'Then why don't you just ask me nicely? I'm a reasonable man. Just ask. Please Mr Argent, if you have finished fucking my wife and don't want her anymore, can I have her back?'

'Derek,' said May.

'Shut up, bitch.' His voice was pitched, jittery.

I couldn't see her face clearly, but I knew this had hurt her.

'Fuck you, Argent.' It is not what I wanted to say, but it was all I could think of. 'He doesn't give a damn about you, May. He's just using you to get out of here.'

'That's not true,' she shouted. 'Go away. You are ruining everything.'

I couldn't see his gun but I knew he had it. To my surprise, I was not afraid. I was in the beginning, but not anymore. As he stepped forward to grab the door, I saw my chance. I lunged at him with the knife, aiming for his stomach.

It was over in a matter of seconds. I lay on the ground, my arm twisted under me. Argent stood above me holding a crowbar. I tried to move my arm. A bright bolt shot from my forearm up though my shoulder.

'That's a nice break you have there, asshole,' said Argent. He reached down and grabbed my upper arm, just below the shoulder, and pulled me to my feet. I grimaced in pain but managed to stifle the cry.

'Now, here is what you are going to do, Teach. You are going to go back to the apartment and lie low for the day. Tell Miss Frenchkiss to get herself and those big tits of hers ready to go – food, clothes, as much water as she can carry. She's good at that. Wait at the apartment. I'll be there by nightfall. I'm assuming the plan is for late. Is that right?'

I cradled my right forearm, nodded. A big welt had risen just above the wrist.

'Good. I'll bring your wife. You get us out, and you can have her back.'

May turned to face him. 'Derek, what are you—?'

But before she could finish, Argent grabbed her by the wrist and jerked her back hard. 'Get back inside,' he snarled. And then to me: 'We split up as soon as we get through the wire. I'll take Frenchy.' He leaned forward and brought his face close to mine. 'You two wouldn't stand a hope in hell getting out of here without me. You need me.' Then he laughed and stepped back inside. 'Now fuck off.'

The door slammed closed.

I stood there amidst the wreckage and watched the spike of the moon rise over the rooftops and tried not to think about any of it.

Walk Right

Beyond the threshold, the unknown beckons. Rules no longer apply. Convention is upended. And all that you think you know about how things work turns out to be wrong. Once you cross the line, there is no return. I have learned, painfully and over years, that chaos has no degrees, and, despite the fractal mathematics, for human purposes, no dimensions. Once invoked, it is complete and absolute. It either exists, or it does not. Chaos can take many forms, of course, and destroy in infinitely many ways. We chose but one.

We now know, all of us who yet survive, that a descent into chaos is more than a loss of order, or the collapse of a certain cherished equilibrium. Reason itself is annihilated, and any notion of control rendered meaningless. We can no sooner govern a typhoon or a blizzard than we can an earthquake, or the deep collision of abducting plates, or the distant implosion of stars and vaporisation of planets. The scale of destruction matters little, in fact not at all, be it the death of individuals, insects, birds, fish, people, or the killing of multitudes, entire species even. I suppose if you want to call it hell, you wouldn't be far off.

It was something Liberty said not long after we had first arrived – a couple of years perhaps – that started putting it into perspective for me, although I didn't realise it at the time. We were sitting out on the point one evening after the birth of his son. He and my wife had just returned from his camp after a day's walk through the bush.

He looked across the water towards the hills where his people were. Our boys, they'll walk this country together, he said.

It's good to think so, I replied.

He looked at me sidelong, stroked his beard, gripped the rock with his toes, once, twice, clenching them down onto the granite. Country's been here a long time.

I nodded. These rocks are very old. More than a billion years. The scientist talking.

Like I said. Be here a lot longer again, too. Liberty stood, tapped the base of his spear on the bedrock. Country doesn't need our boys, mind. Our job as fathers to teach them that. He gave me that look again, harder this time and very clear, looking right into my eyes. Then he turned and started back towards the dark-green edge of the bush. I stayed up there on the point and watched him go. He'd walk all night now, back to his people, back to his woman and newborn son. Just as he reached the trees, he turned and faced me. Teach them to walk right, he said. And then he disappeared into the gathering darkness. I didn't see him again for over three years.

31

By the time I arrive back at the Hamptons, dawn is exploding in a helium fireball. Every particle of sulphur and soot, the radionuclides from Delhi, the strontium-90 that will one day be found in our dried-up bones, all of it ripping apart the sun's fragile spectrum. The building's remaining windows refract gold, arterial red, pulsing caesium. Blinded, I shield my eyes against the glare. As I near the front doors, I can see that someone has dumped a pile of garbage at the entrance, four or five big bags of it, lumped up against the glass. Except the bags aren't bags at all. There is a hand, rigid, upright, crisped into a claw. Feet, legs. The bodies of two men, naked, entwined. One is face down on the pavement, legs spread. The other has been positioned with his chest against the other's back. A piece of paper flutters between his shoulder blades. I have seen such horror in the last few days, and yet at this I flinch, shut my eyes. I move closer, peer down at the paper. It is a poster, like the one Lan showed us a lifetime ago. It is stapled to his back in four places. His friend Dave lies beneath him.

I laid them out together, face to face on their sides, not far from Kwesi. I was spreading the last shovelfuls of dirt over them when Francoise appeared. I told her how I had found them. She cried.

'We should say something,' she said when I was finished.

We didn't known Lan well. His friend not at all. What was there to say? He lived his life the best way he could, tried to find happiness, whatever that meant to him. And now he was gone, like so many others, all of us reaping this poisoned profit, the living and the dead, angels and sinners alike.

Francoise set my arm, splinted it, fashioned a sling from a bedsheet. 'It's not so bad,' she said, 'a hairline fracture that should heal soon.' She didn't ask me how I got it, and I didn't say. I didn't tell her about Argent's plan. I had a plan of my own.

We spent the rest of the day preparing, packing food, water, clothes, tools, wondering if outside, somewhere, we might find a world somehow undamaged, liveable. Then Francoise cut the microchips from our hands, applied one deft stitch to each incision, and we were ready. I told her about Lachie's advice to go south, towards the tropics, to the Southern Hemisphere, where conditions were supposed to be better, and rumour had it that the old were not being persecuted, that there was still food. But I had decided to reveal the details of the escape plan to no one.

May and Argent appeared at the apartment just after dark. We checked our gear, blackened our faces with charcoal, and set out together. I had planned the route carefully. Initially, we headed west, keeping to the darkness. Argent stayed close. I tried to catch May's eye, but she kept her gaze averted. We stopped in a small park near what used to be a movie theatre. Here the garden was still relatively intact and we could crouch in a thicket of shrubs, perfectly hidden from the road. I didn't trust Argent, that he hadn't arranged to have us followed. I checked my watch, scanned the road.

'We wait here,' I said.

Three pairs of eyes peered out at me in the darkness.

'Why here?' said Argent.

I didn't bother to reply.

After twenty minutes we started out again, through the park to the side road behind the cinema, north four blocks and then doubling back to the east along a back alley between two rows of houses, fenced, dark, quiet. We made good time. When we reached the waste plant it was just gone midnight. I knew this place well enough. It didn't take me long to manoeuvre the group across the boneyard and into a narrow depression just beyond the end of the loading dock. 'Everyone okay?' I whispered. Three pairs of eyes nodded back at me in the darkness. 'Now we wait.'

I peered out across the smoking piles of garbage. The glow from the incinerator sent shadows dancing. Shapes rose and caught the light before skulking away across the wasteland. May crouched beside me, her face streaked with char, all its prettiness gone, her hair bundled up under a scarf. She glanced over at me but did not smile. After a moment I felt her hand slide into mine and hold tight. She was frightened. I caressed the knuckle of her index finger with my thumb, an old reassurance. And I remember thinking then that, finally, she knew I loved her still, and that Argent never had.

I glanced at my watch. Anytime now the truck should be arriving. According to Lachie's letter it would unload fuel and food first, and then take on its outbound cargo of recyclables – metals mostly: aluminium, gold and platinum, silicon from circuit boards and computer components, stuff Kwesi and I had harvested. The truck would be in the easternmost bay, the one closest to the boneyard where we now waited. Once the materials were loaded, the driver would open the passenger's side cab door. That would be the signal for us to climb in. We were to hide in the sleeping compartment, in a false bottom under the mattress. I could not imagine how this would work with four instead of two, but I couldn't worry about that now. Just after one o'clock, an eighteen-wheeler pulled into the compound and backed into the bay closest to us. The truck's headlights swept the darkness, forcing us down into the bottom of the trench. I looked over at the blackened faces pushed into the crumbling siltstone, the whites of their eyes shining in the darkness. I signalled 'stay down' and put my finger to my lips. They pushed themselves deeper as the shouts of the men and the clanging of the big cargo doors echoed from the walls of the loading bay.

Unloading the trailer seemed to take forever. By the time the pallets of recyclables were being forklifted into the truck, it was gone two o'clock. We were already behind schedule. Every few minutes I pushed my head up over the lip of the trench and checked the loading bay and the cab, watched the truck sink slowly onto its suspension. May hadn't let go of my hand.

'What's going on?' hissed Argent. 'What are we waiting for?'

'For the truck to finish loading,' I said. 'Sit tight.'

Argent eased his head up, looked both ways, and crouched back down. I watched him reach behind his back and pull out the pistol he'd threatened me with before.

'Put that away, for Christ's sake,' I said, too loud. 'If that thing goes off, we'll have every cop in the place on us.'

Argent glared at me, but he pushed the handgun back into his belt.

Just then the trailer's rear doors slammed shut. The voices of the men receded, down along the bay towards a second truck that was waiting to be loaded. The Peterbilt's diesel engine started up with a cough. Smoke belched from the twin vertical stacks as the driver revved the engine. The truck lurched forward.

Something had happened. He wasn't going to take us. It was the wrong truck, the wrong night. I racked my memory. Maybe I'd mixed up the time, the place. I should never have burned the letter. Or perhaps the deal had fallen through: someone had baulked, lost his nerve. May looked up at me, questioning. The base of my stomach fell away.

The truck rolled forward and then stopped with a hiss of air brakes. The passenger side door swung open and hung there in the dark. The signal.

'Come on.' I clambered out of the trench, pulled May up after me.

Argent followed with Francoise right behind. I grabbed the door handle and swung myself up to the cab step and looked inside.

A flabby-faced man in a stained T-shirt and baseball cap stared at me from behind the wheel, a cigarette burning in his mouth. 'You have something for me, asshole?'

'Magellan,' I said – the codeword.

'Yeah, what the fuck. Get in and make it quick.'

I turned to help May, but Argent clambered up and pushed his way past me and into the cab beside the driver.

'What the fuck is he doing here?' said the driver. 'I was told one man and one woman.'

'Plans change,' said Argent. 'There are four of us.'

'No way,' said the driver, shaking his head from side to side. 'There isn't room back there. The deal was two. That's it. The guards will find you and I'll be up shit creek.'

'Please,' I said. 'We have two women with us. We can't leave them.'

The driver contemplated this new information for a moment. 'Tell you what, I'll take the girls. You two stay behind.' A nicotine smile creased his face.

'We can pay extra,' I said, dropping two of the gold coins that Lachie had given me onto the seat.

The driver glanced at the coins. 'There isn't room, I'm tellin' ya, mister. You won't make it. And if you don't, I don't.' The driver put the truck into gear. 'Now either two of you get in and close the door or fuck off.'

Argent shoved his pistol into the man's side. 'You'll do exactly what I tell you, boy, or you'll end up with a hole the size of my dick in your fucking ribs.' And then to me: 'Get in the back.'

I helped up May and then Francoise, who squeezed into the back of the cab. I closed the door.

'Now get going,' said Argent. 'Just as planned.'

I scrambled into the rear of the cab, which was laid out as a personal sleeping compartment.

'Get out of sight,' the driver called back to us. 'The bed opens up, there is a space underneath. Pull the latch at the front.'

The truck lurched forward, sending May and Francoise tumbling onto the bed.

'Quick,' I said. 'It's less than a kilometre to the first gate. Help me find the latch.'

We fumbled around in the darkness as the truck gained the main road and turned south. I ran my fingers from one end of the metal frame to the other. It was smooth and regular. 'I can't find it,' I shouted out over the diesel. 'For Christ's sake, where is it?'

'Lower,' yelled back the driver. 'Right up under the frame.'

I crouched and pushed my arm up under the steel rib. The rubber sheathed handle was dead centre. I pulled it hard and the latch sprung and one side of the bed jumped free. Francoise was already reaching under the other end. We pushed it open.

The cavity was about as deep as a man's shin bone, and as wide as a pair of outstretched arms. Francoise climbed in and slid to the rear, lying on her back with her arms folded across her chest.

'What about air?' I said.

'Vents on each side,' said the driver. He had clearly done this before.

May crouched beside the box, looking back at Argent.

'Get in,' said Argent. 'I'm staying right here to keep our friend honest.' Argent pulled his cap down close over his eyes, and thrust his hand back over the seat rest, fist closed. 'Here, Teacher-man. You'll be needing these.'

I cupped my hand beneath Argent's fist. Two heavy, gold Maple Leaf coins fell into my palm. White light flooded the cab.

'Get the fuck down and close the lid,' said the driver. 'We're almost at the main gate.'

May was lying on her back next to Francoise. It left a space barely large enough for me to lie on my side. I wedged myself in next to May. I hadn't been this close to her for a long time. I grabbed the handle and closed the lid with a click.

A Desert River

She told me once, when we were first married, that she could only see with her eyes closed.

There, just like in her dreams, the world was so full of colour and pattern that she had to force herself not to process it all, to move back and away so that the terrible detail, the pointillism of a Seurat or the vertigo of a dotted Aboriginal landscape, did not overwhelm her. And she could not wait for the dreams to end so that she could put it all down, pour it out like some waterfall that burst from behind her eyes, each detail flowing down through her arms and her fingertips to the point of her brush, freed somehow from the holding cell of her brain. She did not know where it came from, or why, and when it stopped, drying up like a desert river, she never understood the reasons for her punishment. It was something entirely beyond her control, and contrary to what she had been taught all her life by doting only-child parents, it had no relation to the amount of effort or dedication she afforded it. The paintings, the good ones, the ones she loved and that others sometimes paid for, had always seemed to make themselves, as if she was simply a conduit, a medium.

32

Bumping along inside this metal sarcophagus, with the woman I loved so close, I had a strange feeling of peace. I could feel her breathing beside me, her pulse quick against my hand. Lying there next to her, a certainty came over me, calm and evenly clad. Everything was going to be all right between us. Everything would work out.

The truck lurched to a halt with a loud hiss, pushing us closer. 'Not a sound,' I whispered.

My heart was beating so fast I was sure anyone outside would be able to feel it shaking the truck. What if the guards were equipped with heartbeat sensors, or infrared scanners? I held my breath and strained to make out the muffled voices resonating through the truck's thin metal sheeting. Questions and answers. Long pauses. Tension visceral in the low grumbles.

A loud bang made me jump. May squeezed my hand tight. It was an instinctive gesture, one she had made so many times before on so many nights, back when she was painting and we were happy, and as I closed my hand around hers, I heard her sigh in the darkness.

Another loud bang, like the noise before at the loading bay, someone opening the big rear doors of the trailer. They were searching the cargo. May tightened her grip on my hand. I responded. Time slowed.

How long had we been in this box? It couldn't have been more than a few minutes. I was covered in sweat. I reached above my head and fumbled for the vent, but no matter how I turned the dial, there was no flow. Finally, the doors banged shut and the truck started moving again. Air flowed from the vents. The smells of the desert returned. May slid her hand from mine.

'Just one more checkpoint to go,' I said, a little louder this time, not quite a whisper. 'After the outer gate, we can open the top.'

After what felt like a few minutes but may have been only seconds I heard the engine rev down and felt the deceleration as the truck slowed and jerked to a stop. May reached for my hand. Again, I responded. I could feel her breath on the side of my face.

I put my lips to her ear, whispered, 'I've missed you so.'

A muffled voice from outside was followed by a sharp bang, like an open-palmed slap on a steel panel. More voices, louder this time, angry, shouting. The click of a door opening? Another click. The engine was idling, rumbling, shaking us in our coffin. I strained to make out the words, but there was no distinction to the voices or the syllables, and it was like listening to the bubbled sounds of my best friend speaking to me underwater all those summers ago, his eyes big and bright with laughter through the glass of the mask, the words gargled open-mouthed in the green river water, hilarious.

A sharp crack made us all jump, the clear retort of a gunshot. A yell, another shot, closer this time, much louder, followed by two more. My ears rang with the sound. Then silence. Two slams in quick succession, the cab door closing, and then a gut-shuddering lurch as the truck bounced forward, slamming us back as one into Francoise. She grunted as our combined weight forced the air from her lungs. The gears ground like teeth, the engine revving wildly. And then the metal just above my head burst and something hit the top of my skull and for a moment I lay there blinded, dazed. I reached my hand to my head, searched through wet, matted hair with trembling fingers, slowly becoming aware of the warm liquid trickling into my eyes and down my face. Another series of gunshots rang out and then there was just the sound of the engine gaining speed as we flew though the desert night.

33

We abandoned the trailer by the side of the highway about ten miles north of the intersection with the road from town. Then we doubled back and struck south along the crumbling two-lane road towards the border. Without the heavy load to pull, fuel consumption was much lower, and I figured that with the extra can of diesel strapped and locked to the side we could do at least four hundred miles, maybe more, before running dry.

This is the way my mind works. It is not conscious, in the sense of being planned. Calculation is simply my default, the thing I do when I am not in active control of myself. For May, this single characteristic was always the hardest to accept, so at odds was it with her natural state. Were we ever really compatible? I had always thought our differences would make us more of a whole, stronger together. I could still feel her hand in mine, and I couldn't help wondering what her grip might have meant.

We rumbled along in the darkness, side by side in the front seat of the cab, the headlights washing over a grey ribbon of disintegrating tarmac, not talking about what had happened. I stuck my head out of the window and let the night air wash over me. Argent tightened his grip on the big, flat-set steering wheel. Francoise was between us, the blood on her clothes fluorescing in the instrument panel's glow.

I stared out into the night, into the fifty-mile-an-hour breeze. Since unhooking the trailer and smashing out the rear lights on the cab, no one had spoken. More than two hundred miles now lay between us and the outer gate of our former prison. We needed to make as much distance as we could before the sun rose. If anyone was going to be out searching for us, it would probably be during the day. Soon we would need to find somewhere to hide, and we would need fuel.

Later, we saw the first road sign. Argent slowed the truck as we approached. It was the first marker of any kind we'd seen since doubling back. But the geometry of it was wrong. Closer, we could see that the sign had been bent back almost in half and now hung from a single point on the lone remaining post. Argent pulled up a few metres from the sign so that the headlights were cast full upon it and stopped the truck.

'What does it say?' said Francoise.

'I can't read it,' said Argent, looking over at me. 'Go have a look.'

I took Francoise's hand. 'Come on,' I said.

Argent smiled that smile of his, nodded. We got out of the truck. Argent sat watching us as we walked towards the crippled sign.

'You think he's going to drive off and leave you,' said Francoise. 'And take you with him. I know he will.'

'I'm so sorry. There was nothing I could do. The damage...' She trailed off into silence.

I said: 'I'm sorry too.' It wasn't real or possible in any conceivable way that she was gone.

I reached for the sign and bent it back so the headlights caught its reflective surface. It read: *Redhill 20 miles*.

'Do you believe him?' said Francoise.

Argent hadn't said much. Something vague about a betrayal, shots exchanged, the driver killed and dumped by the roadside.

'I don't know what to think, Francoise.'

We walked back to the cab. Francoise clambered in. Argent put the truck into gear and we moved off, the slightest tinge of pale green now showing against the black of the plain. I took the map from the inside breast pocket of my jacket, unfolded it on my lap and levelled the compass in my hand, orienting the outer dial. Was it level? It was. But the old patterns were smashed now, the recursion splintered and distorted, like standing between two broken mirrors. No GPS anymore, no Google Maps, no way to place oneself in the universe, navigate the chaos.

'Well?' said Argent.

I told him what the sign said.

'The middle of bum-fuck nowhere,' he said.

'According to the map, we're about two hundred and fifty miles from the Gulf. This is Route 23. It should take us all the way to the coast.' The futility seemed immense. Any shred of certainty that remained was gone. It was as if I was outside of myself, watching from a terrifying and indeterminate distance.

'Okay,' said Argent. 'We'll find somewhere to hide this rig and wait out the day. Then we'll set out again at nightfall. At the coast, we can separate.'

'The sooner the better,' I said.

Argent ignored me, and looked over at Francoise and put his hand on her knee. 'You're very welcome to come with me.'

She did not answer, but she made no attempt to remove his hand.

We drove on as day came, checking the road behind us every few minutes. We were alone, for now.

According to the sign at the outskirts, Redhill was once a town of eleven thousand souls. The first sign of its demise was the remains of the gas station, the blue-and-white chevrons of its one-time owner collapsed in the road so that we had to swerve around it. In what had been the courtyard of the station, under the sagging canopy, two rusting steel tanks lay hulked and holed beside piles of dirt.

'Someone dug up the tanks looking for fuel,' said Argent.

Francoise sighed as we entered the town. Skeleton buildings lined the street, stripped of their cladding, ransacked and picked clean, the empty sockets of the windows staring out at each other across a no-man's land of derelict vehicles and stump-lined streets. It was as if a plague had descended upon the place.

'Like Africa,' she said.

We'd heard about this, of course. In the news, and on TV. Towns and cities all across the south abandoned as these latitudes dried up, burned and exhaled their final breaths. Millions of people, impoverished and displaced, had streamed north in the first years of what we now called the Relocation.

'Sorry-ass fucking sheep,' said Argent under his breath as we pressed on through the town, seeing not a soul.

'If there's one thing you can take to the bank,' he said a little while later, 'it's that people are sorry-ass sheep.'

We passed the empty shell of a grocery store, the shelves toppled, the windows shattered by fear and hunger. More shops, more smashed windows. It was all like that. Wrecked and abandoned. At the edge of town, we came to a garage. *Walt's Tires and Brakes*, the sign said. Beyond, the road snaked away through the dry, dead country.

Argent pulled into the garage, rolled the cab to a stop beneath the forecourt canopy, and shut down the engine. A couple of semi-trailer cabs, abandoned, tyre-less, were parked up against a fence that ran the length of the street front.

'If they're looking for us from the air, this will hide us,' said Argent, stretching in his seat.

'I doubt they will waste valuable fuel and manpower on us,' I said, trying to convince myself. Although with Argent, you never knew. May had said that the authorities were blaming him for the riot.

'We have less than an eighth of a tank left,' said Argent. 'I guess about a hundred miles. Maybe less. If we don't find fuel soon, we walk. We can rest in there, out of the sun.' He pointed to the twin bays of the garage, open, doorless. 'Go check if there's any fuel in there. I'll get the jerry can, see what that does to the gauge.'

'No,' I said.

'No?'

'Before we do anything,' I said, 'we are going to bury May. And we are going to do it properly. There's a shovel strapped to the rig. Argent, you are going to help me dig.' I opened the door and swung myself to the ground.

PART IV
Killers

My Few Remaining Days of Immortality

Despite everything, today is better. I write well in the morning, push through into early afternoon. I am making good progress. The thing now is to keep going, to gather my strength and apply it, now when the remembering is most difficult.

I cannot help thinking about Kweku. Allowing for a full day collecting everything on the list and stowing it for the journey, he should be well on his way back now. Perhaps, with luck, I will see him tomorrow, or the day after.

The winds have veered a bit, and this morning the easterlies carry hints of the forest and the scent of distant inland deserts. Afternoons are still dominated by the southwesterlies, which will make for tough going, beating into wind and swell. I wish I were out there with him, braving sea and weather. And if I were to be there with him, I would tell him that I love him, that I am proud of the man he has become. But this is his time now, not mine.

When they were old enough and their mathematics skills sufficient, I taught the boys the General Theory of Relativity, and started them into quantum theory. I also taught them how to build a boat, and how to shoot and navigate by the stars, but I felt it important to ensure that this pinnacle of understanding, the culmination of thousands of human lifetimes of investigation and thought, was not lost. To their credit, and to my great pride, they grasped it quickly, as if it were something obvious and intuitive, which to me it has never been. And they went on understanding it, building their knowledge, exploring the essential wisdom it contains.

There is no now, as we normally conceive of it. Now is as irrelevant as saying here. There are an infinite number of heres, depending on where you happen to be. It depends entirely on your point of reference. The same applies for time. My now, here, bears no relation to someone else's. Of course, on the confines of our small, lonely, oh so fragile planet, we share, at this scale, a degree of common perspective (in this respect at least). But only to a point. Physics decrees that every moment in time exists, forever. Shakespeare's bank and shoal of time is ever shifting, reshaping, fluid underfoot.

And yet, we experience time. We see it; we feel it. Its inexorable arc is there in every tomorrow, in each yesterday, in the turning of the skies and the change of the seasons, in the birth and death of everyone we love. The arrow of time – physicists call this entropy (S), the tendency to disorder. Inescapable, resolute, it marches through the ages, scything down everything in its path, from the smallest life to the highest mountain. Surely the most heartbreaking of mathematical equations is Rudolf Clausius' $\Delta S \geq 0$, which tells us simply that entropy will always increase. Unlike relativity, it is a one-way journey. Everything that is born dies: people and planets, distant galaxies. This is time.

But, now, something has changed. As my life nears its inevitable end, as my finite allotment of days runs down, time has become for me a quantity less of physics than of emotion, of feeling. Each page of this journey I am on brings me closer to this realisation. As I write, I can sense time's warp and bend, feel as it slows to a rain-drop's journey groundward on a cold and cloud-strewn winter's night, and then accelerates again to scythe through a year. I am bending the fabric of space-time, hurtling back to these long-forgotten moments, these places since reshaped by the killer entropy.

Perhaps this is why we create, why we build and paint and write and have children. In a small and fleeting way, we are breaking the rules. By creating order from chaos, we are cheating entropy, and so, in a way, we are cheating death.

Was it Spinoza who said: 'in each instant, here and now, we are immortal'? If so, I have just spent one of my few remaining days of immortality considering just how mortal I am, and by tomorrow I will have journeyed even further into hell.

34

Francoise sat in the dust and tried to keep the flies away from the body as Argent and I took turns digging.

I had found a place outside the chain-link fence that edged the junk-strewn boneyard behind the garage. It had taken us the best part of half an hour to carry May's rag-doll body from the cab and through the maze of rusted-out vehicles and engine parts, through a hole in the fence, and then across the uneven stone-strewn ground to the far side of the little hillock I'd chosen for her.

Now the sun was up, and I could feel the heat soaking into my skin, evaporating the tears that streamed down my face. The grave was knee deep. I stood in the hole hacking at the ground with the shovel. Argent sat on the hillock, looking back towards the garage. Every few minutes he would stand and walk out a hundred paces or so from the grave and peer back in the direction of the truck. Then he would come trudging back, his boots raising little puffs of dust.

No one spoke. The pile of stones and sand grew, and the grave deepened until Argent threw down the shovel and stood waist-deep in the ground staring at his palms. 'My hands are covered in blisters,' he said.

I grabbed the shovel and jumped down into the hole beside him. 'Shut up,' I said, and started digging.

'It's deep enough,' said Argent.

I am no longer the person I was. I know that now, fully. I knew it then, too – at that moment, I think for the first time. I wheeled around and raised the shovel like a bat, ready to strike. Tears streaked my face. Like warpaint, Francoise told me later, or a death mask.

'It will never be deep enough,' I shouted, staring at May's bloodied corpse. 'You of all people should know that.' The bullet that had pierced the truck's side had torn away the top of her head. The exposed bone shone the purest white.

Argent stumbled back against the far end of the pit. He grabbed the edge of the grave with both hands.

'Fuck you, asshole,' he barked. 'I'm done here.' He planted his palms on the ground and started to lever himself up.

I raised the shovel over my head. I don't remember intending to kill him. My dim recollection is of pure fury. I had tried and convicted him, and now it was time to execute the sentence. I started to swing, but just as I did Argent drew his pistol and fired. That part I remember clearly, standing there waiting for the pain, wondering what had happened. Francoise thought I'd been shot, but Argent and I just stood there, glaring at each other, waist deep in the lifeless ground.

That was when Francoise jumped into the hole between us. She told me later that we both seemed surprised, and that we each took a step backward. She turned to me and reached up to touch the point of my elbow, still raised with the shovel over my shoulder.

'Please,' she whispered. 'We already have one to bury.' She looked into my eyes.

I lowered the shovel. 'He killed her,' I said.

Francoise turned to face Argent and took the hot metal of the gun in her hand and tried to push it down, but he resisted, holding the thing level with her diaphragm.

'The soldiers killed her, you idiot,' Argent yelled past her. 'The people who take orders from that fucked-up government your son works for. The same people who sentenced us to that hell hole. They killed her. Not me.'

'If you hadn't pushed yourself in, she would still be alive,' I screamed back. 'There wasn't room. You knew that.'

Argent just shook his head.

I wasn't going stop. 'What in God's name did you do back there, Argent? How could you have been so stupid?'

Argent didn't flinch, just stood there with his weapon raised, staring at us. And then he laughed. 'You want to know something?' he said. 'You would never have made it out. The driver sold you out. He plays both sides. Informs on the buyers, turns in the escapees, keeps the gold.'

I stumbled back a step, bumped the edge of the grave. 'Bullshit.'

Argent shook his head. 'You really are naïve, aren't you? It's not just an act, is it? If it weren't for me, it would have been all of you in a hole somewhere.' He pushed Francoise aside and pointed the pistol at me. 'Now back off, or you'll be joining your wife here in everlasting rest. A romantic end to an unhappy story.'

I stood, unmoved, ready to strike.

Francoise reached up and touched Argent's bare forearm, the one holding the weapon. 'Please,' she whispered. 'For me.'

Argent considered this a moment. Then he smiled and lowered the gun. 'For you, then.' I could see from his reaction that she had successfully conveyed the nature of the reward the words implied. He stuffed the pistol back into his belt, clambered out of the hole, and walked back towards the garage.

Francoise stood with me and watched Argent disappear into the boneyard. 'He'll leave us, you know,' she said. 'He'll take the truck and go.'

'Not now, he won't.' I struck the blade of the shovel into the ground and levered up some sand.

She looked at me sidelong, trying to convey something I was too blocked to understand. She had just saved my life, and after how I had treated her, I didn't understand why.

'Go with him if you want,' I said. 'He seems to know where he is going. Me, I have no idea.'

She clambered from the hole and resumed her position next to May. 'I'm staying right here,' she said.

She watched me bury my wife, as I had buried her husband. And when the first shovelful of sand thumped down onto the drum of May's hollow corpse, she cried as she had the day Kwesi died.

35

The sun was throwing long shadows across the ground by the time I tipped the last shovel of dirt onto the burial mound and crouched to stack a small cairn of stones at the head of May's grave. The sky was clear, I remember, cloudless and bright green. Francoise and I stood in silence a while, and I know that I should have said something profound and meaningful, but all I managed was, 'Rest in peace, my love.'

If I were to have it to say again, I would have thanked her for the joy of our first seven years, and for the gift of my son – they alone were enough for any lifetime. I would have spoken about her great talent and the unique way that she had of seeing things in the world that others could not see, and then somehow making them real so you could see them and feel them the way she did. I would have spoken about the way she had fought her affliction, weathered its cruel peaks and unfathomable depths the best way she could every day. And I would have told her, there by her graveside, that I had always tried to live up to her expectations, despite my failings, and that in all the time we were together I had always loved her and had stayed faithful to her, and that in the end, I was sorry that I had failed her.

But the right words exist only in the future and apply uniquely to the past.

Argent didn't leave us, as I knew he wouldn't. We found him in the garage. He had opened May's bag of provisions and was extracting the last smoked oyster from a tin. 'We wait here until nightfall,' he said without looking up, the oily brown bivalve dripping between his fingers. 'We can't risk the roads in daylight. Not yet anyway.' He dropped the oyster into his mouth, then reached over and picked up Francoise's bag and handed it to her.

'Have something to eat,' he said. 'Keep your strength up. You're going to need it.' Then he smiled at her, a quick upturn of the corners of his mouth and a creasing of the eyes.

I dropped the shovel on the concrete floor with a clatter and walked to the truck. I grabbed my backpack from the cab and returned to the garage. Francoise was still talking to Argent; she quietened to a whisper when she saw me. I sat on the floor in the far corner, as far away from Argent as it was possible to be. Francoise took her bag and found a spot midway between us and sat with her back against the wall. She was filthy, covered in May's blood and the dirt from the grave. She ate a tomato, one of the last from her vine, and took a sip of water from her flask. Then she closed her eyes and was soon asleep.

I wanted to sleep, but I didn't trust Argent. I sat and watched as he rummaged through May's bag. He removed a big tin of peaches and put it into his own bag, then a series of smaller tins of different sizes, tuna and pate and sardines. After he'd removed all the food, he opened May's bag wide and took a long look inside, sniffing at the remaining contents like a wild dog rummaging in a garbage heap. Then he closed it and tossed it aside.

I sat staring at her bag, the same small backpack she'd carried all those years ago when we'd hiked in the Cascades. I wanted to kill him. The realisation frightened me in a way it hadn't before, back in May's grave. This time it was different. Now it was pure, Neolithic. I got to my feet, started towards Argent. Francoise was still asleep. The sun was moving closer to the horizon. I thought of all that had happened since we'd left Canada, of what might lie ahead. I was halfway to him now, only ten paces away. He was looking right at me, eyes narrowed in what could have been a question but was probably a warning.

'Stop right there,' he said, placing his hand on the pocket of his jacket.

I stopped three paces from him, stood hunched forward, jaw set.

'What the fuck do you want?'

I said nothing, just stared down at May's pack.

'I'm done with it,' he said, kicking it across the floor to me.

As soon as I picked it up, my anger dissolved, and all that was left was sadness, a big empty hole inside that I couldn't frame or fill. I retreated to my spot with May's bag clutched to my chest, sat with my back against the wall and closed my eyes.

*

Voices woke me. I opened my eyes to see a man standing in the middle of the garage floor, silhouetted against the evening sky. A shotgun hung from his hand. Behind him was a jeep of some sort, with huge fat tyres and thick steel bars crudely welded around the front and sides. There were other people inside the jeep, another man, younger, and a woman. Argent was standing in the far corner, pistol drawn.

'What business do y'all have comin' here?' asked the young man in a thick Texan drawl. He took a few steps forward and swung the shotgun up by its grip, caught the barrel in his other hand and pumped the action. He was young, definitely not one of the responsibles. The skin of his face was red and pockmarked, the wisps of hair that stuck out from under his cap and sprouted from his chin were fair, golden in the afternoon light. Crudely manu-factured body armour protected his torso, a leather harness plated over with ceramic tiles and what looked like textbooks taped underneath.

'This here is private property,' he said without raising his voice. 'Ya'll is trespassing.'

By now the other man had appeared at the edge of the garage and stood just outside the main doors, a scoped hunting rifle cradled in his arms. 'Drone coming,' he said.

The man with shotgun glanced overhead, nodded.

I stood, moved to place myself between the men and Francoise.

'We are only resting, out of the sun,' I said, arms wide, palms out-turned.

'Gettin' close now,' said the man outside. 'Slowin' down. Interested like.'

'Seems to me they's looking for ya'll right now,' said the man with the shotgun.

'Come nightfall we'll move on,' I said.

The man with the shotgun smiled, revealing a row of tobacco-stained teeth. 'Y'all is eighty-niners. Fugitives from the law.' The last syllable lingered long in his mouth, as if he didn't want to let it go.

'Not from the law,' said Argent. 'From a bunch of thieves. They took everything we have, tried to lock us up. So we're leaving. No crime in that.'

'Damn right they is,' said the man. 'Tried to take away my pappy's farm, move us all away someplace. We said fuck 'em. Hid away.' He glanced back at the truck. Then he turned and stepped out into the fading light, raised the shotgun, tracked a moment and fired. The drone fell smoking to the concrete, shattering into pieces.

'I'm Harley,' said the man, stepping back into the shade. 'Friends call me Har. This is my brother, Aiden.' He held out his hand. 'Y'all is welcome to stay here as long as you like. We got water and victuals in the vehicle if y'all got something to trade.'

We agreed to talk. Harley's brother scrounged up some wood, set it in the middle of the garage floor and soon had a cooking fire going. Harley called out to the car, and a moment later the woman appeared. She stood at the threshold, both hands gripping the edge of the sliding door, peering in at us. She was petite, fair, fine-boned. Her hair was a nest of tangles. Her cotton dress was stained, her sweater holed. There were bright, fresh scrapes on both her knees. If it were not for the heavy swell of her belly, she could have been mistaken for a child.

Harley motioned to her with his chin. She hesitated, shook her head.

'It's okay,' he called to her. 'Come on. Fix us some supper. Everyone, this is my wife, Sue Frank.'

The woman flashed a half-smile and slipped back into the darkness. A few moments later she reappeared with a twine bag, hesitated a moment at the threshold then approached, timid as a wild animal chancing for a treat from an outheld hand. Harley set an overturned crate next to the fire. The woman sat and started unpacking things from her bag: a cast iron pot, a water flask, some vegetables, a chunk of red meat, a cutting board. She produced a small kitchen knife and set to her task.

Everyone gathered around the fire, stared into the flames as the sun set atomic-fireball red and darkness fell. Harley scraped aside a small pile of coals, set a rebar tripod over them. When the woman had finished preparing the stew, Harley hung the iron pot from the tripod. Soon a wonderful smell filled the garage. The woman lifted the lid occasionally, stirred. My stomach was churning. I hadn't eaten since leaving the apartment the night before.

We clustered around the fire in that way people do, as if the flames could impart some wisdom not available in day, waited for the food to cook.

'The government left about a year ago,' Harley said, breaking the silence that had seen us through dusk and into night. 'One day, they just stopped comin' around, trying to get everyone to move north. Mind you, most of the other folk from these parts had already left. We's the last ones, other than the Mennonites out towards Santa Anna.'

'What about the border?' said Argent.

'I heard a while back that they still got troops there, to keep out the Messicans. Though truth be told there ain't many of 'em comin' this way. These days it's more the other way round.' Harley opened the lid and sniffed. 'Lots of folk round here headed south right at the start. Eighty-niners like you all. Talkin' about someplace where there's still plenty of food and things ain't gone and dried up like here, where they ain't putting people in jail on account of their age and nothin' else. Horse shit, if you ask me. Dreamin' dreams 'cause they can't face the way it is. Down there is worse than here, I reckon.'

'Is there any way to cross the border?' asked Argent. 'How well guarded is it?'

'From what I've heard, there ain't no easy way to get through. There's wire, guards, even a minefield on the Messican side they say. They've gone an' started building the wall again. 'Cept now it's the Messicans buildin' it. No way, hombre. The only way is over, or round. Y'all can either fly or take a boat across the Gulf.'

Argent shook his head. 'There's always a way.'

'Yessir, like I told you.'

'I didn't ask for your advice.'

'No, I reckon you didn't,' said Harley, looking over at our truck. 'Tell you what, if y'all is determined on headin' for the border, you need something fast, light, good on gas. You'll never make it in that rig out there.'

'We've done okay so far,' said Argent.

'With all the marauders about, y'all are gonna need something that can go cross country.'

'Marauders?' said Francoise, glancing over at me.

'Yes'm. All round these parts.'

'We can look after ourselves,' said Argent.

'I'm sure you can,' said Harley. 'Still, my Tahoe out there'd be a better bet for y'all. Give me that rig of yours and y'all can have it. Suspension's good, four-wheel drive, and it'll git you twice the miles to a gallon, at least.'

Harley turned to his wife and spoke a few words. She reached into her bag and produced a stack of steel bowls and a handful of metal spoons. She held out the first bowl and Har ladled in the steaming broth.

I looked over at Francoise. She nodded.

'It's a deal,' I said.

'Wait a minute,' said Argent, leaning forward. 'That rig is in good shape, it runs smooth. It's worth ten times that Tahoe. No deal.'

Sue Frank handed Francoise the first bowl. She smiled and mouthed thanks. The woman smiled back. Bowls were handed around. The stew was delicious, chunks of vegetables and what I took for lamb in a salty broth.

'Suit yourself,' said Far. 'But you won't make it to the border with what y'all got left in that tank. Not even the coast. And there ain't no diesel round these here parts that I know of. You, Aiden?'

His brother shook his head slowly.

Argent spooned up the soup without speaking, concentrating on the food until it was gone. He set his empty bowl beside him on the crate, pulled his case close under his arm as if it were a small child, and glared at Harley. Then he reached into his pocket and flipped a small gold coin into the air. It spun across the fire and into Harley's outstretched palm.

'That's for the food,' said Argent. 'Keep the fuck out of my vehicle.'

I got to my feet. 'It's not your truck, Argent. If anything, it's mine. Our friend is right. We can't make it in that thing. We should make the trade and be glad of our good luck in meeting these people.'

Argent glared at me, hunched forward, arms coiled by his sides. 'I warned you, asshole. This is my show. I don't give a damn what you do but stay out of my way.' Then he turned to Harley. 'Throw in water and food, and you've got yourself a deal.'

Har leaned over and spoke with his brother. After a moment he stood and shouldered his shotgun. 'One jerry can of water and this here bag of food. That's all we can spare.'

Argent glared at me a moment and then fished the keys from his pocket and dangled them in his fingers. 'How much fuel is there in that Tahoe? I didn't check it for myself yet.'

Harley was still seated by the fire, a bowl of stew cradled in his hands. He slurped a spoonful, and without looking up said: 'Aiden, take this here guest of ours to the Tahoe and show him whatever he wants to see. The jack, the spare, hell we even got eight spark plugs, one for each cylinder.'

Aiden smirked and stood, swung his rifle up into the crook of his arm and bid Argent towards the darkness with his free arm.

Argent stuffed his handgun into his belt front and bowed. 'After you, my trustworthy friend.'

Aiden looked at his brother, shrugged, and walked out of the firelight towards the gaping silence of the desert night.

Francoise smiled at the woman sitting next to her. 'When are you due?' I heard her say.

'I'm thirty weeks, best I can figure,' said Sue Frank, running her hand across her belly. 'Everyone calls me Frankie.'

'Is this your first, Frankie?'

'Uh-huh. But I'm on my own. There ain't been a doctor in these parts for gone a year, and my mother-in-law gone an' died some months back now.' She reached out and touched Francoise's hand. 'Do you have children?'

Francoise tried to smile but it dissolved into a painful grimace. 'I'm expecting, too. But my husband was killed.' She glanced over at me, held my gaze a moment, and hung her head.

My heart skipped a beat, another. This changed everything. Everything and nothing. I wondered if Argent knew.

'I'm sorry,' I heard Sue Frank say.

'How do you survive out here, Frankie?' said Francoise. The women were whispering now so that I could only catch some of what they were saying.

'We have a spread,' I heard Frankie say. 'Some well water ... my garden. We scavenge ... so dangerous.' Then Francoise's voice in reply, thin like air, barely audible: 'Forced labour ... starvation ... rape ...' Each word hit me like a bullet, separate, devastating, ballistic.

'More soup anyone?' said Har. 'There's a little left.'

'No, thank you,' said Francoise, her voice wavering. 'It was delicious.'

'Is it true what they say?' said Frankie. Her face was covered in sweat. 'About down south I mean. That things there is still normal?' She glanced up at her husband. 'Har says it ain't nothin' but ignorant rumour, but I think we should take our chances. I want to have my baby in a hospital, with a doctor.' She grabbed Francoise's hands and squeezed them. She was crying.

'We've been through this, Frankie,' said Har, taking a step towards her. 'There ain't nothin' down there 'cept dead land and deader Messicans.'

Francoise freed one of her hands and ran a fingertip along the woman's cheekbone, a yellowing echo there I hadn't noticed before.

Sue Frank turned her face away. 'Please,' she said. 'I'm scared.'

'So am I,' says Francoise.

Another Chance

When I was young, before the world changed, I resented time. I couldn't wait for the workweek to be over, for the summer to come or the conference to end so I could be home again with May and Lachie. The unhurried flow of my limitless horizon of days was something to be endured. Now, it barely registers, no matter how hard I try to hold on.

The story is writing itself now, spilling out every morning as if it has been waiting there forever, ready to be told. I sit at my desk and look down at what I have written so far, over two hundred pages. May is dead. Kwesi and Lan and Samantha, and so many others too. I think of everything that must come, these events now predetermined. And I wonder, did we ever have a choice?

I shake my head. Of course, we had a choice. It is nothing but weakness that led me to even consider such a question. And perhaps that, in itself, is part of the answer. We were weak. Too easily misled, too readily captured by our own delusions, we convinced ourselves of our own helplessness. And so yes, absolutely, we could have changed it. In myriad ways and at an infinite number of junctions, other choices could have been made, and each of those decisions would have rippled out through time and space and across all of humanity, and the course of history might have been changed.

And as I look out across the sound and watch a flock of gulls fishing in the light on the water, I know that somehow we have been given another chance. Every day is an opportunity.

36

It had been over three hours since we had concluded the deal, traded vehicles, and resumed our journey south. I didn't have the energy to argue anymore, so I let Argent drive. No one had spoken a word since leaving, Argent's attention fixed on the faded white line ahead, Francoise between us on the front bench seat, her head nodding in half-sleep, a green shadow in the dim light of the instrument panel.

The humidity began to rise – slowly at first, and then after another hour or so, in great wet dollops that glued the clothes to our skin. The night air streaming through the open windows was heavy with the scent of the Gulf, salt and sea and crude oil, and the gut-churning smell of decaying flesh. I looked at my watch and glanced over at the Chevrolet's speedometer. The junction should be coming up soon. We could either continue south towards the Mexican border, or turn east and make for the coast, wherever it was now. I pulled out the map, unfolded it and flicked on the overhead light.

Argent narrowed his eyes. 'What's that map telling you?'

'The road to the coast is coming up. Ten miles at most.' I clicked off the light.

'That's where we part,' said Argent. 'You know what they say about three.'

'Suit yourself,' I said, steady as I could. 'Enjoy the walk.'

Argent laughed a deep laugh that jolted Francoise awake.

'You're a persistent shit, I'll give you that,' he said, wiping his mouth with the back of his wrist. 'Let me clarify. This is where you fuck off. I stop the truck, you get out, and she and I keep going to the border.' He looked over at Francoise. 'I'm calling in our little deal, gorgeous.'

Francoise looked away. 'We can't cross at the border.' Her voice was so quiet I could barely hear her. 'You heard Harley. It is too heavily guarded.'

Argent jerked his head around. 'In deference to Harley what's-his-name, if you have money, there is always a way.'

'No. You won't get that close. Frankie told me they are shooting on sight.'

Argent glowered. 'What the fuck does she know?'

I stared past Francoise at Argent. I'd had enough. 'You go ahead and find out, you blustering idiot. But do it on your own. And by the way, this is *my* vehicle.'

Argent slowed the car and pulled over to the side of the road, rolling for a while on the shoulder, and then braked to a stop. He killed the lights, swivelled in his seat and pulled out his handgun and pointed it at my face.

'Get out of the fucking car,' he said.

Francoise leaned forward, putting herself between me and muzzle of the weapon. 'No,' she said. 'If you want to go south, the Gulf is the only way. By boat.'

'Fine,' said Argent, pushing Francoise back into the seat. 'We'll go to the coast. Now get the fuck out of the car or I'll blow your brains out.'

I knew that this time he wasn't bluffing. I could see his finger tightening on the trigger. Francoise struggled but Argent pinned her back. The black muzzle stared me in the face. It would take my head off.

'Alright, Argent,' I heard myself say. 'I'll go.' I reached for the door. Then I realised. Francoise was right – by boat was the only way.

Looking back, I'm not sure if this was the way it unfolded. Memory has a fluid quality that has always surprised me. But it was something like this, and even if the details aren't exactly right, the outcome was the same.

I turned and faced the gun. 'Can you sail a boat, Argent?'

Argent hesitated. I could see the doubt spread across his face.

'What are you planning to do?' I continued, pressing what I thought might be an advantage. 'Hire a skipper and a yacht? You'll be damned lucky to find a boat that's seaworthy, from what I've heard, let alone a crew. And where is it that you are planning to go? You keep talking about this paradise of yours. If it's any distance at all then you'll have to sail – you'll never find enough fuel to motor. Anything more than a hundred miles or so and you had better know how to navigate.' I took my hand off the door handle and closed it around Francoise's fist. She turned her hand palm up, opened her fingers and threaded them between mine. Her hand was rough, the callouses hard like tree bark.

We sat there for a long time in the darkness at the side of the road. No one spoke. Argent lowered the pistol into his lap and looked outside at the darkened road ahead. He seemed to be weighing up the information, negotiating with himself.

'What deal were you talking about, Francoise?' I said. 'Tell me.'

Francoise clutched her satchel and rolled the flap up into a tight cylinder.

'She comes with me,' said Argent. 'That's the deal, shithead.'

I didn't believe it. Not for a second. I grabbed Francoise by the shoulders and twisted her around so that she was facing me. I tried to look her in the eyes, but she averted her gaze.

'Does he know, Francoise? Have you told him?'

She shook her head.

'Know what?' blurted Argent.

'Nothing,' she snapped. 'It doesn't matter.'

'I want to hear it from you, Francoise,' I said. 'Whatever he has promised you or threatened you with, don't believe it.'

Her face was wet. 'I'm sorry. I...'

'Just remember,' said Argent, his mouth close to the back of her head. 'Teacher here wanted to leave you behind. I'm the one that got you out of there, away from the power plant.'

Francoise clutched my forearm. 'I'm doing it for you,' she said. 'Please go. He will kill you.'

I let go of her shoulder and grabbed my pack. I knew she was right. I opened the door and stepped out onto the gravel shoulder. I looked back inside, but it was too dark and I could not see her face.

'We'll take the map, too,' came Argent's voice from within.

I pulled the folded map from my pocket and dropped it onto the passenger seat. The old V8 grumbled to life. I closed the door and stood back as the car rolled away and gained speed, and then I watched the tail-lights slowly merge into a single red point on the road ahead then disappear.

37

With the moon setting in the west, I checked my watch and started walking. After a few minutes I'd established a good pace, tracking the centreline of a crumbling highway through a deserted land. I had memorised the route I wanted to take, south to the junction and then southwest towards Corpus Christi and the coast. At least a hundred miles, four marathons. In my pack were four litres of water and enough food for two days. I would travel at night and in the cool hours of the morning, at the fastest walk I could manage, resting during the day.

After an hour I estimated I had covered about six kilometres; after two, thirteen. I stopped by the side of the road and sat on the ground and drank. I felt strong. I felt alone. I watched the sky lighten in the east and felt ashamed for what we had done to the sunrise, and I knew that I should never have left her alone with that psychopath.

I reached the junction by early morning, the sun just above the horizon, my shadow jerking long-legged and bone thin across the tarmac, the road signs long since pushed over, the posts burned for fuel, the steel sheeting used for roofing in some recycled shanty town. Since being left at the roadside I had seen not a single living soul, nor bird nor animal of any kind. It was as if the surface of Earth and everything that it contained had died or moved to less-damaged latitudes.

I walked to the middle of the intersection where the camber of the roadways reached an apex, a high point on the flat ground that stretched away as far as I could see in every direction. A twisted line of power poles strung away into the distance like a trampled fence. I figured I must be eighty miles from the coast, less maybe, but I could see no trace of the sea. The air trembled in the rising heat. A clear copper-sulphate sky, devoid of any cloud, spread over me to every horizon.

I checked my compass, sighted southwest, and was about to shoulder my pack when something caught my attention, off to the south in the direction of the coast, a thin dark line bisecting the horizon, almost imperceptible. At first, I thought it was an illusion, some trick of the heat haze dancing above the sand, a finger of dust or vapour. I fumbled in my pack, found my binoculars.

It was smoke, a thin grey tendril rising untroubled into the morning sky about five miles off, no more. At its base I could make out an encampment of sorts: vehicles, slung canvas, movement. Were these survivors, kind souls like Harley and his family, doing their best to live, or were these marauders, the itinerant survivalists Harley had spoken of, preying on those stupid or unfortunate enough to travel those roads alone?

I decided not to take the risk. I would leave the road and move across country, stay hidden for the rest of the day, and come nightfall, bypass the camp to the south and put as many miles behind me as I could before sunrise. I stowed the binoculars and pushed into the burnt, dead scrubland south of the road, looking for somewhere that would swallow me up.

After more than half an hour of trudging, I found a shallow depression between two blunt outcrops of siltstone. I sank to the ground, huddled in the strip of shade under the overhang and closed my eyes. Now that I had stopped moving, stopped thinking, fatigue swept through me. I fought it back, forced myself to drink and eat. Then I crawled to the lip of the outcrop to survey the camp. A slight breeze had come up, and I could smell woodsmoke and the faint but distinctive odour of charred meat.

I focused on the cluster of vehicles, four in all. A tarpaulin was strung between two of the trucks. Just beyond, I could make out the end of an old trailer home, the cladding warped and brown. And standing in a circle, as if engaged in a friendly conversation, were four people. At this distance I couldn't make out their faces. I scanned right, focused on the far vehicle. It was a black four-by-four with heavy welded caging. Farley's Tahoe.

I sank back down into the depression and looked up into the poisoned sky.

38

The sound snapped me from a dazed half-sleep. A single crack, the now-familiar retort of a gun. It came on the dying sea breeze, laden with the chemicals of decay and inundation, the physical result of all that I had warned them would come, so many hours and days trying to convince anyone who would listen, my sceptical students, so easily manipulated by all of the garbage on the internet and in the media, where any hack or grievant could post whatever rubbish they liked, camouflaging it as official, credible, where everything was exactly the opposite of what it claimed, where every site whose tagline claimed to provide 'independent objective information' was guaranteed to be a platform for extremist polemic, where facts and truth were garbled and mashed and cherry-picked to suit agendas so warped that I would, some nights after May had gone to bed, sit shaking at my computer, impotent despair flooding through me, overwhelming me so that I can still feel it even now.

Once, just as the political battle was reaching its crescendo, as it became increasingly clear from the daily news polls that the Repudiation Coalition was going to win, I had made a rare foray into the treacherous wilds of the blogosphere, pointing out the numerous scientific errors and inconsistencies sprouted by the coalition's chief spokesman, a bug-eyed, hugely well spoken and preposterously charming Englishman named Hollinghurst. The lightning speed at which my very short missive was strewn across the world, and the strength and sheer savagery of the backlash, surprised and deeply shocked me. I spent days afterwards trying to reply, as affably and humbly as I could, to the dozens of vitriolic and hateful comments that clogged my inboxes, writing back to each person, trying to present a balanced view and apologising for any offence I may have caused, all the while riven with a deep gut-wrenching unease that I could neither banish nor confront. The whole experience had left me drained and depressed, and I had fallen into a period of dark self-doubt, during which I began to question everything I had believed about people and the future, and the fundamental good in humankind. I concluded then that what people desired above all was misery – their own, but most importantly, others'. They feasted on calamity. Like moths to streetlights, they could not help but be drawn into the blaze where they exhausted themselves in a futile, mindless dance, thrashing themselves to death in the glare. It provided meaning in a meaningless universe.

And now, as I lay in this shallow scrape in the ground, the light of day rapidly fading, the sun long since obscured behind a bank of low slate clouds, I reflected that it had all come to pass. Everything was here, written in this barren ground, in the pangs of hunger in my belly, in May's erasure from the world, in the gunshot that still echoed in my ears. No, I thought, it was worse, much worse.

I reached for the binoculars and squinted through the low-angle light towards the encampment. There was movement now, people moving about between the vehicles. I was sure now that it was Harley's Tahoe. And then I heard men's voices raised in argument, guttural, cave-dwelling brays. A door slammed, an engine roared to life and one of the other vehicles, a big red pickup, tore away towards the road in a tornado of dust. It careened onto the highway and sped off in the direction of the coast.

I swung the glasses back towards the encampment. Three men stood clustered around two other figures, both prone on the ground. One of the men bent over the pair, busying himself with some task, his arms flapping about as he manipulated the bodies. I knew immediately that the figures on the ground were Francoise and Argent. I had heard only one shot. I hoped that it had been for Argent.

I stowed my gear and started to crab my way forward. I needed to get closer while there was still enough light to plan a way in. A series of waist-high outcrops running roughly perpendicular to the road provided good cover, and I quickly halved the distance to the camp. Light was fading fast.

I scanned the encampment again. Francoise and Argent, it must surely be them, seemed to be lying up against some sort of oblong, steel structure – the remnants of an old water trough perhaps. Between one of the vehicles and the trailer an orange light flickered, growing in intensity as twilight passed into darkness. A pang of woodsmoke reached me, soured by the sting of tar. I could make out three of them, their faces and chests barbed in orange firelight. They were standing in a rough circle, passing around a bottle.

After a few minutes one of the men left the fire and walked towards the trailer, where a weak yellow light shone in one of the partially shuttered windows. The door opened, and the man disappeared inside. I took another look at the two men by the fire, and then huddled down behind the low rock shelf to wait.

I awoke with a jolt from some thirst-induced dream, heart hammering, eyes wide. I looked at my watch. Gone two am. I shivered in the cold, my lower back stiff and sore. I scanned the encampment. A quarter-moon had risen and now bathed the landscape in reflected grey light. There was no movement. The fire had burned down. No lights showed from the trailer home. Silence reigned, the quiet of a fast-emptying world.

I slung my pack and moved across the moonlit ground at a run. I had determined that my only hope was to move decisively, as quickly as I could. Speed was the only thing I had left. I reached the first vehicle in a matter of minutes, my breathing regular, a sweat just starting to break. The camp was quiet. I could see the water trough and the two figures, bound and motionless. A pang of dread drove through me. Had they shot one of them, left the other to the horror of a night next to a cold corpse? Nearby, the dying glow of the coals cast dim shadows behind two men asleep under blankets. I slowed to a walk but kept moving. The Tahoe was to the left, close.

I worked my way behind the water trough, crouched down, very close now. It was definitely them. I could see no wounds. I crawled forward, examined Francoise's bindings. Her wrists were roped behind her back and tied to a chain. The chain appeared to be secured to the trough's heavy steel legs. I reached out and touched her hand. It was warm. I snaked under the trough until my face was only inches from her head, reached over and put my hand over her mouth.

'Francoise,' I whispered in her ear. 'Wake up. It's me. Teacher.'

Francoise jerked awake and twisted around to face me, eyes wide. She started to speak, but in her excitement, it came out almost as a shout. I clamped down harder on her mouth, stifling her words, trying to communicate urgency and danger with my eyes. She blinked in recognition, breathed through her nose, the stream of air hot over the back of my hand.

'Don't move,' I whispered. 'I'm going to cut you free.' I set to the rope with my Leatherman. Soon her hands were free.

'Okay,' I said. 'Now move quietly. Snake back under the trough, follow me.'

She started to move and then stopped, grabbed my arm. 'What about Derek?' she whispered, hoarse. 'We can't leave him.'

'Yes, we can. And we will. Now come on.' I pulled her towards me, trying to get her moving, but she tugged back.

'No, Teacher. We can't. They'll kill him. Please. Cut him loose.'

'We don't need him, France.' It was the first time I'd called her that, the name Kwesi always called her.

'He needs us.'

'He doesn't give a damn about us.'

'That's not true,' she whispered, too loud now.

A light flicked on in the trailer. We froze. Someone was moving around inside, coming to the door. I flattened myself to the ground behind Francoise. 'Don't move,' I whispered.

I could hear the screen door creak open and then stop, as if someone were holding it open. I held my breath. The door closed. I listened for footsteps, but the pounding of my heart drowned out the world. I wanted to look up. I wanted to run. After a moment, the light went off. I exhaled slowly, looked up. The compound was dark and quiet, struck in moon shadow.

'Come on,' I said. 'Before they come out again. Let's go. And keep quiet.'

Francoise remained still. 'I'm not leaving without Derek.'

I wondered what had happened between them since we'd parted.

'Please.'

I flipped open my knife and scuttled over to where Argent lay. He looked in bad shape. His face was cut, one eye was swollen shut, and his lower lip had ballooned out. But I could see nothing that looked like a gunshot wound. I put my lips to Argent's ear and was about to speak when Argent turned his head so that we were face to face, only inches apart.

'So you want to leave me behind do you?' he croaked, eyes wide, blazing.

I recoiled but held his gaze. 'Damn you, Argent. Not now. Hold still.' I cut the ropes from his wrists. 'Let's go.'

We walked quickly to the Tahoe, Francoise to the passenger side, Argent and I to the driver's door.

'I'm driving this time,' I said.

Argent stepped back. 'Go ahead, Teach.'

I opened the door, lifting the handle as quietly as I could. The door swung open with a click.

'Before we go, I have some business to look after,' Argent said.

He reached past me and in one quick motion tore open a panel and withdrew his handgun.

I grabbed his wrist. 'No, Argent. Let's go. They're all asleep. Please.'

Argent pulled his arm away and chambered a round. 'Just be ready to roll,' he said, no longer bothering to keep his voice down.

'God damn you,' I said.

Argent strode away. He crossed back past the trough and towards the firepit, where the two sleeping men lay rolled in blankets. I watched as he stood a moment as if looking into the coals, and then he raised the weapon and smashed a round into each body in quick succession, his broken-toothed smile lit up in the flash from the gun's muzzle. Then he walked to the trailer. He didn't rush. It was as if he didn't even care. He swung open the door and went inside. The light came on. Two more muffled shots disappeared into the night.

Francoise and I sat transfixed in the Tahoe, as if watching a drive-in movie somewhere, in better times, when this was entertainment. After a few moments, the trailer door swung open, and Argent ambled out, his case in one hand, a sawn-off shotgun in the other, a large nylon bag slung over his shoulder. As he approached the Tahoe he grinned and whipped up the shotgun one-handed, action-hero style, and pointed it at me across the windshield.

'Move over,' he said. 'I'm driving.'

Storm Coming

*I lose myself in the past each morning, but by afternoon the words
have dried up and I come face to face with the reality that something
must have happened. The journey has never taken this long, even
that first time when we did it, all four us, Lewis just a toddler.*

*Lewis comes down with Mandy, and we have dinner together.
Mandy is looking fine, healthy and happy and very big now. My wife
says she and the baby are doing well. All is where it should be. Soon,
we will be eight.*

*Juliette sends her apologies, Mandy says. She doesn't want us to
see her crying.*

*After the meal Lewis and I go to the balcony and look out towards
The Hope. Stars swirl above us in a milky, cloud-strewn infinity.*

Southwesterlies still blowing, he says.

I wish I was out there with him.

*Me too. Saw Uncle Liberty today. Came while I was working with
the horses.*

How was he?

Said a storm is coming.

When?

Soon.

He'll be okay.

*Lewis puts his hand on my shoulder. Don't worry, Papa. He's the
best sailor of all of us.*

I grip my son's forearm, feel the strength in him.

Maybe he decided to take a few extra days in Albany.

Maybe.

We've done it before.

I remember. Courting the girls.

Now look. Lewis smiles.

I squeeze his arm.

Providence is strong. She'll see him home, Papa.
Yes. She will.

39

We reached the coast as the sun was rising. I had never seen the Gulf before. Growing up, I had heard of the charm of Galveston and the beauty and natural bounty of the San Padre barrier islands. But now they were gone, swallowed up by the rising seas. I'd read about it in the news, a short piece in one of the online dailies over breakfast, back before Marshank-Watson, scanned quickly, just one more story, scarcely believable, numbing. I had learned long ago that what you read in the news was rarely an accurate representation of the facts anyway, and that the imagined idea of something rarely matched reality.

Not here.

Argent stopped the Tahoe on a slight rise and cut the engine. The Gulf of Mexico spread out before us, the early-morning sun painting a sulphurous swath across the dull, oily surface. Pillars of orange flame glowed on the horizon, long threads of black smoke reaching into a lithium sky. The coastline in both directions had that forlorn look of a recently flooded reservoir, a waterline uncomfortable with its new station, sloshing over ground not yet winnowed and sculpted, bays not yet arced.

And everywhere a sodden carpet of detritus, as far as I could see, east and west: a tidal zone of plastic containers of every size and shape imaginable; the trunks of trees, rootwork reaching to the sky in supplication; too many boats to count, hulls holed, masts snapped, rigging tangled, superstructures crushed; a battlefield of dead creatures – exquisitely angled pelican wings, the hideous death smiles of oiled dolphins, heaps of rotting fish. And all of it covered in a thick film of brown oil.

The calm surprised me. Everything seemed quite content in its ruin.

It was the smell that finally overwhelmed us. Although it had been building in strength through the night as we approached the coast, it was not until now, here, that its full force met our senses. Perhaps it was the sight of its source. Francoise reached across me for the door, but it was too late. Her vomit crashed onto me, vile and thin, the colour of the dead land.

She spluttered an apology as I opened the door and helped her out, only to watch her slump to the ground in agony. I put my hand on her back, said something I thought appropriate, but the purging continued, as if her very being was being ripped out and expelled.

It seemed a long time before it was over. I helped her to her feet, wiped her face and arms with a T-shirt from my pack.

She looked up at me. I was covered in vomit.

'I'm sorry,' she managed.

I tried a smile. I was sure it didn't come out as one. 'Don't worry,' I said. 'I'll take them to the cleaners tomorrow.'

'Thank you,' she said. 'Thank you for everything.'

She took the cloth from me and started wiping down my shirt and trousers. The vomit splattered to the sandy ground. 'I'm so sorry. So sorry.'

I allowed her to clean me. I stood rigid and unsure as her hands moved across my chest and abdomen and thighs.

The Tahoe's engine roared to life.

'Let's go, ladies,' shouted Argent. 'We have to keep moving. There is still one more of those bastards out there somewhere.'

Francoise straightened her blouse and climbed into the vehicle next to Argent. I clambered in beside her and closed the door. She reached for my hand on the seat beside her and laced her fingers though mine.

I glanced over and squeezed her hand. 'Go east, Argent,' I said. 'Left.'

'South is the destination,' he said. 'Along the coast to the border. South. That's where things are better. There's nothing left here.'

'You heard Harley. The border is closed tight. The Mexicans

aren't letting anyone cross. East means civilisation, or whatever is left of it.'

Argent scoffed. 'Fuck civilisation,' he said. 'Good riddance.'

Even after everything that had happened, his words hit me like shockwaves.

'The authorities will have notified the border patrols,' I said. 'They'll be looking for us. We won't stand a chance. It's a matter of survival. We're short of food and water, we're almost out of fuel. It's got to be east.'

'I agree,' said Francoise. 'Please, Derek.'

Argent sat clutching the wheel for a long time, the engine idling, precious fuel burning away. Finally, he slammed the Tahoe into gear and turned into the sun.

For the next two hours we followed the makeshift dirt track that wound along the coast. It was slow going. Beyond the tide line, about half a kilometre out to sea, the wreckage of the old world strung out like a halo of regret: the top storeys of buildings, the concrete stained that particularly sad colour of dried blood, clusters of rooftops, some ripped away to reveal the empty stickwork beneath, occasionally the tops of freeway road signs perched on the submerged overpasses of the old coast highway. Farther on, a whale lay where it had washed up, its ridged underbelly bloated and white, its huge flukes limp and motionless. And draped across it all, as far as you could see, a miasma of discarded principles and abandoned hopes.

The fuel gauge crept slowly towards empty as the miles wound by. We had seen not a single living human since leaving the marauders' camp. Was this really what it had come to? Had civilisation finally vanished, as Argent seemed to hope it would? I wondered what Francoise must be thinking – widowed, debased, wandering a ruined world with two men she barely knew? And what would it take for her to survive in such a world? She could probably already guess, whatever 'deal' she'd made with Argent surely just the beginning.

Ahead, just below the horizon, a group of buildings appeared. As we got closer, a small clutch of power poles came into view, then a deviation in the coastline, the mouth of a river, an embayment of some sort.

Argent clutched the steering wheel between his knees, pulled out his pistol and pulled back the action.

'Derek,' said Francoise, reaching over to touch his forearm. 'Please. Put it away.'

Argent looked over at her and grinned wide. You would have thought he was out for a drive in the country. He seemed completely at ease, unconcerned, enjoying it even. Yes, that was it. He was *enjoying* this.

'Don't worry, honey,' he said, stashing the pistol back in his belt. 'Just a precaution. I'm not without honour, you know.'

I shook my head. 'Honour.'

'You heard me.' Argent produced a cigar from his jacket pocket, put it between his lips, flicked out an expensive-looking lighter and puffed the cigar to life. 'I know you consider yourself to be an honourable man, Teacher. Well so do I. I keep my promises.'

'Like you did with that poor bastard in the alleyway.'

Argent smiled big, puffed on his cigar. 'Like I said, I keep my bargains. And I expect others to keep theirs.' He glanced at Francoise.

'You're a murderer and a deceiver. Nothing about you is honourable.'

He laughed. 'If it were up to you, Francoise here would be back at that power station. You hide behind all that pseudo-intellectual bullshit of yours, pretend to care so much about everything, but you're no different from me, and you goddam know it. Time to get down off that fucking white horse of yours, cause the world's changed.'

I said nothing, stared straight ahead. Argent drove on. The little village grew in the distance, a clutch of ramshackle houses huddled around a small tidal harbour, and beyond, on a slight rise overlooking the river, a white spire rising above the drifting smoke like a beacon. A church.

And as the harbour opened into view, I saw them.

'Boats,' I said. 'Sailboats.'

PART V
Prophets

Home

I pull through the cold water, gaze down through the clear, pure sea
to the rocky bottom. Snub-nosed wrasse peer out at me from under
an overhang, their pectoral fins flashing as they balance themselves
against the surge of the swell. Kelp sways thick in the bottom currents.
I catch a glimpse of a blue spotted cray, its antennae twitching in the
fractured darkness between two large slabs of toppled granite. Striped
damsels flit among the slow-growing cold-water corals and the
bright red sea fans. There are abalone here, too, and cold-water
oysters and thick beds of sea mussels that we harvest in the early
spring. I round the point and start for home, each rock and shoal cast
in half a lifetime's familiarity. I emerge where I always do, in the lee
of our point, step on the same flat rocks, pull off my mask, wade
towards our little shingle beach, the water dripping from my naked
limbs.

Hey there.

I run my hands through my hair. Well, hello. I heard you were
round here.

From your boy.

Lewis, yes.

Your other boy still not back.

Not yet.

Good boy, that boy.

Sure is.

Sure is.

Black fella.

Partly.

Although it is colder now, Uncle Liberty is dressed as he was when
I last saw him, in his favourite footy shorts. Thick curls of grey hair
cover his chest. His soles are bare. He taps the base of his spear against
a rock, nods.

Black fella just the same.

I reach for my towel, rub myself dry. I suppose he is.

Eight days, says Liberty.

Eight.

I once walked to Adelaide. Took me most part of six months.

You're joking.

Nope.

That must be over a thousand miles.

Like I said.

Long way.

Met some other black fellas here and thereabouts. Stopped for a rest now and again. Kept walking.

What did you do when you got there?

Turned around and came home. He tapped his spear again, looked me in the eyes, and then turned and disappeared into the bush.

40

We trundled into the town at around midday. A warren of sheet metal and plywood shacks lined the narrow dirt road that snaked up the hill. Plastic tarps shivered in the sea breeze, the smells of woodsmoke and shit mixing with the strong chemical odour of the sea. A few permanent buildings emerged from the clutter: an old clapboard house with a stately veranda, a relic of another time, paint peeling, the windows shuttered tight, and further on up the hill, another similar structure set in a dusty square.

Vehicles were parked out front, an old Cadillac all fins and cones, and several large-tyred pickups in various states of distress. From here you could see down to the estuary, the rainbowed surface of the Gulf stretching away to a flare-studded horizon. A series of booms had been strung across the narrowest point of the inlet to keep the oil from washing into the bay, where about a dozen boats swung at anchor. A makeshift wooden pier extended from the end of the town's main street. On the other side of the inlet was what appeared to be a docking area, with a few shipping containers scattered around a boat ramp and several vessels out of the water, up on trestles.

Argent slowed the Tahoe to a stop and shut off the engine. The front door of the house opened, ejecting a burst of male laughter, the fractured notes of recorded music, the higher-pitched squeals of women. A man stood in the doorway, eyes narrowed against the sun. Tall and well built, his hair glowed in the backlight. He clutched the railing, raised his hand to shield his eyes. He was looking right at us.

'Don't look away,' said Argent. 'Don't show weakness.'

The young man stood a moment and then staggered to the front steps. He stumbled, lurching into the dusty street, muscles flouncing beneath a dirty singlet. He climbed into one of the pickups, started the engine. The vehicle jerked back, tyres spitting dirt, and then rocked away down the hill.

'Well, here it is,' said Argent. 'Civilisation.'

I pointed down to the boats. 'You want to head south, Argent. So do I. There's the way.' With the right boat we could sail all the way to South America if we had to.

Argent looked over at Francoise. For once he seemed unsure. He opened the car door and stepped to the ground, the sun highlighting the bruised and swollen flesh around his nose and eyes. 'You two stay put,' he said, securing his pistol in the waistband at the small of his back and flipping the tail of his shirt over to make sure it was covered.

'Come on, Francoise,' I said, getting out of the car.

'I said wait here.'

'No way, Argent. From here on, we stay together.'

Argent shrugged and paced across the hard-baked dirt towards the building. Francoise and I followed him up the steps of the front veranda and through the door. The room exhaled a hot breath of alcohol, cigarette smoke and sweat. We stood a moment blinking in the smoke as our eyes adjusted to the shuttered darkness. A makeshift bar lined one wall where half a dozen men stood drinking. Under a harsh light at the end of the room, an unattractive woman with large, pendulous breasts danced on a makeshift stage. A few men sat watching her, others turned and stared at us, at Francoise. She moved closer to me, took my arm.

Opposite was a ceiling-high double screen of heavy wire caging that divided the room. Behind the cage were rows of shelves stacked to the roof with everything we had once been so used to seeing at our local supermarket: dry goods, packaged food, toilet paper, and beyond, rows of humming refrigerators and freezers. Nestled into a recess in the caging was a counter protected by thick plexiglass, behind which stood a square-headed giant with a pistol holstered to his thigh. Farther back, protected by another screen of glass, a man with a long grey beard peered out at us over a pair of dirty bifocals. He frowned as we approached.

Argent strode directly towards the counter like he owned the place. 'I want to speak to the boss.'

The old man gave a nod, waved the guard back and came to stand behind the counter. 'Welcome to Ephesus,' he said. His face was shot with deep-red blotches, the skin scaly, eczemic. He was dressed in a long white robe, a cassock almost, held in place with a length of nylon rope tied about his prominent gut. The scar of a seven-pointed star was burned into his forehead. He scanned Argent's face, looked Francoise up and down – took his time doing it. 'If you are looking for a doctor, I am afraid we have no such blasphemy here.'

Argent reached a coin through the opening in the plexiglass, placed it on end on the counter and gave it a flick. 'I want to do some business,' he said.

The coin spun on its edge, blurring into a sphere. The old man watched as the orbit slowly decayed into a saddle and then rimmed flat. He picked up the coin, turned it over in his fingers. 'Sovereign,' he said.

'That's one ounce of pure gold,' said Argent. 'The only currency worth shit.'

The old man stood and thrust the coin into the pocket of his robe. 'Not the only one. Come with me.'

We followed him past the dancer, through a door, up a flight of stairs. The place was a relic from another time. Hardwood floors shone under fluted light fixtures. High ceilings graced beautifully panelled walls. The old man led us into a private study with a big, polished-oak desk and two leather chairs, a big window behind and a bookshelf lining one wall. The dense grain of the old first-stand wood glowed in the afternoon light that streamed in through the half-closed shutters. He sat behind the desk and signalled us to sit.

Argent took the chair closest to the door. I offered the other chair to Francoise, but before she could sit the old man raised his hand. 'Gentlemen sit,' he said. 'Not women.'

'I prefer to stand,' I said.

'Suit yourself.'

I stood next to Francoise.

Overhead, a flat wooden frame covered in cloth began to sway gently. A cooling flow of air bathed the room. In the far corner, almost obscured in darkness, a man sat on the floor pulling the rope with his foot, a twenty-first-century punkah wallah.

'Now,' said the old man. 'Drink with me.'

He clapped his hands and the door opened. A tall black woman entered carrying a silver tray and walked to the desk. Francoise gasped.

'Bourbon for our gentlemen friends, Camille,' he said.

The woman placed the tray on the desk next to a leather-bound copy of the Holy Bible and poured bourbon into three crystal tumblers. She was completely naked.

'Good girl,' he said, pointing to the floor at his feet. The girl got to her knees and disappeared under the desk. The old man looked up at us and smiled, revealing a mouth empty of teeth. 'Upon conclusion of our business, feel free to enjoy her as you like, gentlemen. On the house. You see, my friends, the angels are restoring the natural order of things, as prophesied.' He raised his glass.

'I want to leave,' Francoise said. She grabbed me by the hand and started to pull me towards the door.

'No, Francoise,' I said, resisting. 'I'm not letting him out of my sight.'

She let go of my hand, but she didn't leave.

'Please, gentlemen,' said the old man. 'The whisky.'

Argent drank.

'You are not drinking?' the old man asked me.

I shook my head.

The old man frowned, addressed Argent. 'I saw you admiring the house,' he said, his voice thicker now. 'It was built in a time when men of wealth and substance commanded and were obeyed, could shape destinies in a world still undiscovered, uncharted, could satisfy their hungers unfettered by petty bureaucrats and cloying governments, free to worship God as they chose.' He arched his back. 'This time has come again.'

Argent put his empty glass on the old man's desk. 'Enough bullshit,' he said, glancing at me. 'I want a boat. A sailboat.'

The girl's head was moving in long strokes now, muffled murmurs coming from deep within her throat. The old man closed his eyes as a long sigh escaped from his lips. Then he leaned forward, opened the Bible and flicked through the pages, found what he was looking for. He stabbed the point of his index finger onto the page. 'It's all here,' he said, twisting long strands of his beard between thumb and index finger. 'Ezekiel.' He read:

'"Now is the end come upon thee, and I will send mine anger upon thee, and will judge thee according to thy ways, and will recompense upon thee all thine abominations. And mine eye shall not spare thee, neither will I have pity."'

'"And you shall know I am the Lord,"' said Francoise.

The old man nodded. 'The woman knows her scripture.'

'The woman's husband...' She didn't finish, glared.

The black woman emerged from under the desk and left the room.

'Heading south, are you?' said the old man.

Argent frowned. 'Depends.'

'I would advise you to reconsider. Any stories you may have heard of Eden are blasphemy. The equator has been ravaged by the angels, laid waste by the seven plagues. What remains is in control of pirates, miscreants. Godlessness rules.'

'As it clearly does here,' said Francoise.

The old man tapped his finger on the desk, ignored her. 'Here. This is where the world begins anew, my friends. The world as it should be, as it was always supposed to have been, before we lost the true path set out in scripture.'

'A sailboat,' said Argent. 'I want to buy one.'

'The good Lord has seen fit to deliver several to us. In fact one was towed in by the boys this morning. The vessel is in poor shape, mind you.' The old man retrieved the sovereign from his pocket, considered it a while then took another long, deliberate look at Francoise. 'I see that you have something to offer in return.'

I could feel Francoise shiver.

Argent pointed at the coin. 'I have more of those. She's mine.'

We Can't Stop It, But We Can Use It

I sit on the rocks and gaze out to sea. Nine days now. The weather is worsening day by day, an Antarctic cold front coming in. I try not to think about it, the possibilities – good and catastrophic.

My fingers trace the sharpened clasp of a fossil bivalve stuck here not so long ago, ten thousand years perhaps, before it was covered over and cooked and up-thrust into the ragged Cenozoic limestone cliffs that fringe this part of the coast. It was here, in this very place, that I started teaching the boys geology, first awakened them to the distant past, the formation of continents, the appearance and extinction of species.

How old are you, Kweku?

You know, Papa.

Tell me.

Laughs. Eight.

And me?

I don't know. Old.

Fifty-three.

That's right, Lewis.

What is the difference?

Forty-five. Lewis again.

Forty-five what?

Years.

What is a year?

You are as old as the Earth going fifty-three times around the sun. Kweku.

Right.

Nineteen thousand, three hundred and forty-five days. A big smile.

Good, Lewis. What is a day?

The time it takes the Earth to spin around one time.

And this clam, here in the rock?
Three million, six hundred and fifty thousand spins.
Time is moving, said Kweku.
That's right. Time is motion.
And we can't stop it.
No, we can't stop it. But we can use it.
How, Papa?
Now that, son, is up to you.

41

It was evening by the time the old man led us down to the shore in his Cadillac. We followed in the Tahoe. The boat had been hauled out of the water and now lay cradled in a wooden trestle a few metres from the shore. Its hull was covered in oil, and the deck was a tangle of wire and bent poles. She looked in bad shape.

'She washed up not far from here,' the old man said, reaching up to pat the wood-plank hull. His hand came away covered in a film of crude. 'The good Lord's bounty to the righteous.'

His eyes settled on Francoise. 'She'll take some work, mind you,' he said, gaze unwavering. 'But then that has always been the advantage of wood. I voyaged to the island of Patmos in a wooden vessel, long ago.' He waved towards the river embayment, a dozen or so craft bobbing on the current. 'All of this fibreglass is very difficult to repair. Resins and epoxies are required. The devil's technology.'

The old man reached into his cloak and pulled out the same Bible we'd seen in his office. Gilt flashed as he leafed the pages. 'Genesis,' he said, placing his palm flat on the page. 'It is right here, my new friends. "And I will wipe mankind, whom I have created, from the face of the Earth". It could not be clearer.'

He closed the book, held it before him a moment, then slipped it back into his cloak pocket. 'But we here are blessed. Soon, we will never hunger again, nor will we thirst, the sun will not beat upon us, nor any scorching heat. The Lamb has led us to springs of living water and has wiped the tears from our eyes. The great tribulation is upon us, after a thousand years of waiting it has come, just as I had prophesied that it would. We are the chosen generation. Exult. It is all part of God's great plan.'

Argent laughed. 'God does not exist, my friend. I can't put it any plainer for you. Superstition, that's all it is. A simple-minded replacement for science and rational thinking. An abdication. I can't understand what is happening, so I won't even try. I'll just make up some bullshit myth and enforce blind faith. Imagine where we would be if we had always thought this way.'

'Yes, imagine,' said Francoise, frowning over crossed arms.

The old man smiled. 'One does not need to imagine, my friend,' he croaked. 'Look around you. The seven angels have come. A third of the Earth has been laid waste. A third of the living creatures of the sea have died. Wormwood has poisoned the waters, and the stars have been struck from the sky. The horsemen have arrived, my children. Two hundred million of them to slay humanity. This is the harvest of rationalism, your so-called science, the blasphemous alchemy of Newton and Einstein, the scourge of feminism and homosexuality, the usurpation of the natural order of things.'

The old man looked at each of us in turn, and then fixed his gaze on Argent. 'Only we, the sealed, the repentant, will survive. We have food, water, everything we need. The Lord provides.'

'And the Lord taketh,' said Argent. 'In that, I agree with you. Everything had to be swept away. And soon, we can start over.'

I should have realised then, of course. But even with all we'd be through, it was beyond my comprehension. We are human, after all, and frail. Until we see for ourselves, we cannot truly believe. And sometimes not even then.

'It is late,' said the old man. 'You are welcome to camp here for the night.' He offered his hand to Argent. 'I am Saint John, High Priest of Ephesus, one of the seven great churches of scripture. I will return in the morning, and we may converse more. Perhaps we can conclude an arrangement.' He clutched at his Bible, ran his fingers across its cover. 'Perhaps you might even be convinced to join our community, to help us rebuild the world as God intended it, to find everlasting salvation. We need new blood.'

'Perhaps,' said Argent.

'In the meantime, please stay here. We have strict rules of entry to the community. No visitation after dark.' The old man took another long look at Francoise. 'God's will be done.' Then he turned and disappeared in his Cadillac back towards the village.

'Saint John,' said Francoise. 'They were talking about him. The men at the camp. The other one who left, he might come here.'

'He may be here already,' I said, standing back and looking at the boat stranded on its cradle.

'So, what do you think, Teach?' said Argent. 'Can you sail this thing?'

I did a circuit around the vessel, clambered up the ladder to check out the cockpit, went below. She was sturdily built and appeared well equipped. As I looked around the cabin, I could hear Argent's voice through the open porthole.

'Shangri-la,' he was saying. 'That's where we're going, babe. We'll start over. It's a clean slate. Almost biblical, don't you think? The deluge, God's wrath. The old bastard has a point, in his way.'

'That woman,' said Francoise. 'The way he treats her.'

Then silence, Francoise perhaps expecting a response and not getting it. And then: 'Do you think he will come looking for us, that other man from the camp?' Fear in her voice.

'It's alright,' I heard him say. 'I'll look after it.'

Francoise again: 'You heard what he said. Is there really somewhere left, where all of this...' If there was more, I didn't hear it.

I moved closer to the porthole. They were there, just feet away from me.

'Don't worry, just stick with me,' I heard Argent say, voice lowered.

By now I knew why Argent wanted Francoise – the physical attraction was obvious – and it was clear that Francoise was using that to protect me. What I couldn't understand was why Francoise had insisted I cut Argent loose back at the camp. Whatever the reason, I'd heard enough. I clambered up the gangway and stood in the cockpit, looking down at them. Argent had his arms around Francoise's waist. When they saw me, she pushed him away.

'Well?' said Argent. That smile again. 'Is this thing seaworthy?'

I climbed down the ladder and stood with one hand on the boat's hull. I felt lightheaded, perhaps from the vapours coming from the bay, or all the radiation I was now sure my body had soaked up over the weeks. Something inside me had gone away. 'Can be,' I said.

In truth, she was pretty banged up. The rigging needed a complete overhaul. We would need wire, tools. The hull looked sound, but I would have to inspect it more thoroughly before I could know for sure. There was a full set of sails, but we would need to check them for holes and tears. I hadn't seen sheets or halyards. There was an old Yanmar diesel engine, but the propeller was gone and the drive shaft was bent – probably when she ran aground – so there was no way we could motor. At first glance, the cabin was pretty well fitted out. There was a kerosene stove that would run on just about anything, a couple of berths forward, self-steering gear, a working compass in the cockpit.

'I'd say yes. It can be made seaworthy. If there are places closer to the equator that have escaped the worst, then this is the best way to get there.'

'We'll trade the Tahoe for it,' said Argent. 'And some gold if we have to. What about water?'

'There are two water tanks. One forward, one aft. Both empty. What we need is a new driveshaft for a Yanmar twelve horse, a desalination pump, and a wind generator. Or solar panels. And diesel fuel.'

'If it's here to be had, I'll get it,' said Argent.

'And some wire for the rigging.'

Argent frowned. 'Anything else?'

'There is one more thing,' I said. 'A boat needs a captain.'

'Does it, now?' Argent pulled his pistol from his belt, withdrew the magazine, checked the top round, and pushed it back into the grip with the flat of his palm.

I stood my ground. I did not want Francoise to see me buckle again. 'Do you know how to sail, Argent? How to navigate?' My voice was shaky, unconvincing.

Argent laughed. 'No, Captain. But you do.' He shoved the pistol into his belt at the small of his back and winked at Francoise. 'You two stay put,' he said. 'This time I mean it.'

'Where are you going?' said Francoise.

'To get that stuff we need.'

'We stay together,' I said.

'Look, Teach. If we are going to do this, we are going to need food, water, tools, like you said. I'm going to find out what there is, and who has it. And then I'm going to make sure we get it, one way or another.'

'Please Derek,' said Francoise. 'You heard what Saint John said. If you get caught—'

'I'm not coming to bail you out, Argent,' I interjected. 'Again.'

Argent's face creased and he shook his head. 'I won't be long. You two get busy. Do as much as you can to get this thing ready to sail. Sounds like they haven't had a chance to go through her yet, find out what she's carrying. Do an inventory of what we've got.'

'We haven't slept for days,' said Francoise. 'And we're almost out of water.'

'The sooner we leave here the better,' he said, clambering into the Tahoe.

Francoise and I watched the truck disappear up the hill, a few lights flickering in the sea mist across the embayment, the church a grey shadow above, barely visible in the evening haze.

42

We moved methodically from bow to stern. I worked above deck, Francoise in the cabin. I could hear her rummaging below, opening and closing lockers, moving objects about the cabin.

What we discovered was a vessel prepared for an extended open-sea voyage. Saint John clearly was not yet aware of what he had salvaged. The forward storage holds were stocked with every kind of non-perishable food imaginable – things that we hadn't seen in months, years. The unrestricted plenty of another time, carefully packaged and labelled, then wedged neatly into every available space: UHT milk, tinned pears, fruit salad from Australia, peas, green beans, baked beans, tuna, anchovies, salmon, pate, sealed plastic containers of rice, flour, oats, lentils, salt, sugar, coffee, four-litre jugs of spring water, at least two dozen of them. In the main cabin holds we found candles, flashlights, batteries, a complete set of tools, motor oil, spare parts for the diesel engine, a hand pump, kerosene for the stove, a solar charger. The galley was fully stocked with kitchenware – basic, sturdy stuff – knives, pots and pans. Books lined the port shelf: Slocum, Chomsky, McCarthy, Dawkins, *Ocean Passages of the World*, Shakespeare. There was Melville, Marcus Aurelius, Dostoyevsky, Hardy, Tolstoy and Hugo. A man's ship, Francoise said, opening a battered copy of *All the Pretty Horses*. She ran the palp of her index finger along the handwritten inscription on the title page, tilted it so I could see: *For Daniel, November 1998, from your loving wife.*

An escape planned but never achieved.

We worked until dark. I managed to reconnect and tighten the stays and the shrouds. The roller furling system for the jib was smashed, but I cleared the wreckage so that we would be able to hank on the foresails by hand, the old way. I cut away the old vang and roped a new one, rigged a bosun's chair and inspected the masthead, ran new halyards. It wasn't perfect, but it would do. We couldn't motor, but we could sail.

By nightfall, Argent still wasn't back. I joined Francoise below, lit the kerosene lamp. A warm glow spread through the snug, wood-panelled cabin, lit up Francoise's face. Her eyes were red and swollen. Dirt streaked her cheeks. I sat beside her. She produced a tin of tuna, opened it, and handed me a fork. I stared at the pink flesh. She nodded for me to go ahead. I sank the tines of my fork into the meat and flaked back a chunk, raised it slowly to my mouth, cupping my hand under the fork to catch the dripping juice.

'Go on,' she said. 'Eat.'

But despite the hunger groaning inside me, I hesitated, sat there with the liquid dripping from the fork into my cupped palm.

'What's wrong?' she said.

I studied her face, sought to find an answer to her question. She hadn't eaten any of the tuna yet either, seemed to be waiting for me.

'It doesn't seem right.' It was the best I could come up with.

'I know. Eat.'

I put the fork into my mouth, closed my eyes, let the tuna melt on my tongue. Francoise took a piece, chewed. We finished the tin and then opened another, pulling out the flesh and shoving it dripping into our mouths, washing it down with long slugs from one of the jugs of spring water. We ate in animal silence, and afterwards we threw the empty tins over the side.

I explored the bilges, removing the access panels, lying on the floor, running the flashlight's beam along the inner hull, over the oily water that still had not drained away. Inside the aft bilge, tucked at arm's length atop one of the wooden ribs of the boat's frame, I found a sturdy plastic drybag about the size of a thick paperback. I pulled it out, dripping wet, smeared with oil. It was heavy, tightly wrapped. I unwound the tape, opened the bag, looked inside.

'What is it?' Francoise whispered.

I reached in and withdrew a roll of US one-hundred-dollar bills, a box of nine-millimetre shells, five magazines, and a handgun. It was an automatic, black, oiled and gleaming in the lamplight. It had *Made in Israel* stamped on the side.

'Now we're even,' I said.

Francoise was staring at me, eyes wide. 'Do you know how to use it?'

'I think so.'

'Have you ever used one before?'

'No.'

'Give it to me.'

She weighed the gun in the palm of her hand, pushed in one of the empty magazines, worked the slide a couple of times, and pulled the trigger.

'Where did you learn to use a gun?'

'In the war. They showed us how, in case.'

She opened the box of shells, slid one into the top of a magazine. Then she dropped the empty magazine from the gun, pushed in the loaded one, worked the slide back and let it snap forward. She sat there on the cabin floor and cradled the gun in her hands.

'Can we make it to South America in this?' she whispered.

I was staring at the weapon. I knew enough to understand that it was loaded and ready to fire. 'Yes. We could go halfway around the world in her if we wanted.'

She nodded. 'Will Derek come back?'

'Honestly?'

She nodded.

'No.'

'Did you see the way Saint John was looking at me?'

'Yes.'

'Do you really think Derek would betray us, after everything?'

'Yes,' I said. 'Without hesitation.'

'He says he has a place we can go. He wants me to go with him.'

'He's lying. Don't believe him for a second.'

She sat and watched me, not saying anything.

'Did you see the whale?' she said.

I nodded yes.

'How could we?' she groaned. 'How?'

'I don't have any answers.' I had long since given up trying to make sense of the decisions we had made, or indeed if any had been made at all.

'We didn't try hard enough.'

'Some of us didn't try at all.'

'At first, I tried, I really did. But the war ' She looked up at me, her eyes glassy with tears. 'It was too much. The weapons were so horrible, you have no idea. I just couldn't face it anymore. All those young boys...' She trailed off into silence.

She was right. I had no idea.

'An extermination,' she whispered. 'That's what this is. A third or more of everyone and everything, of every living creature, gone. And this is only the beginning. You know that don't you?' She raised the gun, and before I could stop her, she put the muzzle into her mouth.

'God, no,' I said.

She was looking right at me, her eyes wide, imploring.

'Don't, Francoise. Please.' I was shaking my head back and forth. 'You did a lot more than most of us.' As slowly as I dared, I reached up and put my hand over hers. She didn't stop me. 'Please, Francoise.' I could feel her shaking. 'Please don't. Don't leave me.'

She narrowed her eyes. A question.

'We can do this, together. Please, Francoise. I need you.'

She pulled the gun from her mouth, closed her eyes. 'My God,' she whispered. 'What have we done?'

Spin, Earth, Spin

Rain thunders on the roof, sweeps over us in thick Southern Ocean sheets. The storm started last night and has been raging ever since. Gale-force winds howl through the trees, shaking our handmade windows in their frames. My wife gives me a cup of tea, sits next to me in front of the fire. I slept poorly last night, bothered by a sore throat that I have tried to ignore but seems to have worsened since the storm began. I can feel it creeping down towards my lungs. She urges me again to rest, to take a break from the writing, which she knows is taking a toll on my strength. I tell her that I am feeling a bit better today, a lie she sees past right away. I tell her that it's not the years but the miles, an old joke we share more frequently now. Where has it gone, that unrelenting vitality that used to course through me like a deep, wide river? That sure flow of energy that I always took as a given. Get up, run twenty kilometres before breakfast. Days without sleep, piloting through rough seas. Cutting and hauling stone, building a house for my family, day after long day. All of it, lost to the spinning Earth.

She puts her hand on my forehead. You're running a fever.

It's nothing.

You must not swim. It is too cold. She takes my wrist in her hand, looks into my eyes. Your heart rate is up.

I'm anxious.

We all are.

Finish your tea and go to bed. I will be in soon to give you something to help you sleep.

I do as I am told, lie under the roof and listen as the storm gathers.

Spin, Earth, spin.

43

We worked late into the night, getting the boat as ready as we could. By three in the morning, Argent still hadn't returned. High tide would be sometime around dawn. That would be our first and only chance to sail on the ebb. With any luck, we could leave without him.

We sat in the cockpit under a starless sky and shared a cup of tea. A deep grumbling sound came to us. It seemed to be coming from the town, from somewhere up on the hill.

'Sounds like voices,' I said.

'A crowd.'

I stood and gazed across the darkened inlet towards the town. A faint red light painted the side of the church steeple.

'It looks like a fire,' said Francoise.

'No smoke.'

The sound came again, a surge of raised voices, cheering, as if we were standing outside a sports stadium, back when such trivialities still mattered.

'Argent's up there,' I said.

'He'll come back.'

'What happened, Francoise, back at the camp?' I'd been on the edge of asking her so many times but hadn't been able to work up the courage. I expected her to wave it away, but to my surprise she seemed to want to talk.

She told me how, not long after leaving me at the roadside, they'd encountered a makeshift roadblock and been forced to stop. A man had emerged from the darkness with an assault rifle aimed at their faces. They were taken to the camp, chained, and questioned. The men, four of them, had discovered Argent's case and after trying in vain to open it, had tried to get the combination from Argent. The gunshot I'd heard was a failed attempt to blow open the locking mechanism. They had made their collective intentions towards Francoise very clear.

'Derek told them that if they harmed me in any way, he'd kill them all,' she said.

'And he did.'

'He did.'

'What about the other one, the one who left?'

'They argued among themselves. About me.' She swallowed hard. 'The one who left was younger. He insisted that they tell Saint John about us, about me. He must be here by now. I'm surprised Saint John hasn't put it all together yet. Maybe he's playing for time. I don't know.'

'And now Argent is up there, alone. Maybe that's what all that cheering is about. Maybe he's selling us out right now.'

'He saved me back there.' It was dark and I couldn't see her face, but I knew that she was crying. 'And then you did.' She took my hands in hers. 'Is this really what it has come to? Has civilisation finally vanished?'

'Argent seems to hope it has.'

'Look at that poor girl, Sue Frank. And Saint John's slave woman. We're living in the Dark Ages, for God's sake. Well, I can't live in this world. I can't live as chattel. I won't. Do you understand?'

I nodded. Yes, I did understand.

Francoise went below to get some sleep. I lay in the cockpit, head propped against the bulkhead, and watched the sky lighten over the Gulf. A bank of low cumulus clouds pearled the horizon. Platform fires danced in the distance. It was almost beautiful. It *was* beautiful. It had no right to be, but it was – as if nature, despite the unspeakable harm that had been done to her, was simply unable to stop being beautiful.

I closed my eyes a while, tried to sleep. When I awoke, Francoise was asleep on the saloon berth under a wool blanket, her arm tucked under her head, knees gathered up to her chest.

Boats bobbed at anchor in the bay. A haze of smoke drifted over the town under a grey dawn sky. Argent still wasn't back.

The sun came, illuminating the damage of the world. Soon, Saint John would return and inspect his property. And when he did, we would lose it all. Our hopes for survival were here, in the womb of this vessel. It was time. We had to leave now. We had to get the boat into the water, despite the damage, rig up the foresail and head to sea before they had a chance to follow.

High tide wasn't far away now, judging from the industrial jetsam lining the shore. The wind was fair. We wouldn't have another chance until late afternoon. I clambered down the ladder and inspected the trestle. It was wheeled. All we had to do was push it to the skidway, about ten metres away, and gravity would do the rest. Francoise and I could probably do it alone.

By now I was starting to think – hope – that Argent had either been caught or had decided to go his own way. More likely, he'd sold us out altogether. I wasn't going to wait around to find out. I swung down into the cabin.

'Wake up, France,' I said, kneeling to the bilge plate, reaching in, grabbing the bag and pulling out the handgun.

Francoise sat up, blinking the sleep from her eyes. 'What are you doing?'

I opened the box of shells and loaded ten rounds into a magazine, pushed it into the handle as I'd seen Francoise do. I'd never used a gun before, but how hard could it be? Point and shoot.

'Get up. We've got to leave. Grab two of the white sheets – ropes – with the blue threading from the forward starboard locker, and the big blue sail bag. Get them ready on the forward berth and open the hatch. Then come down and help me push this thing into the water.'

Francoise disappeared forward. I slid down the ladder and walked forward and pulled out the chocks holding the frame's wheels in place.

Francoise was down now and joined me at the stern. 'Are we ready? Do we have everything we need?' she croaked, still half asleep.

'We don't have a choice, Francoise. We'll have to make do.'

'What about Derek?'

'He took the truck and his case. He's not coming back. This is our only chance.' I braced my shoulder against the frame. 'Now push.'

Francoise leaned to the frame. The frame creaked and moved an inch, and then ground to halt. Something was blocking the wheels. I ran to the front of the trestle and kicked a stone out from under the camber of one of the front wheels. It didn't help. After fifteen minutes we had moved the boat less than a metre. It was too heavy, the wheels too rusty. Slack water was near. We were running out of time.

Up in the town I could see a group of people on foot moving up the hill towards the church. A car trundled past them in the same direction, and then another, drawn to the steeple, its Baptist clapboard bathed in low-angle morning light. And then, on the land breeze, came the sound of bells.

It was Sunday. It seemed a long time since I had even considered what day it was, let alone what month. Did it even matter anymore, with nowhere to be, the future a blank? Sunday. If Saint John really was the pastor here, then he would be in the church right now, surely, preparing to deliver the sermon to his lost congregation.

A rap on the hull broke my reverie. I spun in the direction of the noise and crouched down and looked under the hull. Someone was standing on the other side of the boat. Another rap on the hull, open palm on wood, two, three times. I pulled the gun from my pocket, held my breath. I could see Francoise's red sneaker-clad feet immobile at the stern. The church bells pealed, calling the flock.

If it was Saint John standing there, or one of his men, he had come for his boat. He would inspect his salvage and find the treasure it contained, and any chance of a deal would be gone. Perhaps if we stayed hidden somehow, he would go away, and we would be able to get the boat to water in time. But hide where? He was too close, and it was now very clear that we had shifted the boat. We were thieves. Shame swept through me like wildfire, surprising in its intensity, ridiculous.

I scanned the open ground beyond where the man stood. He appeared to be alone. If there was another option, I abandoned it when I saw one boot rise and step slowly towards the stern. The trailing boot remained planted, did not pivot in the turn. The motion looked awkward but prevented disturbing the gravel underfoot. After a moment, the trailing foot rose and came down gently onto the gravel without sound. Francoise still had not moved. Because of the curve of the hull, I couldn't see her or signal to her without stepping out and away from the hull.

I rose from my crouch, ducked under the bow and pivoted sternward, taking the stranger by surprise from behind, surprising myself in the process. 'Don't move,' I said, pointing the gun at the man's back.

He spun around to face me. 'There you are,' said Argent. 'Jumpy this morning?'

I let the gun hang in my hand and doubled over. After a while I caught my breath. 'I thought you'd gone,' I said. Hoped.

He flashed a half-smile, looked at the trestle and down to the water's edge. 'Launching so soon?'

'We thought you'd gone your own way. You said you'd be back in a few hours.'

'I said I'd be back. I'm back.'

'We need high tide to leave. That's soon. If we can get this thing into the water, we can go.'

Francoise was now standing just behind Argent. 'You should see what we found on the boat,' she said. 'Enough food for at least a month, water, tools, maps. Everything.'

'And a nice new nineteen-eleven,' said Argent, glancing down at the gun in my hand. 'Nice piece.'

'Now we're even.'

He smirked. 'Too bad it's not loaded.'

I looked down at the foreign object in my hand.

'You forgot to cock the slide,' he said. 'That chambers the round, sets the hammer.'

I pulled back the slide, let it go.

'There you go.'

I raised the gun again, pointed it at his chest.

He backed up a step. 'Be careful with that thing.'

'Like I said. We're even now.'

'Maybe,' said Argent. 'But we have other things to worry about.' He motioned with his chin up towards the church on the hill. 'Our friend Saint John the Baptist up there is far more than just a religious nutjob.'

'Revelations,' said Francoise. 'All that talk last night of Patmos and Woodworm and the seven angels is from the last book of the Bible, the words of John – the end of the world.'

'Well, he's making the most of it,' said Argent. 'I spent the night up there with him and his mob. They are in business. They make deals. They scour the coast for salvage, ships, cargo, people, whatever they can find.'

'We heard noise from up there,' said Francoise. 'It sounded like a football game.'

Argent shook his head. 'Hardly.' He made eye contact with Francoise. 'It was a public trial. More like a mob lynching. The young one. The one who left the camp.'

Francoise gasped.

'He was accused of abandoning his post, of allowing the three others to be killed.'

'But he left before you...' Francoise cut herself short.

'He changed his mind, went back. He got there after we'd left. Found them dead. That's why he got here after us.'

'So, they know you did it,' I said.
'No, Teacher. They know *you* did it.'

The Aegean of My Youth

I am on an island. It is hot. The sky is blue. The blue of my youth. As I climb, the Aegean spreads out before me like a sea of diamonds. I am thirsty, so thirsty. Near the summit is an old monastery. Drawn to it, I enter the garden, the wrought-iron gate rusted from its hinges, the stone walls crumbled, the limestone worn, edges blunted. Centuries-old cypress trees, withered and brown, creak and groan in the wind. Toppled gravestones, the names of the dead long since eroded, whisper to me. The ground is ash, burned away. I walk up the path towards the main arch. The worm-eaten doors are open wide. Inside it is dark and cool, empty. Shafts of dusty light stream down from the high windows, illuminating a deserted nave. The worn flagstones are cool on the soles of my bare feet. I have been here before. When or how I cannot remember. In another dream perhaps, for this is surely a dream. I know I should leave this place, but I want to stay, to see that blue again, to feel it, but also to find the thing that is calling me, drawing me into the deep bowels of this place – a voice. I can hear it now, echoing through the stone beneath my feet. There is a door, heavy pounded metal and ancient oak, stone stairs leading down. The air grows cooler as I descend, heavy with moisture and must. Water is flowing somewhere below, I can hear its turbulence surging through the narrow passageway, buffeting the mortared blocks of stone. The voice comes again, clearer. Release me. Please. Still I descend. The stone is cold and wet. I pull my hand away, look at the moisture beading on my fingertips. Now I know that this is no dream. It is real. I emerge into an underground cavern, the roof high above in the darkness, invisible. I sense it only by the reflection of sound. A subterranean canal courses before me, stretching away into the darkness, the water surging over the stone. I fall to the ground, lie at the edge and put my lips to the water. I drink. The water is sweet, fresh, cold. I drink long, eyes closed. I can feel the water flowing over my tongue and down my throat, filling my withered cells. I open my eyes and look deep into the water, my lips still kissing the smooth surface. The water blisters slightly, wetting my face. I pull back. A face is staring up at me from just below the surface. Dark eyes, a wide grin, rows of sharp teeth, smiling at me.

44

I looked out across the remnants of the Holocene coastline, the sun ascendant over the Gulf. Argent had betrayed us, had come back to rub my face in it. I pointed the gun at his chest. I'd never killed anyone before.

Argent looked at the gun shaking in my hand. 'Relax,' he said. 'I've made a deal with them, bought us some time.'

'I don't believe you.'

'The kid was his son.'

'Which kid?'

'The kid they were accusing. The one who left the camp. They were going to execute him for deserting his post. The old man was going to do it himself. Can you believe it?'

'I'm long past disbelief.'

'Well, I prevented it,' said Argent, that curious smile of his creasing the edges of his mouth.

'How?'

'By telling Saint John what happened back at the camp. That I was one of the hostages, which was true. That they tried to open my case, which was true. That they beat me up, threatened to spit roast the girl. That they'd argued about her – his son insisting they take her back to Saint John, the others wanting to keep her for themselves – which is also true. I told him that it wasn't his son's fault. All true.'

'Except you made me the killer.'

He grinned wide. It was a practised smile, symmetrical, designed to show off his perfected teeth, two of which were missing now. 'Served my purposes.'

I tightened my finger on the trigger. 'You lying bastard.'

'Think about it, Teach. You're smart. Or you keep saying you are. If I'd told them it was me, what would they have done? They would have killed me, then come down here, killed you and taken Francoise here into slavery. You've seen what *that* looks like.' He paused, reached behind his back, drew his own gun. Before I could react, he dropped the magazine, caught it in his left hand, then worked the slide, ejecting an unspent round that he also caught in his left hand. 'This way, I tell them that I will deliver you, the killer, to them. They just need to give me some time to set it up. I made out that you were some kind of special-forces type, steal into camp, take on three guys all on your own, blow them all away. Made you out to be the devil himself.' He laughed that way he did. 'Shit, Teacher, they're scared as hell of you. Imagine that.'

'Jesus Christ,' was all I could manage.

'I bought us some time is what I did. So why don't you lower that gun?'

'You sold me out.'

He thrust his pistol into his belt. 'Think what you like, asshole.' He looked down at the gun shaking in my hand. 'You're not going to hit anything like that.' The way he said it you would have thought it was a sling shot or a water pistol that was trained on his chest. 'Push your right hand right up as high as it'll go against the grip safety – that curved thing at the back. That's it. And use two hands, for Christ's sake.'

I held the thing as he'd said but my anger was gone, replaced by something else. By now Francoise was with us. She stepped in front of me. I lowered the gun.

She turned to face Argent. 'There is no way that they will trade for this boat once they know what's inside.'

'I wouldn't be so sure,' said Argent. 'It's not the boat they're interested in.'

'I don't want to know,' she said.

I pushed the pistol into my trouser belt like I'd seen Argent do. 'How much time do we have? Slack water is in less than an hour.'

'That should be enough,' said Argent. 'Help me get this stuff aboard.'

Argent pulled the Tahoe up close to the boat and we unloaded the stuff. Somehow, here in the middle of nowhere, he'd managed to get most of what we needed. You had to hand it to the guy. He'd got diesel and water. The drive shaft he'd found was brand new, still in its original packaging. So were the solar panels. The rest was a chandlery of close-enoughs and wild guesses, items that could perhaps, with some work, be modified for their intended use. A grudging admiration lodged itself beside my hatred.

I set the driveshaft box on the ground near the sailboat's stern, grabbed the toolbox from the cockpit and set to work. Francoise and Argent started loading the water, roping the big, twenty-litre containers up onto the deck and stowing them below. Then they hoisted five jerry cans of diesel fuel aboard and funnelled them into the tanks. We worked without speaking as the sun climbed over the wasted coastline.

As the sun rose, so did the heat. And with the heat came the vapour, a smog of volatile hydrocarbons that choked the air and seared my lungs. Soon, I was covered in sweat. A thick benzene humidity clung to me like a sodden wool blanket, heavy and constricting. My eyes streamed. It was more than half an hour now since Argent had returned. The water in the estuary was calm, rainbowed with oil. Slack tide was close. We needed to go. I had managed to remove the old driveshaft, but I was struggling with the new one. My head was swimming, and it was hard to focus. I couldn't seem to align the bushings, and every time I thought I was close the assembly would slip out of place and I'd have to start over. Finally, on the fifth attempt, I managed to set the bushing. I needed a break. I tried to stand, but as I did my vision started to collapse. I dropped to my knees and pushed my head to the ground, trying to breathe.

Slowly, too slowly, I came around. I had to keep going. Soon it would be too late. I pushed myself up and went back to work. This time it went a lot better. It didn't take me long to set the new prop in place. I checked the assembly. It seemed good. The shaft spun freely and without any visible wobble.

When I emerged from under the boat, Argent was standing over by the Tahoe. From the back seat he grabbed the shotgun, his silver case, and the black bag he had taken from the marauders' camp, and put them on the ground. Then he levered up the vehicle's hood and with a deft flick of his wrist opened a switchblade. I watched as he reached in and pulled out clumps of wires and tubes and tossed them to the ground as if he were gutting a fish. He turned, looked back at me and grinned, then picked up the bag, the shotgun and the case and walked over to the boat.

'No way back now,' he said. 'Ready, Captain?'

I wiped my hands on the sides of my shorts and bladed the sweat from my eyes. 'We don't have a choice,' I said. 'We have to go now.'

'Right then,' he said. 'Let's do it.'

'Everyone push.'

We leaned into the hull, but even with three of us pushing, the trestle would not budge. Three times we tried, to no avail. The casters were seized.

'Hold on,' I said, scrambling up the ladder. I grabbed a hammer and a can of WD40 from the toolbox, jumped back down to the ground and bent to one of the casters. I applied the lubricant, let it seep in a moment, and then hammered at the housings, short hard raps that rang out across the bay like the peals of Sunday bells. 'Now try.'

We wedged our shoulders against the wood and pushed. This time the trestle budged a little, and then a little more. After a few minutes we'd managed to move it another metre, maybe a bit more. Not nearly enough. The tide had started to turn. We stopped, panting in the cloying air, then kept going. We crouched low, driving our feet into the gravel, pushing with all our strength. And then it was rolling, creaking over the plank-wood ramp, picking up speed. Then we were to the break in slope and the boat started to roll on its own and we stood back and watched it clatter down the ramp and crash into the water with a whoosh, the hull listing at first and then righting itself.

I looked back towards the village. A car was flying down the hill, trailing a plume of dust. Argent had seen it too.

I grabbed the bow line and paid out scope until the little boat was clear of the trestle and floating free. 'Okay,' I shouted, 'everyone on board. Quick.'

I waded into the warm water and moved towards the boat. The bottom fell off quickly, and soon I was chest deep. The chemicals burned my skin. I pushed off and started swimming towards the boat, trying to keep my mouth above the oily surface.

I was first aboard. The others followed. I pulled Francoise, dripping, up into the cockpit. She turned away, towards the gangway, murmuring thanks, peeling the shirt away from her chest. A second vehicle was careening down the hill.

I took my place behind the wheel. We were already moving, drifting oceanward with the ebbing tide. I turned the wheel to direct the bow towards the middle of the estuary, away from shore. Then I cinched down the wheel ratchet and jumped forward. From the foredeck I reached down into the open front hatch and pulled out two coiled sheets and the red sail bag I had asked Francoise to prepare earlier. Soon I had the big foresail flying. We were a couple of hundred metres from the launch point now, picking up speed.

Saint John's Cadillac reached the boat launch and slid to a stop in a crash of dust. Two other vehicles followed. When the dust cleared, I could see Saint John standing at the water's edge, waving his arms in the air. He was screaming. We could hear him clearly, his voice carrying on the land breeze that was blowing us out to sea. 'The girl is mine,' he kept saying.

'So that was the deal you made,' said Francoise, frowning.

'I had to make it worth his while.' Argent raised his hand to wave at the men on the shore.

'Don't, Argent, for Christ's sake,' I said. 'Any minute they'll start shooting at us.'

'Not yet they won't. They'll try to catch us first.' He looked at me, his eyes intense, strained with fatigue. 'He wants his breeding stock. How else is he going to repopulate a new world?'

Francoise shuddered visibly.

Saint John and his men were running to their cars now, tearing back up the hill. As the foresail filled, we picked up speed. Within minutes the cars reappeared further up the estuary, at the small dock. Men clambered into two low-slung craft tied to the wood-plank jetty.

'Boston Whalers,' said Argent. 'Their pursuit boats. This should be fun.'

All I could do was shake my head. This guy was truly crazy. He seemed to feed on conflict.

We were almost clear of the estuary now, almost to the Gulf. The sail was full, and there was that sound of the water rushing against the hull. We were going well, but there was no way we could outrun the speedboats with their powerful outboard engines.

'What are we going to do?' said Francoise.

'Just wait,' said Argent. He sat back in the cockpit and pulled a cigar from his jacket pocket, flicked a lighter and puffed smoke into the sail. He looked as if he was on a Sunday joyride.

Soon I had the main up. I urged the boat on, ratcheting in the big headsail with quick quarter turns on the winch handle. The boat was heeling over, and Francoise moved to the high side of the cockpit. The men at the dock were almost indistinguishable now, tiny specks.

A loud rip above our heads startled me. A neat hole bloomed in the sail, about the size of a dime. I could see the sky through it. And then, a fraction of a second later, the distant retort of a gunshot. I pushed Francoise to the floor of the cockpit and crouched low above her just as the teak planking below us splintered with a loud crack. I turned the boat so that she heeled over hard, putting the hull between us and the firing. Two more rounds split the air above us.

Argent had moved to the high side of the boat and was standing in plain sight, one hand clutching the backstay, the other waving his cigar in the air. 'Don't worry, babe,' he shouted. 'If they're shooting at us, it means they aren't chasing us.'

I brought the bow further into the wind. The boat heeled and Francoise was thrown against the low side of the cockpit bench. She winced in pain. We were so far over now that the water was boiling over the deck rail and we were staring right down into its oily depth. Another round cracked into the hull. I could feel the impact through the cockpit floor, hear the wood splinter. More rounds tore through the sail. Argent was laughing, oblivious. He stood against the railing, braying like a madman, taunting the men on the shore.

PART VI

Supplicants

Patterns

I close my eyes and listen to the falling snowflakes of a Bach cello suite. There are patterns everywhere, if we want to see them. Designs in nature's smallest creations, in the largest scatterings of the universe. In the ribs and sails of an insect's wing, the unique branching of the oldest oaks. It is there, hiding in plain sight, in the ever-changing sculptings of the sea and the rhythms of the sky, and yes, even in the flows and eddies of death and time and in the mysteries of human relationships.

Randomness is the illusion. It has taken me a long time to reconcile myself to this fact.

For most of my life, I could not see the patterns, and so I was blind. May could see them, I know now. Perhaps it was only on an intuitive, artistic level, but she could see them well enough to be able to translate them onto canvas. Perhaps that was why the chaos of the relocation and everything that happened after we were moved south sparked something inside her. She was seeing through the mayhem, making sense of it, connecting with it through both her poles. I still have one of the paintings she did there, the one of the riot. It's on the wall, near the door to the veranda. Every time I look at it, I shiver.

I have always been a determinist. Early on I thought that chaos, randomness, and entropy were the enemies. Pattern was logic. Logic was predictability. And in predictability was safety. Now I can see how wrong I was, and how that fundamental way of looking at the world prevented me from doing what I now know I should have done. All the patterns I could see were illusions. And the real patterns, the ones that mattered, were beyond my comprehension.

At the beginning, I was convinced – passionately sure – that we were connected at some fundamental level, as souls, as minds. Then as that feeling faded, I began to doubt whether it had ever been there at all. Now I know it was real, all of it. Those early morning walks up into the mountains, just the two of us, and all that as yet untouched glory spread before us as if it would last forever. But that is the nature of pattern, all pattern. There is no stability in it. It moves and changes, winds and meanders, and then comes on like a fury, only to abate again into a new and different type of calm. It is part of the camouflage. Mathematical catastrophe. The trick is to see through it.

45

Towards mid-afternoon the wind died. The Anthropocene coastline and the dead remnants of the barrier islands had long since vanished behind us, and all that remained was a sky empty of clouds and the desolate circumference of the horizon. We drifted in an endless slick of oil. It was hot, and without the breeze the air was heavy with hydrocarbons. I could feel my mind starting to drift.

Argent was sitting with his back to the cockpit bulkhead, eyes shielded behind reflective Ray-Bans, mouth crisped tight. Françoise had gone below, and I could see her feet at the end of the main cabin berth. I called to her to come back on deck. The vapours were heavier than air and would accumulate in the cabin. Her feet stirred a moment and then settled. There was no answer.

Argent looked up at me and hauled himself down the main hatch, appearing a few minutes later with Françoise tottering in his arms. He grinned up at me, almost comic now with his missing teeth, and pushed her up the gangway. She flopped down onto the cockpit bench. Her face was pale, her eyes narrowed against the sun. I pulled off my cap and was about to put it on her head when she wrenched herself around and stuck her head over the side. Her body heaved, and I could hear the splatter of vomit on oil and a moment later the acid odour of half-digested food. She lay like that for a while, hugging the deck, her head on her arms, panting in the heat.

I raised the binoculars and scanned the northern horizon, but there was only the string of abandoned oil-production platforms we had passed hours ago, rusting and derelict, tiny now in the distance, and the empty grey of the Gulf. I estimated we were some fifty nautical miles offshore, maybe more. With the mainsail up, I had poled the jib to catch whatever breath of wind there might be, but the sails flapped uselessly, and there was no wake whatsoever on the surface.

I left the wheel with rudder centred and cinched, took a deep breath, and went below to the galley. Dizzy, I opened the locker beneath the stove and found three new dish towels. I poured a quarter-litre of water from one of the small plastic bottles into the aluminium sink, dumped in an eighth of a box of baking soda, and soaked the cloths thoroughly in the mixture. The air above deck was foul, only marginally better than below. I handed a cloth to Argent and one to Francoise, folded mine in half and held it over my nose and mouth, sealing it as best I could against my skin. Francoise smiled thinly at me and pushed the cloth over her face. Argent did the same. It was an improvement – psychological as much as anything – but after a few minutes the vapours seemed to have grown in strength and I knew that if something didn't change soon, we would all be overcome.

I had not wanted to try the engine. I wasn't sure about the driveshaft and I feared that motoring through the slick would make things worse by stirring up the oil, releasing even more of the volatile compounds – but our options were few. I looked out across the water for any ripple or sign of wind and down at Francoise and Argent, their eyes closed, the wet rags smeared ineffectually to their faces. They looked asleep, unconscious, dead.

I reached into my pocket and pulled out the engine key and inserted it into the ignition. It would not fit. As I bent down to inspect the panel the blood rushed to my head. I staggered forward onto my knees and pushed out my free hand to steady myself. I stabbed the key into the panel, missing the lock hole altogether. My hand seemed impossibly large. I felt as if my fingers were made of foam. My head was spinning violently now. Francoise was out, a lick of drool spilling from the corner of her mouth. Argent's eyes were closed. I knew I was next. I looked up at the mast, the sails hanging limp in the dead air. Altitude – that was what I needed. Even a few metres would make all the difference. I managed to pull myself up and clamber to the top of the cabin housing. Even here the air was better. Holding the boom for support I made my way forward to the mast. Then I grabbed the main halyard in one hand and hauled myself up until I was standing on the boom.

Here, my head was a full three and a half metres above the surface. I sniffed at the air. My sense of smell was almost gone, but I could tell that here it was purer. Slowly, my head cleared a little. I wrapped my legs around the mast and using the halyard I shimmied up, gaining height, until I reached the spreaders. A breath of cooler air bathed my face, wicked the sweat from the back of my neck. I closed my eyes, dizzy still from the vapours. This far above the deck each yaw and roll of the hull sent me swaying far out over the water. I clung tight to the mast, gulping in lungfuls of clean air, trying to purge the toxins from my blood, knowing that if I fell, I would be overcome before I could make it back to the boat.

I stayed there a long time, looking down at the oiled surface of the sea, the boat swaying beneath me as the sun moved closer to the horizon. To the north, three orange flares spun long, vertical threads of black smoke from deepwater rigs that had exploded in the sudden sea-level rise and storms of four years ago. Neither the companies nor the government had had the resources to deal with the disasters, and ever since the fires had raged and the deep reservoirs had poured forth their epochal store of crude oil into the Gulf.

It had all happened so fast, this unravelling. In his letter, Lachie had described some of it. As the rains around the globe shifted poleward – Hadley cells behaving exactly as the models had predicted they would, exactly as I had taught my senior high-school students they would – crops failed everywhere. Prices skyrocketed. Tens of millions died of starvation in Asia and the subcontinent. The changing rainfall patterns threw already eroded terrestrial ecosystems into freefall. During the Repudiation, successive Brazilian governments had promoted widespread development of the Amazon. Roads and rail lines were cut, concessions offered, land cleared and burned. Big new mines were opened, and dams built. Then, in one fire alone, one-third of the remaining forest burned away, leaving a moonscape of ash and smouldering stumps. The Amazon, a perennial carbon sink, became a net emitter. The new Brazilian youth government, combating unrest and food riots, was powerless to fight it. It burned on and on, month after month, the TV screen a daily conflagration of unimaginable dimensions, the fires of hell itself, the smoke blanketing Calgary and most of North America, and even on some days London and Madrid. Then, as the war deepened, they just stopped reporting it. News was banned, replaced by official government announcements and a steady barrage of light comedy. As far as anyone knew, the fires were still burning now. We knew people were still starving.

I thought of Lachie, running through every word of his letter again in my head, still unable to come to terms with what it contained, the despair in his words. Lachie was tough and resourceful, I told myself. He would find a way through. He always had before.

From high on the mast, I looked down at my companions, unconscious in the tiny cockpit, adrift in a vast wasteland. And there was nothing I could do for them. Forgive them, I thought. Forgive us all. For we know not what we do.

Everything Was Possible

I haven't thought about Lachie for weeks, months even. Too long. God, I miss him.

I have never believed in God.

The evidence disproving His existence is everywhere. No supreme intelligence would ever have allowed this cataclysm, and if it had, as Kwesi believed, then it was no deity worthy of worship. And if the reward for a corporeal life of piety is eternal life in empyreal radiance, absolution of all sin, then nothing here matters anyway. No, Argont was right: religion is nothing but superstition, a weak-minded salve for the terrifying implacability of truth.

And the more I think about it, the more I suspect that this is exactly why we lost our way so badly, why history unfolded the way it did. The power of unrestricted social media for all gave us the ability to destroy truth. By forcing each of us into our own orbits of belief, no commonly held fundamental truths remained. And in that way, and very quickly, all was lost. We lost the ability to causally link action, or inaction for that matter, to consequence. Everything was possible, and so nothing was real. I think it was Tolstoy who said that, or something like it. We forgot that this life, here on Earth, is all we have, and all that matters.

And yet, as I did high above the deck of that boat so long ago, I close my eyes and pray with all my being for my son, out there somewhere, alone on the raging sea.

46

As evening approached the temperature fell. I shifted my weight, still perched on the spar high above the deck. To the East, a thin strip of the surface seemed to break away, flashing from hydrophobic mercury to rippled copper. I pulled myself to my feet, balanced on the spreader and peered into the distance. But it was gone. My eyes were offering wishful mirages just when I needed them most. I rubbed my eyes and stared hard. There was a definite interface, there, almost at the horizon. I watched it disappear and reappear in the haze, shifting, lengthening, widening and contracting again, until I was sure. It was the edge of the slick.

Charging my lungs with air, I slid down the mast and jumped into the cockpit. Francoise and Argent lay as I had left them, unconscious. This time the key slid home first time, and I flipped the switch, centred the throttle and pushed the starter button. The engine fired and then spluttered and died. I counted to ten and tried again. This time the engine took, roughly at first, belching smoke from the stern exhaust, rattling and pinging below my feet. I gave her some revs and the engine smoothed out. The splash of water aft told me the sea-water cooling pump was working. I let it idle a moment and then eased the engine into gear. We started to move. There was almost no vibration. I had done a better job than I had thought. It didn't take us long to get clear of the slick.

*

It wasn't until after dark that the wind came up. We had been clear of the oil for a few hours, and my dizziness had been steadily replaced by a brain-shattering toxic hangover. At least the air was cleaner now, and the wind was freshening quickly from the south. I raised the sails and trimmed up for the first tack, east-southeast by the green glow of the cockpit compass. The sheets creaked as they tightened under the load and the boat heeled into the tack, the water hissing past. I looked at my watch, hit the timer for a two-hour tack, cinched down the wheel and stood on the high-side rail and watched the little boat slide through the dark water.

Francoise and Argent were still sleeping off their chemical overdoses. They would feel like hell when they came around, but they were alive, breathing clean air now, their chests rising and falling steadily. I checked the compass heading and looked up into the spreading canvas. We were moving. The air was clean. We would be okay. But I still had the problem of Argent. Despite recent events, and though I had saved his life back there, and most probably he ours, I knew that he wouldn't hesitate to get rid of me as soon as it suited him. His designs on Francoise were as clear as those of that lunatic Saint John. I had to be careful, for both of us.

I found Argent's metal case stashed deep inside the starboard berth locker. The black duffel bag Argent had taken from the marauders' camp was there too. I picked up the case, examined its keypad and locks. From the way he'd described its treatment at the hands of the marauders, I had expected to see at least a few dents and scratches, but the polished surface was flawless. Whatever was inside was important enough for Argent to kill for. Inside the duffel bag, buried under a convenience-store aisle of brightly coloured junk-food packages, was a shotgun, four boxes of twelve-gauge shells, another handgun, several boxes of nine-millimetre ammunition, and a wad of old-issue American cash. I stashed the guns and ammunition in the forward berth under the storm sail, put the bag and the case back where I had found them.

By now my head felt as if it was splitting open from the inside. I fumbled for the medical kit, sprung the lid, spilled the contents across the chart table and to the floor. Nausea flooded my senses, pushed me to my knees. I searched through the strewn packages, managed to find a box of painkillers, punched the pink and white codeine tablets from their foil envelopes, swallowed them one after the other, drank down half a jug of spring water, sprawled there on the floor of that tiny cabin in the middle of a poisoned sea.

Francoise had been right. Luck had handed us this lifeboat just when we had needed it. I slipped the box of painkillers into my pocket – the others would need them when they finally came to. From the sound of the water moving over the hull, we had picked up speed. I went above. The wind was rising, and a noticeable swell had developed. Francoise and Argent were still wedged into the low side of the cockpit where I had arranged them.

I went back below and sat at the nav station and flipped on the chart-table light. It flickered and steadied. The batteries had charged. I opened the chart table and found the ship's log. Inside, Daniel Menzels' neat hand recorded their last voyage, just over two years ago. A shakedown cruise from Miami to Key West and back. *Providence* had been provisioned for a long voyage, probably south. Everything still had a pre-departure newness to it. But then some calamity had befallen them. Either they had not had a chance to get to the boat, and it had been unmoored and cast to sea in one of the recent hurricanes that had lashed the coast, or they had been swept overboard early in their journey, and *Providence* was left to wander the seas alone, a post-Repudiation *Marie Celeste*, until Saint John's men had found her. And despite everything, despite losing May and not knowing where my son was, or even if he was alive, and despite the wreckage all around, I knew then that I wanted to survive, to live, to hope for something better, some chance to make things right again, even in just the smallest way. Aloud, I thanked Daniel and his wife for their foresight.

Suddenly, the bow pitched up, held for a moment, and then crashed down the lee of a wave. I steadied myself and swung up into the gangway as a gust of wind hit the sails, heeling the boat over momentarily so that the rails were awash. I looked out across the lonely darkness of the Gulf. The wind was rising and had backed to the southwest. The swell had grown and was now overlain with a chop that thudded against the hull. A storm was coming.

47

I could tell that Francoise had no idea where she was. She sat for a long time, disoriented and groggy, looking out into the night, the wind whipping her hair. She closed her eyes and slumped her head to her knees. Later, she described to me her profound shock at the ferocity of the storm. Slanting rain stung her eyes. Knifepoints of pain twisted in her brain. The scream of the wind through the rigging deafened her.

With each wave the ship was pitched up, up towards the screaming heavens, to tremble there a moment at the crest so you could look out at the torn surface of the ocean stretching away as far as you could see, until the wave was past and you were falling, down in gut-hollowing free-fall with the sea towering all around until the bone-crunching impact as the bow disappeared down into the black water, and for that eternity you believed with all your being that the ship would be swallowed whole, that there was simply no possible way that it could ever survive such a maelstrom, until finally she struggled free, shedding that burial weight of water in silver cascades as you were lifted up again to reach the next crest to do it all over again.

She had not expected any of it: the violence of the water, the way it wrenched the boat like a rat in a terrier's jaws, the noise, the malevolent impersonal fury of it, the blackness of the shroud that covered the world. I'd been in storms before. But never anything like this.

Argent was just coming to when a huge wave hit the boat. Half awake, he was thrown against the lifelines and toppled back into the cockpit. Francoise scrambled over to help him, reaching him just as another wave hit. Water flooded the cockpit, and she was knocked sideways. I reached out for her, helped her up. Then I handed them each a life jacket. Once she had put hers on, I tied a length of line around her waist and made it fast to one of the cleats, then handed another rope to Argent, signalled him to do the same. He was in bad shape, reeling, sodden.

Another wave broke over the cockpit, sending Francoise crashing down on top of Argent. The cockpit was full of water and for a moment they were gone. Then they reappeared, coughing up water. The boat yawed violently.

Argent stared up at me, wild-eyed. 'Where are we going?' he shouted over the gale.

I pointed astern. There was just enough diffused moonlight to reveal a surface in turmoil, waves whipped to enormous heights, bigger than I had ever seen or imagined.

'Away from that,' I yelled.

Argent grabbed the wheel frame, pulled himself up and looked at the compass. 'We need to go southeast, goddam it. This takes us to fucking Mexico.'

We held tight to the frame as the boat slid down the back of a wave.

'Are you insane?' I shouted.

'Mexico is fucked. We can't go there.'

'I'm trying to keep us alive,' I yelled. 'Heading doesn't matter now. Weather does. Sit down and hold on.'

Another wave twisted Argent to the cockpit floor, still clutching the steel tube frame of the wheel mount. He pulled himself back to his feet, muscles straining, but Francoise pulled him back. She was soaked, her hair running in sodden shivers across her face. 'Teacher knows what he's doing,' she shouted.

'You owe me,' Argent spluttered. 'Without me you'd be back there having Saint John's babies.'

'I don't owe you anything.'

He grabbed her wrist, squeezed it hard. 'You ungrateful little bitch. Who do you think bought this boat, sabotaged their Whalers?'

'Leave her alone,' I screamed over the wind. 'So help me Argent, let go of her right now.'

Argent looked up at me, still holding her wrist.

'Or you'll what?'

She glared at him. He glared back a moment, and then suddenly the anger was gone, and he bent forward just as a stream of vomit spewed from his mouth over the cockpit floor. He doubled up, gasping for breath.

'You're seasick, Argent,' I yelled. 'Probably high from the chemicals too. Go below. You need to lie down. Please.'

'We are going the wrong way,' he said, pushing her away. 'This is not the plan.' He jammed the heel of his hand into my chest and grabbed the wheel, wrenching it hard to starboard.

The boat yawed violently. Argent had put us beam to the weather and now we were completely exposed. The next wave knocked the boat over onto its side, sending Argent and Francoise overboard.

48

I hung on to the wheel, my feet dangling in the water. The boat wallowed on its beam, the cockpit half underwater, the mast parallel to the boiling surface of the sea. I could see the two lines still cleated into the cockpit, but no sign of Argent or Francoise. The waves, if anything, were getting bigger. They pounded us again and again, shaking the little vessel to its core, burying us in thick, heavy water. Time seemed to slow. No. It *did* slow. Individual raindrops moved past me, met the surface of the water. The mast spreaders dipped in and out of the waves. Lightning sheeted the horizon, illuminating the surface of the sea so that I could see all the way to the edge of the world. And then suddenly we were lifted high into the air, and for a moment it was as if I were weightless, floating there above the cockpit, hanging on to the wheel, knowing that if I let go, I too would be lost. I knew that the boat should right itself, that the weight of ballast in the keel should eventually bring her back and that all I had to do was hold on, hold on, but for a terrifying moment it was if all that I knew to be true, the certainties of mass and gravity and moment, had abandoned us. And I remember thinking how small we were, how utterly insignificant in the face of this rage. This indifference.

But slowly, *Providence* came good.

The cockpit drained. As the storm jib caught the wind, we gained some speed. I set us head to wind to protect us a little, backed the jib, locked the rudder. The boat shuddered as another wave hit us. A wall of water crashed over me. I reached for Francoise's line, started pulling. She was down there somewhere. I could feel her clawing for the surface, the line shuddering as she fought. I kept pulling, reeling her in, the weight of her there in my hands, burning through my shoulders. And then suddenly the line went slack, hung there in my hands limp and dead. She was gone. I shouted out for her, scanned the boiling surface all around me.

And then she was there, bursting to the surface, gasping for breath.

My heart restarted. I guided her to the stern, pulled her aboard. She looked around, dazed, shivering. 'Where's Derek?'

I grabbed Argent's line, hesitated.

'Pull him up,' she gasped.

I stood there, the line in my hands.

'What are you doing?' she said. 'Pull him in.'

I started bringing in line. But there was nothing there. The rope was slack.

'He's gone,' I said. Part of me hoped he was gone. A big part. She knew it. I stopped pulling, stood there looking at her, the rope dead in my hands. We have talked about it since, Francoise and I, that delay. For the first time in my life, I was absolutely prepared to cause the death of another human being.

'You will be just like him,' she said, grabbing the rope. She started pulling.

I watched her struggle with the line, the storm spinning around her. A lifetime passed, a nanosecond. It was as if everything had stopped, had started to go backward. Time's arrow was broken, its law repealed. Every manner of thought hurtled through my brain, an ataxia of every for-and-against I have ever considered. She is not strong enough. He is too heavy. She is good. He is evil, will kill me if he gets the chance. Life is fleeting. Death is everywhere. Slavery has returned. God has abandoned us. May is dead. Sun. Stars. Graves. Dolphins. Guns. Mountain forests. Delhi. Kazinsky. Smith, those lips, those yellow cat's eyes. Famine and murdrum and snow and every kind of cold. Dark fission clouds heavy with atomised cities. Sleet and sun, unrelenting heat. A beating heart, a gull's wing. Pain in blades and arcs, filling deep ocean trenches. Love and loss, and surely after a hundred thousand years of history, we should all have known better, known more.

I grabbed the rope and started pulling.

Time resumed.

Then the weight came on and I knew he'd been sent deep. I hadn't had time to size the line properly, there was far too much slack. We pulled together. Hand over hand, shoulders straining, slowly, we pulled him in. When he reached the surface, his eyes were closed and for a moment he bobbed there in the wind-whipped spume, his skin as grey as the water surrounding him. I thought he was dead. And then his body convulsed, and he opened his mouth and spewed out a stream of grey bile. Gasping for breath he started flailing towards the boat. We hauled him aboard. His leg was broken and there was deep cut in the back of his head.

This time, he went below without a word, leaning on Francoise.

For You

When I wake it is still dark and I am holding on to the fragment of a dream. I am alone and I know that something is missing, something irreplaceable and utterly unique, never to come again.

My throat is not so sore this morning, and the headache that plagued me all night is gone. I throw my coat over my shoulders and walk to my desk. The rain has come, as Liberty said it would. The heart of the storm can't be far behind.

I settle in, start to write. It goes well. I get carried away. After a while, I stop and re-read what I have written. The sun has risen, and the rain is falling harder now. I line out a sentence I don't like, another. There is always a better phrase, and you must leave space for the reader.

Later, after I have finished for the day, Lewis comes over. He leaves his hat and coat at the door, palms the rain from his beard.

How are you, Papa?

Doing better today. How's Mandy?

Good. Ready.

Don't worry. Your mother is the best doctor I know.

I could say something about that, he says with that smile of his.

I smile too.

I'm not worried.

Good.

He looks past me, at my journal still open on the desk.

Still writing your story?

Getting close to the end now.

How will you know when you're done?

I guess that will be when I've said all I need to say.

Makes sense.

It's for you. You and your brother. And your little ones.

Anything in there we haven't already heard? He smiles at me.

A lot.

He considers this, nods, the smile lingering in his eyes.

Will you read it when it's done?

Sure, Papa. Of course. He touches me on the shoulder. Got to go now. Taking Cass and Star to the upper paddock.

Okay, son.

I watch him wind his way back up the hill in the rain.

49

When she stuck her head up from the gangway, hours later, a fine rain was falling. I was still at the wheel, had stopped counting the hours. The wind had fallen off and veered. Wispy cirrus clouds feathered the sky. The storm had passed. We were absolutely alone, and I had no idea where we were.

'Water in the cabin,' she said. 'Lots of it.'

'How much?'

She chopped at her shin with the blade of her hand.

'And Derek's in bad shape. I set his leg, sewed his head and stabilised him, but he's lapsed back into unconsciousness.'

I started the bilge pump, let it run. Francoise made us hot chocolate. We sat side by side in the cockpit and sipped, watching the sky clear.

After an hour, the water level in the cabin was still rising. The more water we took on the deeper we sat and the slower we went. The pump was running at full speed. I checked the seacocks, any of the other obvious sources of leakage, but they all appeared to be sealed up tight. The batteries would give us another hour of pumping at most, but after that we would soon be dead in the water. We could start up the engine to charge the battery, but the water was already lapping at the cylinder heads. I couldn't risk it. We would have to deploy the solar panels Argent had conjured up in Ephesus, connect them to the battery, then one way or another, find the leaks and plug them, and do it fast.

While I set up the solar panels, Francoise began bailing. She tied a length of line to the handle of a plastic bucket and for the next hour she stood in the cockpit pulling up bucketfulls of seawater and dumping them over the side, one after the other. After a while, the batteries died and the pump rattled to a stop, its reassuring hum replaced by the silence of a thousand miles of ocean. Francoise glanced up at me, her face set hard. Sweat poured from her face, drenched her arms and torso. I tried a smile, as much to encourage myself as her, and she flashed back something that might have been a question, or a doubt unresolved, and went back to work, hauling up the water as quickly as she could, grunting as she heaved each bucketful overboard.

I got the panels connected and took over with the bucket. Slowly, we were making progress. The water level in the cabin was dropping.

Francoise rested a while in the cockpit, then went below to check on Argent. After a while she reappeared and reported that his fibula was broken just below the knee – a bad fracture – and he had suffered a severe concussion. He was still unconscious but was breathing regularly. Once he had murmured something, as if in a dream, but he had not stirred since.

Towards mid-afternoon, we were foaming along in a light breeze under a strange turquoise sky windrowed with puffy white clouds. The sea was calm, all traces of last night's storm gone. After a couple of hours of bailing and pumping we had lowered the water level in the cabin considerably, but I had still not been able to find the source of the leaks.

With the immediate danger past, I opened one of the lockers and brought out a coiled line, tied one end to a stern cleat, flipped the other end through the life ring, fastened it with a quick bowline and tossed it overboard in a long arc. Soon the orange life ring was bobbing along behind us like a fishing lure. I stripped down to my shorts, grabbed a swimming mask and set *Providence* hove to. Soon, we were nodding a slow back-and-forth course into the wind, almost stationary.

'Take the wheel, Francoise,' I said. 'Just hold her here. I'm going overboard to inspect the hull. If anything changes, just shout.'

It didn't take me long to find them. After the sludge of the Gulf, the water here was clear and pure, cool on my skin. I stayed in longer than I should have. I don't know how long. A long time.

When I clambered back on board, I felt better than I had in days, weeks. I stood and let the breeze run cool across my body, felt the water drip from my limbs. I could see Francoise staring at me. Later, she told me how surprised she'd been to see me like that, so thin and pale, skin and bone, so unlike Kwesi.

'Three holes,' I said. 'Pretty close together, just below the cockpit, portside. Bullet holes.'

Her eyes widened a moment. 'Can you fix them?'

If we kept *Providence* on a beam reach with the wind over the port rail, we would be able to keep that area clear of water long enough to jam a couple of plugs in. 'Saint John may have been crazy, but he was right about one thing – wood is better than fibreglass.' I stowed the mask, pulled in the life ring. 'How's Argent?'

'He won't be very happy when he comes to.'

'Do you believe him?' I said, towelling myself dry. 'About this place he has?'

'Yes,' she said. 'I do.'

'Has he told you where it is?'

'Just that it's south, somewhere in Central America.'

'Do you want to go there?'

'Do you?'

'I don't know.'

'Do we have anywhere else to go?'

'If you put it that way.'

She was standing close to me now, just the wheel separating us. The breeze blew her hair in long streams about her face. Sun blushed her cheeks. The clean air was doing her good.

'Derek said something about the riot,' she said, as if she had been holding on to this for a long time, waiting for the right time to tell me.

I waited for her to continue.

'The demonstration was a diversion,' she said. 'He organised it that way from the beginning, as cover. He had a way out, but something went wrong.'

I thought back to the mayhem of that morning, the dying man in the alleyway with his phone and his gold coins and his gunshot wound, and Argent disappearing up onto the rooftop. 'He told you that?'

'When I was setting his leg.' She looked into my eyes a moment and I knew she was thinking about Kwesi.

'It doesn't surprise me one bit.'

'Why on earth would he tell me that?'

'Don't listen to him, France. He's trying to manipulate you, mess with your mind.'

She considered this a moment. 'He was in a lot of pain.'

I couldn't believe that she was still defending him. 'Let's get to plugging those holes,' I said, turning away, hoping she couldn't see the anger in my eyes.

We put *Providence* into a steady broad reach. Francoise took the wheel, and I went below. I found the holes pretty quickly. Two bullets had ripped through the planking just forward of the engine and lodged into a main spar. Another had driven into the engine mount, narrowly missing the block. I dug them out, three little hardened points of metal. In one of the toolboxes, I found a series of wooden plugs of various sizes. I mouthed thanks to Daniel Menzels again as I trimmed the plugs and then hammered them home. With a bit of caulking, it wasn't long before the cabin was dry.

*

Two hours later, as the sky began to darken, we went below together to check on Argent. He lay as Francoise had left him, on his back, mouth slightly open, eyes closed, arms folded across his chest. She sat beside him on the edge of the berth, and I watched as she lifted his head and checked the bandage and then dripped some water from her bottle onto his tongue. Black and grey wire stubbled his chin and jaw; his lips were thin and cracked by the sun. I noticed that his lashes were very dark and thick. His eyes opened.

'Derek,' she said.

He grabbed her arm. 'Don't cross here.'

'Don't cross where,' she said. 'Derek? I don't understand.'

'It's ready. Everyone has been paid.' His voice cracked like those dried-out plains I'd run through to rescue him.

'Derek?'

'The bank.'

'Rest,' she said.

'Belize,' he whispered, reaching up and squeezing her arm. 'That's where we have to go.'

She held her breath, put her ear to his mouth.

'The sanctuary. The Maya Mountains.' He exhaled and released his grip.

'Derek,' she whispered, but his eyes were closed.

And all the time I was thinking: so much easier to end a life than save one.

Holding On

The storm rages with a savagery born of decades-long forcing. The big trees outside our bedroom window groan and creak, bent by the gale. Rain pelts the windowpanes. Water floods the gutters, streams from the eaves, chokes and gullies its way down the hillside to pool debris-thick in the swales behind the beach. In my fever I imagine swollen torrents eating away the rock and soil beneath our feet, scouring out huge, gaping voids, uprooting trees and toppling the big rocks that anchor our cove, carrying them away to the sea. It is then that I see Kweku. He is clinging to the branch of a mighty gum tree that holds desperately to the cliffside. I call to him, reach out in the darkness, but he cannot hear me. A bolt of lightning splits the night, and for a moment everything is lit harsh and blue, the stone walls, the window curtains Francoise sewed from scraps of children's clothing, the driftwood side table Lewis fashioned for us when he was ten, our copy of Herodotus there beside me, and I know that Kweku is still out there somewhere, riding the storm alone, and that it was my fever that transported him to me. I pick up my notebook and pen, write a while, write this.

I am still writing when Francoise appears at the door.

You called out.

Sorry. I was dreaming.

It is the fever. She disappears, returns a few minutes later with a mug of tea. Drink, she says. This will help.

I sit up, mouth thanks, drink, wince at the bitterness of it.

One of Liberty's remedies.

I nod, take more.

Lewis has been keeping watch, she says, her hand cool on my forehead. Still nothing.

He's holding on.

Yes.

So am I.

Good. She takes my free hand in hers. You can greet your new grandchild soon.

When?

Any day now. Mandy's doing well.

How is Lewis?

Worried. For everyone.

That's Lewis.

A worrier. Like his father. She smiles.

Do you remember the storm, on Providence, *when we almost lost* Argent?

Her smile disappears. Is that what you were dreaming about?

No.

She glances at my notebook. You were writing it.

Yes.

She looks at me a long time, staring into each of my eyes in turn. I know why you are doing this, she says. I really do. And I understand. But you need to leave it for a while, my love. You need to get better. Then you can go back to it.

50

It was just before sunset when I saw the gull.

At first, I wasn't sure it was a bird at all, it had been so long since I had seen any living wild thing. It soared high above us, gulf-streaming along on invisible thermal currents, tracking our course. With a flick of its wings, it dropped down until it was just off the stern, its breast snowdrift white, the eye keen in its black mask, the wings powerful, sublimely engineered. I watched the gull as it bore in and then stood off, sometimes abeam, its head crooked towards us, watching us, sometimes falling back, neck craned towards the surface, watching for any jetsam we might release, then gaining altitude again, finding the warm rising air.

I cinched up the wheel and grabbed one of the leftover pancakes from the galley and climbed back into the cockpit. As I crimped off a piece of the pancake, the gull drew closer. He was just astern now, almost level with the boom, watching me. I tossed the piece of food high into the air. The gull swooped in, flaring his wings to a stall, caught the morsel cleanly in his beak and gobbled it down in one go. Francoise beamed in delight as the gull skimmed the surface and regained position astern. He was watching us intently now, a survivor where there were few, one who had learned to scavenge among the wreckage without ever becoming any less wild.

'You are beautiful, aren't you?' Francoise said to the gull.

I tossed out another piece of pancake. The gull caught it smoothly, without braking this time, and swooped back astern, closer now so that we could see the fine detail of its plumage, the soft stratocirrus grey of the flight feathers, the red circumference of the coal-black eye and the small nick in the lower beak, some healed wound. The bird was watching us intently now, watching the rest of the pancake.

'Isn't he magnificent?' she asked, smiling, her hair streaming in the breeze. In that moment, she looked happy.

She looked at me, gazed into my eyes a moment, and turned back to the gull. I threw the last bit of food, and the gull snapped it up.

'Come back tomorrow and we'll give you more,' said Francoise.

The gull held on for a time, tracking the boat as we hissed towards the darkening horizon, until finally, perhaps sensing that its luck had run out, it drifted off, gained altitude, and disappeared towards the setting sun.

We were making good progress. Over a hundred and twenty nautical miles today, I figured. The plugs I'd driven into the hull were holding, for now anyway, and the cabin was dry. The solar panels were working, charging the batteries. With a day of sun tomorrow they would be at full charge. I had patched the bullet holes in the Genoa, three in all, sitting down with needle and palm, the old-fashioned way, stitching over squares of canvas.

Francoise was below, busy in the galley. Soon the smell of garlic and onions was wafting topside, incredible. From the wheel I watched her working, her long hair braided up, the back of her neck sunburnt a deep ochre, one hand on the frying pan handle. She was humming to herself. I didn't recognise the melody, but it was gentle, a children's lullaby perhaps, and as the sun sank into the sea, I thought that I could see a tinge of blue haunt the sky like a childhood memory, and for a moment I forgot what had brought us here and who was missing. But then it all came back, and I cursed myself for my contentment.

We ate in silence, sitting in the cockpit side by side, tin plates balanced on our knees. She had made spaghetti in tomato sauce laced with garlic. I couldn't remember ever enjoying a meal so much. Afterwards she took the plates down to the galley and brought up two steaming mugs of sweet tea. We sat watching the sky darken, hands wrapped around the warm mugs, the boat's phosphorescent wake spooling out behind us like the plotted course on an empty map.

'*Providence* is stocked for a family of four,' said Francoise. 'Man, woman, two children under ten. You can tell from the clothing aboard. I wonder what happened to them. I hope they're alright. I feel as if I know them.'

'There is a copy of Herodotus on the bookshelf down there.'

'And Maupassant and Proust, and lots of Dr. Seuss. I loved those books when I was a little girl. That was how I learned English.'

It told you something about a person, the books they travelled with. I let off the main a little.

'How far is it to Belize?'

'A thousand nautical miles. Maybe more.' I still wasn't exactly sure where we were.

'Did you hear him?' she whispered. 'The sanctuary in the mountains. The bank.'

I nodded in the darkness, checked the compass. One five zero. On this heading, at this speed, in ten days' time we would either run straight into Cuba or the Yucatan peninsula. Belize lay south of there, through the two-hundred-mile gap between the two, just around the corner. That was a lot of water.

'My son—' I heard myself say before cutting short, my throat tightening.

Francoise waited a time, then said: 'Tell me.'

I swallowed hard. 'Lachie told me that the government's experts were saying that certain parts of the equatorial territories may have fared better. The climate models always predicted that the poles would heat up most, that the mid-latitudes would dry out, and that the tropics, in some places at least, would be less hard hit, especially at higher elevations, in the mountains. Lachie told me that the government had intelligence that supported this, although the equatorial countries were trying to downplay it, as you would expect, making a lot of noise about crop failures and food shortages, trying not to attract the attention of northern powers.'

'Argent's story makes sense then.'

'Some.'

And then after a time she said: 'Can we sail a thousand miles?'

'In this? Absolutely. Even during that storm, we were never in danger.'

'It didn't feel that way to me.'

'It never does when you're in it.'

'Then we can go anywhere.'

'The boat's not the limiting factor. It's us.'

'We have enough food for a month more, at least,' she said. 'It makes me feel guilty.'

I reached out for her hand. She didn't pull away. I turned to face her. In the darkness I could see the whites of her eyes, the flash of her teeth. I put my arm around her waist, pulled her to me. It didn't feel awkward. We stayed like that for a while, the cool sea air, so much purer now, caressing our faces. And then she drew closer, and we sat together and listened to the sound of the water moving against the hull for a long time.

Later, I woke from a dream. I was lying on the cockpit bench, a cushion under my head, one of Daniel's jackets zipped up under my chin. Francoise was asleep below, tucked into the main saloon berth. *Providence* was secure, trimmed nicely in a quartering breeze on a calm sea. Above me, dark shapes progressed across the heavens: the mast, the shrouds, the ghostly mainsail. At first, it didn't register – it had been so long. Then I saw it, just abeam the masthead, something I hadn't seen in years. A star.

51

It was the star that did it. Just that few minutes was enough, lying there in the cockpit, watching that light shimmering unhinged and lonely in the darkness. I started thinking that maybe, finally, after all we had been through, that there might be a way.

I must have gone back to sleep, because when I awoke the star had spun down to the horizon and now hung suspended just above the water, strobing like a pulsar. I watched it hover there, anticipating the moment of its extinction, but instead of sinking below the horizon, it got steadily brighter. I pushed myself up, watched as it started tracking back behind us. And then the sound came, almost imperceptible at first, then growing quickly, the hum of an engine, approaching fast.

I jumped up, felt the adrenaline kick through my body and slam into my heart. We were running without lights. I held my breath, watched the light steady, then turn and dim. At first, I thought they might pass us by – whoever they were. They looked to be setting a course far to our stern. Their engine beat a steady rhythm. *Providence* held to her reach, clipping through a calm sea. Soon the light was gone, and we were alone again, tracking south towards the equator.

When the light reappeared sometime later it came on fast, straight for us. There was no doubt now. I called for Francoise to wake up and fetch the gun. I tightened the main, winched up the jib, nudged *Providence* higher. By the time the searchlight caught the sails, we were heeled over hard, cutting nine knots.

'Who is it?' called Francoise from the cabin.

'I can't tell. Coast guard maybe.'

'Out here?'

'I want you to stay below until we find out.'

'I'm coming up.' She started up the gangway, the pistol clutched in her right hand.

By now the cockpit was lit up like a service-station forecourt back when you could still buy gasoline and drive where you wanted. I raised my hand to shield my eyes. 'No,' I shouted. 'For God's sake, stay below.'

She stopped just inside the gangway, stared out at me. I knew what she was thinking. 'Just be ready,' I shouted. 'And hold on.'

By now the spotlight had us trapped like a twentieth-century bomber on a night run over some European city. I raised my hand again, waved in greeting. They were close now, had swung around off our portside quarter, standing off maybe fifteen metres or so, matching our course and speed. It was an open-sterned cabin cruiser with a flying bridge and a big outboard engine that spewed smoke. The man at the helm was looking out at me through the cabin window as he manoeuvred closer. Another was standing on the beam railing, leaning out towards us as if to catch our forestay in his outstretched hand. He was wearing cut-off jeans and a stained T-shirt – so definitely not the coast guard. The third man played the spotlight over us from bow to stern and up to the masthead and back, finally fixing on me. I pulled the peak of my cap lower over my eyes, nudged *Providence* away, again putting distance between us. They matched my manoeuvre almost immediately, drew in closer, almost within reaching distance.

'*Hola*,' shouted the man on the railing, waving his free hand in a motion that might be interpreted as a signal to slow down. Or maybe it was to speed up.

'Hold on,' I shouted, snapping the wheel hard to port. *Providence* hit the other boat hard amidships. The man on the foredeck was flung overboard. I saw the man on the searchlight topple over, the beam swinging away until it was shining up into the empty sky. As I soon as I felt the sails fill, I wrenched the wheel to starboard and put *Providence* into a powerful broad reach. Soon we were bathed in darkness.

'Hand me the gun,' I said. 'But keep out of sight.'

'They don't look like the coast guard.'

'No.'

'What are you going to do,' she said, palming me the gun.

'Make it as hard for them as I can. Hopefully, they'll just give up and go away.' As long as the wind held, we had a chance. I crouched low, checked the gun, made sure the safety was on and pushed it under my trouser belt. I hoped I would be able to work it if the time came, prayed I would not have to find out.

'Hold on,' I shouted, bringing *Providence* sharply about. As soon as I had reset the sails I fell off until we were running with the wind on our starboard quarter.

'What are you doing?' called Francoise.

'Doubling back.' Maybe we could lose them, but I doubted it.

And yet, we had put some distance between us, and they now appeared to be heading off in the wrong direction, following our previous course. I tightened up the sails, urged *Providence* to give us every knot she had.

Steadily, the light dimmed, and sometime around midnight, it disappeared altogether.

52

As day came, the wind died. All that morning we drifted on a flat, dead sea under a strontium sky. The sails hung lifeless from their gallows. By midday the heat was unbearable.

We were lying in the cockpit under the awning when I saw it, just a speck on the horizon. Through the binoculars I made out a small craft, moving quickly, white spray jumping about its hull. It was coming towards us.

I watched it come on. After a while I could make it out unmagnified. It was heading right for us, at speed.

'What is it?'

I handed Francoise the binoculars. 'It looks like our friends from last night.'

She frowned. 'Don't let them...' She swallowed her words, reached out to steady herself.

'Don't worry, France. I won't.'

'I'm going to check on Argent,' she said as she disappeared down the main hatchway.

I thought about starting the engine but decided against it. The notion that we might have fuel on board would only make us more of a prize. Maybe it wasn't the men from the night before. It could be a customs boat, I told myself. Perhaps law and order still existed here. I stood at the wheel, the binoculars dangling on their strap around my neck. As it got close, the speedboat slowed and settled into the water, engine idling. They were moving alongside, perhaps twenty metres away now. It was the boat from last night, the same three-man crew. One of them was shouting something in Spanish. His voice bounced across the water. I waved at them, smiled, my insides running steeplechase.

'They are asking you where you are going,' Francoise whispered up to me.

I nodded, stood, pointed south. More shouting from the speedboat.

'They want to know why you rammed them last night. Tell them it was an accident, that you're sorry. *Accidente. Desculpeme.*'

I shouted it out, shrugged my shoulders. The men on the boat laughed, glanced at each other. The helmsman called out again.

'They want to come aboard,' Francoise said. 'They ask if you have any food or money.'

I smiled, opened the port cockpit locker and pulled out the fishing rod, held it up, pointed at it. Then I pulled out the pockets of my shorts, stood with my hands open. I could make out the men's faces now, bearded, rough-looking. One of the men was making ready a coil of rope. He wore shorts and a stained red T-shirt with the sleeves cut off. The man at the wheel was shouting, pointing.

'They ask if you have anything to trade. They are coming alongside.'

'No,' I shouted back, shaking my head. I started the engine, gunned the throttle, put some distance between us.

As they closed the distance, one of the men drew a gun. It was a pistol of some sort. Then he pointed at *Providence*'s cabin, yelled something in Spanish.

'He asks if you have anyone else on board. I think they saw me.'

They were close now.

'*Estoy solo,*' Francoise whispered up to me. 'Say it.'

'*Estoy solo,*' I shouted back to them. 'I have nothing you want.' I doubted they understood English.

Again, I swerved away, and again they closed. I was about to reach for the pistol when the driver gunned the engine. It happened so quickly I didn't have time to react. *Providence* shuddered as the speedboat's steel prow rammed us forward of amidships. The force of the collision sent me toppling backward as *Providence* rolled and yawed simultaneously. The last thing I saw was one of the men leaping from the foredeck of the speedboat, airborne between the two vessels.

When You Get There

She is sitting in the chair beside my bed. Outside, the storm rages unabated. She looks up from my notebook which lies cradled in her lap.

Kweku? I ask.

She shakes her head. Nothing.

Ten days.

Twelve.

Really?

You have been in a fever for two days.

Something must have happened.

We have to trust him. That's all we can do.

Yes. We must. I do.

She opens my notebook to the last written page, runs her index finger along the final line. You are still writing.

I have to.

She says: It doesn't end here.

No.

Please be careful.

I nod. I can't do it without you.

I know.

All this time, you've never told me what happened.

I know, she says. But I will.

When?

When you get there. When Kweku gets home.

PART VII

Sinners

Lucidity comes in bursts. Francoise staring out at me through a veil of blood. The look of surprise on her face, the gentleness of her voice as she works on my head. A gull swooping across an empty sky. But in between there is only chaos. The dirt behind the garage at my childhood home, all of my plastic soldiers afire in their positions. Mid-air in the moment between leaving my motorbike and hitting the windshield of the car, the bugs squashed on the car's hood, the newly mown ditch. Stumbling through the sleet, May's body in my arms. Pain breaking like surf, picking me up and spinning me deep so that there is no up or down, only the roar of it filling my head. Burning buildings. Faces staring up from the ground, eyes filming over with dirt. The smells are there, too. Blood. Death. Volatile hydrocarbons, radionuclides, and the pervasive odour of burn. It is as if everything I have ever seen or done is coming at me at once, every thought and dream and vision come unstuck, until the tide of it overwhelms me completely and then there is nothing.

When I come to, night has fallen. I am lying in the cockpit, covered in a blanket. The sails are down, and we are adrift. The sea is calm. A few stars peek through a layer of high cloud. I reach for my head, explore the bandage with my fingertips. I remember the noise of the impact, the other boat so close, just off the starboard beam.

I close my eyes, try to sit up, but a wave of nausea pushes me back down. I lie panting, covered in sweat. I call out for Francoise. I must talk to her, ask her what happened, tell her... What? How to get *Providence* under way again? Where to point her? How to navigate in an empty sea with nothing to guide you and nowhere to go? A wave of pain rolls over me, picks me up and drags me across another dead reef. I can feel the coral skeletons ripping into my flesh, tearing into my brain, and then I am gone, drowned.

I awake sometime later, panting but lucid. It is night. Sea air flows cool over my face, down into my lungs. We are still adrift. The pirates' boat is tethered to *Providence*. I can hear her gunwales thudding gently against *Providence*'s wooden hull, and I calculate that the frequency of the collisions and the length of the pauses in between must equal the period of the swell, and that the swell has come probably from some much deeper part of the Atlantic, or perhaps from farther still.

Light glows in the cabin. I push myself up, slowly, fighting to hold back the dark peripheries of unconsciousness. When I look below, I see three bodies, one of whom I instantly recognise as Argent, lying heaped on the cabin floor. Blood covers everything. I can't see Francoise.

I reach for the topside cabin railing, pull myself to my feet. I call for her, move closer to the gangway. She is sitting at the forward end of the main saloon. Her eyes are open, stark white orbs set in a mask of dried blood. The left side of her face is swollen, misshapen. She stares past me. A handgun sits on the table in front of her. And beside her, laid out under a blanket on the main settee, is one of the pirates.

'France.' My voice is barely audible, just a croak.

She looks up at me as if I am unknown to her, an intruder. She reaches for the gun.

'France, it's me. Teacher.'

She tightens her hand around the pistol. Her eyes narrow and she juts her chin out, but she does not reply.

'France.'

She closes her eyes.

I brace myself against the gangway rails, try to swing one foot onto the first step. But as I do, darkness closes in. I just have time to step back and lean against the cockpit seat before I black out.

When I come to Francoise is sitting next to me. She has washed her face and is wearing a clean blouse and fleece jacket. I try to speak, to ask her what happened, but she shushes me and places her hand on my chest.

'Don't,' she whispers. 'You need to rest.'

'How long have I been out?'

'Three days.'

I take a breath. Surely not. 'No way.'

'Your skull is fractured. There was bleeding on the brain. I have operated, but you must rest.'

'Operated?' I wasn't hearing straight.

She shakes her head. 'Not now.' Other than the bruises on her face, she seems unharmed.

'Jesus, what happened?'

'Not now. Rest. You are not out of danger.'

'Argent?'

She shakes her head, closes her eyes. 'No.'

I think of the storm, pulling him to the surface. 'And the other one, down there?' I can barely speak the words.

'Gunshot to the lower abdomen. Internal bleeding, perforated intestine. I have repaired the worst of the damage and stabilised him.'

I shake my head. I can't imagine it. 'With what?'

'With whatever there is.'

I can form no words.

'I am accustomed.'

Of course. 'Will he live?'

'Yes.'

'That's good.'

'Is it?' she asks.

'Yes.'

'You must rest,' she says. 'Please.'

'Cut their boat loose,' I say. 'If someone sees it...'

'Don't worry,' she whispers. 'Now, sleep.'

I reach for her hand, hold it to my chest and close my eyes.

54

She sits on the gangway step and wipes the sweat from her eyes. Her patients are resting quietly, the living and the dead. She has cleaned Argent, sewed up his wounds, set him out on the opposing bench in the saloon, covered him over with a blanket. But the other two bodies remain where they fell, open-eyed and stiff-set. In the heat, they are starting to bloat and decompose. Already the smell is overpowering. She must dispose of them, but alone, there is no way she will be able to haul the bodies above deck. Each of them is double her weight. She will have to wait for me. But that could take days. The thought makes her physically ill. She breathes hard, fights back the nausea, steadies herself, gazes out across the water.

Her hand is clasped over the winch. There is dark blood under her fingernails. The winch handle is still in its pouch against the bulkhead, still standing by as if nothing has happened here. But the answers are all around her – the jib sheets, the pulleys, the swinging boom arm. The whole of this machinery makes her feel suddenly strong, capable, a survivor here amidst all this death. Soon she has one end of the spare jib sheet tied to the first man's ankles, threaded through the pulley block that runs on the underside of the boom, and around the big main winch. She fits the winch handle into the capstan, spins out the slack and starts cranking. The rope bites into the dead man's ankles, goes taught. Slowly, the body begins to move. With each turn of the handle, the corpse twists across the cabin floor. She keeps winching, her arms burning, demonic. Soon she has him hung in the gangway, head down like a marlin. A tendril of dark liquid spins from his open mouth. His eyes bulge with the pressure of unregulated fluids responding now only to gravity, all vascular control inoperative. When she has winched as far as she can, the feet touching the base of the boom, she pulls the vang aft, the body moving with it until the head and shoulders hit the upper step. Securing another rope around the body's midsection and tying it off to the starboard jib winch, she cranks the corpse onto an angle. The head thumps against the handrail and then swings free. From there she can open out the awning on the starboard side, swing the boom out over the water, and lower the body into the sea.

In her revulsion and desire to see the thing gone, she considers letting the rope go entirely, but she knows that the rope is valuable. With the body floating, she leans over the side and cuts the rope away from the ankles, then stands back and watches the body disappear into the depths. The last things to vanish are the eyes, open still, as empty as her soul.

By the time she lowers the second body into the water the sharks are circling. She counts at least three of them, big grey brutes that start attacking the body even before she has a chance to cut it away. Their sudden appearance surprises her. With big shakes of their ugly heads, the animals tear the carcass apart in a few seconds. All of this she kept to herself for a long time.

*

The wind dies completely. We drift for days, her two patients in and out of consciousness, the boat steadily south and towards the coast, pulled along by the current. She is doctor and nurse, feeding and cleaning us both, checking wounds for infection, monitoring recovery. My moments of clarity are more frequent now, longer. We talk, she tells me some of what happened. She wishes she could take an X-ray to determine exactly the extent of fracturing. She knows it is extensive. I am lucky to be alive. Fortunately, there does not appear to be any more fluid on the brain. The pirate is improving, too. She is pretty sure that she has repaired all the internal damage, has done a complete debridement. His wounds look clean and there is no sign of infection. He is young and strong. She keeps his wrists bound with the plastic zip-ties she found in his pocket, the same ones they used on her. She keeps the gun close.

A day later, she buries Argent at sea, hoping that the sharks have moved away. She sews him into a square of the forward berth linen, offers a prayer, lets him slide into the deep. She scrubs the cabin clean like a madwoman. By now a light breeze has risen. It is coming from the east, from the Atlantic, from Africa. She checks on her prisoner, then climbs onto the pirates' launch. On board she finds charts, some money, fishing rods and tackle, more weapons – another AK47, a handgun, knives, boxes of ammunition, even a couple of hand grenades. Disappointingly, there is no food, but the launch's water tanks are almost full. After transferring everything she can to *Providence* she prepares to cut the launch loose, as I have been urging her to do. We cannot get under way with the launch aside, and towing it under sail will be impossible. I tell her to untie the stern line, throw it over the transom. She is about to move forward to let go the bow line when I see a flash of movement inside the cabin.

A massive jolt of adrenaline floods through mc. I stagger to my feet, start towards the gangway. The man is standing in the cabin, a knife in his hands. I signal to Francoise, point below. She nods, wraps her hand around the grip of Argent's gun, withdraws it from her pocket. By the time I reach the main hatchway, the man has managed to sever the tie around his wrists. He stands in the galley staring up at me, a kitchen knife in one hand, the other braced across his bandaged torso.

Francoise stands beside me, levels the pistol at him. Her hands are shaking wildly. '*Baja eso*,' she shouts. Put that down.

The man looks at her a moment, appears not to hear.

She fills her lungs, repeats herself, with more control this time.

He does not drop the knife. Instead, he takes a step back, deeper into the cabin. He is rubbing his free hand along the length of the bandage that encircles his torso, as if to locate the exact point of the wound.

'*Tu?*' he says.

She nods.

'*Porque?*'

'*Soy doctora.*' It is reason enough. I know it always has been.

He looks down at his midsection. '*Una doctora con arma.*' A doctor with a gun.

She stares down at her attacker, tightens her finger on the trigger.

'Don't, France,' I say, reaching for her arm.

'I have done my duty,' she hisses, her voice trembling. 'Without me, he would be dead now, fed to the sharks like the others. Do you hear?' she shouts in Spanish. 'You live because of me.' She knows very clearly that he must pay for what he did, and that she must be the one to enact justice.

She is about to pull the trigger when I put my hand on the gun.

'France,' I whisper, 'you can't.'

'He...' she begins, cannot continue.

'We can't, France. We just can't.'

'They almost killed you,' she says. 'I thought you were dead.'

'Not like this,' I say again. 'Please.'

Slowly, I guide her hands towards the deck, lowering the weapon.

The man drops the knife to the cabin floor, stands staring at us.

'What will we do with him?' she says. 'I don't want him here.'

'Put him back in his boat. Set him adrift.'

The man smiles, an ugly crease across his cruel mouth. Does he understand?

She shudders. 'He will come back. We killed his friends. He wants revenge. Look at him.'

'I can disable the engine. By the time someone finds him, we will be far away.'

She considers this, does the calculation. 'If they find him,' she says.

'We can give him some food and water. Give him a chance.'

'It is more than he deserves.'

I take the gun from her hands, point it at the man. 'Tell him to lie face down on the floor.'

'*Tírate al suelo*,' she shouts. '*Boca abajo*.'

He complies.

'Tie his hands behind his back. Ankles, too.'

She fishes a tie from her pocket, steps down into the cabin. Despite the hours spent nursing this man back to health, something fundamental has changed. She forces herself closer, step by step, until she is standing above him. I can tell that the thought of physical contact with him fills her with revulsion. She looks back at me.

'I can't,' she says.

'Yes, you can, France.'

She closes her eyes, breathes. The knife he was holding is there on the cabin floor by her feet. She reaches down and picks it up. Then she kneels on his back and places the point of the knife on his neck, just below the jaw. The carotid artery is there, just below the skin, pulsing, full.

'*Una doctora con un cuchillo*,' she says.

Soon she has him trussed up and is back in the cockpit. She shows me the weapons she collected earlier, now stowed in the cockpit lockers. I pick out one of the two AK47s, check the magazine, pull back the bolt. Then I go to the stern and fire off a few single rounds, then a burst on automatic. When I turn back to face her, I say: 'Practice.'

The painkillers Francoise has given me aren't working. My head is pounding. Every movement sends a bolt of pain spearing through my head, as if my skull has been skewered from temple to jaw. I manage to clamber down into the other vessel, detach the outboard engine and drop it into the sea. She follows me, does another search of the vessel, finds a couple of mobile phones, an old GPS, a marine radio. It all goes overboard.

Soon we have our attacker above deck. I hold the rifle ready, levelled at his chest. Fear pours from him. He is jabbering in his coarse Spanish, asking for forgiveness, to be let go, pleading to be allowed to live.

I motion with the gun for him to move to the railing. "Tell him to turn around, face the water."

She tells him. He complies. He is crying now, invoking the Virgin Mother.

'Tell him to get on his knees.'

'*Arrodíllate*,' she says.

'*Por favor*,' he whimpers, pleading to her in Spanish.

I watch as she listens, see her countenance soften a moment. 'What is he saying?'

'He says he has a wife, a daughter. That he used to be a fisherman, but that now there are no fish, that everything is dying. He is just trying to provide for them. He says he is sorry.' She cuts the tie around his wrists. '*Vamos*,' she says. '*Recuerda esto*.'

He stands, glances back at her as if not quite believing what he'd just heard, and then scrambles into his boat. She unties the line. He stands in the stern looking back up at us as the boats slowly disengage and start to drift apart.

'Now let's raise the sails and get out of here,' I say.

I set the gun down and take the helm. Françoise starts raising the main. A light breeze begins filling the sail. Our attacker stands in the stern of his disabled boat, watching us move away. The main is half up now, Françoise cranking the winch. The other boat is about five or six metres away when the man suddenly drops to the deck. When he reappears a moment later, he has a gun in his hand, a pistol of some sort.

'Look out,' Françoise shouts as he fires.

I turn the wheel hard to port, turning *Providence* towards our attacker. Another shot cracks out as the wind catches the main and slams Providence hard over. A second later we broadside the speedboat with a sickening crash of wood on fibreglass. The man loses his footing, topples to the deck. With the two vessels locked

PAUL E HARDISTY

together, I grab the rifle and jump up onto the coaming. The man is lying on his back, looking up at me. I glance down at Francoise a moment, raise the weapon and take aim. On full automatic, I empty the magazine in a few seconds.

The Cloud-Shadowed Sea

It is just before midday when I set down my pen. The storm has passed.
Thick beams of sunlight stream between low-slung cumulus, track across
the becalmed surface of the sound. I go back, read through what I have
written today. Having recalled all of this, having done it together, the
events now seem somehow clearer than when they were happening, as if
only in retrospect are we able to see the true nature of things.

I am putting my notebook back into its drawer when I hear it. A lone
voice lifted on the breeze. I stand, pull my coat around my shoulders and
shuffle out to the balcony. Francoise joins me a moment later.

Did you hear that?

It's Lewis, she says.

We stand, listen. There it is again. Definitely Lewis, excited,
getting closer.

We look back towards the head. Lewis is flying down the pathway,
a blur between the rocks. He sees us, stops, waves his arms above his
head, points out to the sound. Providence, he shouts. It's him.

We turn and look out to sea, scan the horizon. Nothing. I shuffle
inside, grab the binoculars, sweep the sound, the cloud-shadowed sea
and the distant rocks of The Hope.

By now Lewis is next to us, jumping up and down, pointing.
There, he shouts. There! Come on, Papa, can't you see? Just beyond
The Hope.

I refocus the glasses, register the two islets. And then I see. Two
white sails.

My heart jumps. Joy floods my wretched body. It could be anyone,
I say.

No way, shouts Lewis. It's him, Dad. Look at the way he's
rounding The Hope, cutting close to the reef like he always does. It's
him! And before I can answer, he's gone, sprinting away towards the
beach, calling out to Mandy and Juliette at the top of his voice.

55

After a few days, I was able to start moving about again. We were making good way, moving steadily south. Somewhere ahead, still below the horizon, lay the east-west belt of Central America – Nicaragua, Panama – and then the main bulk of South America – Colombia, Venezuela. Dangerous places all, lawless and violent. At least we were well armed.

I was sitting at the chart table when Francoise came below. She put a CD into the player. Soon, Mozart filled the cabin with order and hope. She stood over me, running her hand over the back of my head. Earlier that morning she'd cut my hair and shaved off my beard, insisted on doing it herself.

'You are healing quickly,' she said.

'I have a good doctor.'

She was smiling. Her hair was wind-blown, full, lofted with salt. There was sun and wind in her face. She looked healthy.

'What did you say to him, just before he got onto the boat?'

She looked at me, not understanding.

'*Recuerda esto.*'

'Remember this.'

I nodded, understood.

'Do you believe Argent's story?' she said. 'His sanctuary.'

'It makes sense, I suppose.' Anticipating the political backlash, Argent set himself up a bolt-hole in the tropics, in a part of the world where he thought he would be safe. To do that, though, he would have had to consult the scientific literature in depth, or be advised by someone who knew what they were talking about. And while Argent had shown himself to be incredibly knowledgeable about the phenomenon, he had consistently misinterpreted the causes and effects. Why would he so vehemently deny that climate change was real, and then invest time and effort in protecting himself against exactly what he denied existed?

Francoise looked down at the chart. 'Shangri-la, he called it. Paradise. He was dying. Why would he lie?'

'All he did was lie.'

'I think he was telling the truth.' She placed Argent's case on the map in front of me. 'Open it.'

I hinged open the lid, glanced back at her.

'Go ahead. Have a look.'

Slowly, I went through the contents, withdrawing each item and placing it on the map table. A stack of one-ounce Australian kangaroo gold coins encased in a clear, hard plastic roll. Title deeds for property, in Spanish, some names of places I didn't recognise. Bank account details for Crédit Agricole. Two Australian passports, one with Argent's picture and the name Randolph Artemis Hume, the other in the name of Denise Arabella Hume. I stared at the photograph. It was her.

'How did he...?'

'I don't know.'

'He was planning this.'

'Keep going.'

I reached into the case. More gold coins, stacks of them, ammunition for the pistol, a set of keys, a tiny black notebook no bigger than a credit card filled with strings of numbers – codes and designators. A map of Belize marked up in coloured pen. A mobile device. And stacks of cash, thousands of dollars – so much I couldn't count.

I took a breath, held it a while, put it all back in the case.

'He told me everything, just before he died. We should go to Belize.'

I pulled out the coastal chart, unrolled it across the table. The coast of Belize, pre-inundation, was guarded by three strings of islands and reefs, once a tropical garden, a diver's paradise of coral and white carbonate sand islets set in clear, aquamarine waters. I remembered seeing holiday brochures, back when May and I were first married. Most of the islands and reefs would be gone now, I supposed, based on the sea-level rise data I had seen, the effects of warming on the hyper-sensitive coral, the forcing out of the algal symbiont on which the host matrix depended, leaving a dying skeleton of bleached rock, something I'd done lessons on for my year-twelve biology class before the Repudiation. Navigation would be difficult, especially at night, without landmarks or beacons, drowned islands lurking beneath the surface, waiting to tear us open. I looked at the chart, at the cleft in the coastline and the Gulf of Honduras littered with islands and ring-shaped reefs.

'I don't know, France. Something tells me that Argent was just setting us up – it would be his parting shot. We go in there, trying to claim what is his, and we end up in jail. Or worse. I wouldn't put it past him.'

'You weren't there with him. I was.'

'I don't know.'

'I am asking you to trust my judgement. We're close. We need fuel and water. We should go to Belize.'

'I don't trust him, Francoise. Alive or dead.' I was sure that it was a trap, that Argent would reach out even now to impose his will on events. 'We should keep going south.'

Francoise didn't say anything for a long time, just stood studying the charts laid out on the table. 'I know Derek was telling the truth.'

I said nothing.

Then she opened the galley freezer, reached inside and withdrew two small Ziploc bags. The clear plastic was frosted white. She considered them for a moment, as if weighing them in her hand, and then put them on the table on top of the chart. 'I know,' she said, 'because he told me to do this.'

'What are they?'

'Open them.'

'Why don't you just tell me what they are?'

'No,' she said. 'I want you to see for yourself.'

I picked up the first bag, pulled it open. The object inside was wrapped in medical gauze, frozen hard. It was the size and shape of a sausage. I looked up at her.

'Unwrap it.'

I unwound the frozen gauze. By the time I was down to the last wends, I knew what it was. 'Jesus, France.' A finger.

'He told me to do it. Just before he died. He said we needed his print to access the safety-deposit box and to open the security gate.'

'And the other one?'

'His eye. For the retina scan.'

An Old Man's Tears

I hold my son in my arms, feel his solid bulk so close to me, his powerful chest. I don't want to let him go.

Kweku laughs, squeezes me harder. It's okay, Papa, he says.

We were so worried, I say. He has already survived the inundation of kisses from his mother and been reunited with his wife and child.

We sit down to breakfast all together. Francoise has made pancakes. Everyone crowds around, anxious for his news.

I made it to Albany in good time, Kweku says between mouthfuls. But I was late getting away. It took me longer than I expected to get everything on the list. And I met some people, so I decided to stay longer. It was what saved me. I was only a day out when the storm blew up. I ended up running back to Albany, holed up there while it passed through.

Lewis slaps him on the back, grinning wide. Juliette wraps her arms around his neck, kisses him again and again on his bearded cheek.

Everyone in Albany was very distracted, he continues. A lot is going on. He looks over at me, smiles. Things are getting better, Papa. The war is over, they say. All the wars. Countries are rebuilding, working together. Australia, too. Apparently, there is a new leader in America who is helping to lead the way.

Francoise reaches for my hand, holds tight.

And, Dad, you'll never guess.

I look into his eyes. What?

His name is Armstrong.

Whose name?

The American President. President Armstrong.

Kweku smiles big. Lewis guffaws. Mandy and Juliette exchange glances. I am not sure I have heard correctly.

Lachlan Armstrong. He pauses, searches my face.

It's him, says Lewis. It must be.

He's the right age. Born in Canada, a senior advisor to the Lejeune youth government during the Relocation. Kweku reaches for his bag, pulls out a newspaper. Here, he says. Read. It's all there.

Lachie. For the second time in less than a day I am overcome with joy. My boys, my grown sons. Alive. After everything they were forced to face, the hardships and perils, after all our failures, our terrible betrayals. Standing strong. Walking right.

I hide my face in my hands and weep like a child, like an old man.

56

Later that night, I took a sight on Venus. I checked the ship's chronometer, found the Greenwich hour angles and declinations in the nautical almanac, and calculated the altitude intercept. Then I plotted an apparent position based on the earlier noon sight and using the azimuth line of Venus, set a line of position. I labelled it 'Venus 1805' in pencil on the chart. The process calmed me.

Back on deck, Francoise was at the wheel, holding course south-southwest. I caught the flash of her eyes in the starlight. Bracing myself against the main hatchway, I sighted Sirius, higher now in the night sky. This allowed me to cut a line of position for Sirius 1815, advance the Venus LOP to match the time of observation of Sirius, and plot this on the chart. I went back several times to check my calculations. Finally, though, I had it. In the glow of the navigation-table light, a point on the chart where the two lines crossed, our position: three hundred and thirty nautical miles to the northeast of Belize City. If the wind held, we could be there in four days.

When I climbed back into the cockpit, Francoise was staring up into the sky. I stood next to her, looked up. We were alone, with nothing but the eyes of a billion stars to watch over us.

*

Three days later Francoise was sitting alone at the bow, her feet dangling in the waves. She smiled back at me, from one end of our little world to the other. The winds were fair, the sea calm. We were making good progress. I gazed out across the water at the endless pattern of wave and ripple, infinitely complex and yet so simple. The sea was bluer here, the air clearer. The planet would recover. This realisation came as a certainty, undiluted by fear or doubt, pure. Maybe we could, too.

And then I saw them, so faint at first that I didn't dare cry out for fear of being wrong. But there they were, very clear now above the haze, a range of purple, cloud-topped mountains strung out along a distant coastline. I shouted it out, pointed. Francoise waved back, smiled; she'd seen it too.

As the coast revealed itself, scale returned. Progress could be measured, individuality recovered. Strings of islets appeared – remnant coral atolls – and beyond, a green coastline without sign of human habitation. The stars had shown us the way. We had used geometry and reason to fix a point in the midst of an infinite sea. Before, when the satellites and communications systems still worked, it was as simple as pushing a button. The GPS in my car had allowed me to drive without thinking, without using a map. Just do what the voice told you. Perhaps that had been our problem all along, all of us. We just followed the voice. And it had guided us to a dead end.

Without Us

It takes me a long time to walk the couple of hundred metres down to the shingle beach. Juliette is patient with me, little Leo strapped to her chest. I cling to her arm, lean up against her lissom frame when I need to rest. Time seems to be running faster now, but I know it is only my perception of it. The strength I took for granted most of my life has left me. My bones are frail and stretch up against my skin. How did it happen so quickly, this passing of days?

Juliette sits me down on a piece of bleached driftwood, runs to the water's edge and takes hold of the prow of the dinghy. Lewis and Kweku are unloading the last of the supplies from Providence. *I watch as they jump out and help Juliette pull the dinghy up onto the shingle. Soon they have everything stacked on the beach, and Lewis heads up the hill to fetch his horses. Kweku and Juliette walk out to the point. I can see them standing together, close but not touching, looking out to sea.*

Good about your boy.

Liberty is standing next to me, twisting the base of his spear stick in the shingle.

Jeez, Liberty. Don't do that, mate.

Do what?

Appear out of nowhere like that.

This ain't nowhere.

That's not what I meant.

Still.

Still.

Good about your boy.

Sure is.

Good boy, that.

Yep. Sure is.

Liberty shifts his weight from one bare foot to the other, pushing the balls of his feet into the shingle. He doesn't speak again for a long time, and I don't break our silence. He told me once, not long after we first arrived here, that it was the length of quiet that could occur between two people that was the true measure of how close they were. He didn't use those words.

Finally, he says: And good news.

You've heard?

News travels. Good slower, mind.

That's the truth, I say. Always.

Your boy that one too. In America.

So it seems.

Second chance for you mob.

Yeah, maybe. I hope so.

Get it right this time, he says.

We'll try.

Young fellas gotta do it without us now.

Then he taps the base of his stick three times against a flat stone, looks into my eyes one last time, turns away and disappears into the trees.

57

We arrive just before dusk, the lights of the city winking on, the sun already behind the mountains. A few ships swing at anchor in the harbour, a rusty freighter, a twin-masted schooner, several small powerboats, a merchant ship that looks as if its main superstructure has been torched – blackened streaks above the portholes, the topmost steelwork mangled, a few containers strewn at odd angles across the deck.

I lower the sails, start the engine, make for the red flashing beacon at the tip of the southern breakwater. Beyond, the low white buildings of Belize City rise from the water. Woodsmoke drifts across the bay, sweet and pungent, and with it the smells of ripening sugarcane, rain on black earth. We are past the breakwater now, its unweathered granite blocks glowing in the last of the light. At its landward terminus, I can make out a jetty and what appears to be a harbour master's control tower. I manoeuvre *Providence* past another freighter. We gaze up at it as we pass, a vertical wall of rusty, riveted steel that dwarfs us. A crewman stands at the rail, smoking a cigarette. I raise my hand. The crewman frowns, flicks the butt of his smoke into the sea and disappears.

Light is fading. Francoise takes the helm. I go forward and make ready the anchor, a small Danforth with thirty metres of chain and a sturdy rode. When we are about a hundred metres from the harbour control building, I signal her to idle the motor. Soon we are drifting away from the breakwater on a gentle land breeze. I drop the anchor, let the rode run through my hands until I feel the Danforth's flukes dig into the bottom. I pay out scope and cleat the rode, then check our position against the city's tallest building and the breakwater beacon. We are holding, secure. I breathe in the land. We have arrived.

Francoise puts Argent's case on the cockpit bench beside me and opens it. 'He said to go to the bank.'

I reach into the case, pull out a stack of gold coins sealed in clear plastic. 'It was all about this.'

'Yes.'

'Argent protected himself. Left everyone else to rot.'

'But it didn't turn out like he planned.'

I hesitate a while, then say what I'd been wanting to say for days now, but had never been able to utter. 'He said I was just like him.'

'You're not.'

'You saw what I did back there.'

'You had to.'

'I am a murderer. He was right.'

'No.'

'Yes.'

'You cannot think that way,' she says, reaching for my hand.

'There is no other way I can think.'

'Yes. There is. For both of us.' She pulls out a little black notebook and a one-thousand-dollar bill. 'He wrote it all down here, the instructions.'

That night we sit in the cockpit and eat the last of the tinned fish with some steamed rice. The lights of the city dance over the water. It looks like one of those impressionist paintings that May loved so, random daubs of colour scattered over the black water, a few star points there too, shimmering in the breeze.

'It almost looks normal,' Francoise says.

'Abnormal, you mean.'

'Like before.'

'We can't ever think that way, Francoise.'

Two hours now since we sailed into the harbour, and no one has come to enquire about our presence. It is as if the whole place is asleep. 'Tomorrow I'll go to shore and register our arrival,' I say.

'Shouldn't we go straight to the bank?' Francoise sips her tea, blows on the steam.

'I'll go right after. You stay here with the boat.'

Francoise frowns. 'We should keep together.'

'No, France. I want you here, with everything ready to go. We may have to leave in a hurry.'

'You still don't believe him, do you?'

I put down my mug, consider this again. A few of the anchored vessels are displaying lights, as maritime convention demands. I go below and switch on *Providence*'s masthead light, still pondering the question. Despite Argent's apparent dying wish, and the severed body parts, I am convinced that tomorrow morning I am going to walk into that bank and never walk out.

'Let me see those instructions.'

She gives me the thousand-dollar note. I have never seen one before, didn't even know such a thing existed. I flick on my Maglite, examine it back and front.

'You can see there, where he wrote on it,' she says.

Two words and some symbols are scrawled across the top of the bill, and beneath, a string of numbers, bloodstains. Argent's writing is almost illegible. It looks like: $\alpha\Omega$ *Mersenne 3*.

'It's a code,' she says, 'so the bank manager can identify you. He explained it to me. "Mersenne 3" is the third Mersenne Prime: two to the third power minus one. You need to remember that. The numbers below are a combination. I've cross-referenced it.' She opens the black notebook, points to a series of figures. 'Here,' she says.

I shine the light across the page.

'What we need is in the safety-deposit box. You need a combination, a finger swipe and a retina scan to open it.'

I turn the note over, examine the watermark. 'The bank manager will know that I'm not Argent.'

She examines the photo in Argent's passport, reaches up and touches my five- day stubble. 'You have the same blue eyes.'

'We could be brothers,' I say. She does not laugh.

'He told me they have never met. If they question you, say

you've lost weight, that you've been ill. Carry his case. Speak the way he did.'

'You mean like a heartless, selfish bastard.'

Francoise frowns. 'He also told me that the previous bank manager was killed in an uprising. His name was Chenault.'

'I'm not going to fool anyone, Francoise. Argent knew that.'

'When he told me about this, he thought you were dead. He said I had to do it.' She pauses. 'Perhaps I should go. I am his wife, after all. It is my photo in the passport.'

'No way, Francoise. No way. If we're going to do this, it will be me.'

'Besides, it's the code words and the scans they want. If you have those, they aren't going to quibble over a passport photo.'

I think it over.

After a while, she whispers: 'If you really don't want to go, we can just use some of the money in the case, buy supplies, and keep going.'

'Keep going where?'

'Just going.'

'Eventually, we're going to have to stop somewhere.' I am not sure if I am trying to convince myself to stay, or to leave. 'Is that what you want, Francoise? Do you want to keep going?'

She shakes her head slowly. 'I don't want to go back out there.'

I nod. She hasn't told me the whole story yet, of what happened after I was knocked unconscious.

'The last thing he said—' She stops herself short and puts her hand on my forearm, where the break was. 'Aren't you tired?' she whispers. 'Don't you want somewhere to rest, to be safe?'

I say nothing.

'He died saving us. We owe it to him. We owe it to ourselves.'

'I don't owe him a goddammed thing.'

I know she is tired. So am I.

I Have Given Them Names

*Francoise sits beside me, takes my hand in hers. He is back, she says.
Now I will tell you.*

*She tells it slowly, without embellishment. She describes it
carefully, as if the events of so long ago had happened only yesterday.
She tells of Argent's intervention, the wounds suffered by each of the
men and how they occurred and their result. I have seen it before,
she says. This is what happens when the thin skin of civilisation is
ripped away.*

*The collision. I saw you fall backward. And then men's voices
shouting outside, and the sound of them on the cabin roof above me.
I looked up into the cockpit. You were lying in a pool of blood. You
weren't moving. Two men jumped into the cockpit. I remember their
voices. One deep and rumbling, the other higher pitched, with a
strange lisp. They were speaking in Spanish, talking to the man in
the other boat, the one who seemed to be in charge. His voice was
raspy, as if he smoked too many cigarettes. He said: See what you can
find below.*

*There was nowhere to hide. One of the men started down the
gangway , his foot on the first step. Argent's duffel bag was on the
settee opposite me. I'd just had time to pull it out of the locker before
the collision. The man stopped on the second step and turned back to
talk to one of his companions. The muzzle of a gun hung down from
a strap over his shoulder. It was an AK47. I'd seen enough of them
during the war, the hateful things. I lunged for the bag and opened
it. The man was staring at me. He looked surprised. I fumbled inside
the bag, feeling for Argent's shotgun, the one he took from the camp.
But it was gone. The man raised his weapon and smiled.*

*I hid it, I say to her. I didn't want Argent to find it. I should have
told you.*

She nods, closes her eyes, continues.

The man was laughing, moving towards me, the gun pointed at my midsection. He looked down at the bag, crouched down and pulled it towards him, not taking his eyes off me. He opened it with one hand and pulled out a wad of cash, then a strap of gold coins. A smile creased his face. There was a big gap where his front teeth were missing. He asked me if there was anyone else on the boat. His tongue lisped between the gap as he spoke. He sounded like a cartoon character. I pretended not to understand, shaking my hands, shrugging my shoulders.

Una mujer, Gaptooth shouted back over his shoulder. A woman.

I have given them names, she says to me. Though they do not deserve it. She continues.

Another man appeared in the gangway. He was heavier-set, thickly muscled. He had on a New York Yankees baseball cap. He grabbed the duffel bag from Gaptooth and looked inside, then he stared at me. He told Gaptooth to tie me. Their Spanish was rough, uneducated. I struggled, and Gaptooth hit me in the face with an open hand, hard enough to cut my lip. He tied my hands behind me with a plastic tie. The hard plastic cut into my skin, the pain made me cry out. Yankee laughed.

I am going to tell you what they said. I remember it all. All of it. Write it down.

She pauses, looks deep into my eyes. This will be the only time.

I nod.

He said: Before we are done, we will hear more of this, no?

Can we take her? asked Gaptooth.

We'll see how good she fucks, Yankee replied.

She pauses, breathless. Do you want me to continue?

Only if you want to.

Gaptooth laughed and pushed me to my knees. They started searching the cabin, taking everything of value and stuffing it into the duffel bag – tins of food, the kettle from the stovetop. They ripped the radio from its brackets and emptied the locker beneath the sink of all of the cleaning things – dish soap, scouring pads, everything. It was … I don't know. They were like animals.

342   PAUL E HARDISTY

I thought of you up on the deck. I thought you were dead. They said you were dead. Argent was still in the forward berth, unconscious. They hadn't found him yet. I was alone, and I wept.

She is crying now, but she keeps going.

The big one, Yankee, was in the cockpit going through the lockers, throwing things over to the other boat. Gaptooth was going through the saloon lockers. He opened the portside locker and looked inside. He must have seen something he liked because he leaned into the locker. After a moment, he pulled his head back up, looked over at me, grinned stupidly and put his gun on the far berth. Then he pushed his head deep into the locker, reaching in with one hand, the other holding up the locker lid.

That's when it started, she says. All that happened from there. Do you want me to go on?

Yes, I whisper.

She nods, fills her lungs, exhales, does it again.

It was my chance. Gaptooth was rummaging head down in the locker, the lid open above him, one hand gripping the edge. I threw myself onto the lid. The frame crushed through the bones of his fingers, and the clasp came down on his spine. He struggled and at first I held him down. His screams echoed inside the locker as he bucked under me. But without my hands to steady me, I fell to the floor. And then Gaptooth was up. He screamed at me, kicked me away before I could get to his gun. Three of his fingers hung from threads, pouring blood. And then Yankee was there, staring at us. Gaptooth was crying, cradling his hand. Yankee picked up Gaptooth's gun and shouted at him to shut up.

They were like children, she says, looking up at me. Do you understand? They were lost and frightened.

I nod, although I am not sure I do understand. Even in this she is able to show compassion.

She continues. Then they beat me.

But by then I didn't care anymore. You were gone. There was nothing to live for.

Jesus, I whisper.

Do you understand now why I never...?

Yes. I'm sorry. So sorry.

And yet we are here.

Yes.

After they stopped beating me I lay on the cabin floor for a long time. I could hear Yankee shouting instructions to the man on the other boat and Gaptooth's whimpers as Yankee told him to hold still. I'm going to kill the bitch, he said. Look what she did to my fucking hand. And then Yankee telling him to hold still, calling him an idiot. You can do what you like with her, he said, but I'm going to fuck her first, and, eh, Miguel, you want to fuck the mujer too, cabrón? And then Gaptooth lisping, Okay, you and Miguel fuck her, and then I fuck her, and then I kill the dirty bitch. That's what they said. Word for word. I will never forget. I knew it was the end. I was glad. It is important you know this.

I write it. I say nothing.

She continues. Yankee pulled me to my feet. He touched my cheek with the back of his hand, gently, then brought it back and slapped me hard. Then he grabbed the front of my blouse and ripped it open. He tore off my bra and grabbed my breasts. The other men were watching. Then he pulled out a knife and brought it up to my face so I could see it. He cut my clothes off with it. All of them. He positioned me on the edge of the table. The other men moved forward. I closed my eyes. I could smell them.

It Would All Have Been for Nothing

It's not until later that day that we continue. I can see the strain of the remembering in her eyes, in the darkened furrows above her brows. It has taken a toll on both of us. She sits beside the bed. I prop myself up, take my pen. I start to read back the last sentence from before.

I know what I said.

Sorry.

She nods. It takes her a while to start.

It was then that Argent burst from the front cabin, a gun in his hand. From there it all happened so quickly. The men turned towards him. Argent pointed his pistol at Gaptooth's torso and then lowered his aim suddenly and fired. For a long time I have wondered why he did that. Now I know that I was too close, and he did it to protect me. The bullet shattered Gaptooth's knee. He fell, screaming. After that it was chaos. Yankee stumbled back, and Argent shot him through the chest and then in the middle of the forehead. He fell back into the other man, pinning him as he struggled to raise his rifle. Argent took aim, but just as he was about to shoot, Gaptooth lunged at him and knocked his legs out. They fell to the floor in a heap, clutching at each other. Argent managed to twist himself under Gaptooth just as the other man fired. I saw the bullets hit Gaptooth's body, and then Argent raising his pistol. He fired three times. The man with the rifle fell, his face...

She stumbles over the words, closes her eyes a moment.

His face was gone.

Jesus, I say.

It took me a long time to get Argent out from under Gaptooth's body. He had lost a lot of blood. I was shaking so hard I could barely open the medical kit. Argent looked at me and reached up and touched my chin. Now you really owe me, he said. He was soaked in blood. His and Gaptooth's. I reached under him, but there were no exit wounds. Two rounds had gone straight through Gaptooth's abdomen and into

Argent's stomach. I had seen this kind of wound before, far too many times. I knew he didn't have long. Not much you can do, he said, looking down at his midsection. At least I went out fighting.

He asked about you. I told him you were dead. He seemed disappointed. I asked him for his gun. He looked into my eyes. He knew what I was thinking. Don't, he said. I told him that there was nothing to live for. Yes, he said. There is. I hid my face in my hands and started to cry. That was when he asked me to get his case. The sanctuary, he said. It's real. A paradise, with everything you need. I set it up years ago, as an insurance policy. At first, I didn't believe him. He told me to hurry, that there wasn't much time. He opened the case. It's all there, he said. Everything you need. That was when he told me what to do, and how to do it, every detail.

The finger, I say. The eye.

She pauses, thinking back. Yes.

Now use it, he said, or it would all have been for nothing.

I sat there, naked among the bodies, covered in blood, shivering in the heat. I spent a long time looking into Derek's eyes. You remember his eyes. Those steel slivers floating in that sky-blue background. Empty. All that time I was holding his gun, the barrel still warm from the killing. I was calm now, sitting there. I remember the sound of the sails flapping in the breeze and one of the halyards tapping on the mast and it reminded me of a book I had read once, a long time before, about a wind-blown signal lever sending out a random signal to a dying world. My hand was shaking, and the gun was tapping against my thigh. I thought of my mother, of her disapproval of Kwesi and our marriage. I thought of you.

You were lying face down on the cockpit floor. Blood pooled around your head. I looked out over the water. I had always thought that it would require great courage, great determination. But I felt none of that. I took one last look at you and cleared my mind. I was so surprised when I saw you move that I almost twitched my finger that last fraction.

Jesus.

There. I've told you. Now you know.

58

Early next morning I check the anchor, inflate the dinghy, and make *Providence* ready. I brief Francoise on what to do if she needs to leave in a hurry. She is a good sailor now, has learned quickly. From Argent's case I take four gold coins, ten thousand in cash, the black notebook and the two passports. I shove Daniel Menzels' Israeli-made Desert Eagle nine millimetre and an extra magazine into my pocket, fold the thousand-dollar note scrawled with Argent's hand into my shirt pocket, and slip *Providence*'s registration papers into my backpack along with a bottle of water.

A fishing boat chugs hopefully past the beacon and out to sea. An old pickup truck trundles along the top of the breakwater towards the harbour master's station. I climb down into the dinghy. Francoise looks down at me from the cockpit.

'If I'm not back in three hours, I want you to get out of here.'

She wipes the back of her hand across her cheekbone. 'You don't understand, do you?'

I push off, slide the oars into the locks. 'Understand what?'

'Anything.'

Truer words never spoken. I pull hard on the oars, head for the jetty. She stands in the cockpit watching me go. It takes me just a few minutes to reach the jetty, a couple more to walk to the harbour master's building. I pass a couple of burnt-out vehicles, their sides punctured with bullet holes. The building's wooden siding is torn away in places, peppered with the same holes. A couple of the front windows are boarded up. I look back, wave to Francoise. She waves back.

An official is sitting behind a wooden counter in a tiled lobby. An old rotary phone sits on the desk, its plastic faded and cracked. A ceiling fan turns overhead. The man is small, his face gaunt, as if he has been on reduced rations for months. His uniform is

stained, his officer's cap holed, the gold braid on the peak frayed.
He smiles as I approach, revealing stained, cracked teeth.

'*Buenos dias, extranjero*,' says the official.

I place *Providence*'s documents on the counter. The official
scans them in silence and after a while places a heavy logbook on
the counter. He finds a blank page and starts filling in the top line
with a disposable plastic pen.

'You have come from United States?' he says in accented
English.

I nod yes.

'Things are very bad there, yes?'

'Very.'

'We too have had trouble.'

I nod.

'I have seen you arrive last night. Name of vessel?'

I tell him.

'One crew?'

'Yes, sir.'

'Passports.'

I place the two Australian passports on the counter. The officer
flips through them, studies each photo page.

'*Señor* Hume, do you have a visa for Belize?'

'I was under the impression that one could be purchased on
arrival.'

'That is not the normal procedure.'

'What is the normal procedure?'

'You should apply in your home country.'

'Things there are very bad.'

'Yes. Nevertheless.'

I glance back over my shoulder at *Providence* swinging at
anchor. 'Surely we can reach some accommodation.' I reach into
my pocket, extract a banknote, close it in my fist and place my
hand palm down on the counter.

He narrows his eyes. 'Are you offering me a bribe, *Señor*?'

'No, sir,' I say. 'I am paying for a visa.'

'A boat was found drifting off the coast two days ago, *Señor* Hume,' he says still looking at my hand with the note underneath. 'With a dead man inside. He was shot many times, murdered. What do you know about this?'

Another mistake. We should have sunk the boat, let the sea take the body. I try to look grave. 'Nothing,' I say, sure I look exactly like what I am: a man who is bad at lying.

The official glares at me. 'And what might we find if we search your boat, *señor*?'

I can feel the situation unravelling. The AK47 is still aboard, the other stuff. Francoise is out there alone. 'What kind of boat was it?' I manage.

'A speedboat.'

'Please, sir, look out there.' I point to *Providence*. 'You can see my boat. It is small, a sailing vessel. My pregnant wife is on board. We are hardly equipped for murder and piracy. Please search her if you wish.' I decide then and there that I will not allow myself to be detained. I will run if I have to.

The official glances past me, considers this a moment. 'Of course, *señor*. I am not accusing, only seeking information.'

'Of course.'

The official scans the passports again. 'What business do you have in Belize?'

'I bank here.'

The official looks at me with widening eyes.

'Mr LaBarge at the Crédit Agricole is expecting me.'

The official smooths his shirt front, closes the ledger and replaces it in a drawer beneath the counter, then picks up the phone. A conversation ensues. The official covers the receiver with his palm. 'Señor LaBarge asks if you have a word for him?'

A word. 'Excuse me?'

'He asks for a word from you. One word he says is sufficient.'

The banknote. 'Mersenne,' I say.

The official repeats it, then replaces the receiver in its cradle. 'Señor LaBarge is expecting for you.'

My pulse halves. 'And I would like to purchase a visa.' I must be Argent. I open my hand, revealing a new one-thousand dollar note. 'Will this cover it?'

The official takes the note and slips it into the pocket of his waist coast. 'Welcome to Belize, Señor Hume,' he says, banging arrival stamps into our passports.

59

Outside, it is already hot, the sky that new, hopeful shade of pale aquamarine. An open launch full of passengers chugs out towards the nearest freighter, the one we skirted on the way in. The men are standing, packed into the small craft. *Providence* has swung around into a light sea breeze and is now closer to the jetty. The cockpit is empty. I scan the foredeck, look for movement in the portholes. Perhaps she is lying down. I walk back along the jetty, get as close to *Providence* as I can, call out. One of the men in the launch turns to look at me. I wait, call out again. Nothing. I was only in the station twenty minutes. Fear rises inside me like a sickness, a realisation. I push it back, call out again, louder this time, her name skipping over the water. The launch disappears behind the freighter's dark hull and then she is there, emerging from the main hatch, standing in the cockpit, waving to me. I can see her smile from here. Relief blooms through me, an under-standing, and something else. I wave back, point across the harbour towards the cluster of white buildings. She gives the thumbs-up. I start along the jetty towards the city. Responsibility, a sense of duty, that's what I feel. It feels good.

It isn't hard to find the bank. It is the tallest building on the main waterfront avenue, the big Crédit Agricole sign above the main entrance. I stride along the top of the seawall, my feet a full three metres above the main road, perhaps a metre above the water level opposite. Buttressed, thick as a four-lane highway, the concrete structure arcs around the entire harbour like a long, squat version of the Hoover Dam, except that the Hoover Dam's reservoir is empty now, has been for a long time. Clearly, the city has prepared itself for sea-level rise, both the gradual thermal expansion that had been happening for decades, but also for the sudden one-metre jump that occurred a few years back when the eastern third of the Greenland ice sheet destabilised – quickly and without much more than a few months' warning. Without the wall, the whole place would have been underwater. It must have cost a fortune to build.

A few cars ply the avenue, people on bicycles, pedestrians in ones or twos. Other than the boarded-up windows and the occasional burned-out hulk of a car, the feeling of normality is palpable, like a memory of childhood. I stop across from the bank and, clutching Argent's case to my chest, I start down the steps to the road.

I enter a cool, marble lobby. Two security guards are sitting behind a table beside a metal-detector station. One is very tall and thin, the other slightly less tall and thin. They stand as I approach. I want to turn and run, but I know it is too late for that, in every way. The taller guard places a plastic tray on the table and pushes it towards me.

'Señor LaBarge,' I say.

The less tall guard points at the tray. I fix his gaze, nod. Without looking away, I place Argent's case on the tray.

The tall one raises his eyebrows, picks up the phone, speaks, waits. '*Nombre?*' he says.

'Hume.'

He mispronounces the name back into the receiver, then nods at his colleague. They usher me through the metal detector. I pass through, no alarm. The less-tall guard places my case – Argent's case, with his gun inside – on the table, motions for me to open it.

I shake my head. 'No.'

'*Ábrelo,*' he says. 'Open it.'

I cross my arms.

He repeats himself. We go through this several times. Finally, the taller one picks up the phone. After a brief conversation he nods, and the less tall one hands me back the case and points to the elevators.

Señor LaBarge is a lean man with dark, intelligent eyes and a thick head of dark, longish hair. He sits behind a big glass-topped desk and searches my face through rimless spectacles, the passports spread before him.

'It must have been a very difficult journey, Mr Hume.'

I nod.

'The world has become a very dangerous place, as you predicted it would.'

I do my best to remain expressionless.

'And now your preparations have paid off.'

I nod again.

'We were starting to become concerned. You are overdue.'

'I was...' I clear my throat, steady myself. 'We were detained.'

'We expected you by air.'

'Change of plan.'

'That is understandable, with all that has happened.'

'I understand you have had problems also,' I say.

His brow knits in a question.

'Chenault.'

LaBarge nods, frowns. 'Yes. Very sad.'

I stare like Argent. 'You have something for me.'

'Of course.' The banker opens a folder and removes a red dossier. 'I took the liberty, when informed by the Immigration Department that you had arrived, of preparing a statement on the status of your investments, Señor Hume.' He looks up at me, slides a form across the desk. 'But first, as a formality, if you could please provide me with your key details, investment account numbers, and signature. And of course, the complete password.'

I place Argent's case on the desk, scan the form. Using Argent's gold pen, I scrawl the code sequence across the top of the paper. I have practised Argent's handwriting, but it doesn't come out right. 'Alpha, Omega, third Mersenne Prime,' I say.

The banker nods. It doesn't take me long to complete the form. I sign it as I had practised the night before, slide it back across the table.

He stares at the form for a long time. Sweat blooms at my temples, sluices down my spine. I shift in the chair. There is still a way out. I could get up right now, stride to the elevators, out past the guards, and be back to the boat in a few minutes.

Finally, he looks up. 'Most international markets have continued to operate amazingly well, despite the turmoil. The systems have proven to be quite robust. It is remarkable, actually.' He pauses, removes his glasses, polishes them with a small black cloth. 'Your investment strategy was sound, Señor Hume, both in terms of timing and direction. The shorts have outperformed the long options by a considerable margin. As instructed, all profits have been converted to bullion, half held here in our vaults, the other half at the property.' He points to the ground. 'Very secure.'

Most of the names are unfamiliar, but the numbers make my head reel. My hands are shaking.

'Are you quite well, Señor Hume?'

I push my hands below the desk, try to breathe. 'It was a very difficult journey.'

'Of course.' The banker rises, straightens his tie. 'Now, if you would like to access your safety-deposit box, I'm sure you are anxious to get to the mountains. Please come with me.'

I follow him along a corridor, down a flight of stairs and through a set of heavy steel doors. Uniformed guards usher us into a plush anteroom lined with red velvet and mahogany. A series of doors lines each side of the room. At the far end, a massive circular vault sits half open, a complex arrangement of locking bars and sets ringing the polished milled steel.

'Box number, please, Señor Hume.'

I reel off the number I have been repeating in my mind for the last two days, the one Argent scrawled on the one-thousand-dollar note. LaBarge nods to an orderly in a dark suit, who disappears into the vault. One slip, and I will be exposed, and Francoise will be alone. LaBarge offers me a seat. I shake my head, no, remain standing. It is hot. Sweat pools salty and biting in the depressions above my collarbones, in the corners of my eyes. I blink hard. After what feels like a long time, the orderly reappears carrying a long, polished metal box.

'At your leisure,' says the banker, unlocking one of the anterooms.

I am alone. The room is a small private office, complete with desk, telephone, computer terminal and printer. I scan the walls and ceiling for surveillance cameras but see none. The box sits on the desk before me. I take three long deep breaths, wipe my forehead with my sleeve, try to steady myself. Other than a keypad on one end, the box is featureless, smooth. I consult Argent's notebook. I punch in the twelve-digit string Argent scrawled on the banknote. A mechanism whirs and the keypad panel rotates away, replaced by a black pressure pad. I unwrap Argent's finger, press it down onto the pad. The thing spins to life again and a third panel with a clear lens appears. I unwrap the eye, careful not to touch the cornea. The nerve endings are shrivelled, the pulped tendrils dark, flaked with dried blood. I imagine Francoise cutting it out of Argent's lifeless skull. The thought makes me shudder.

I press the cornea to the lens, push the button. A red light snaps on, extinguishes. The box whirs again and the keypad returns. I stare at the thing. What does it want? A second string of numbers? Perhaps the retina scan hasn't worked. Maybe the eye's structure has decayed too much. I punch in the numbers again, restart the sequence, arrive again at the optical scanner, once again press the cornea to the glass lens. The keypad returns again. Shit. What did France say? Argent was very specific about the safety-deposit box. Without what's inside, you get nothing.

I stand, pace the room. Have I forgotten something? It won't be the first time. If the scanner won't accept the retinal image, we have nothing. I start thinking that maybe that's not so bad. We have the boat after all, and each other. I fill my lungs. I will try one more time. I go through the sequence again. This time, when the scanner appears, I hold the eye further away from the lens, as if it is my own. Three green lights appear and the latch springs open.

I open the lid, look inside.

It is not what I expected at all.

Get It Right This Time

I wake from a fitful sleep to the sound of the bedroom door opening. Francoise is standing in the hall in her nightdress, an oil lamp in her hand. Lewis is standing next to her. Their whispers fill the room with urgency.

What is it?

Mandy is going into labour.

And with that they disappear down the hall. A few moments later I watch the lantern light make its way up the hill, here on the edge of the world where we have lived a lifetime almost as my great-grandparents would have, or their grandparents before them, without the permanent day and unrelenting noise of the time we left behind not so long ago. I am going to be a grandfather. Perhaps I already am.

I lie in the darkness, listening to the sound of the waves on the shore, the rhythm of the ocean. Even this we tried to corrupt, and in this too we have failed. We have failed. I smile, alone in the darkness. I smile. To think that we even tried.

This morning, when dawn comes, I will write. The story is almost told. But the most difficult part remains. And though I have known the truth for a long time now, and have somehow learned to live with it, never before have I forced myself to articulate it, to truly understand it. But now I know that I must, that it was always the ultimate goal of this journey, to stare open-eyed into the pure anarchy of it and acknowledge the truth. My strength is failing. If I don't do it now, I fear I will never be able to summon the courage. Liberty said it, after all. Get it right this time. Young fellas gotta do it without us. They need to know.

60

The sun is low in the sky by the time we reach the foothills. Rows of roadside eucalypts – planted, LaBarge says, to depress the water table – throw long shadows across marshes and raised fields of wheat, vegetables, sorghum. The land looks fertile and productive.

'Much of this part of the country's agriculture has been preserved,' says LaBarge. 'I suppose we have you to thank for that, Eminence. You and your colleagues.'

Argent, Eminence? His preferred honorific? It wouldn't surprise me. We drive on, I say nothing.

'As you saw, the city has survived. The pumping system was installed at the same time as the sea wall and is functioning as designed. The coastal dykes have performed well, despite several storm breaches in the last few years.'

I nod, try to catch Francoise's eye. I haven't had time to explain much to her, just those few minutes on *Providence* and in the dinghy rowing back to the jetty while LaBarge waited on the quay in the car. So far it seems I have managed to pass myself off as Argent, or rather Hume. Francoise has played her role as Mrs Hume to perfection: arrogant, spoiled, entitled.

Mountains loom ahead, the foothills vivid green in the afternoon sun, the peaks darker, dotted with white puffs of cumulus. Soon we are climbing, the vehicle bumping along a narrow gravel track through thick forest, the canopy towering above us in a cathedral arch. Cool air swirls through the windows. After a few miles, the road cuts through onto an open ridge. The coastal plain spreads beneath us, the wetlands and marshes shining like silver patchwork among the green fields. The city, tiny now, stands nestled within its protective wall with the long, raised causeway running landward, an island city on a flooded coastline.

LaBarge slows the vehicle. Ahead, at the far end of the ridge, hidden at the edge of the forest, a checkpoint appears, the first we have seen.

'As requested,' says LaBarge, rolling the car to a stop before a steel barrier. A soldier in camouflage uniform appears from a concrete bunker. He wears a jungle cap and carries an assault weapon on a sling across his chest. When he sees LaBarge, he stands to attention and salutes.

'They have arrived,' he says in Spanish to the soldier.

The soldier raises the barrier, salutes again as the vehicle rolls past.

'The guards are well paid and disciplined,' says LaBarge. 'The fortifications are second to none, built by American engineers.'

I glance at Francoise. Argent spoke of paradise.

We re-enter the rainforest. Mist creeps through the foliage. Part of me cannot believe that places like this still exist, that they haven't all been burned away in the wildfires that raged for years across every part of the planet. After another five kilometres or so, LaBarge takes us onto a side road that leads west. We cut through a pass, the peaks towering left and right, the vegetation different here, sub-alpine, the trees stunted, rooted among boulders and cliffs, and then back down into more forest.

LaBarge slows down. 'We have arrived, Eminence. I hope you will find everything in order. Everything has been completed to your exact instructions. I have verified it personally.'

Francoise looks at me a moment, mouths: *Eminence?*

I shrug my shoulders.

'You have done well,' I say, trying to emulate Argent's tone and demeanour. 'You will be rewarded.'

LaBarge smiles, nods and sinks back into the seat, smug behind his sunglasses. We come to a tall steel gate that seems to emerge directly from the vegetation. A high wall topped with coils of razor wire runs off in both directions. LaBarge pulls a remote from his pocket and punches a series of numbers into the keypad. 'And your touch key, of course,' he says, pointing to a steel post at the side of the road. I reach into my pocket, pull out the small black disc attached to a Paris Saint-Germain key chain, which was the only other item in the safe-deposit box. I hand it to LaBarge and he touches the disc to a sensor pad set into the top of the post.

The big doors slide open.

'Of course, you can reprogram the access codes as you like,' LaBarge says, handing me back the device.

LaBarge eases the late-model Land Rover through the gates and up the freshly raked gravel drive. When we arrive at the house, he rolls the vehicle to a stop. We sit, open-mouthed.

For the next two hours, LaBarge leads us on foot through the estate, proudly describing each feature. There are acres of gardens, thriving plots of every kind of vegetable and grain, orchards, hothouses. A mill and granary nestle in the hillside. Past a screen of trees, we come to a promontory built into the rock. Beneath us, a quilt of terraced fields, small and well tended, each a colour and texture of its own, cascades down the hillside towards a green valley that snakes away through the mountains. It is breathtakingly beautiful. Francoise grips my hand, squeezes hard. Is this now ours? I remain silent, acknowledging LaBarge only with brief nods, knowing that if I were to speak, I would surely betray myself.

The house is built into the side of a rocky outcrop, nestled into a saddle in the hills. From the outside it is almost entirely hidden by trees and cascades of flowering vines, bougainvillea and wisteria. A long, elevated balcony runs along the front of the building, giving it a colonial look. LaBarge throws open the front door. Inside it is cool and fresh. Hardwood floors glow under rich oriental carpets. Room leads to room. A games area with full-size snooker table, a massive library filled floor to mezzanine ceiling with books, a sumptuous living area, cosy ten-seat cinema, a modern, fully equipped and stocked kitchen leading on to a formal dining room. In back a swimming pool and jacuzzi. Francoise counts six bedrooms. The master suite leads out onto the balcony. We stand gripping the railing, looking out across the darkening valley to the sweep of the mountains.

'And of course, the entire estate is completely self-contained, as requested,' LaBarge continues, checking his watch. 'The bunker is accessed from the basement, directly below us, and connects via a tunnel through the hills to the armoury and shooting range. The private airstrip is only two kilometres away by secure road. The solar-power system has been designed with multiple redundancies and ample storage. There is also thermal energy from the deep wells, and a reliable, high-quality aquifer provides all the fresh water you could ever need. Garden and farm staff have been on site since completion, of course. The house staff – cooks, maids, personal attendants – will be moved into their on-site quarters tomorrow. I will be back in the morning to introduce you to Hernandez, head overseer, and direct the final preparations myself.'

I say nothing, stand motionless. Is she thinking what I am thinking? Feeling what I am feeling?

LaBarge's brow creases. 'Is something not to your liking, Eminence?' Francoise squeezes my hand.

'Eminence?' says LaBarge.

'Sorry,' I stumble.

LaBarge clasps and unclasps his hands, looks down at his shoes. 'Please, Eminence, if there is something...'

I know we are balancing on the thinnest wire, with a long way to fall, but I cannot answer.

'We were expecting something grander,' said Francoise, looking disappointed. 'He is wondering if you have been feathering your own nest, rather than doing what you have been instructed to do.'

LaBarge staggers back a step as if hit by a sudden gust of wind. He bows low. 'I can assure his Eminence that all is as instructed. I can provide a complete set of accounts and ledgers confirming how the money has been spent.'

'Good,' says Francoise. 'Bring them tomorrow.'

'Of course. Of course. Tomorrow.' LaBarge bows again and backs away to the door, closing it behind him. A moment later we hear the truck start and drive away.

We stand looking at each other.

'Thanks,' I say.

'You're welcome.'

'Attack.'

She nods. 'What would Argent do?'

'You're right. Sorry. I was just so, I don't know. Look at this place. This whole time. It's beyond belief.'

'He suspects,' she says.

I nod. 'What do you think he'll do?'

'It depends on how scared he is of being wrong. And how venal he is.'

'Then we have to reinforce that fear and amplify the consequences of error.'

'And promise to reward him.'

'Jesus,' I say. 'What a way to live.'

She reaches for my hand. 'Eminence?'

I try to smile. 'He started calling me that as soon as he'd seen that I'd retrieved the key from the safety deposit box.'

'What is this place?' she whispers.

'A monument to Argent's ego.'

'And you are Argent now.'

'Eminence.'

'And all of this? Is it ours?'

'You heard him. If we want it, yes.'

'It is very beautiful, the gardens, the fields. But so much.'

I stare out across the hills.

After a while she says: 'What did you find at the bank?'

I swallow hard, still reeling. 'The truth.'

'The truth about what?'

'About everything.'

'What do you mean?'

'There was something else in the safety deposit box, besides the key.'

'What was it?'

'Instructions. No, more like a testament. Short. Four pages.'

'What did it say?' she draws closer, but I step away.

'What's wrong, *chéri*?' It is the first time she has called me that.

'I'm sorry,' I say after a time. 'I shouldn't have told you. I said it was the truth. That was wrong. It was nothing. Just a piece of fantasy. Shit Argent trawled up from the depths of his twisted mind. Don't worry about it. What matters is that we are here. And now we need to figure out what we're going to do.'

61

I clutch the thin sheaf of papers in my hands and re-read the letter for the third time. I know in that moment that I have been profoundly and forever changed. I see my life's efforts for what they are, the wrong answer to the wrong problem. I am a murderer. Shame is too tepid a word for what I feel. When I woke this morning to the sound of vehicles entering the compound, there was a moment, a fraction of a second, perhaps, in the no-man's land between unconsciousness and realisation, when the possibility that what I'd read had been a dream burned itself into my brain like an auto-beacon through the fog. I wanted it to be a dream. More than I have ever wanted anything. Certainly, and with conviction. But time harks no pity, and I know now that everything has changed.

I walk to the balcony and look out across the compound at the trucks disgorging workers, and beyond to the rumpled hills and the flat sea basking under an intermediate sky. It all happened. All the things that might have been, all the other possibilities and options and alternative pathways, have now been forever reduced to this singular present. And from this our time of anarchy, there is no way back.

I think of Kazinsky and Smith and their newborn baby, somewhere in the Canadian Rockies I can only hope; of Lachie, wherever he might be. This is the wreck we have left them, and they are going to have to do the best they can with it, because it's all they've got. It sounds heartless, but it's the truth. The truth. I feel like screaming the word aloud, crying it out to the heavens. The truth. The only thing that ever mattered.

I cycle a breath, fill my lungs again with this re-engineered air. Below me, forty miles away, *Providence* waits, swinging faithfully on her anchor, and beyond, all of the changed world. I grip the rail and try to fight back the anger pushing up inside me. I haven't told France yet, haven't shown her the letter. How do you inflict such a thing on someone you love? This realisation flows through me, not as a surprise, really. More like a release, the trip of a capacitor.

I wonder again if Argent's letter could be true. Surely not. It is beyond imagining. Who could even conceive of such a thing? But it is all there. The whole story. All the data and the computer modelling. The moment of realisation, the pivot as he so clinically puts it, when they realise that they can force a new reality, one from which they will emerge in control of whatever is left. And then the plans and arrangements, the global coordination. Argent and his partners considered everything, developed detailed contingencies for every scenario, anticipated reactions and counter-strategies, ran detailed physical models and cost-benefit analyses. And as it progressed, successful beyond their wildest hopes, they doubled down, channelled funds and wielded influence, fuelled the reactions of governments, companies and communities, manipulated public opinion, used the awesome power of AI-driven social media to destroy the truth and create their own. Everything and everyone behaved pretty much as predicted – fear and greed are powerful motivators – except that the whole system, man and nature, responded much sooner and more violently than anyone anticipated. And of course, by the time enough people finally figured it out and started to take meaningful action, it was too late.

I can't decide if it is pure opportunism, or undistilled evil. Maybe it's both.

France emerges from her bedroom dressed in a long, flowing silk kimono, joins me at the railing. As she does, LaBarge waves up to us from the compound, clipboard in one hand, a cigarette burning in the other. I offer the slightest tilt of my head. LaBarge smiles.

'He is worried,' she says. 'And suspicious.'

'We are going to have to be careful.'

'It appears the staff have arrived,' says France.

'So many.'

'And so many young women.'

'You noticed.'

'It is difficult not too. They are all so beautiful.'

I turn to face her. 'Can you see now, what this was all about, France?'

'Last night you spoke of the truth. Is this it? Is this what you meant?'

'No, France. Not this.' I reach into my pocket and hand her the letter. I can't hold it from her any longer. She will have to make up her own mind about it.

She takes the paper, unfolds it. I watch her read the title, printed in bold capital letters across the top of the page. Yes, Argent gave it a title. It is called:

THE FORCING.

She reads. It takes a few minutes, as if she is having trouble making out the words, their meaning. After she has finished, she folds the paper and slips it back into my shirt pocket. For a long time, she says nothing, just stands staring out towards the sea.

We watch the trucks leave through the main gates and the last of the workers disappearing off through the gardens towards their new living quarters.

'It's not possible,' she whispers finally. Her voice is low, distant, resigned.

'Argent wanted you to read this. Even when he knew he was dying, he could have let it go. That's why he told you.'

'I can't believe it. He saved me, saved you.'

'Think about it, France. Not only did he want you to see this, he wrote it *for you*. Other than the key, there was nothing else in the safety deposit box.'

'That's ridiculous. Why would he have done that? How could he have?'

'So you would know, France. So someone would know. It was

an insurance policy for his legacy. He wanted you to know that *he* did this. Him. He played the whole world and won. What use would it have been if no one ever knew?'

She sits silently, staring away into the distance.

'It all would have been for nothing,' she says after a time. 'It was one of the last things he said.'

'Exactly. He knew what would happen. He and his colleagues understood it all, how the earth's climate system worked and how it would respond. And once they realised what the price of fixing it would be, and who would have to pay, they did everything they could to force it along, to push the system towards collapse, while preventing action to stop it. They knew what would come, bet on the outcome, and prepared themselves with places like this. That whole time, we thought they were a bunch of luddites, ignorant and greedy, not understanding the science or not wanting to, not caring about the future or even about their own kids. But that wasn't it at all. It was intentional, France. The whole thing. The biggest short ever conceived. Brilliant.'

She shudders visibly under the fine silk. 'What did Saint John say? "And after the world has been wiped clean, we, the alpha-omega, will begin again".'

'Saint John prayed for this. But Argent, he used it.' Guilt and dread and remorse and a thousand other things I cannot describe clutch me like a panic.

'It doesn't seem possible,' she whispers through her tears. 'That anyone could think that way. No. I refuse to believe it.'

'Not possible? Look back through history. It's the rule, France, not the exception. It's who we are. All of us. That's what he was trying to tell us. We're just like him.'

She looks away, somewhere across the world. I can only guess.

'We can't stay here,' she says after a time. 'I won't.'

'We'll go back to *Providence*.'

LaBarge is crossing the courtyard towards the house now, carrying a bulging briefcase.

'And then, after, where will we go?'

I think about this a while. About the size of the world, and the new, old difficulties of moving across it, of all the things we took for granted, back before. 'What did the letter say? "I had them determine where the good places would be"?'

She nods. '"And I picked the three best."'

'It will be here somewhere.'

'The library perhaps, or the computer room.'

'I am going to ask LaBarge.'

She nods. 'It will be protected. Do you still have the eye, the finger?'

'In the freezer.'

She nods. 'The gun?'

I place my hand on the small of my back.

'Be careful,' she says, reaching up on her toes to kiss me on the cheek. It is the first time she has ever done that.

'We'll find a way,' I say. I believe it. For the first time in a long time, I believe. 'And we'll do it on our own.'

'And then,' she says, 'we will begin again.'

62

I look out across the dark water. Providence foams along beneath us. Francoise is asleep in the main cabin below. The compass glows on its gimbals as we track the Earth's magnetic field, south-southwest.

It wasn't hard to leave. LaBarge showed us his ledgers, anxious to please, and then went back to the city in another vehicle, leaving us the Land Rover. I found the information we needed in the library – precise coordinates to small stretches of the planet where the effects that had ravaged much of the rest of the world had been muted by the remaining core of southern polar ice. We waited until nightfall, packed up as much food as we could carry, along with a few books and a couple of gold bars from the vault, loaded it all into the Land Rover and drove off. No one questioned us; no one tried to stop us. The guards waved us through the checkpoints, saluting as we went.

When we reached the harbour, Providence was there as we'd left her, swinging serene on her anchor. The harbour was quiet and the sky clear. We loaded the bags into the dinghy and rowed out under the stars, the dark water all around reflecting the lights of the city. Then we took a last look back at the dark mountains, raised anchor, and slipped out of the harbour.

I cradle the gun in my lap. I think again about Argent's letter and all it revealed. I think about Francoise, about the new life she is carrying, about the world that Kwesi's child will inherit. And I wonder, is it an act of selfish madness, bringing this new person into being? Or is it the ultimate rebellion, the most powerful expression of hope imaginable?

I hold the gun in my hand, feel the coolness of it, the weight. Then I stand, stretch, check the wheel and the mainsheet, and slip the gun into my pocket where I can find it if I need it. I think back to all that has transpired, the journey south, the camp, our escape, finding the sanctuary. I think of all those who have died, of those we have saved and lost. Names come, faces, moments. I wonder what it can all mean, this strange and violent history being made. We have covered so many miles, fled halfway around the world with more to go. Argent thought he could run away and hide. That whole time, he thought it was about a place, a destination. But he had it wrong. We all did.

It's not a place to live we need to find, it's a way of living.

Tomorrow and All the Days Before

I scrawl my grand-daughter's birthdate and the name of this place at the bottom of the page and set down my pen. I push myself away from the desk, look out again over this beautiful bay to the dark headlands and the ocean beyond, watch the white clouds scuttling across the horizon.

A great weariness comes over me. I know now that this is more than just a statement of witness. In going back, I thought that I might somehow reverse the flow of time and so create, at least in my own mind, a semblance of order from the chaos. I hoped, too, that I might find an explanation for what had happened, for why we did what we did, what led us to this. In truth, I don't know if I am any closer to either. But I do know that I am no longer ashamed. I did my best, in the best way I could, despite my weaknesses and imperfections, as did countless others. In the final reckoning, we are all angels and sinners both. And we will be okay.

The way I see it now, we simply lost our way. Increasingly ruled by time, a measure of our own creation, we lost sight of the natural rhythms of the places around us and began to believe that we were masters of everything we saw and touched, and so we ceased to wonder. A caesium-133 atomic clock keeps time faithfully to one second every one hundred and thirty-eight million years. But we forgot that in the end, there are only moments, those exquisite portions of eternity between dawn and the next sunrise. Some – too many – pass without register, forgotten, as if they had never existed. Some dwell in the timeless ache of loss, blurring into a woe of years. But the good ones, the really good ones, come into being with a gleam through the trees as you make your way together up the hill that overlooks the sea, then linger in the steady sunlit country of the uplands, resting when the sun is high under the shade of an ancient tree and then going on again as the shadows lengthen across the land and blissful darkness beckons.

Twenty-eight thousand, nine hundred and sixty-seven days I have lived. And in them I have experienced more than most, seen more than my measure of hate and horror and waste. More, I hope, than my grandchildren will have to face. I have seen the truth destroyed and rise again, as inevitably it must. I have watched the loved deceived and the cherished buried. Joy too, I have had, and love. And through it all I have come to understand that days – tomorrow and all the days before – are all we have. Their sum is the finite truth of our lives. And how we decide to use this precious ebb of time is what will determine the fate of the world and of all those we love.

I can feel it even now, this turning of the world. In the caress of the waves on the shore, in the hiss of the foam across the shingle and the scuttling of crabs across the rocks as the tide floods. I can feel it in the high blue of day and the deeper blue of the ocean, in the air moving through my lungs, captured and held as another wave laps the beach and runs away again as I let it go, let it go, each moment held, held, there in the sky, in the water, in the living pulse of this sacred Earth.

*'Oh, my servants who have transgressed against themselves,
do not despair of the mercy of Allah.'
Sura 39:53, Holy Qu'ran*

ACKNOWLEDGEMENTS

I wrote the first version of this book twelve years ago, based on an idea that came to me fully formed when camping on Woody Island, near Esperance off the coast of Western Australia. And while the core idea, characters and plot have remained essentially the same, I was never able to get it quite right. Conveying the bleakness of a world ravaged by the worst of climate change within a compelling story, while maintaining a line of hope, and doing so in a way that didn't trivialise the issue in any way, was a challenge that I could not overcome alone. Several failed versions died quietly, and for a while I had abandoned it altogether. It wasn't until the first big Covid lockdown that I had the time to come back to it, and with the help of my editor West Camel and publisher Karen Sullivan, found a way to bring all of those elements together.

Thanks to Heidi, Zac and Dec for their unwavering support, no matter where I go and what I do.

This book is dedicated to my dad, who died as I was finishing this eighth and final version of the book, and who had read a couple of the earlier versions and urged me to keep working on it.